D1431146

RECKLESS IN LOVE

The Maverick Billionaires, Book 2

Bella Andre & Jennifer Skully

RECKLESS IN LOVE

~ The Maverick Billionaires, Book 2 ~

Meet the Maverick Billionaires—sexy, self-made men from the wrong side of town who survived hell together and now have everything they ever wanted. But when each Maverick falls head-over-heels for an incredible woman he never saw coming, he will soon find that true love is the only thing he ever really needed...

Sebastian Montgomery rose from nothing to become one of the most powerful media moguls in the world. Yet beneath the seemingly perfect façade of his life, the past still haunts him. Because when he lost his parents in his teens, he also lost his faith in love. When he discovers Charlie Ballard and her incredible metal sculptures, he is awed, inspired—and he can't help feeling things he swore never to let himself feel again. Soon, Sebastian wants not only Charlie's art, he wants her as a woman, too. More than he's ever wanted anything in his life. And what a Maverick wants, he always gets...

For Charlie, Sebastian offers the commission of a lifetime. Creating a magnificent sculpture for his new headquarters is a dream come true, but falling for the spellbinding billionaire isn't part of the plan... until his luscious kisses entice her into total recklessness. He fascinates and captivates her, and as Charlie learns more about the dark depths of Sebastian's past, all she wants is to heal him with her love. But can a man who has grown up thinking love is toxic ever believe that true love is real?

Dedication

To Doris Beach and Judy Moffett
For all the miles you have walked and all
the inspiration you have given us.

A note from Bella & Jennifer

We are both so thrilled with the outpouring of love for our Maverick Billionaires! Thank you to all our readers.

In the pages of **Reckless in Love**, you'll meet a lovely woman named Francine, Charlie's mother. Our inspiration for Francine comes from two wonderful ladies, Doris Beach (Jennifer Skully's mother) and her friend Judy Moffett. These two ladies start every day with a smile. Their lives are filled with happiness, and they bring joy to everyone around them, especially to their families. And every day, they walk a mile despite the debilitating arthritis that makes each step a battle. But nothing ever stops them. Doris and Judy have been best friends for over thirty years and this year, each celebrates her 90th birthday. They both gave their time to tell their stories, share their inspiration, and make this tale real for our readers.

A huge thank-you to these courageous ladies. May we all live our lives as they do. And happy birthday to you both!

Happy reading,
Bella Andre & Jennifer Skully

p.s. Each book in the Maverick Billionaires series can be read as a stand-alone novel. However, if you would like to find out how it all began, please check out _Breathless In Love_, Will and Harper's love story. And watch for Matt's story, coming soon!

CHAPTER ONE

Charlie Ballard had one hell of an imagination.

Sebastian Montgomery marveled at the garden of creatures fashioned from junkyard scrap glowing beneath the hot California sun. A magnificent lion roared, its flowing mane a fabrication of railroad spikes. An elephant trumpeted—literally, its trunk shaped from two trumpets fitted together, its body and legs forged from various old musical instruments. Two rams, their ginormous antlers constructed of rolled corrugated-tin roofing, were pitted against each other in a battle to the death. There were smaller works as well—lizards cut from what appeared to be rusted car doors, and some strange, scorpion-like insects built with nuts, bolts, screws, and claws formed from the blades of old pruning shears.

Ms. Ballard's artwork spoke to something deep in Sebastian's core that was as primal as the beasts she'd welded with the blaze of her torch. Her vision was so clear, so pure, that a sense of awe radiated through his chest. Awe at the way she put it all out there—her energy, her whole soul, and every ounce of passion, for everyone to see—and how in her brilliant hands, metal came to life. Inanimate objects became real. Became *magical.*

Her metal menagerie touched his soul, if for no other reason than the fact that she'd constructed something so momentous from everyday junk.

To most people, this acre lot in the Los Altos Hills area of the San Francisco Peninsula would look like a junkyard filled with car parts; tractor seats; saw blades; pitchforks; barrels of nuts, bolts, nails, and rivets; and metal scrap of everything from ancient barbecue grills to sewer grates. But Sebastian understood that they were her art supplies—and were far more important than a green lawn or fancy landscaping. The fact that her house and detached garage had seen better days in no way detracted from the genius of the artistry strewn across the property.

Sebastian removed his suit jacket and rolled up the sleeves of his white dress shirt as he headed toward the ramshackle single garage, through which he could hear the screech of welding equipment. His heartbeat was already well into overdrive from the incredibly beautiful sculptures—and his fingers were itching to sketch everything around him. He got his first sight of Charlie standing in beams of sunlight streaming down through two Plexiglas-covered holes in the roof, her protective face shield up now and her welding torch off. Sebastian's heart stilled in his chest with renewed wonder.

Because he finally knew what *true* beauty was.

Charlie's temples and forehead were dented from the welding mask while her glossy hair shone with hues of red and gold in the sunbeams cascading from above. She snapped a restraining hairband loose and ran her fingers through lusciously messy curls, letting them spill over her shoulders. Sebastian was instantly caught up in a vision of burying his hands, his face, his mouth in all that incredible red hair.

Removing a heavy smock that safeguarded her arms and body, she revealed a pair of stained and faded farmer-style overalls, beneath which she wore a tank top. Her arms flexed with a fine ripple of muscle, a gorgeous creation of bone, sinew, muscle, and smooth skin.

Of all the works of art on Charlie Ballard's land, the woman herself was by far the most stunning, more radiant and fierce than any sculpture could ever be. So stunning that only one thought remained.

He had to have her.

At last, she turned sparkling green eyes in his direction. "You're here," she said as if she'd been waiting for him all her life.

And when he answered, "Yes, I'm here," for a moment he actually felt as if he'd discovered his destiny.

That thought was pure whimsy; he'd found his destiny the first time he stood on a stage and encouraged people to change their lives. But everything about Charlie Ballard and her creations made him feel as though he'd walked into a fantasy. One where the normal rules didn't apply, and the only thing that mattered was passion—passion for both the art that surrounded him and the woman who'd created it.

Which was why he didn't hold back, didn't bother to act nonchalant. "You're a genius."

Her eyes went wide with surprise at his compliment for a split second, before she smiled at him. One perfect smile that rocked his world yet again. "Thank you."

She didn't ask him to tell her which was his favorite piece, didn't press for more compliments, and he was struck by her quiet confidence. It was something he'd found to be extremely rare when most people were desperate for as many ego strokes as they could get.

"Let me introduce myself." He held out his hand, dying to feel her skin against his. "Sebastian Montgomery."

"Charlie Ballard."

An electrical charge ran through him as she slid her hand into his. Perhaps he shouldn't have been so deeply affected. Her grip was firm, with a ridge of calluses along her palm. She wore no flowery scent, just the heady aroma of woman and the metals she worked with. His world was filled with women who glittered with jewels and smelled like designer perfume. But Charlie Ballard sparkled with life, and all her contrasts intrigued him. The gorgeous red hair and steel-toed work boots. The sexy tank top and old overalls. The slightly upturned nose and kiss-me lips that she'd hidden beneath a welding mask. Lips that were now curving into a ghost of a smile, as if she'd felt that same zap of electricity when they came skin to skin.

He nearly asked if he could kiss her. Instead, he forced himself to keep that question under wraps for the time being. "Is Charlie short for something?"

"My parents named me Charlotte. But as we all soon discovered—" She held the baggy overalls out to each side with a grin. "—I was more of a Charlie."

No, even at first glance he could see she was both—the beauty and the tomboy. Beneath the drab fabric, he could easily guess at her curves, the indentation of her waist, the taut length of leg. Again, the urge to sketch her—and all her magnificent creations—was stronger than it had ever been for him before.

Sebastian's art broker, Xander Smith, had set up the appointment for three o'clock. Xander would have attended, but a last-minute crisis demanded his attention. Now Sebastian was glad he'd had the chance to see the elephant and the fighting rams for the first time with no one else around. And he definitely didn't want to share his time with Charlie.

He'd already told her she was a genius. Reminding himself that going on about her beauty at this stage in the game would definitely be pushing things too far, he said, "I'm a bit early, but I'm glad that gave me time to tour your garden."

She laughed, and the sound was throaty, deeper than he'd expected from a woman who was almost a foot shorter than he. Granted, he was tall at six-three, and her work boots added a couple of inches to her height, but her head still didn't reach higher than his shoulder.

"I wouldn't exactly call it a *garden*," she said in a smooth, soft tone that only served to stoke his attraction to her.

As they talked, he led her back out into her yard, wanting to see her beauty amid all the splendor she'd created. "How about a menagerie?"

She smiled again, and he simply couldn't control his response to it, his body heating up several degrees just looking at her. Just standing so close. Her smile was as beautiful as everything else about her, even the lingering dents in her forehead from the face shield and the shimmer of perspiration on her cheeks and upper lip.

"Now that's a diplomatic term." Her smile was wry as well as beautiful. Intelligent too. She rested her hands on her hips, her boots planted apart in the dust and gravel. "Mr. Smith said you liked my dragon."

"Please, he's Xander and I'm Sebastian. And like most art brokers, he prefers to keep things understated. But I don't. Which is why you need to know I think your dragon is magnificent."

"Magnificent." She repeated the word as though she was more than a little surprised by his reaction to her art. She tipped her chin at the collection in the yard. "Most people call it junk."

Sebastian was impressed by how well she hid any sense of offense at the word *junk*. Still, he'd built his career on looking beneath the surface of people, and he could see that it did, in fact, hurt her. Maybe only a little, but he knew all too well how the small hurts could add up. Especially when it came to one's art and creative dreams.

Forcefully pushing away the thought of the dreams he'd given up so long ago, he told her, "I'm not most people. And I appreciate beauty when I see it."

"I'll take genius," she said with another smile. "I'll even let you get away with magnificent. But beauty?" She shook her head. "That's going a bit too far."

"No, it isn't. Take the elephant, for example. I'm amazed by the way the instruments fit the contours of the body, the legs, even the ears. How did you do it?"

"I used the bells from a couple of old sousaphones I found."

She said it as though it had been the easiest thing in the world, but he knew better. Knew just how hard it was to bring your vision to life. Knew, in fact, that it could be impossible to see that vision work out just right. But she'd done it not only with the elephant, but also with every other creature in her garden. And with an effortlessness that blew his mind.

"I suspect you're the only artist on the planet who can take the bell from a sousaphone and make it look as if an elephant's ears are flapping."

She tipped her head as if he'd just performed an astonishing feat. "Nobody's ever seen the intended effect before. I had to beat them into submission, of course—bend the rims, manipulate, and add to them, but that's exactly what I was going for. Flapping ears." She caressed the tubes forming the basic structure of the animal's haunches and he swore he could feel the heat of her touch all along his own muscles. "I used the tuning slides and the rest of the sousaphones back here. I've always thought musical instruments were like diamonds, that you should never throw them away."

He turned to find her startlingly green eyes on him again. The marks of the mask were starting to fade, leaving a beauty so pure, so fresh, it stunned him all over again. Even if her art hadn't blown his mind, Charlie herself was worth the price of admission to her backyard art museum.

"You found all this in junkyards?"

"And thrift shops. Parents make their kids join the school band, but after two years those kids hate it. And bye-bye trombone." She threw out her arm, and again he saw the play of muscles in her shoulders and along her throat. "I saw the sousaphone first. It looked like an elephant's ear—and suddenly I knew I needed to bring him to life." She spread her hands to encompass the structure made up of saxophones and horns, tubas and flutes, even drums. "It took me five years to find all the instruments."

"Five years?" She continued to surprise him. "For one project?"

"I worked on other pieces at the same time. And I also teach welding over at the junior college."

"It still shows a great deal of dedication to one vision." He understood that kind of dedication. At the age of eighteen, he and his four best friends, the Mavericks, had vowed to get out of the Chicago hellhole of a neighborhood they'd been born into and strike it big. They'd all made good on that pact. Clearly, Charlie Ballard had the same kind of single-minded vision.

"Five years of dedication to a piece of junk I can't even give away," she said with a smile. A smile content enough that he suddenly wondered if she'd ever really tried to find a buyer.

"Are you going to try selling it to me?"

"Do you want her?" Her eyes lit with humor as she nodded toward her small house on the other side of the acre. "I could use a new roof."

This time, he was the one laughing out loud. "Maybe one day I'll succumb to the need to take the elephant home with me, but today I'm not here for the elephant, the ram, the lion, the lizards, or the scorpions."

"Scorpions?" She shook her head. "They're Zanti Misfits from *The Outer Limits.*"

"You mean that sci-fi TV show from the nineties?"

"Not the remake," she said with obvious disgust. "The original."

He was hard-pressed to fight back his grin at just how much fun it was to talk with her. He couldn't remember the last time fun had factored into his relationship with a woman.

Especially a lady he was senselessly attracted to. Not only was her art magnificent, but so was she. He wanted her with a sweet kick of desire low in his gut.

"Tell me more about these Misfits." Lord knew he'd felt like one when he was a kid, living with two alcoholics who often forgot they even had a son.

"They used to do TV marathons of *The Outer Limits* when I was a little kid," she explained. "They had the worst special effects, but the stories were great. 'The Zanti Misfits' was my favorite episode—all about expecting the unexpected. My dad had a big barrel of nuts, bolts, and screws in his workshop, and I was so inspired by the show I swear they seemed to build themselves. They were my very first sculptures, and every once in a while, even though I already have a zillion of them, I have to make another."

Suddenly, Sebastian realized there were Misfits creeping around everywhere. Small compared to the rest of her work, they were still fierce little creatures, their pruning-shear claws ready to snip the toes off trespassers.

"Is that how you get your ideas?" He wanted to plumb her creative depths, her mind. Hell, he wanted to delve into every single part of her. "You see something that inspires you and you just start building?"

"Sometimes," she mused, and appreciated that all his questions didn't seem to bother her. "Or sometimes it's a place, like the church in San Francisco where you saw my dragon sculpture." The sun created a rainbow of reds in her hair. "A dragon was meant to sweep its tail over the path, barely missing Sunday parishioners. So I walked inside and asked if there was any interest in my building one for them."

Every day Sebastian put himself out there in a seminar or book or TV presentation. Through his company, Montgomery Media International, he strove to help other people fulfill their destinies, something he found extremely gratifying. But though it seemed he didn't have any secrets, the truth was that he'd never offered strangers a piece of his heart and soul. And he sure as hell wasn't willing to expose what he created to anyone, deliberately keeping his drawings locked away in his den at home. He was the exact opposite of Charlie, who was so easy about his visit to her studio, so relaxed in answering his questions, so carefree about the idea of asking a church if she could build them a sculpture of a dragon.

Then again, Charlie's talent was in performing a miraculous metamorphosis of junk heaps into amazing creatures, whereas his talent was in helping people transform themselves. He'd wisely given up his dreams of being an artist a long time ago, had accepted as a teenager that he'd never see his work hung on a gallery wall.

He ran a hand through his hair, not sure why he kept spinning back to the past today. Especially when it was the future he was far more interested in—one that had Charlie Ballard playing a starring role.

"I'm glad the church was smart enough to be interested. And I hope they paid you well for the dragon. It's unlike any sculpture I've ever seen."

"It's Chinatown and everyone loves the dragon at Chinese New Year, so I gave it to them. The dragon couldn't have lived anywhere else." She gestured to her crowded garden. "Not even here."

He supported numerous charities, but he still frowned upon hearing that she hadn't been paid for her work. "You don't need to give your sculptures away for free."

She raised an eyebrow at the slight scolding in his tone and answered him back just as firmly. "I do just fine, thanks."

He liked that she had an independent streak, her spirit matching her strong, lithe body. He liked everything about her a great deal, in fact. And yet, she really did need that new roof, one she could easily afford if any other collectors discovered her talent. And if she were willing to charge for her art's true worth.

What, he suddenly wondered, was holding her back from being the superstar that lurked inside her? With her talent, she brought out the majesty in mere junk, like revealing the swan hiding inside the ugly duckling. She had huge vision and saw shape and form in things that no one else could even begin to imagine. So why wasn't her metal statuary displayed all over the world, in museums and buildings and parks?

Sebastian vowed to find out. But first he needed to convince her to work with him. "I'm opening a high-rise office in San Francisco at the end of September." He'd taken over an existing structure and was rebuilding it to suit his needs, including a production studio. It would be his new headquarters and that of the Maverick Group as well. "There's a fountain in the lobby center." He let silence beat for three seconds. "It needs you." *I need you.* The thought hit him hard, right in the solar plexus, where no other woman had ever gotten to him. "It needs one of your sculptures."

"You want to commission me to design something?" She still sounded as though she couldn't quite believe what he was saying.

Had no one ever let her know just how extraordinary she was before today?

"I'm planning a grand opening for the building, attended by friends, business associates, clients, customers, art enthusiasts. The fountain and its statue—the one you're going to create for me—will be the centerpiece of the event." Her work would be seen by everyone who was anyone in San Francisco and beyond. But it was more than her work that he wanted people to discover and appreciate. "We won't just unveil your art, we'll unveil *you* to the world too."

She didn't jump at his offer. Didn't do anything for long enough that he actually began to worry she might say no. Though he couldn't understand why she would possibly turn down his offer.

"Well," she finally said, "I am off school for summer break. Classes don't start again until the fall."

He eased closer, catching the perfume of woman and sparks. He wanted her art—and *her*—more than he'd ever wanted anything or anyone before in his life. "Is there anything else standing in your way?"

She paused again, her expression shifting in ways he couldn't quite understand. There was excitement there, but also wariness and continued confusion. At last she said, "No, I guess not."

Now that her mind was made up, she looked at him directly, her eyes glittering like emeralds. In an instant, the spark of desire lit between them again.

"What exactly did you have in mind?" she asked.

You. In my bed. For a month straight. Longer than that. For as long as I can convince you to stay.

But what he said instead was, "A stallion."

The sweet and sultry sound of her laughter made it nearly impossible not to reach for her, to drag her into his arms and find out if her mouth tasted as sweet as it looked.

"Somehow that doesn't surprise me." She gave him a slow blink, then a sexy arch of her eyebrows. "Although I was thinking more in terms of a T-Rex."

"A killer dinosaur?" His own laugh rumbled up. Only his fellow Mavericks could make him laugh so easily. But despite her baggy overalls and vast skills with power tools, she was worlds away from being one of the guys.

She pointed at the garage. "Didn't you see my masterpiece inside?" She said the word *masterpiece* far too mockingly.

He spoke the absolute truth. "I saw only you."

She stilled, blinked, and the afternoon heat wrapped around them, tugging him another step closer. So close that he could practically feel the heat radiating from her skin to his.

"You really should see the T-Rex." She murmured the words as if they were talking about moonlit nights rather than a vicious dinosaur made out of all manner of sharp castoffs. "I'm building it out of road signs riddled with bullet holes. Battle-scarred, but alive and kicking despite its hunters."

"Isn't the T-Rex the hunter?"

"They're misunderstood," she supplied simply. "But the truth is, even if you like him, I have to let your space speak to me first. And if you want me to build something for you—" She held his gaze, her finger just short of tapping his nose. "—you have to let the space choose what's right."

Charlie's property clearly needed more than a new roof. But instead of rolling over like most artists who were desperate to sell their work, she wouldn't be pushed. He was amazed that she appeared to be as open as her art—no artifice, nothing to hide. No smoke, no mirrors. Easygoing Charlie-not-Charlotte. And he found her more attractive than any glittering, cosmetically enhanced celebrity or society woman he'd ever dated. More intriguing.

More *everything*.

"Deal. The space chooses the sculpture." He reached for his checkbook, then pulled a pen from the pocket over his heart. He wrote the numbers, signed his name, and handed her the check.

She read, gripping the paper tightly between her fingers as if a sudden gust of wind might whip it away. But when she raised her eyes, her beautifully lush mouth was a flat line. "This is a joke."

"I never joke about a hundred thousand dollars. I know that whatever you fill my empty space with will end up being worth more than that, Charlie." As he held her gaze and said, "A hell of a lot more," he wondered if she understood that he was talking about far more than her work.

Because something told Sebastian that Charlie just might be his destiny after all.

CHAPTER TWO

One hundred thousand dollars.

Charlie stared at the check. She couldn't believe it. But there were the numbers, written out in all that lovely script. The man's handwriting was as beautiful as his face. And his clothes. And especially his body beneath the expensive suit pants and shirt.

Of course she'd recognized Sebastian Montgomery's name when his broker called to make the appointment. She couldn't open her Internet home page without seeing the face of the media mogul and self-help guru. But she'd refused to let herself get worked up. Especially when his broker told her that Mr. Montgomery had a *mild* interest in her work after seeing the dragon. She'd figured he'd look at her junk and walk away like pretty much everyone else did.

Instead...the fabulously gorgeous billionaire had just written her an enormous check for a piece of her *magnificent* junk.

Was it possible that he had more money than sense? It wasn't too great a stretch to assume that all filthy-rich people were a tiny bit off their rockers, was it?

His sleek black luxury vehicle, which sure as heck hadn't come off any showroom floor because she'd never seen anything like it, was covered in dust from her dirt-and-gravel drive. And yet somehow, even after tromping through her dusty acre, his white dress shirt was pristine, his slacks were still perfectly creased, and his shoes had actually retained their shine. Lord if the man didn't smell good too, like sun and long stretches of white sand beach. Whereas she was dressed in stained overalls, an ancient tank top, and filthy work boots. Not to mention her hair had to be sticking out every which way.

She hadn't expected Sebastian to make her skin heat and her breath catch. And she *definitely* hadn't expected him to write her a six-figure check.

"I guarantee it won't bounce."

Normally she would have laughed or made a joke. But she was holding on to ninety-nine thousand too many dollars to remember how to do either of those things. All she could remember was how to be honest. "I'm overwhelmed."

True honesty, however, would be to admit that she wished she'd run a comb through her hair, put a little gloss on her lips, and swapped out the overalls and boots for a dress and heels. Even if the only fancy outfit she owned was as outdated as the house and in not much better shape. She'd never worried about her looks, but this man brought out a need in her to be, well, feminine.

And yet, even though she wasn't looking at all pretty right then, somehow he managed to make her feel appreciated. *Desired*. All with just a look.

Oh God...she was *way* out of her depth.

But did she ever need that money. Desperately. And not for a new roof either. She knew she'd appeared casual, aloof even, when she'd assumed he'd offer her a few hundred dollars for a sculpture. But this kind of money was life-changing. In the best possible ways.

"No need to be overwhelmed," he reassured her. "I know you can do this for me."

Actually, she'd be doing it for her mother. With that much cash, Charlie could finally get her mom out of the substandard care facility in Fremont that was all Charlie could afford, and into the great facility in Los Gatos. The new retirement home had an entry fee that Charlie hadn't had any hope of raising until Sebastian Montgomery walked into her life and literally handed her the chance to make her mother's life better.

One hundred thousand would take care of the entry cost and pay for a few months. And if Charlie could keep up the fees for five years, then her mother would be guaranteed a room in the facility even if they ran out of money. It was a gamble, though, because if she couldn't make the monthly payment, Charlie would lose the deposit along with having to move her mother again. But what if Sebastian Montgomery's project were the beginning of everything, opening other doors that might lead her to the financial miracle she desperately needed?

So even if she was more than a little stunned by how much he seemed to like her sculptures—and though the idea of stepping into a glittering and glossy world like his for any length of time was daunting—Charlie knew she couldn't blow it. Stuffing down the inner voice that said a world like Sebastian's was beyond her, she said, "Scratch the overwhelmed part. When do I start?"

"I like your enthusiasm."

When he grinned at her, it was impossible not to grin back. He was the best-looking man she'd ever set eyes on, the kind of guy who could turn a girl's head, to use the old phrase.

Hers had turned the second she'd spotted him standing in the doorway of her studio.

"I'm sure you'll want to see the space as soon as possible, so I'll pick you up tomorrow at eleven and you can inspect the lobby in full sunlight."

When he wanted something, he obviously didn't waste any time. A part of her wanted to spend some time inventorying her junk in case something fit when she saw the fountain, but with the check practically burning a hole in her hand, she said, "Eleven sounds perfect."

"We should talk about your workshop too."

She could read the look in his too-sexy brown eyes; he thought she lived in a dump. She knew she should renovate the old garage, but she couldn't waste money on something that worked, even if it wasn't perfect. "I know the garage doesn't look like much, but—"

"There's a barn on my property in the Hayward Hills that I've never used. It'll work great as a workshop for you, especially if you decide to construct something larger."

A part of her resisted the idea of leaving the studio she'd always worked in. But she'd be stupid to turn down his offer for that reason. "I'd like to check it out first," she said. "It's opposite the commute, which is good. Although—" She looked over at her dusty old truck sitting by the garage. "I'm not so sure about my truck holding out for too many daily commutes." These days it was practically held together by rubber bands.

"There's a guest bungalow on my property. You can stay there and avoid driving back and forth." He paused before adding, "Unless you have a husband or boyfriend who might object to my whisking you away."

She'd had a few serious boyfriends. Serious, at least, until they'd eventually come clean about expecting her to do "normal" things like clean up the yard and throw out all the broken pieces of instruments and gates and tools that she'd so carefully collected over the years. At first a man might tell her she was a breath of fresh air. But in the end, it turned out that none of them actually appreciated all the mixed-up, jumbled pieces that made Charlie who she was any more than they appreciated the mixed-up, jumbled pieces that would become her sculptures.

"There's no one to object to a little whisking." She hoped he didn't catch the slight edge to her voice. She was happy being alone, of course. But sometimes it still stung a little bit to know that she hadn't been enough just the way she was for any of the guys she'd been serious with.

"Good." Sebastian was clearly pleased to hear that she was single. Pleased enough that she had to wonder if the attraction she'd felt between them was more than just a figment of her overactive imagination. "Then the bungalow is yours to stay in and the RV barn is your studio."

Every need a girl had, he provided an answer for. He made her want to throw caution to the winds, to just be reckless and say yes. *Yes* even to the things he didn't say, but that she felt simmering between them as they negotiated the details of the commission.

There was something about him. Not just his over-the-top good looks or his self-possession and command, but the way her body reacted to his nearness and her skin overheated—and not from the hot afternoon. He made her heart beat faster and harder than usual. She'd never paid attention to a man's smell, but Sebastian smelled *incredible*.

But as sorely tempted as she was by her reckless urges—and how badly she needed his hundred grand—she'd never respect herself if she just fell at his feet the way she guessed plenty of women already had. "How far from your house is this guest bungalow and workspace?"

He held her a moment with those deliciously cocoa-brown eyes. "Down the hill. Maybe a quarter of a mile."

Okay, so the buildings weren't exactly next door. Still, she could never take his money if it were tied to anything but her art. And there was only one way to know for sure. She had to ask the hard question. "You're not expecting anything from me other than a sculpture, are you?"

"I'm expecting nothing more than the unexpected." She appreciated the way he tossed the Zanti Misfits back at her. "The commission is yours. The house and the barn are there simply to make it easier for you. I'll pay for all the materials you need as well. I want whatever it is you're going to create for me and my building. Nothing else is *expected*." He emphasized the word.

But anything can be given. She heard that loud and clear.

No question, this man had the charm to talk anyone into anything. He'd just dealt her all the good cards. She'd be closer to her mom's nursing home, at least until she could get her moved. She wouldn't have to fork out for materials—not that the stuff she got from junkyards cost a lot of money, but the tools were expensive—and she'd get to stay in a bungalow where the plumbing probably worked a heck of a lot better than hers. She'd have a huge workspace at her disposal. This commission could open doors for her so that she could actually be an earning artist.

Yet there was more. So much more, considering that she could actually feel the heat of his body and the touch of his eyes in the simmering sensation that flowed between them. Wanting him had seemed natural from the moment she'd seen him silhouetted in the sunlight outside her garage. And, if she wanted him for the summer weeks that they were near each other, something told her she could have some very sexy fun with this gorgeous man too. Charlie didn't have weird hang-ups about sex, and she definitely didn't have expectations anymore when it came to men ever appreciating her idiosyncrasies in the long run. If it happened with him, it happened.

She might decide to be reckless when it came to pleasure, but she'd make sure to be careful about letting herself fall in love with the beautiful man who had just changed her life.

Charlie folded the check and shoved it into the front pocket of her overalls, closc to her heart. "You've got yourself a deal."

CHAPTER THREE

At eleven on the dot the next morning, Sebastian picked Charlie up in a limousine that quickly became covered in the dust of her yard. Rather than overalls and steel-toes, she'd chosen a pair of dark-wash, slim-fit jeans, a peasant blouse, and sandals. She'd been pleased to find one pair of jeans that didn't sport burn holes from stray sparks off her arc welder.

Sebastian seemed to approve of her outfit as she slid in beside him and he said, "Good morning," in a deep voice that was enough to raise her temperature several degrees, turning the air-conditioned interior of the car positively sultry.

"Nice ride," she told him as she appreciated the soft leather with the slide of her palm over the seat. The limo was over the top, true, but he was a rich man and she could already tell that he did everything with style. And clearly enjoyed every second of it. "Although you didn't have a driver with you yesterday, did you?"

"I didn't want to split my attention between you and the road today."

Her breath caught at the simple way he'd just told her that she mattered to him, both as an artist *and* as a woman. He always had just the right words. The fact that it was also his job didn't make their impact any less.

"You've probably been working all morning and didn't take the time to eat. So I brought you brunch." He waved a hand over the spread he'd provided. "Bagels, cream cheese, and lox." Sebastian tapped the coffee carafe. "And this is a special Arabian coffee imported by a friend of mine."

She didn't know which smelled better, him or the coffee. Both made her mouth water. He looked seriously scrumptious in another suit. She wasn't necessarily partial to the executive type, but Sebastian Montgomery was rapidly changing her preferences on a lot of things.

"Sit back," he told her as he poured her a cup of coffee. "I'll serve you."

A blush crept into her cheeks as she was instantly hit with an explicit image of him serving her breakfast in bed. He set her cup on the console, then slathered cream cheese on half of a sliced bagel, topped it with lox, and passed her the plate.

"You're too good to be true."

He fixed her with a gaze that was as sultry as she felt. "No. I *am* that good."

"And cocky about it too." She couldn't hold back her smile—couldn't see a reason to.

He laughed, and she felt the sound rumble through her. "So I've been told."

A certain amount of cockiness was probably good in his business. And the truth was she didn't find it at all unattractive. Not on him, anyway. Somehow, it only added to his charm.

She dumped a pile of sugar and cream into her cup, but he took his coffee black and didn't make a bagel for himself. "Aren't you eating?"

"Like I said, I want to concentrate on you." When he sat back and asked her, "Why welding?" the full force of his concentration felt like a warm stroke of heat along her body. "From the research I've done, it's not something a woman usually gets into."

He'd done research? Only on her profession? Or had he tried to find out more about her too? "My dad was a welder by trade. I was an only kid and he didn't have a son, so I was it." She'd loved that father-daughter bonding in his workshop. "He was a patient teacher."

"I'm sure you are too." Sebastian caressed her with his gaze, moving from her eyes to her cheeks to her lips, as if he were memorizing every feature.

That, too, was part of his charm and his art of persuasion: total focus. "I love teaching," she told him. "And I try to be patient. Although, I'm afraid I don't always manage it."

"Someone like you, with such a clear vision..." He smiled at her. "I've worked with artists before. I understand wanting things exactly the way you want them."

He was talking about art, but the word *want* hung between them in the back of the limo, making her even more aware of just how close he was...and the fact that it would only take one small move for her to be on his lap.

And for his mouth to be beneath hers.

She'd told herself yesterday that she would be okay with starting something physical with Sebastian at some point. And he'd been clear about not expecting anything from her other than art. Nonetheless, her sculpture still had to come first so there would be no confusion at any point about his commission getting tangled up with hot, sweaty, yummy sex.

Considering they hadn't even made it to the site yet, she deliberately put a halt to thoughts of getting naked with him. Instead, she talked about her dad. "My father worked on bridges, high-rises, mall projects. He did stuff in oil fields too, on the rigs. And pipelines. A lot of the pipeline work was in remote areas so he sometimes had to leave us for a while. I missed him when he was gone. But he missed us just as much."

"He sounds like a great dad." For a moment, Sebastian's gaze seemed to turn inward, as if he were looking back into the past at his own relationship with his father. One that she sensed from the expression on his face might not have been the best in the world.

"Most of the time," she said as he came back to her, "we moved with him. A lot of the projects he worked on could last for a year, so we didn't stay in any one place for very long."

"How did you feel about moving all the time and leaving your friends behind?"

Charlie didn't mind his questions, not when he seemed genuinely interested in her answers. No man she'd ever been with had given her so much pure, concentrated attention. Being the center of such focus could quickly become addictive.

As addictive as she suspected being Sebastian's lover would be.

"Sometimes it was freeing to start over, with everything new and fresh. But at the same time," she found herself admitting, "I have no idea what it's like to have friends I've known all my life." Wanting to learn more about him too, she asked, "Did you move much?"

His eyebrows went up in surprise as if he'd expected her to know his story, probably because he was so famous that most people already did. "Born and raised in Chicago. I've known my friends since I was a kid. They're like my brothers."

She hadn't given in to the urge to do a Google search on him last night, hadn't let herself give in to any doubts about their new arrangement. Whatever she learned about Sebastian, she wanted to come straight from the man himself, and now that he was talking, she wanted more. "You all still see one another?"

"We have several business ventures together. We're known as the Maverick Group."

"But that's business. What about spending time with them for fun?"

He looked a little surprised by her follow-up question, as if most people didn't differentiate between personal ties and business ones. Likely, she thought, because most people wanted something from the sexy billionaire. The thing was, when it came to Sebastian Montgomery, she could see how complicated *wanting* could be.

She wanted to make the sculpture for his building. She also wanted him as a man.

Just how intertwined those things were going to get, she wasn't sure. Something told her, however, that both could very likely end up being the biggest highs—and the greatest pleasures—of her life...

"We were all together in Chicago for July Fourth. It was a great time." He grinned at her and said, "You would like everyone. And I'm sure they'd like you too."

Again, pleasure suffused her at his words. He truly did know how to make a person feel special, just the way her father always had. "How many Mavericks are there?"

"Five. Evan, Will, Daniel, Matt, and me. Daniel's parents, Susan and Bob, raised us, right along with Daniel and his little sister, from the time we were all about twelve or thirteen years old."

"They must be very generous."

"They are," he answered with undisguised fondness. "Susan, Bob, and the Mavericks made me the man I am today. I owe them everything."

There was nothing cocky about him now. The way he shared credit for his success was both humble and sweet. Even a billionaire, with all his money, needed a friend to unload with. Whereas Charlie's only true confidante was her mom...and for the most part Charlie tried to shield her mother from the problems in the outside world. Francine Ballard had enough of her own problems to deal with.

"We'd do anything for each other. We're all godfathers to Matt's kid." He smiled as he thought of the child, his beautiful face transforming yet again. "Noah's a great little boy."

By that look, she knew with perfect certainty that Sebastian was also a great godfather. She wanted to ask about his parents, since he hadn't mentioned them, but before she could Sebastian said, "We're almost there. What would you like to know about the building before we arrive?"

Wait...they were almost there? It felt as though five minutes had passed in the limo, not thirty. That's what being the focus of Sebastian Montgomery's attention did—made the outside world do a fadeout so that there was only him, his maleness, the deep timbre of his voice.

"Everything," she replied. "Tell me everything."

They both heard the sensual undertone beneath her question at the same moment. She'd always been curious, always been drawn to power. It was why she loved creating and delving deep into magnificent creatures like lions and dragons. But she'd never been drawn to anyone as much as she was to Sebastian. From the first moment, she'd been powerfully aware of him and had wanted to know, wanted to experience *everything* with him.

But for now, they each pretended it was all about his building as he said, "It's an existing structure that I had gutted. There are all the necessities—a helicopter pad on the roof, a fully equipped gym and swimming pool on the tenth floor, and my production studio on the thirtieth."

She almost laughed out loud at his definition of *necessities*. A helicopter pad had never quite made it on to her list.

"We've constructed a central lobby with escalators up to a mezzanine that overlooks the fountain. People will need to walk all the way around it to reach the elevators in the back. Everyone will see what you create from all possible angles."

She was well aware that this was a big project he had hired her to do. Despite how easily he'd written her the check, she sensed that he wasn't the kind of person who threw money away. Yet it wasn't until this moment that she truly felt the awesome pressure that came with such a commission.

"I probably shouldn't tell you how terrified I'm feeling, should I?"

He reached out and put a hand over hers. The touch sizzled through her, instantly shifting terror to something hot and hungry instead.

"You should always tell me what you're feeling. *Always.* And you should also know that I have full faith and confidence that you can do the space justice. That's why I chose you."

The weight of his words—and his gaze—settled over her. It wasn't that she doubted her abilities. She thought her creations were pretty cool. But this was a whole different level. One where plenty of other people would be seeing her art...and judging the way she took the crazy jumble of her vision and made all the pieces a reality.

"Expect the unexpected," she reminded herself, saying what had become her mantra so many years ago almost under her breath.

"I always do," he agreed with a smile. "And then I make sure I'm prepared to deal with whatever comes. Especially when the unexpected is more beautiful, intelligent, and captivating than I ever could have dreamed."

Charlie's head, her body, her heart were all still spinning as they pulled up to the curb. Sebastian opened the door and drew her out of the car, their hands linked. And as they stood on the sidewalk, closer now even than they'd been in the limo, the heat arcing between them was electric.

Explosive.

So explosive that she had to pull her hand away just to keep a little sanity. And remind herself that the commission needed to come first. *Before* all the hot sex she was dying to have with him.

She forced her gaze away from his to take in the immense skyscraper rising above them— and that was when her breath left her lungs for the second time that morning.

Windows reflected the surrounding buildings and the San Francisco Bay. High on the glass façade a monumental sign proclaimed to the world in huge blue letters that the building belonged to MMI. To Sebastian Montgomery, who *was* Montgomery Media International. A wooden construction barricade walled off the front while a covered walkway led to the entrance.

Inside lurked a completely different world. Traffic noise was hushed. At least three stories high, the lobby ceiling was made entirely of glass that grew up out of the floor at the front and curled over, allowing a wide strip of sunlight to pour down from between the surrounding buildings. Above them, the curved balustrade of the mezzanine provided an overlook. The floor appeared to be polished marble in varying shades of gray and black swirled through with cream. A broad belt of sunshine crept across the marble toward the huge circular fountain filling the lobby center. Charlie put a hand to her mouth, mesmerized as beams of light slid up the sides, and the fountain's tiles seemed to glow with iridescent color—blues, greens, and reds, like a hummingbird in sunlight.

"It's magnificent," she whispered to Sebastian, wondering how on earth she could do it justice.

"I agree," he said in the same hushed tone, but his gaze was on her, not the fountain. "Totally magnificent."

CHAPTER FOUR

Magnificent. It was more than just a word to Sebastian, encompassing not only Charlie's beauty but also the wonder with which she took in everything around her.

"Did you plan the light show this way?" Her voice was quiet, as if they were in a sanctuary.

"It lasts only a short time as the sun moves through at noon. Then the effect is gone."

"You'll have people coming here just for this sight." She held her hands up to the ceiling, the sky, her skin glowing like that of a goddess in the sunlight streaming over her. "And it's not even hot."

"Low-E glass reduces the heat."

"You thought of everything."

"That's what I do." In Sebastian's experience, if you didn't account for every detail, if you didn't understand absolutely everything about the people you dealt with, life could go completely down the tubes.

But he'd never imagined this moment, standing close to the most beautiful, talented woman he'd ever seen. So close he could barely keep from shoving his hands into the thick, gorgeous red masses of her hair and tasting her.

Devouring her.

"Can you already see what the space needs?" He grinned as he added, "A T-Rex, maybe?"

Her smile was a radiant curve. She'd put her palms against her neck, her elbows together in front of her, as if the posture increased her concentration. Tipping her head one way, then the other, she looked up, turned a circle, then stopped in the same spot she'd started from. "I love my T-Rex, but he's not right for this space."

Watching her work, getting to be a part of her creative process, had a physical effect on him. A need to touch, to taste, to explore. To try to satisfy all his cravings for her right here, right now. Yet at the same time, it went beyond sex. Because he wanted to be a part of that inner life, to touch the inner woman, to explore her genius. During his early morning meeting, he'd even found himself imagining how he wanted to sketch her. Instead of paying attention to the details of the negotiation, he couldn't stop thinking of her.

Sebastian had never felt this way about a woman. Not until Charlie.

Then, when her eyes suddenly met his, he was hit with another one of those electric jolts as she said, "I know what you need."

You.

"Tell me."

"A chariot race. Like in *Ben-Hur*." Her arms came out, encompassing the whole, then her fingers curled as if she were creating her vision out of water that wasn't even flowing yet. "Four horses running so fast they're almost flying. The chariot bouncing so hard, it throws its driver, then slams on its side, snaps its wheel, and the magnificent stallions gallop headlong, dragging the broken carcass of the chariot behind them." She tilted her head as if she was already looking at the sculpture in the middle of his building. "Can you see it?"

"Yes, I see it. The horses breaking free of all attempts to control their power—of everything holding them back—so they can run as fast as they were born to go. It's what all of us truly long for."

The images were so alive in her head that it would have been impossible for him not to see them too. But even clearer was *Charlie*, red hair on fire in the sun, her features shining, the light coming from inside her as well as outside. Her eyelashes lay lush against her cheeks as she closed her eyes for one long moment of vision. Her excitement was like fuel, making his heart beat faster, his blood pump harder.

"The fountain has to blow the water up, right under their feet, like it's earth and dust roiling beneath their beating hooves. Can you do that?"

"Yes." For her, he could do anything. He *would* do anything. Everything she wanted. Everything she needed. He would be her patron. He would show her work to society, introduce her to his world. And he wouldn't rest until she'd conquered it all.

She pivoted on her heel and grabbed his forearms, her touch branding him. "It was meant to be here. I can see it so clearly."

Her eyes were the deep verdant green of a forest when the sun hits the leaves after a hard rain. Her skin was flushed pink, her fingers warm, her grip on him unrelenting. Their eyes locked for an endless moment.

Then her gaze fell to his mouth. Her breath came harder, and she licked her bottom lip. She held more tightly to him, her body leaning closer...closer... He wanted his mouth on hers. He wanted her lips on his. He wanted to taste and touch and never let go.

"Sebastian," she said softly, with the same awe he'd heard when she'd seen the light come shining through just minutes before. "Do you want it?" She could have meant the statue.

She could have meant the heat that sizzled between them.

"God, yes," he said, his voice so full of need it almost hurt as it rose up from his throat. "I want it all."

He was barely a heartbeat from tangling his fingers in her hair and crashing his mouth down on hers when his brain replayed her question from the previous afternoon: *You're not expecting anything from me other than a sculpture, are you?*

He'd promised her there weren't any strings attached to the commission. Which meant that even though he wanted to kiss her more than he wanted to take his next breath, he'd never forgive himself if she thought the price of her art was sex.

"Do you believe I want your chariot as much as I want you?"

She paused, just long enough that he knew her answer even before she said, "Maybe."

"Maybe," he said slowly as he let himself take one more greedy glance at her gorgeous mouth, "isn't in my vocabulary."

"It isn't usually in mine either," she told him in her delightfully straightforward way. "Then again—" She smiled and her eyes sparkled in the rain of sunlight. "—I can't think of the last time I was so tempted by a billionaire. You are going to adore my chariot and horses."

"I'm sure I will." He couldn't imagine anything about her that he wouldn't adore. That he wouldn't crave. "Your new workshop is all ready for you."

"I've got some things to wrap up first. Let's make the move to your workshop the day after tomorrow. Plus, I've got to load all my welding equipment into my truck." She ticked things off on her fingers. "The MIG and the TIG. My torch. My plasma cutter. And any parts I can use from the yard. It will be better if I just drive my truck over."

Charlie spoke easily about trucks and trailers and torches. But he could see that she was beautiful and accomplished enough to fit into any world in which she chose to live. He would open a new universe to her, one full of glittering possibility, and he knew instinctively that his world would embrace her completely.

He wanted to take her upstairs to the helipad right this second and fly her off to his estate in the Hayward Hills so she wouldn't have a chance to change her mind. But he'd already learned that Charlie was as fiercely independent as her work. Was it because she'd moved around so much as a kid? Or was there another reason? Had someone in her past disappointed her and made it difficult for her to trust others? Sebastian understood that all too well, knew just how hard it could be to trust that the people who were supposed to be there for you would actually be there when you needed them.

Whatever her reasons, he knew for sure that dragging her to the workshop on his property as if he were a caveman would be a mistake. A big one. So instead of insisting she start today, he said, "I'll send a trailer with some guys to help with the loading. It'll be easier than trying to get everything in your truck."

Just as she had when he'd offered her the commission yesterday, she didn't jump at his offer. Instead, she took the time to turn it over in her mind, before she finally nodded. "That will work great, thank you." She tilted her chin at the fountain and when she touched him again, her hand on his arm, everything inside him stilled, absorbing her heat, her closeness, her heady scent. "The sun show...it's almost over."

He put his hand over hers on his arm, bound her to him as the wide swath of sunlight made its final arc across the floor, just as the chariot and its stallions would. "The horses will look like they're racing through an arena." Shining, alive. Like her.

And then, in the next moment, it was gone, leaving the fountain in the shade of the building's façade. But he could still see the brilliant vision as if it were a mirage lingering on his horizon.

"It will be spectacular," he told her. "*You* will be."

He felt the slightest tremble of her hand beneath his, before she took a deep breath, then smiled into his eyes and said, "That's the plan."

* * *

Francine Ballard's gnarled fingers gripped the walker's handles. Charlie's natural tendency was to let her mother hang on to her, so that Charlie could keep her steady and safe. But her mother had to do things on her own, and since Charlie was a chip off the old block, she understood that was better for her mother's wellbeing.

"Just two more passes along the hallway," her mom said. She walked the halls four times a day for exercise. *Use it or lose it*, she always claimed. And it was true that without the workout, she would have been in a wheelchair years ago.

As soon as Sebastian had brought her home from their excursion to the city, Charlie had jumped in her dusty old truck and rattled across the Dumbarton Bridge to Fremont. She couldn't wait to tell her mother all about her new project, but for the next few minutes she didn't want to break her concentration.

"Hello, Gladys," her mom called through an open door as they passed.

"You go, girl," the gray-haired lady called back. "Hi, Charlie." Gladys was ninety and bedridden, and she loved soap operas in the afternoon. She could recite everything that had happened over the last ten years on each of her favorite shows as if the characters were her relatives.

Charlie's mom had lived at Shady Lane for the last two years. But there was no shade, no lane, and no garden. There were only concrete walls, linoleum floors, beige paint, the underlying scent of cleaning fluids and medicines, and the competing sounds of too many televisions tuned to different channels.

Charlie had come to her parents late in life, and she'd still been a toddler when her mom was diagnosed with severe degenerative osteoarthritis. Though she'd been in her early forties, Francine's joints had begun to collapse. After years of pain and increasing loss of use, she'd had her first operation in her fifties to fuse three of the vertebrae in her spine. She'd soon had to give up sewing and needlework, which had been her joy. Since then she'd had all the joints in her fingers replaced, except the pinkies, which were etched into a permanent curl. Her ankles had disintegrated and were now held together by steel and bolts and staples.

But at seventy, her mother still walked a mile of hallway every day. Because Francine Ballard never gave up.

Charlie smiled at her mother as she moved at a snail's pace beside her, her mom's head barely coming to her chin now that years of arthritis had compressed her spine. "Okay, I need a short rest before I finish my walk." Her mother plunked her bottom down on the walker. In a compartment beneath the seat, she kept a book and a purse with her reading glasses, tissues, a brush, and her lipstick. Today's outfit was a skirt and sweater set in a dusty rose color. She had her hair done once a week in the nursing home's salon, and Charlie did her nails when she visited. It didn't matter that her fingers were bent in odd directions, her mom loved the pretty pink polish.

After resting a minute, she said, "Okay, I'm ready to keep going now."

Charlie put her hand beneath her mother's elbow and helped her up so that they could steer back into the central hall. This wasn't a bad place, but the staff was overworked and didn't have time for anything extra. The residents never went on outings. The food, though nutritious, was often unidentifiable. The worst, though, was the lack of anywhere to sit outside, to smell the flowers and get a little sun to heat old bones. Charlie often took her mom out for lunch or to a nearby park, but those excursions weren't the same as having a lovely garden she could go to whenever she wanted. She knew her mother would adore the gardens at the Los Gatos facility. Instead of walking institutional hallways, she could stroll through lush greenery and fragrant flowers and read her book in the shade of a leafy tree, in the gazebo, or by the koi pond.

At the end of the hall, her mother let out a long, satisfied sigh. "Another lap done. Let's sit in the lounge." Francine shared a room with Rosemary, who was nearly deaf and had the TV on so loud, Charlie couldn't think, though thankfully it didn't seem to bother her mother at all.

They parked her walker outside the lounge, and her mom made her way to the sofa, moving hand by hand across each chair back she passed, while Charlie brewed tea. She'd brought china mugs with her because her mother claimed tea tasted better in bone china, especially if the cups had been warmed with hot water. For herself, Charlie pushed the whipped coffee button, creating foam on the top, then added milk and sugar to both her mother's cup and her own.

At the opposite end of the lounge, a TV blared for the six residents seated in front of it. A sallow-skinned lady, who must have been new since Charlie didn't recognize her, slept in an overstuffed chair kitty-corner to the sofa her mother had chosen.

Charlie carried the two flowered mugs, setting her mother's on the coffee table. "I brought your favorite." From the shopping bag she'd slung over her arm, she pulled a pink box from a fabulous bakery only a few blocks away, two china plates, and pretty paper napkins, then placed one half of an almond bear claw on the china. In the old days, her mother had made the most delicious pastries. But she'd had to give up baking when the pain of standing too long became excruciating, not to mention what all the measuring, mixing, and spooning had done to her fingers.

"This is so yummy." Her mother savored the pastry in little bites, enjoying every morsel. "Now tell me what has you positively glowing."

Charlie had known her mother would see what she was feeling. *Glowing* was the perfect word for it. "I've got a new commission. A really big one."

"That's wonderful. I'm so happy for you, honey. You deserve it."

Just like her father, Charlie's mother had always believed in her art. They'd lost her dad to cancer seven years ago. She and her mother had taken care of him together at the end, with the help of Hospice, who'd come in twice a day. As close as she and her mother had been before, that difficult time had forged an even deeper bond between them.

"Tell me all about the commission."

Tell me. Sebastian had whispered the words to her, and she'd wanted to tell him everything. Not just about her vision for the chariot, but all the secrets she kept buried down deep. Even from herself.

"My work is going to be shown off in a high-rise in San Francisco at the headquarters of a company called Montgomery Media International."

"That sounds familiar," her mother said, frowning a little as she tried to figure out where she'd heard it.

"Sebastian Montgomery is pretty famous." Charlie had assumed he'd be some glib TV personality, all looks and fast talking, but there seemed to be so much more to him. "He's on TV a lot and in the papers. That's probably why it sounds so familiar."

Charlie felt a thrill just saying his name. Or maybe the thrill came from the heated memory of the moment she'd put her hands on him and said, *Do you want it?* Even better had been his response. *God, yes. I want it all.*

Charlie's stomach did a slow roll of desire just from remembering how the sparks had flown like crazy between them that morning. She wanted him with an intensity she'd only ever felt while working on her art—and every sign indicated he felt exactly the same way—but he hadn't crushed his lips to hers. Hadn't given them a first, desperate taste of each other. Instead, he'd asked her if she trusted his intentions. Asked her if she truly believed that he wanted her art as much as he wanted to take her to bed. And when she'd hesitated...

"What does he want you to create, dear?"

Magnificence.

He not only seemed to believe Charlie could do it, but he was also truly determined to make sure she didn't think her six-figure paycheck came with any naked, sexy strings.

"The lobby has an enormous fountain, and I'm going to create a chariot with stallions, a horrendous race, foam flying, dust billowing."

Her mother clapped her hands, her fingers so crooked, they barely made a sound. "Like *Ben-Hur*. Oh, I loved that movie and Charlton Heston." She sighed dreamily. "He was so handsome." Her mother would have been a teenager when the movie came out. "I take it Sebastian is pleased with your vision?"

Charlie grinned. "Very."

Her mother's eyebrows went up as if she'd just realized there was more to the story than a great commission. "Is he gorgeous?"

"He's very good-looking. But this is business." At least for right now.

She didn't want to get her mother all worked up that Charlie was finally going to have some romance in her life, only to disappoint her if nothing happened. Or if something *did* happen, and then Sebastian turned out to be like all the other guys she'd dated, eventually becoming frustrated with the fact that she wasn't a neat and tidy package of a woman. Odds, Charlie knew, were on that one. Finding someone who liked her just the way she was— junkyard and all—would be a tall order, indeed. Good thing she already liked her life. Apart from her worries about her mother's care.

"He's going to pay me a lot of money, Mom. Enough to get you into that place in Los

Gatos. Remember we toured it last year? Magnolia Gardens."

"Charlie, that's so far out of our league."

"He's paying me a *lot* of money, and I don't know what I'd do with all of it if I didn't use it to put you somewhere that at least has a garden. And good food too."

"The food's fine here."

Her mother hated that Charlie had to put money toward her care. But they were family, and she'd do anything for her mom. "I want you to live where you can feel the heat of the sun on your skin and smell the blooming flowers."

"Charlie. Sweetheart. You should be saving for your own future."

"They have more staff. More doctors." Charlie lowered her voice. She didn't want to insult anyone here, but she needed her mother to understand how important this chance was. "There's physical therapy and hydro baths, all the things that can help ease your pain. I want that for you. It will make *me*—" She tapped her chest. "—feel better."

Her mother stared deeply into her china mug, as if there were leaves at the bottom that would predict the future. "Your father wasn't good at saving for retirement. And all his medical bills just ended up being so big." They'd had insurance, but so many things were only partially covered. "I'm so sorry it's all fallen on you, honey."

"I'm not sorry, Mom."

"But you could use the money to fix the house."

Five years ago, Charlie had sunk all her money into the property because it was perfect for her studio, such as it was, and it was close to the college where she taught. The land was valuable, the house, not so much. But if she'd realized her mother would need full-time assisted living, she would have made a different choice. "Your care is more important to me right now. Let me do this. Please."

"You always could wrap your father and me around your little finger." But her mother was smiling. "I would love to smell the flowers and sit out in the sun more often."

"I'll start making arrangements."

"Thank you, honey. You're too good to me. You always have been." Her mother patted her hand. "Now, tell me more about your Sebastian."

"He's not *mine*, Mom. He's just an art patron." But even as she said it, she knew Sebastian could never be *just* anything. Especially when he made her body heat and her heart race as though she were having palpitations.

And when she was already counting down the hours until she saw him again.

CHAPTER FIVE

It wasn't just a trailer. Sebastian had sent a freaking semi with four burly men who lifted her heavy equipment as if it were so many down pillows.

They'd arrived at ten on Friday morning. Fifteen minutes later, Sebastian flew in. Literally. In a helicopter, for God's sake. His pilot landed at the edge of her property, just beyond the junkyard of parts. Charlie couldn't imagine ever having that kind of money. All she needed was enough to take care of her mom and keep her own roof from falling in and she'd be perfectly happy.

Then again, as Sebastian crossed the junkyard to join her on the drive, it occurred to her that maybe there were a couple of other things that could also make her happy. Most of them having to do with getting naked with the beautiful man coming toward her.

"I missed you yesterday." It was one heck of a *good morning.* Almost as good as the way he put a hand on her arm, stroking her skin. "Everything going okay?"

Charlie tried to pretend there was nothing over-the-top about a helicopter sitting in her yard or a billionaire driving her wild with nothing but a simple touch. To use her mother's word, he was *yummy* in a pair of butt-hugging jeans and a short-sleeved black shirt that defined every hard muscle and emphasized just how broad he was in a way his suit hadn't.

The often buried feminine voice inside of her told her she should have worn something better than her overalls and steel-toed boots. But it was moving day and she hadn't been sure whether he would show up, or merely send his guys.

Boy, had he shown up.

"Totally fine." She was glad she sounded completely normal, not starstruck. Or like a teenage girl whose heart was back-flipping at how incredibly handsome he was in the sunlight. "We're making sure everything gets strapped down." She called out to Jerry who had a jet-black mustache, "Don't forget the ladder."

He waved an acknowledgment as he rolled a dolly holding her barrel of nuts and bolts up the ramp and into the cavernous semi.

"I didn't need you to rent a trailer this big, Sebastian."

"How many barrels of nuts and bolts are you bringing?"

"Just one."

"And barrels of screws?"

"Only one."

He cocked an eyebrow as he asked, "How about barrels of monkeys?" in such a deadpan tone that she almost missed the joke.

Who would have thought that a billionaire could be adorable? She could get so attached if she let herself, she thought, as she answered his question just as seriously. "Seven. One for each day of the week."

"Now that I'm watching them load everything in, I'm thinking I should have sent a bigger trailer." He leaned close, so close that she was hit with a sudden rush of heat. One that had absolutely nothing to do with the hot sun. His bare skin brushed her, the dusting of hair on his arm soft against hers. She wondered if he had hair on his chest. How thick it was. How soft. And what his skin would smell like if she burrowed her nose against him. "Before we're done, you'll have everything in the yard stowed inside the trailer."

He smelled so good that she almost lost her train of thought, almost forgot she couldn't let him be right about absolutely everything, including the fact that she would probably need most of the semi for her equipment and supplies. "I'm only taking essentials."

She surveyed the property for anything else that might turn out to be essential, and of course she found plenty that was. Half an hour later, the trailer was packed with her equipment, her barrels, her parts, extra bottles of argon and other gases used in the welding process, boxes of protective gear, solder rolls, tubing, and miscellaneous tools. The last thing she needed was her suitcase.

When she walked out of her house with it, Sebastian rushed forward to take it from her. Though she could easily carry it, she appreciated his good manners. Someone had clearly raised him well.

"I've never met a woman who can pack for two months in a carry-on."

"As long as there's a washing machine in your guest cottage, I don't need to bring everything I own." She'd packed sundries like shampoo and toothpaste, work clothes, shorts, tops, her one good pair of jeans, a pair of sandals, her iPad, chargers. At the last minute, she'd thrown in a couple of sundresses.

"You are the queen of low maintenance."

"You do realize you're saying this to the woman who just filled up an entire semi with junk, right?"

"That's your art." He stowed her suitcase carefully in his helicopter. "It's a vocation, not maintenance." He said it with complete sincerity, despite the fun he'd made of all her barrels.

A vocation. Not junk. No guy she'd ever been attracted to had felt that way about what she did.

"Okay." He dusted off his hands. "We'll take the helicopter, and the guys can meet us."

The helicopter. It was hard to hold back a *wow.* Or to ignore just how badly she wanted to experience flying in a helicopter. But she needed to make sure she could come and go freely from his property while she was working on the chariot and horses. "That sounds like fun, but I need to drive my truck."

Sebastian eyed her dusty truck beside the garage. "You're free to use one of mine."

"You have a truck too?" Until now, she'd managed to be cool about his wealth—and everything he was offering her—but the question came out before she could stop it.

He simply grinned and said, "What can I say? I've liked playing with them since I was a kid. And honestly, I'd feel better having you drive something more reliable."

She looked at the dirt barely holding her truck together. He had a good point. Still, she was wary about agreeing to anything too quickly. Not when she'd been so careful to make sure she could easily take care of herself without depending on a man.

"No strings, Charlie," he reminded her in a soft voice.

She believed him. But what about the strings she might want to tie on at some point in the future? What if she fell for him? What if she let herself believe in him the way he seemed to believe in her already?

Don't borrow trouble, honey. It was something her mother had said to her more than once when they were taking care of her father, and then again when she had to move into the nursing home. *Just try to appreciate the good things we already have.*

"Thanks, I'd appreciate the loaner," she finally said, giving him a smile to let him know she truly meant it.

"Then we're ready to go." He circled his arm above his head, and a beat later, the helicopter's rotor blades started to whirl.

Sebastian held out his hand, offering her the adventure of a lifetime. Days spent with a billionaire and all his toys. A six-figure commission. Entrée into a glittering world of future art patrons.

There would also be pressure. Pressure to create. Pressure to fit in. And plenty of time to wonder if in the long run Sebastian might not be quite as charmed by her menagerie or her very unique quirks as he seemed to be right now...

No. She wouldn't let herself borrow any more trouble. She couldn't let this chance slip through her fingers just because she was afraid to step into shoes she'd never worn before.

Reminding herself that this was the life any artist in her right mind would die for, Charlie put her hand in his and let him sweep her away.

* * *

Half an hour later, Sebastian brought Charlie's suitcase into the guest bungalow. She'd filled almost an entire semi with her equipment, but she had only one small suitcase.

Sebastian couldn't begin to describe how attractive that was. Not that she needed any help in that department, given that he'd been seriously hard-pressed not to kiss her at least a hundred times this morning.

"I hope you'll be comfortable here."

"Comfortable?" She turned in a circle. "Look at this place. It's *huge.*"

There were four bedrooms that he'd equipped with flat-panel TVs, stereos, game consoles, and computers. The bathrooms all had a large jet tub, sauna, and rain shower. Sliding glass doors opened onto a deck and hot tub. And the kitchen was fully stocked with top-of-the-line appliances.

"I can't stay here for free. I have to pay you rent."

He'd be damned if he took a dollar from her. "I'm providing accommodations so that you're at your best when you're creating. Room and board is part of our deal."

"I don't remember *this* being part of the deal." She waved a hand. "All the luxury. A brand new truck at my disposal. Helicopter rides."

But he'd seen how much she'd enjoyed it, the way she'd been glued to the window when the pilot had flown them out over the Bay. Once upon a time he'd been floored by the view from above too, but these past few years he was always in a hurry just to get where he was going. Today, however, he'd reveled in her excitement and appreciation.

Thinking how much he'd appreciated the view—and her too—he said, "My truck is safer, this guest cottage is closer to the big workshop here, and the helicopter is easier and faster than sitting in traffic."

"I get all that, but you know it's not what I meant. It's just too much, Sebastian. Too much for some artist that you've hired to build a sculpture for your office building."

She was right about so many things, so flawless in her vision for her sculptures. But she was wrong about this. Nothing was too much for her. And soon, he'd make sure she knew that she deserved everything that would be hers once the rest of the art world finally discovered her incredible talent.

For now, though, he needed to know something. "Is it about the luxury itself? Or because you don't want to feel obligated?"

She frowned. Took a breath, then blew it out. "Honestly, I'm not sure."

"I wasn't born into money." He wanted her to know where he was coming from just as much as she wanted to be understood. He didn't want her to judge him for his wealth or find him lacking because of it. "I don't take any of it for granted. But I've got it now and I enjoy it. And I hope you'll let yourself enjoy it too, Charlie."

He moved to the couch and held out his hand to her, and just as she always had before, she paused. He found himself holding his breath until, finally, she put her hand in his and let him guide her around the coffee table. She was about to sit on the leather sofa when she stopped to remove her boots first. No question about it, his foster mother Susan would *love* her.

Charlie rubbed her feet on the thick rug as if it were fur, then curled up into the sofa and propped her chin on her hand as she said, "I would never begrudge you your wealth. I know you've worked hard for it. That's not why I'm feeling uncomfortable." She bit her lip as she worked to put her feelings into words for him. "What if I fail?"

He immediately hunkered down in front of her, so close that their heat mingled, forming one aura out of two. She'd been so confident in the lobby of his new headquarters, so sure of herself standing in the doorway of her dilapidated workroom. He hated to think he could have done anything to change that. That he might have done anything to hurt her in any way. Even though they'd only just met a few days earlier, hurting her was the very last thing he wanted to do.

"The money changes your feelings that much?"

"Maybe." She ran a hand over her face. "Or maybe it's just performance anxiety."

"I know we haven't known each other very long," he said slowly, "but I can't imagine you care that much about what people think of you."

"Not people." She paused and he could swear a world of emotions shot through her beautiful eyes and over her stunning face. "You."

"You already know what I think." He smiled at her. "But I'm more than happy to tell you again how magnificent you are."

He'd been hoping to see a smile, but she simply sighed and admitted, "I'm not used to anyone paying me for my work. Especially not the amount you paid."

One hundred thousand dollars honestly wasn't a huge amount to him anymore. But he understood that it meant a hell of a lot to her. Still, he wouldn't allow it to diminish her now, or to strip away her confidence. "Do you want to work for free?"

"No."

He was glad her answer was so quick and to the point. "Then take the space and the luxury I'm offering. And don't worry about anyone's expectations, Charlie. Because I already know you're going to blow them all away."

"How do you do it?" She stared into his eyes. "How do you always know the right thing to say?"

Because I grew up with a father who never did. Sebastian knew firsthand just how important it was for words to heal and inspire, rather than hurt and cut.

But this was about making sure she was okay, not going back into a past he'd already dealt with, so he gave her a different truth. "You make it easy, Charlie."

The smile she gave him now was blindingly beautiful. "Okay. I'll take what you're offering. And I'll stop worrying about expectations. At least," she added with a small uplift of her eyebrows, "until the next time I do."

Even as he laughed at her totally honest response, he knew that it would be so easy—and so damned good—to sweep her up into his arms, carry her into the master bedroom, strip off her clothes, and make love to her the way he'd been fantasizing about ever since he'd first set eyes on her, since the moment her husky laughter had resonated deep inside him.

Though he felt compelled to make sure she didn't think there were any sexual strings attached to the commission, that wasn't the only reason he'd worked like hell to lock down his control. By now, his feelings for Charlie were definitely not along the lines of a simple fling. They had the potential to be big. Big enough that he needed to know more about her, more about how they fit together outside of bed, before they jumped into it. The last thing Sebastian wanted was for him and Charlie to end up destroying each other the way his parents had.

Waiting to have her might very well kill him, but he forced himself to put some distance between them. Rising to his feet, he held out his hand. "Are you ready for the workroom?"

Disappointment flashed in her eyes for a split second, but when she let him pull her to her feet, all traces of hesitation were gone as she said, "Let's get started."

* * *

Charlie stood in the sunbeams streaming down through one of the four skylights in the roof. It sure as heck beat the holes and Plexiglas in her garage that served as her light source.

"I love it." Which was pretty much the biggest understatement in the world, considering it was beyond her wildest expectations. Just like the bungalow. Just like the six-figure check.

Just like Sebastian.

Two days ago, she could never have imagined a man like him stepping into her world. Yet now, she could barely think of anyone—or anything—else.

Even his barn had style and panache. Suspension pulleys hung from the ceiling, and workbenches lined the walls, along with cabinets, tool chests, and storage shelves. He'd promised to rent her an air compressor, and a brand new one stood in the front corner. The movers had rolled in her equipment, lined up her barrels, stacked her boxes, and laid out her parts on pallets.

Just as she'd said to him a few minutes earlier, there were big expectations in an environment like this, especially when a hundred thousand dollars was on the line. She'd felt the first wallop when he'd handed her the check, then again watching the glorious light show in his building, and once more when they were soaring in his helicopter with the brilliance of the Bay beneath them, the sailboats gliding across the water, the cars marching along the freeway like ants. And though he'd been nothing but nice, she'd felt like an ant under his heel that could be crushed at any moment.

At least, until he'd knelt beside her and asked if she wanted to work for free.

With one simple question, he'd helped her see that the only boot heel crushing her was her own. If she let it. Which she wouldn't. She wouldn't allow the money—or any success that came—to change her. Instead, she would revel in this perfect place—and in being near Sebastian—for as long as it lasted.

This, she was coming to see, was Sebastian's power. How with one sentence, he'd opened her eyes after she'd shut them because she was letting fear and worries get the best of her.

"I should let you settle in, unpack your boxes, arrange your stuff, and make the place your own."

He sounded like he didn't really want to leave, and a deep desire for him to stay tingled inside her. She wanted to show him every piece and how it worked. The urge to keep him near—and to bring him much, much closer—was so strong that she had to retreat a pace so it didn't spill over.

"It's a long way back to your house from here." The property covered acres of rolling hills, now brown and dry in the summer sun, and they'd reached the bungalow and outbuildings along a winding driveway leading from his helipad. His house was almost invisible beyond another rise at least a quarter of a mile above them. If this was what his guest bungalow and barn looked like, she could only imagine the opulence of his home. He'd said he hadn't been born with money, and she wondered how he'd gotten used to all of this and how long that had taken. Would she ever feel like she fit in a place like this? In a limo or helicopter? Or would she only ever be truly comfortable in her ratty overalls and steel-toed boots? "Are you sure you don't want to call your helicopter to fly you up?"

He barely stifled his laughter. "Are you begging for trouble?"

Yes. She wanted his brand of trouble. Badly. "You're such a good sport I can't help myself." And she hadn't yet stopped being surprised by that fact. "It's fun to give you a bad time."

"Bad?" The heat that radiated from him nearly jolted her farther back into the room. "Normally, I wouldn't care for the sound of that. But with you, I like the way *bad* sounds."

Oh God, her knees actually went weak at the thought of just how good she already knew it would be.

"Would you like to have dinner at my place tonight?"

She had no idea what was in the bungalow's cupboards, though she suspected he'd had them fully stocked, along with the refrigerator. She could cook passable meals, though nothing like her mother's. But the truth was that she'd rather be with him. And she had no urge whatsoever to lie to herself when the truth looked and smelled as good as he did. "I'm usually starving by six, if that will work for you."

"Six is perfect."

For one long moment after he said the word *perfect*, she couldn't take her eyes off his lips, could barely resist the urge to devour him.

But she hadn't been on his property an hour. And it was only a matter of days since he'd given her a six-figure check. Only remembering those two facts could have stopped her from giving in to the steamy air enveloping them.

Sebastian had told her he didn't want her to think his desire for her art came with strings. When they finally did come together, Charlie didn't want any of those material things in the way either. Just heat. Just desire.

And pleasure.

"Thank you for the helicopter flight here. For loaning me your truck. For the beautiful bungalow. And, most of all, for knowing just the right thing to say right when I needed it."

His gorgeous mouth turned up into a smile that made her want to forget all about her decision to keep sex and art separate for a little while longer. "Until tonight."

The two simple words falling from his lips sounded like a promise.

Or, better yet, a dare.

CHAPTER SIX

Thank goodness for the little sundress she'd thrown into her bag at the last second. Otherwise Charlie would have been totally underdressed for the terrace, the table setting, the view.

And, most of all, for Sebastian.

He was wearing slacks and a button-down shirt that molded perfectly to his chest. Whether executive style, casual, or something in between, he made her pulse sizzle. She could actually feel her blood's rapid thrum through her veins.

She raised her wineglass. "Your house is amazing."

A Spanish style, it was bordered with a breathtaking profusion of hydrangeas, azaleas, camellias, and rhododendrons. Inside, the floors were terrazzo tile inset with Spanish mosaics. The furniture suited, as if it had come from an old hacienda.

The table on the terrace was intimately small, his knee close to hers, his scent as delicious as the food and more intoxicating than the wine. They were seated on a cozy terrace on the side of the house, with a view of the rolling hills, the suburban towns sprawled below, the San Mateo Bridge, the waters of the Bay, and the outline of a distant San Francisco. As Sebastian tapped his glass to hers with a *ting* of crystal, she felt the echo of its ring inside her.

"I'm glad you like it. But I didn't design it."

People rarely designed their own homes. But for some reason Sebastian seemed to think this was a failing on his part, even though she was fairly certain he hadn't trained as an architect. "Tell me about the art on your walls," she asked him, partly because it was all exquisite, but even more because she hoped it might give her more insight into the man behind the perfect face and the always immaculate clothes.

"I choose things I like, things that catch my eye, regardless of how much anyone else thinks they're worth."

Monet. Degas. John Singer Sargent portraits. She was all but certain they were the real thing, rather than prints. But there were also oils, watercolors, drawings, etchings, and a great deal of photography. He had an eclectic collection of art all over the house—sculptures by a relatively new artist named Vicki Bennett, Haitian ceremonial masks, wooden marionettes from Thailand, Burmese tapestries, elaborately feathered and beaded Pueblo kachina dolls, scrimshaw carvings, Satsuma vases.

His collection made the fact that he'd chosen her to create the fountain statue even more important—as though he actually thought she might be up there with all these brilliantly talented artists. Sebastian definitely wasn't a snob when it came to art. He clearly didn't care what anyone thought about his choices. Only that he loved them.

Another point notched in his favor.

A knock came and when Sebastian said, "Come on over, Rory," the waiter rolled a trolley through the open patio doors. Hmm, were they called waiters when you were in your own home? She honestly had no idea, and had never expected to find out. Just as she'd never expected to fly over the Bay Area in a helicopter.

Or earn a hundred grand for one of her sculptures. She honestly wasn't sure when she'd finally believe her work was worth that much money...

Smoothly, Rory removed their empty plates, stacking them on the bottom tray of the trolley. Dinner had been brochettes of beef, tomatoes, and roasted red peppers on a bed of risotto, plus broccoli seasoned with pepper and lemon. Charlie's eyes had practically rolled back in her head when she tasted the beef, and Sebastian seemed delighted by her enjoyment, his gaze fixed on her mouth. He hadn't touched her, yet somehow she felt as if his hands were doing delicious things to her all the while. If a breeze hadn't blown through, she might have had to fan herself.

"English trifle," Rory announced, placing their bowls with a flourish.

"Oh my," Charlie gasped. "That looks delicious."

"Thank you, Rory," Sebastian said. "You've outdone yourself tonight."

Sebastian wasn't just polite and complimentary with his staff. He was downright friendly and clearly didn't expect to be called *sir* or *Mr. Montgomery*. Given how well he was paying Charlie, she suspected Rory wasn't being stiffed, either.

"Did you make all of this incredible food, Rory?" When the man nodded, she nearly leapt out of her chair to hug him. "I haven't eaten so well since my mother's last Thanksgiving feast."

Looking pleased by her compliment, Rory topped up their wine, then rolled his trolley back in the way he'd come.

She picked up a spoon and had just dipped into the whipped cream, custard, and raspberry sponge cake of the trifle, when Sebastian said, "Wait. It will taste best if you eat it like this."

Taking the spoon from her fingers, he brought it to her lips. "Close your eyes and let the flavors meld."

His voice was low, seductive, and she almost groaned. Not just because of the rich, sweet taste on her tongue. It was because she wanted more.

So much more of *him*.

"Good, isn't it?"

So good.

His sexy smile heated everything above the table. His knee against hers heated everything below. But then he leaned back and said, "Tell me why a beautiful woman like you isn't attached."

While his compliment made her blush, the conversational shift was so abrupt that she almost laughed. They'd spent the meal talking about her teaching, her art, the seminars he gave, the Mavericks.

"That's a nosy question." And one she wasn't sure she was ready to delve into with him yet. She'd rather he just kept feeding her the trifle.

But when he grinned and agreed, "Very nosy," her heart did a triple-time dance. The man's grin was killer. As was his focus on wanting answers when he asked again, "So what's the reason?"

"I'm a busy woman with two careers, and men take a lot of work." She paused before deciding that two could play this game. "So I prefer not to keep them around for too long." Nothing she'd said had been a lie. She'd simply left out the part about *why* she hadn't kept any of the men around for very long—and how it might all have been different if she'd ever found anyone who appreciated her exactly the way she was, quirks, junkyard, and all.

"Your attitude is both refreshing and a little disturbing."

"I like refreshing," she said, although she'd heard that one plenty of times from the men she'd been with. They always found her *refreshing* at first. Until that became the problem. "But disturbing?"

"Well, if you're a guy who actually *wants* to stick around..." He wasn't teasing her anymore. In fact his gaze was surprisingly serious. "In any case, I hope you're not done with me yet tonight, because I have a surprise. If you'd like to stay a little longer."

Her heart already beating faster after the way he'd fed her the trifle, it now flipped completely. Stay? *God yes, please, more than anything.* But she needed to at least *seem* cool and collected. So she reached into her bag and retrieved a small box. "I have a little surprise for you too."

"A woman bearing gifts." Something about his comment made it seem as if he was usually the bearer of gifts, rather than the one receiving them. Setting the present on the table, he opened the flaps and reached inside, pulling out a small Zanti Misfit. Its eyes were made out of bolts and its pincers crafted of pruning shears. Sebastian lifted his gaze to hers for one intense moment before he rose from his chair to hunker at the edge of the terrace next to several terracotta pots filled with greenery. Placing the Zanti, he turned the creature slightly. "Perfect."

Yes, she thought as she let herself drink him in for a long moment, he really was. Cool and collected? Around Sebastian? Who was she kidding?

"I'll treasure it, Charlie. Always. Thank you."

She'd meant it simply as a small thank-you for all he was doing for her, but seeing how much he appreciated the miniature sculpture filled her with unexpected joy. "You're welcome."

He held out his hand. "Time for my surprise." As his fingers closed around hers, a thrill went through her, right down to her sandaled toes.

With nothing more than the touch of his hand, he made her feel reckless. Crazy. Yes, he was handsome, rich, and as mouthwatering in a suit as he was in jeans. He had a voice that strummed all her nerve endings, along with a touch that made her skin come alive and her body want to dance in age-old rhythms.

And yet, what she was feeling for him somehow went deeper than just his looks, his voice, or his touch. She'd never thought to give a man one of her Zanti Misfits before. And she was certain that no other man would have appreciated it as much as Sebastian did.

Her fingers tucked in his, he picked up their wineglasses in one hand, then led her through the formal part of the house, past his library, and into a smaller, more intimate room with a fully equipped entertainment center that rivaled the one in the bungalow. Black and white photos of forests and mountains and waterfalls adorned the walls. He splayed a hand toward the couch. "Make yourself comfortable."

She had visions of not only taking off her shoes, but sliding out of her sundress and panties too. Oh boy, she had it bad.

With a remote on the heavy wood coffee table, Sebastian turned on the TV. Several pieces of equipment lit up as he pushed buttons.

"We're going to watch TV?" They were both exercising a great deal of self-control tonight, presumably to make sure the line between art and commerce didn't blur on her first night here. But while she hadn't thought he'd jump her right away, she hadn't expected him to turn on the TV either.

"I found something special for you." He sat down beside her, taking his half of the sofa out of the middle, her bare feet pressing against his thigh.

A movie began to stream. There were no opening credits, just a large, old-fashioned off-the-air symbol she hadn't seen in years. Then the voice told her to sit back, because she was no longer in control of her TV set.

"Oh my God." She gasped out a little laugh. "I can't believe you found 'The Zanti Misfits.'"

"I had to find out why you made an army of them. And I'm really glad I did, now that I have my very own."

She instinctively knew he was telling the truth—that he hadn't done it to impress her, but had simply wanted to know what inspired her. Which made perfect sense when she considered his career as a motivational speaker. He had to *know* people.

Still, it stunned her that he was so interested in knowing *her*.

"Popcorn," she said, to resist throwing herself at him. "We need popcorn."

Hitting Pause on the remote, he reached for a house phone on the side table and asked Rory if he could bring them popcorn. He seemed even closer, warmer, melting her all the way through as he sat back a moment later, pointed the remote, and the Zantis started their mischief.

* * *

The show delighted Charlie, though Sebastian was sure she'd seen it many times over. And he was delighted not only by the way she snuggled into him, but also by how natural she was. He couldn't imagine any of the women he'd dated in the past decade licking the salt and oil from her fingers as they shared a bowl of buttery popcorn. Although it was hell keeping himself from grabbing Charlie's hand and licking each finger clean, one slow swipe of his tongue at a time.

By the time the credits rolled—she had curled into him by then and her hair was soft against his skin—he was aching with need. He wanted to take her to his bed, wanted to spend the rest of the night learning every curve and hollow of her gorgeous body with his mouth, his hands.

But for the first time in his life, he knew he couldn't do that. Because Charlie already mattered. Mattered a hell of a lot. Which meant he needed to figure her out first. Needed to be sure that they were the right fit in every way, rather than merely in bed, where he already sensed no one would ever fit him better.

"So?" She shifted to look at him. "What did you think?"

"It had a lot more screaming than I thought it would." The way she'd spoken of the show had been so upbeat. "And it seemed like no matter how good a plan people made, things went wrong anyway. I kept looking for the happy ending."

"The happy ending is right there in front of you," she told him, her body swaying slightly as she leaned in to make her point. She was so warm, so sensual, that his blood heated even as he warned himself to cool it. "The screaming woman ended up figuring out her life *and* they all triumphed in the end."

Sebastian was amazed that Charlie saw positive messages in a plan gone totally wrong. Ever since his parents had gone completely off the rails, he'd spent the past two decades on constant alert for the ways things could go wrong. Then he devised the right fix before everything got sucked down the tubes. He was always moving, planning, doing, acting—and encouraging others to do the same. But Charlie soothed something inside him with her unselfconscious laughter and relaxed sensuality. She inspired him too, with the way she approached her art so openly. So freely. Plus, she felt absolutely perfect against him.

"What were your favorite shows when you were a kid?"

In an instant, he went completely still inside, the relaxed feeling gone as if it had never been there at all. Sebastian didn't hide his history from people, but he'd learned how to talk about his childhood on stage and in interviews without getting upset about it. He used his past as an example, treating his story as an object lesson in his talks: You didn't have to be controlled by your past, but you *did* need to make sure you learned from it so that you wouldn't end up repeating those mistakes.

But he knew he couldn't do that with Charlie tonight. Not if he wanted her to know more about him than the billionaire façade right there on the surface.

"Are you okay, Sebastian?" she said softly, breaking through the fog he'd let descend around them.

He stroked her cheek, her soft, warm skin helping to bring him back to her. "Just thinking."

Thinking about how he hadn't watched TV as a kid because he'd been too busy looking after his parents. As far back as he could remember, they'd drunk too much and partied too hard. When they were drinking, they'd had huge fights, but they'd never hit each other or him. Mostly they'd just loved to party, staying out till all hours of the night until their bodies gave out, forcing them home to pass out in their bed. Or as close to their bed as they could manage. Once his mother had recovered from their latest binge, she'd always promised they'd change their ways. But then his father would reel her into another drink, another party, another *great night out.*

Until the day things went from great to deadly in the span of a heartbeat.

Sebastian had learned that you could love someone with all your heart and still be the worst thing for them. Like his dad had been for his mom. Each other's worst enemies. It was a lesson he'd never let himself forget—just how much love could hurt and how toxic it could be when two people were a bad fit for each other.

Finally, he told her, "I didn't watch much TV. I grew up in a seedy neighborhood of Chicago and my parents were alcoholics. TV wasn't a priority." Keeping them alive was. Until he couldn't even manage to do that anymore.

Her lips parted, then her gaze moved over his face like a caress. When she put her hand on his arm, her heat highlighted his cold skin and how easily she warmed him up again. "That must have been tough. That's why your friends mean so much to you, isn't it? Because they were there for you when you needed them?"

He not only appreciated her questions— none of the women he'd dated had wanted to know more about his past than they could read in an interview or hear him speak about from the stage—but how matter-of-fact she was about it. Concern without pity. Strength and support without anyone being considered weak.

Charlie Ballard was an extraordinary woman. So extraordinary that he understood less now than ever about what could possibly be holding her back from the glittering success she deserved. With her heat seeping into his bones, his marrow, his heart, he silently vowed to give her the world. Whether she was ready for it or not.

CHAPTER SEVEN

The words had rolled off Sebastian's tongue as if they were no big deal. *I grew up in a seedy neighborhood of Chicago and my parents were alcoholics.*

Maybe most people let him get away with that because they were so wowed or intimidated by the billionaire with the entire world at his feet. But the pain she'd heard—the pain he'd clearly been working so hard to hide—made Charlie desperately want to reach out to him, to help him in any way she could. Even if it was just by listening, she hoped he'd know he wasn't alone.

"You're right. If my friends hadn't been there..." There was little inflection in his voice, but from the way he played with the ends of her hair, curling it around his fingers in a repeated loop, she knew that what he was saying bothered him. "My parents were big partiers. My mom might have been able to make it on her own. But my father was always about the next party. Until he burned them both out."

"You took care of them, didn't you? Even though you were just a kid." She wished she could absorb the pain of his childhood and erase it, but for now, the stroke of her foot along his leg was a small connection he seemed to appreciate.

"I did my best." He rubbed his cheek against the top of her head, obviously needing comfort. Comfort she so badly wanted to give him. "But when my parents couldn't hold down jobs anymore, I moved in with my friend Daniel's parents for good. I was about thirteen then."

Thirteen. Just a child. Anyone else who had grown up in Sebastian's shoes would have been filled with darkness. But even as he exposed his past to her, he was sweet, caressing, gentle.

"They must be wonderful people."

"Bob and Susan have greatness in them. Kindness. Caring. They had it tough too, but they still shared everything they had with us. Everything and more."

She recognized the love threaded through every word—not only when he spoke about Bob and Susan, but also about his parents. "What happened to your parents?" Something told her she should slide her hand into his before he answered.

"They fell off the wagon one too many times." The pain of their passing expressed itself in the slight tightening of his fingers around hers. "I was a senior in high school when Mom had a bad fall. She never recovered and died a couple of weeks later."

"Oh, Sebastian." Even bracing herself hadn't helped. She still felt the pain of his loss arcing through her...just as she knew he had to feel it himself.

"A few weeks later my dad died in a drunk-driving accident. Luckily he didn't hurt anyone else."

Heartache spread to her entire body. To have to use the word *lucky* while talking about his father's death?

It speared her, all the way to the core.

She slid her hand from his to take his face in her hands. "I'm sorry." Not that she'd asked, but that he'd had to live through it at all.

"I am too. They were good people. Good people who couldn't beat their addiction."

It was an amazingly kind way of looking at the situation. But even though kindness was great, so, Charlie knew from personal experience, was anger. At least in small doses, if only to purge it from your system.

Had Sebastian ever given his anger wings—or four wild horses to drag it on a chariot through the streets until the wind, and the rain, burned it out?

"How did you get from there to—" She paused and swept her hand in front of her to encompass the huge house and property. Even the helicopter now waiting for its next flight in the nearby hangar.

"I'm a big talker." Now that he was no longer telling her about his parents and his childhood, the tension began to leave his body. "I didn't go to college, but I always liked telling people what to do. I especially liked it when they listened." He grinned. "And, of course, when their lives got better as a result. A talk-show host who liked my shtick gave me my first big break."

"What you do isn't a *shtick*." She'd never seen him in action, but he couldn't have achieved all this—he owned a Monet, for God's sake—with mere magic tricks or smoke and mirrors.

"You're right, I should erase that word from my vocabulary." She swore she could see him silently do that. *Erase erase erase.* "I truly do believe every word I say, every piece of advice I give." He smiled at her. "And the rest is history."

"You make it sound so easy. As though anyone could build an empire and make billions."

Pulling her hands down, he held them and locked his gaze on her eyes. "You *can.*

Believe in yourself. Push for what you want and deserve. It *will* manifest."

Her head spun at how quickly he'd twisted the focus around to her, making her feel slightly uncomfortable with the intensity of his gaze. Or maybe, if she was being totally honest with herself, she wasn't uncomfortable with Sebastian, but with all of the big changes she could see coming down the pike. His words from the first day he'd come to her workshop replayed in her head: *We won't just unveil your work, we'll unveil you to the world too.*

Her roof might sag, but her life had been comfortable. Of course she wasn't averse to being a big success, but was she ready for it?

"I'm already manifesting," she quipped in an effort to relax a bit about it all. "You saw my dragon in Chinatown and now here I am, poised to create something amazing."

"Definitely amazing," he murmured as he pulled her into him, his arm deliciously warm across her shoulders. "Tell me more about yourself. From the way you speak of your parents, I can tell they were good ones."

"They really were. My dad taught me everything about welding. My mom taught me everything about cooking." She grinned at him. "Only one of them succeeded at getting through to me, though."

Though he smiled back, by the way he slid his hand through hers as he asked, "Where's your dad now?" it was obvious that he already suspected the answer.

The familiar ache bloomed in her chest. "He died of cancer seven years ago. With Hospice help, Mom and I took care of him to the end. We let him die at home the way he wanted to."

Sebastian squeezed her hand and dropped a kiss on the top of her head. "You've very brave, Charlie."

If anyone should know about bravery, it was Sebastian. But their pasts weren't something to compare, so instead of saying that, she simply leaned into his comfort. "I loved my mother before that, but it brought us even closer." They'd created an unbreakable bond, weeks where they were everything to each other, offering support, one holding the other up when she would have fallen, sharing a glass of wine at the end of an exhausting day after her father had finally slipped into sleep. All that despite her mother's debilitating arthritis.

"And where's your mom?"

Sebastian had revealed his worst to her. Now it was her turn. "I had to put Mom in a home two years ago." The agony of that decision—and the overwhelming guilt— squeezed her heart inside her chest. "She has osteoarthritis, but hers is extremely severe and started in her forties. She's in constant pain." She winced at the memories of her deterioration, but her mother was stoic. What on a scale of one to ten would have been a nine for Charlie, Mom smiled right through. "I hate what the disease has done to her."

It was doubly hard to know the extent of her mother's pain and not be able to do a thing about it. She wanted nothing more than to take care of her mother herself, but her place was more substandard than Shady Lane. Her mom had reached the point where she needed help dressing, washing, even putting on her shoes. Charlie's bathroom had an old clawfoot tub that, as strong as Charlie was, she had trouble getting her mom in and out of. It was an accident waiting to happen. Then there were all the times her mother had been alone because Charlie had an irregular schedule—teaching during the day, with night classes three evenings a week, often not arriving home till eleven o'clock. She'd had visions of her mother falling and then lying there for hours before Charlie returned.

While she'd explained about her mother, Sebastian had caressed the back of her neck, giving her warmth and comfort that eased the knot of tension. Now, he folded her into his arms, his tenderness bringing her close to tears when usually she tried to be as stoic as her mother.

"Can she take pain meds?" He soothed her with long, sweet strokes down her back.

Charlie shook her head against his chest. "She's already on a bunch of stuff, but you build up a tolerance in time, and it doesn't do much."

"What about an operation?" His voice was a warm rumble against her ear.

"She's had them all. There's only so much they can do." She pushed away from his comfort and put the flat of her hand on his chest. "But with the money you gave me for the chariot, I can move her into a great place in Los Gatos with beautiful gardens to stroll through. She pushes herself to do a mile every day with a walker in the hallway. Otherwise she'd be in a wheelchair."

"Now *that* is amazing. And so are you." He held her with his dark, beautiful eyes. "It's incredibly selfless to use the money for her care. I should have doubled what I gave you."

He was too much. Not only that he listened with such attentiveness when most people had to jump in with their own story—but that he was moved enough to even think of handing her more than he already had.

"You've already given me more than anyone else." She savored the strong beat of his heart beneath her palm. Sharing with him didn't take away her mother's pain, but somehow it eased Charlie's anguish. "It's more than enough. More than I can still wrap my head around."

Just as she could barely wrap her head around the heat the two of them generated, simply sitting on the couch talking about their pasts.

As he ran his hands up her arms, over her shoulders, into her hair, and cupped her nape, she was palpably aware that her inner voice, the one reminding her to keep her hormones in check, had long since shut itself down. She'd wanted to make sure that she and Sebastian had clearly carved out the lines between business and pleasure before they became lovers—and she'd wanted to make sure she wasn't letting herself fall into another relationship where she started out *refreshing* and ended up with her heart broken.

Though she didn't have nearly all the answers to her questions, what he'd shared with her had touched her deeply.

She still didn't want to risk messing up the business arrangement between them by jumping into bed, especially not when her mother's future care depended on it. And yet, drawing in a deep breath of his scent, all male with hints of soap and raspberry trifle, she could no longer repress the part of her that was dying for a kiss. One heady kiss she could dream about at night.

His mouth was so inviting. And when he said her name—*"Charlie"*—barely above a soft whisper but heavy with need, she simply couldn't resist the pull of his desire any longer.

He leaned close, but she was the one who closed the final distance between them. She parted his lips. Or he parted hers. She couldn't be sure. All she knew was that he was the sweetest thing she'd ever tasted.

His tongue danced with hers, his taste drugging her. She moaned and his arms wrapped her close. Her fingertips to his jaw, she rubbed the soft end-of-day stubble. The length of his body was hard against her, all that relentless muscle. And she couldn't help letting herself go, throwing her arms around him, pressing her breasts to his chest, her leg against his thigh.

He consumed her, kissing the very breath from her. It was, she silently acknowledged, what she'd wanted from the moment he'd stood outside her workroom, the sun blinding her and turning him into a silhouette of metal calling her to shape him, mold him, take him, make him hers.

His fingers curled into her hair as he devoured her as though she were a delicacy he'd never tried before and couldn't get enough of. His groan made her crazy for more—his whole body on hers, his hands all over her. He made her want to be reckless, made her want to give him her body, her heart. Her very soul, if he wanted it. Right here. Right now. Made her want to throw her worries and her wariness to the wind. Made her want to pretend she'd never been hurt before. Made her want to believe that *he* would never hurt her.

She wanted to taste and touch every part of him, but the way he was loving her mouth was addictive. Overwhelming. Tantalizing.

So damned good that she would have been completely lost if he hadn't drawn back, his heart pounding as swiftly as hers, his eyes the deep, intoxicating color of whiskey.

"Wow," she said, more an exhalation than a word.

"*Wow* is exactly right." He trailed a finger across her lips. "The perfect first kiss." But instead of diving back in to see if the second would be even better, he said, "Do you believe it yet?"

"Do I believe what yet?" she asked, even though she was pretty sure another of his kisses could make her believe anything.

"That I want your chariot and respect your talent as much as I desire you?"

Two days ago, when they'd been standing in the atrium of his new building, he'd asked her the same question. And though his kiss had made her feel reckless and borderline desperate for more, it hadn't made her a liar.

"No." She hadn't even begun to build the chariot, and though it had taken shape in her mind, he couldn't possibly see it as clearly as she did—at least, not clearly enough for it to be anywhere near worth the check he'd written. "Not yet."

"You will." He licked out against her lips, and it was almost enough to send recklessness to the forefront again. "Soon."

She smiled through the desperate ache to kiss him again. "I hope so." Because until that moment came, the ache would only keep growing.

He stood, held out his hand. "I'll walk you home."

She put her fingers in his. "It's not that far."

"It's a few more minutes with you."

Oh God. He was to die for.

Wrapping her beneath his arm, he kept her close on the walk down the hill. The wind came up, whipping away their voices, but talk wasn't necessary. There was just the sweet feel of his body against her side and his protective arm around her.

At the bungalow door, he turned her in his arms and took her face in his hands. As his gaze roamed her cheeks and her lips, she almost felt as though his mouth were on her. After a long pause in which she found herself holding her breath, he finally lowered his lips to her forehead for a soft, sweet kiss.

Then he said good night and walked away.

CHAPTER EIGHT

Charlie was so damned sweet, her skin so soft, her body so supple and strong, yet so giving. Leaving her with nothing more than that peck on the forehead was the hardest thing he'd ever done. He had always been a fairly patient man, at least compared to the other Mavericks, but with Charlie his patience was being sorely tested.

But he could tell she wasn't ready yet. And if he was honest, he wasn't ready either—not when there was so much about her he still needed to uncover. Which was precisely why he headed straight for his workroom upstairs—it was little more than a walk-in closet off his bedroom—and flipped on the light. Other than the stars shining through the window, the room was unadorned but for supply cupboards, a bureau full of sketchbooks, a comfortable chair, the side table, and a standing lamp.

After all these days of dying to sketch her, he finally chose a pencil and a drawing pad. The medium he used didn't matter. No one but Susan, Bob, and the Mavericks knew he drew.

Growing up poor and hungry with parents who were rarely around made it hard to have big dreams. And the ones you had, you learned to keep to yourself. After all, by the age of twelve so many of his dreams of a happy family and normal life had died that he knew to steal this dream away for himself. Drawing was what he did alone in his bedroom when his parents were partying with their "friends," as though sketching could somehow drown them all out, make them go away, and make everything better, at least for a little while.

Until the day his father found one of his sketchbooks during a bender. Sebastian knew it was his own fault—he'd been careless and had forgotten to shove it beneath his mattress with the others. Even all these years later, he could still hear his father's voice. Slurred, like it so often was, but clear all the same. *You drew this crap? All these pictures of me looking like shit? Like a goddamned drunk?*

As far back as Sebastian could remember, probably to age five or six, it wasn't just creative urges that made him draw everything and everyone around him. It was also his need to understand people. He'd drawn the kids at school, his teachers, the bus driver, and of course, his parents. Because if he could figure them out, then maybe he could fix them.

The sketchbook his father had torn through had been filled with sketches of his dad during—and after—his last bender. Sebastian had simply wanted to know why his father was so attracted to the high that he refused to give it up, even when their lives were falling completely apart because of it. Maybe if Sebastian knew *why,* then he could finally figure out how to make the drinking stop. And if his father stopped getting wasted all the time, Sebastian had been sure his mother would follow.

But those dreams were slashed the night his father had laughed in such a cruel, devastating way as he ripped out Sebastian's sketches in big fistfuls of paper, his wasted friends laughing right along with him. *My stupid, worthless kid thinks he's an artist. But he's nothing,* his father had declared. *I'll show you where your pictures belong, you little shit.* He'd thrown Sebastian's drawings into the fireplace, and when they'd lit and flamed, his father had toasted his friends with another bottle, another shot, another pack of cigarettes.

All the while, Sebastian's mother was passed out on the couch in the corner. Sebastian never knew if his father told her what had happened, or, honestly, if his father even remembered what he'd done. But it didn't matter.

The damage had been done. Sebastian now knew just how worthless his dreams really were. How crazy. His father was right—he'd been kidding himself to think he could actually be an artist.

Sebastian didn't draw for years after that, not until the itch in his fingers got so strong that he couldn't stop himself from doodling in class. He still remembered the first time he drew again, the way his hand shook, knowing what crap he was at being an artist. And yet, at the same time, it was such a huge relief to let out the urges again.

The first time Susan had seen one of his doodles, she'd marveled at it, the opposite reaction to his father's. Sebastian knew it wasn't because he was actually talented, but simply that she had the eye of a mother, not an art critic. Eventually, though, he decided it would be okay to draw if he was simply using it as a way to work through his thoughts and feelings, to figure people out. But never again art for art's sake. Never with any dreams attached. And that was fine, since his dreams had completely changed once he'd finally grown up.

Ever since the moment he'd set eyes on Charlie, he'd wanted to try to capture her unique beauty and her irrepressible spark, even if he didn't have a prayer of actually doing her justice. Of course, he'd make sure she never found his drawings.

He flipped past a dozen sketches of his parents in the sketchbook before he found a fresh page. It still grated on him that he'd never been able to shine a light on their addictions. Though they were no longer alive, he was still drawing them, still trying to understand why they'd lived their lives as they had—why they'd chosen booze and parties over a life with him.

On the fresh page, he put pencil to paper and quickly worked to try to bring Charlie to life beneath his fingers—her beautiful, expressive eyes, filled with heartache and pain but also with such joy it floored him. He hated that he didn't have the skills to get what he saw in his head onto the paper, but at the very least he hoped the pencil would reveal things he couldn't see with the naked eye. There was so much he wanted to figure out about the woman who commanded his attention like no one else ever had.

Charlie had been helpless to cure her father's illness, and now clearly felt helpless to ease her mother's suffering. Just as he'd been helpless against the liquor in his parents' cabinets. It hadn't mattered how much gin or beer he poured down the drain or how little money there was in the house, somehow there was always enough for another bottle and another party.

Susan and Bob Spencer took him in on the nights when his own parents seemed to have forgotten they had a son. His thirteenth birthday had been just around the corner when his mom woke from a drunken stupor long enough to ask where he'd been the night before, telling him that he was *her* son and he needed to come home to her. She'd helped him throw out the bottles, and he'd thought things would change. He thought he mattered to her. He'd had hope for a whole week. Until his dad wanted to have a little fun, just a night out, one night.

Once again they forgot they had a son who desperately wanted to see them clean and sober. He'd moved in with Bob and Susan on his thirteenth birthday. This time, neither of his parents had seemed to miss him.

Over the next five years, no amount of AA meetings, rehab, or liquor down the drain had done a thing. He'd suffered with them through the DTs, but they'd never stuck it out. The moment his back was turned, they'd find another drink. Until finally his mother had fallen, hit her head on the edge of the coffee table, and never woken up again. He'd often wondered if his dad had died in that car crash because his luck had finally run out? Because guilt had finally soaked through his sodden conscience? Or was it simply that Ian Montgomery couldn't live without his wife Olive?

Sebastian had created a billion-dollar career out of helping people change their lives for the better in every possible avenue—career, relationships, health, family. But the concept of *love* still twisted him up in knots. He knew firsthand that you could love someone with everything in you and still be the absolute worst thing for them. Sure, there were couples like Bob and Susan, who would do anything for each other, but then there were couples like his friend Evan and his wife Whitney. There was no doubt in anyone's mind that Whitney was toxic and would be Evan's destruction. As far as Sebastian was concerned, you always had to be ready to walk away from a love like that. But he didn't think Evan ever would. Not only because of his loyalty, but also because he was holding onto hope with an iron grip.

Sebastian hadn't allowed himself to hold onto hope against all odds again, not since that day his mother had sworn she'd stop drinking if he came home, and then surrendered the first time her husband had tempted her with another party, another night out, another drink.

An owl hooting outside his window brought him back to his workroom and the drawing of Charlie beneath his hand. Looking down at it, he knew he'd never been involved like this before. So involved, on such a deep level already, that he was tempted to draw a self-portrait next, to try to figure himself out this time.

To try to figure out *love.*

Love wasn't something he'd been looking for. Wasn't something he thought he'd be able to trust in for himself, after his upbringing. But could Charlie change everything?

Had she already?

Working to push away his memories of his parents for good this time, he refocused his thoughts on Charlie as he continued to fill in the flowing locks of her hair, then sketched the lines of her cheekbones, her jaw, her nose. Yet he still saw nothing in his drawing that shed light on why she hadn't reached her career potential despite her brilliant talent and skill.

His pencil swirled, giving life to her luscious lips, the ones he'd tasted and craved with a soul-deep need. Dammit, that was the problem. He was so focused on the physical, on his desire—on *himself* rather than her—that he couldn't see beneath the surface of what he drew.

He nearly crushed the pencil and pad in his fist. This always happened, this moment where his frustration at his poor skills made him want to rip out the pages just the way his father had and burn them to ashes.

Knowing he wouldn't be able to see beyond his memories tonight—or his desire for Charlie—he tossed aside the pad. But he did know one thing for certain, knew it even without drawing her. Charlie badly needed a cure for her mother's pain. There had to be some treatment—an operation, an advanced drug, something that would help. He might not have been able to fix his parents, but he'd spent his life trying to make up for that by building an empire facilitating positive change for as many people as he could.

He had all the money in the world to find the best doctors and the best medicine. He would find a way to help Charlie's mother. And maybe knowing her mother had every dime of his billions working for her would clear the roadblocks from Charlie's path to achieving her true potential.

She had already brought him more than she could know, first by letting him watch her creative mind take flight in the lobby of his building. Though he would never be an artist himself, it was incredibly satisfying just to be near one of her caliber. And then she'd given him so much again tonight, listening to every word about his parents, and knowing just the right thing to say when he needed it. She'd been there for him in a way no other woman ever had.

Charlie might think she was the one who needed him. But Sebastian already knew the truth.

He was the one who needed her.

CHAPTER NINE

Charlie got up early Saturday morning, planning to don her overalls and work boots first thing. But how could she resist luxuriating in a shower that had two heads and practically massaged her scalp? And, honestly, she would have been a fool not to make the most delicious coffee in a contraption that added whipped cream, chocolate, *and* Almond Roca syrup. But though the fridge was stocked and she could have cooked for a week out of the staples in the cupboards, she made herself settle for cereal with fresh blueberries. It was time to get out to her fabulous new studio before she frittered away the whole morning in luxury.

As soon as she walked in, she got to work hooking up the MIG, the TIG, and the compressor, hanging her tools on the pegboards, and setting out her barrels of nuts, bolts, and screws. This was always what she taught her students—to start each project by being as organized as possible. Because once the vision kicked into overdrive, you wouldn't want it to end up flying out of your brain because you had to stop to look for something in your workshop.

That was when she found the barrel of plastic monkeys Sebastian must have slipped in. Laughter bubbled up and over, joining the desire that was still humming inside her from the night before. Her lips tingled from his kiss, and she swore she could smell him too—that luscious, sexy smell all his own.

"Okay, it's time to get to work," she chided herself.

"You know what they say about all work and no play."

She darn near jumped out of her steel-toes. "You scared me." She put her hand to her chest, her heart beating hard and fast, and not just from fright. He really was the most beautiful man she'd ever set eyes on, yummy enough to eat. His white polo shirt showed off his tanned, muscular arms. Moments before, her fingers had itched to start a few welds, but now all she could think about was kneading his flesh like a purring cat.

Then she whirled, pointing at the barrel. "Oh my God, the monkeys." She laughed. "I love them."

Something decadent and delicious sparked in his eyes as his gaze played over her mouth. "I wanted to hear you laugh, just like that."

An answering flame flared up deep inside her. She could almost taste last night's kiss, and she knew he was remembering it too, as his eyes traced her lips. She was in danger of diving on him if she didn't say something. "Well, a barrel of monkeys will certainly do that to me."

"Actually, I came down to see if I could help."

Given that fluttery feeling she got whenever he was near, she suspected he would be more distraction than help. She shot a glance at his pressed slacks and shirt. "You're not dressed to help."

"You've got me," he said, holding up his hands. "The real reason I'm here is because I wanted my day to start with seeing you."

God, the things he said to her.

I saw only you.

I didn't want to split my attention between you and the road today.

I'm more than happy to tell you again how magnificent you are.

You make it easy, Charlie.

It's a few more minutes with you.

After learning about his parents and the life he'd had as a kid, she'd found so much to admire about him. The way he made her melt from the inside out was like the whipped cream on this morning's coffee, that special little treat that made her taste buds *ooh* and *aah*.

She drew in a deep breath because he made her feel lightheaded. Which, she quickly decided, was unacceptable in her workshop despite how much she had come to like being with him. This was her studio while she built the chariot and stallions and she needed to control it. It would be one thing if he were one of her students—she couldn't stop thinking how much fun it would be to bring them here to see what a fully decked-out workshop looked like. But he wasn't her student. He was her patron. And she was here to build him a $100,000 sculpture for his San Francisco high-rise.

"It's nice to see you too," she said as gently as she could, "but—"

"Get out?"

How could she not laugh out loud again? "Actually, if you wouldn't mind helping me move these car doors first, that would be great. And then," she added in a teasing tone, "you can go."

He looked really pleased to get to stay a while longer, and her heart thumped a few extra beats as he carried the doors over to where she wanted them and his biceps flexed big and strong beneath his shirt.

"Are you planning to use these for the chariot?"

"Yup. I can grind them down to bare metal, then shape them."

"Tell me about your equipment."

She loved teaching. Plus, even if she should be kicking him out and getting to work, the truth was that she was glad to spend a few more minutes with him. Laying her hand on the first machine, she said, "This is a TIG welder—that stands for tungsten inert gas. It works on just about any weldable metal, including dissimilar metals. It's also good on round pieces."

"Fascinating," he remarked. "I'm dying to watch you work." His voice was low, and it set off a distinctive thrill inside.

"It will be a while before I begin putting pieces together. I've only just started a diagram. I'll show you." She opened her iPad on the workbench, then tapped an app to display the drawings she'd recently added. "I find a picture, import it, then flesh it out. Mostly I get the feel of the lines of whatever I'm making." She traced her finger along the bunched muscles of a stallion.

He leaned over to put his elbows on the bench, his hip bumping hers. And for a moment, she forgot everything except the feel of him against her...and how good it was. Nearly as good as his mouth had felt on hers the night before.

Giving herself a quick mental shake, she refocused on the tablet. "The app isn't designed for what I'm doing. But it works." She showed him the bit of work she'd already done—a galloping horse and a chariot.

"I've only just hired you for the project and yet you've already put together a vision of it." His gaze roamed her face, as if he were memorizing her features so that he could capture them on canvas. From out of the blue she suddenly found herself wondering if he'd painted any of the artwork in his house, even though he'd never said anything to her about being an artist himself.

"I dream these things at night," she told him. "Right before I go to sleep, I'm planning, visualizing. Then, while I'm dreaming, things are created."

"You're amazing, Charlie."

No one had ever built up her confidence like this. Her father had praised her, and her mother always believed in her, but neither of them had seen the same vision in her work. She tried to do that for her students, whether they were learning a trade to take into the workforce or creating a masterpiece. But for Sebastian, the ability to help a person see his or her own uniqueness was innate.

And so was his ability to make her admit things she hadn't planned on giving away. "I've never had anyone tell me I'm amazing. Or magnificent." She wanted to grab him, kiss him, wrap herself around him. "It's nice. And also a little overwhelming."

"I'm overwhelmed too, Charlie."

When she could get her breath back at his unexpected statement, she had to ask, "Is that a good thing?"

He paused for several long beats. "I hope so."

They were standing together on the precipice of something that had the potential to be great. Unfortunately, she knew from personal experience that *great potential* could turn to *great disappointment* really fast.

Finally, she broke the heady silence between them. "I want to visit my mom this afternoon, so I'd better get to work."

"I'd like to come with you." At the mention of her mother, something changed in the air. She couldn't say exactly what, except that he seemed to vibrate, not with tension so much as intent. "If you don't mind."

"That's very sweet of you, but you've already spent so much time with me, and I know how busy you must be with work."

Honestly, the thought of a man who filled his remarkable home with dazzling, priceless art strolling into Shady Lane was horrifying. He would look at the institutional walls, ancient linoleum floors, and cramped rooms and be appalled that she could allow her mother to live there. Shady Lane was clean and passable, but there was none of the luxury he was used to.

He touched her cheek, sending sparks of electricity through her. "You create amazing art. And she created you, so I'd like to meet her."

Lord, he was sweet. So sweet that she felt churlish for saying no, especially when, besides Charlie, her mother didn't get any visitors. Francine Ballard would love to meet Sebastian, a man who would treat her like royalty, give her his whole focus, make her smile.

So despite all the inadequacies shrieking inside her, Charlie said the only thing she could. "She'd like that a lot."

When he smiled his appreciation, then left her to do her work alone, she actually had to bite her lip to stop herself from begging him to stay.

* * *

"What beautiful flowers." Francine Ballard bent her head to inhale the fragrance of the blooms Sebastian brought her. "Thank you so much."

Charlie's mother was a tiny thing, her back bent and her fingers crooked, but she had a smile that lit her face. With her curved lips and sparkling eyes, he saw Charlie in her.

"It's so nice to meet you, Mrs. Ballard," he said formally. "I'm Sebastian Montgomery."

Resting on the seat of her wheeled walker in the nursing home's lobby when they entered, she'd risen at the sight of Charlie, keeping steady with a grip on both handles. "Sebastian, please call me Francine. Let's put my flowers in the lounge so everyone can enjoy them. I'll lead the way."

She signaled her departure, turning the walker and heading past the nurse's station at a slow and steady pace. Despite the pain she must feel with each step, she didn't give up. He admired her tenacity.

"Looking sharp, Albert," she sang out as she cruised past an old man with cataracts that practically obscured his irises. Albert raised his hand in greeting, and Charlie patted his knee as she passed, drawing a smile from him.

Shady Lane was more like a hospital than a home. The floors were plain linoleum, the primary lighting fluorescent, and the chairs populating the lobby and halls resembled those in a doctor's office. The pictures lining the hallway walls had probably been purchased in bulk. Open doorways revealed two beds to a room with only a privacy curtain separating them. TVs were mounted in either corner, competing volumes screeching out into the hallway. Windows in the rooms were small, most with blinds closed. They passed a comatose woman in a bed, her mouth sagging, her curtain open as the nurse adjusted something on her monitor.

He hated himself for thinking it, but this wasn't a home. It was a place people came to die. He understood now why Charlie had stared at the check he'd written as if it were a lifeline. That money would change her mother's life. He wished he'd written double the amount, but he knew Charlie would never have taken it.

"Did you do your walk already today, Mom?" Charlie asked, leaning in close enough to Sebastian to give his heart a kick with her sweet scent.

"Three rounds. One more to go." Francine pointed to the pink bakery box in Charlie's hand, eyes twinkling. "I want to hear all about the sculpture you have planned for Sebastian's building, so let's have tea first."

She parked her walker by the open lounge doors, then moved from chair to chair, holding the back of each one, until she slid onto the cushions of the sofa. At least here, the furniture appeared more comfortable. A larger TV than those in the rooms sat against the wall at the opposite end, surrounded by a grouping of chairs.

"Sorry, Mom, I forgot the china cups and plates," Charlie said as she headed to the coffee service on a long bar against the far wall.

"I'll survive," her mother answered sweetly. When Sebastian sct down the vase in the middle of the table, she said, "Lovely—now sit." She patted the sofa beside her, then winced.

"Are you all right?" The sudden pain on her face stole his breath away.

"My hand is simply acting up." She rubbed the center of her palm as best she could with her crooked fingers. "Now tell me all about this marvelous building of yours."

He was still reeling from the pain he'd seen shoot through her, but she was already past it. Amazing. "Charlie's pieces will bring the place to life."

"I hear you have a fountain. And lots of glass to let in the sunlight."

She didn't look longingly toward the window that faced the parking lot, but he knew she needed a garden. Flowers. Sunshine. Charlie would use every penny of her commission to provide those things for her mother.

"Here's your tea, Mom. Sorry about the paper cups." She set down a cup filled with milky liquid in front of her mother and another for Sebastian, the coffee black and steaming.

He smiled his thanks while Francine said, "Don't worry about the china, dear. This is just wonderful." Then she whispered to him as Charlie returned to the coffee bar for her own cup, "She's so good to me. I don't know what I'd do without her. Most people don't receive any visitors at all, but Charlie comes at least twice a week, often more."

He thought of all the lonely people in nursing homes, their final years spent in a bed without a single visitor, a curtain providing their only privacy. It made him appreciate Charlie even more. She wasn't merely a talented artist and a dedicated teacher. She was also a loving daughter.

She carried another cup, plus three paper plates balanced along her arm as easily as if she'd been a waitress in a past life. "I could have gotten that," he said, getting up to take one of the plates.

"I'd rather you two enjoyed chatting with one another." She pointed to the whole bear claw he held. "That one is for you." She handed half a bear claw to her mother and kept the other half for herself.

"We always share," Francine explained. "I could never eat a whole one." She took a bite, eating with a dainty sound of pleasure. "Aren't they to die for?"

He couldn't help but turn his gaze to Charlie as he said, "Totally to die for."

As they ate, he noted that each of Francine's feet was encased in an ankle brace, and her fingers bent at odd angles. When she spoke, her voice quavered as if the muscles of her throat didn't quite work properly. Lines he associated with someone fifteen years older than seventy crisscrossed her face as though her pain had risen to the surface and marked her forever. Yet she chattered happily as if her body hadn't turned against her, and she was dressed in her Sunday best, a pretty blue skirt with a flowered sweater. She told them stories about this resident or that, and they laughed good-naturedly at the antics of the people she lived with. She wanted to know more about his new headquarters and what Charlie would be doing for him. Her mind was sharp, and she was interested in everything.

Last night, after he tossed his sketchbook, he'd opened his laptop and read everything he could about degenerative osteoarthritis, from the Arthritis Foundation to WebMD. He'd looked up eminent surgeons, doctors, facilities. Sebastian understood how it felt to watch one's mother live in such agony. His parents had brought their troubles on themselves, but he'd still felt the pain of watching them fall apart, the anguish of not being able to do anything. He didn't want that for Charlie.

So he would fix it.

* * *

Her mother had been completely charmed by Sebastian, just as Charlie had known she would be. "Thank you for coming to see my mother. She loved the flowers and all the attention."

"I see where you get your strength, and your joy for life." He gave her a smile before turning his attention back to the road. "Your mother has both in spades."

Sebastian hadn't said a word about the state of the home, but she'd seen his eyes taking in everything, from the floor to the walls to the furniture. He would have had to be blind to miss any of the second-rate accommodations.

"I'm going to call Magnolia Gardens on Monday to put Mom's name on the waiting list. I know she'll love it there. The gardens are gorgeous."

"How long before she'll get in?"

Her own sense of guilt almost made her imagine for a moment that there was censure in his words. "Maybe a couple of months."

"Do they have good doctors?"

They were adequate, but honestly, she was more concerned about the environment her mother would live in. "They're good, but they can't do much for Mom except manage her pain."

He switched lanes on the freeway before saying, "I've been doing some research on the Internet. There's a hand surgeon at Stanford who's the top in his field in severe degenerative osteoarthritis. And an orthopedic surgeon down in Santa Cruz specializes in ankles."

Staring was all she could manage. Charlie didn't blab to everyone about her mother's problems, but she had told a teacher or two, her dean, the secretary. None of them had tried to help before, though. Only Sebastian, who had immediately jumped in.

"I can't tell you what it means to me that you thought of her, even before you met her. But I've taken her to all the doctors. She's past anything they can do." At least nothing she could have afforded beyond what Medicare paid for. Charlie couldn't stop another stab of guilt.

They'd reached their exit, and he let the car roll to a stop at the light. "There could be new surgeries, new treatments that have been developed in recent months. Maybe it won't help. But it couldn't hurt to see the doctors." He looked so earnest.

For her mother's sake, she had to let Sebastian try. Somehow she'd find the money to pay for consultations with these new specialists. Putting her hand over his on the steering wheel, she looked straight into his eyes, held him there a long moment even though the light changed. "Yes. Let's try."

But the new worries about money were already twisting inside her by the time he said, "I'd like to help with Magnolia Gardens too—see if I can grease the wheels to get your mom in earlier."

It wasn't his fault that a chill ran down her arms. Sebastian was the kind of man who would always offer help when he thought it was needed. But he'd already given her a humongous check. She couldn't take any more. Even her mother wouldn't approve if she took money from him she hadn't earned.

"The check you gave me will more than cover her move." And only a few months after that, but she'd somehow figure that out too. "You're doing enough already."

As it was, she didn't know how she'd ever pay him back.

CHAPTER TEN

Charlie clearly hated seeing her mother in pain, hated Shady Lane, hated that she couldn't take care of her mother herself. But Sebastian could help her with all that. *If* she let him. Maybe he'd pushed too hard about her mother's condition, but what good was his money if he didn't use it to help a woman in pain? Especially when it meant a great deal to him that for one afternoon, she had made him feel he was part of their family, for a little while at least.

That evening, after Charlie politely turned down his request to have dinner together again, Sebastian returned to his drawing. In fact it was that politeness that told him she'd shut down on him, just put up a wall to all the heat and sparks between them.

In his workroom, he downloaded the app she'd shown him. He was up on most of the latest technologies, but this one had slipped by him. Easy to use, it took only a few tries before he had it figured out. Charlie imported photos she then manipulated, but the app simulated just about any medium for drawing. He chose charcoals with a textured background.

He started with her eyes, those beautiful, expressive eyes. They could have been her mother's eyes—bright, laughing, with a hint of pain always lingering behind them. But Charlie had her pain too, springing from an emotional well deep inside her. On the iPad, he filled in her cheekbones, the slope of her nose.

Unfortunately, an hour of drawing still didn't bring the insight he needed. He'd had the stupid hope that the app itself would somehow reveal her in a way his sketchbook hadn't. He shut it down in frustration.

At least there was one thing he knew for sure he could do right. He hit Will Franconi's number on speed dial, knowing his friend would answer if at all possible.

It took two rings. "Hey." Will's voice was almost drowned out by a blast of noise around him.

"Where the hell are you?"

"Santa Cruz Beach Boardwalk. The Edgar Winter Band is doing a free concert on the beach. It's a madhouse here. Jeremy wanted to come."

There was a loud shout, but Sebastian couldn't make out a thing.

"He says free fun is the best kind," Will translated. "He gets that from Harper."

Jeremy was Will's soon-to-be brother-in-law. He was a great kid, though at eighteen, he wasn't exactly a kid anymore. Jeremy's older sister Harper was a special woman, and she fit Will even better than a finely made suit. His friend was finally happy after all these years, so happy that Sebastian had added them to his *exceptions* list. No toxic love between them, that was for sure.

"What do you need?" Will asked.

"That new venture you've got going with the British company. The signature bone china. I need three china mugs and three matching plates."

For two beats, all he heard was the crash of music. Until Will said, "Do you need to have your testosterone levels checked?"

"No more than you for putting the deal together with them in the first place. It's for a friend."

"A woman friend?" He could actually see Will's raised eyebrow.

"Her mother."

"Her *mother*? Whoa, man, if you're getting a gift for her mother, that sounds like some serious stuff."

As Will said it, Sebastian felt the truth deep in his core. He'd never been more serious. "Can you order it for me ASAP?"

"Hold on a minute. When do we get to meet her?"

Sebastian knew that Charlie would love Harper, Jeremy, and Will. "I've got to convince her to spend time with me first."

"She's not yet convinced?" Will made a considering sound. "Now that I hear she's not just slavering at your feet like all your other women always have, I *really* want to meet her."

Sebastian laughed. "You going to help me or not?"

"You want ultrafeminine, flowery, or classic?"

Will was trying to gauge the type of woman Charlie was. "All of the above." She was the perfect combination of tomboy meets feminine. There was Francine to consider too.

"We just received the first shipment, so I'll courier the pieces to you tomorrow. And if the china convinces her to fall for you, you owe me big time."

"Thanks," Sebastian said to the dead air, but the silence was golden. Charlie wouldn't have to drive back to her place to pick up the china she'd forgotten, and she and her mother would have a one-of-a-kind tea set.

There were so many things he could do to make Charlie's life easier. All he had to do was convince her to take them.

Tea cups. His money. And him.

* * *

Charlie hadn't been sure whether Sebastian would show up at her workshop this morning after the way she'd refused his offer of dinner last night. But here he was, looking sexier than any man had a right to be in his dark slacks and crisp white button-down shirt. *A billionaire's uniform,* she found herself thinking, and one he wore exceptionally well, despite having been born into extreme poverty and despair.

All night and into the early hours of the morning, the incident with her mother had wedged itself somewhere between her throat and her heart. *Incident* wasn't the right word. Nothing had actually happened. She'd accepted his offer to try to help with her mother's medical condition while turning him down on Magnolia Gardens, then lain awake berating herself for not having done enough to take care of Mom in the first place. Lack of funds was a sorry excuse.

But neither of them mentioned her mother's illness as he entered her workshop bearing warm blueberry bagels that tasted as if they might have been fresh out of the oven.

"I can't wait to watch you work." He sounded like he was talking about a strip tease instead of metal cutting. Boy, could he switch on the sizzle, heating her up like plasma, turning her into molten metal.

She took a bite of the bagel, then began to pull her hair up into a knot. The next thing she knew, he was helping her put on her smock and work apron, his fingers lingering on her skin. Her breath went, her skin tingled, and even though she really did have a ton of work to get started on, she couldn't resist twining her arms around his neck and going up on her toes to steal a kiss.

A sigh of pleasure fell from her lips as they touched his, *gentle* spinning to *desperate* in less than the span of a breath as he tangled one hand in her hair and used the other on the curve of her hip to bring them close. So close that she could feel his heart beating against hers as he deepened the kiss. Taking. Giving. Delighting.

When she finally drew back, his eyes were dark with desire and she was breathless from the feel of his hard muscles pressing into her, his strong arms holding her tight. It wasn't even ten in the morning, yet the atmosphere was positively sultry. Honestly, she was glad that Sebastian made her forget every thought that had kept her awake last night, at least for a little while. There was only the sweet anticipation of his kiss, his touch, even the way he looked at her with those dark eyes of his, as though he could taste her.

"Boy, am I glad I dropped by this morning."

She knew he didn't have time to spend with her in the workshop, just as he hadn't had any spare time to visit her mother. Not when he held the reins of a billion-dollar company, one that depended on his inspiration and charisma first and foremost. Which only made the time he did spend with her sweeter.

"I am too," she said, before forcing herself to step out of his arms and reach for two sets of safety goggles.

"Put these on and stand over there." She pointed to the far end of the workshop.

"You want me to sit in a corner and shut up?" Clearly, people rarely told billionaires where they could and couldn't go.

"At least I'm letting you stay today," she said with a laugh. "But only as long as you don't mess with my concentration." Because Lord knew, he was too darned sexy, even in goggles. How was that possible? Simply because he was Sebastian. He lived and breathed sexy.

Be still, my beating heart.

When he didn't head for the corner, she said, "I'm sure you never just sit back and let someone else do the work, do you?"

"Actually, a big part of my job is observing people." He raised one eyebrow and curved his mouth in a half smile as he finally began to back away. "But watching you is pure pleasure."

She gave him a look, even as everything sizzled inside her. "Go. Sit. I need to concentrate."

She'd clamped a car door to a table she'd made out of sawhorses. She was still in the design phase, thinking about angles and curves and materials, but she wanted to demonstrate the process for Sebastian, so she was jumping ahead. He was so eager to see how everything worked.

Or maybe, she thought with a smile she couldn't quite contain, it was just that he was eager to torment her with the promise in his eyes. Well, if and when the time came, she was going to enjoy tormenting him just as much...

She let the machine and the noise and the sparks drown him out. Work. Create. Cut. And yet, all the while, she felt him watching her. Her pulse pattered faster, a sweet, hot feeling—to be his focus, sense his attraction, and know that he wanted her. The potential for something huge between them tantalized her. There was still the business-versus-pleasure thing, but after sharing their pasts with each other and taking him to meet—and charm the socks off—her mom, she knew they weren't strictly business anymore.

Still, Charlie didn't want to simply jump into bed with him. Not until she knew for sure that he wouldn't expect her to change who she was. Because it felt like he already meant too much to her to be *just* a fling...and it would break her heart into a million pieces if she let herself fall, only to end up shattered if he didn't actually want *her.*

She finished the cut, shut off the plasma arc, and studied the work after pushing up the shield and goggles. Again it occurred to her that it would be really fun to bring her students into this workshop to see firsthand what it was like to build such a big piece from the ground up.

"Looks like a perfect job to me," he commented as he rose from his seat to check it out.

She'd done better. But she hadn't had him for a distraction either. "I need a Dumpster." At home, she had a small one behind the garage.

"Don't you use every piece for something or other?" He was close enough by then for his breath to whisper over her cheek, his body heat arcing over her like the electrical current of the plasma cutter.

She almost shivered. "Not *every* piece. I have enough of a junkyard as it is."

"Then a Dumpster you shall have." She wasn't sure how he made it sound as though he were giving her jewels. And when he traced a finger over the metal, she felt as if he were running his hands over her body. "Is this the front of the chariot?"

"Yes." Her answer came out husky. He pushed aside a few wisps of hair that had escaped her knot, and when he dropped a kiss on her throat, it was the hardest thing she'd ever done to force herself to tell him, "It's time for you to go now."

"Already?"

"You're too distracting."

He was grinning as he removed his goggles and headed out of the workshop, clearly pleased that he had such a strong effect on her. But around noon, he reappeared with a picnic basket laden with gourmet cheeses, fruit, and a variety of crackers. He'd spread a blanket on the grass outside the bungalow.

"You don't have to keep feeding me," she said as she took a cracker spread with warmed Brie from his fingers. "Especially when I know you couldn't possibly have time for all this."

"You wouldn't stop to eat if I didn't. And I need to eat too."

"I eat." Except that he was right—she often became so involved she didn't notice her hunger until her stomach rumbled as loudly as the compressor. Just the way it had when he'd tempted her with the picnic treats.

He smiled, reading her mind. "Knew it." He gave her another cracker, this one with a mouthwatering Cambozola cheese.

God, she could get used to this treatment. Did he sweep all his women away like this?

As soon as it hit her, she hated the thought of *his women*. It wasn't fair to him, her being judgmental like that. As if she were saying that because he was rich, he must use his wealth to make his conquests. Especially when she didn't feel like a conquest.

She felt treasured.

After the scrumptious lunch, they sat side by side at the workbench, her iPad propped up, the chariot drawing on the screen, his hip pressing lightly against hers. It was so familiar, so sweet.

So intimate.

"Have you decided what you want to use as the floor of the chariot? Another car door?"

She breathed in, out. Tried to calm her racing heart—and ever-growing desire. "No. Not a door. Something else..." The words trailed off as she traced the lines with her finger.

"What if you used a tile mosaic for the base?"

She tipped her head one way, then the other, picturing a mosaic before saying, "What if we accented with some of the tiles you used on the fountain?" Her mind began to sprint at the same speed her heart was from his nearness. "When the sun hits, the tiles will sparkle like rainbows. We'll have to make sure the angle is right so it gets enough light. We can set the mosaic in a metal form so I can weld the body of the chariot to it."

"The design could be free-form. The tiles can be chipped so they're not square."

Their ideas built on each other. "We could even add other irregular fragments, like broken crockery. I've seen garden stepping stones made from bits of china plates." Her excitement rose, not just for the chariot they were creating together as though they were a team, but for him—his body so close, his thigh taut against hers, his male scent all over her.

"That's brilliant."

She scanned him again, right into him, past his good looks. "*You're* brilliant. I would never have thought of mixing the two mediums, metalwork and tile work." She thought of the anger he must still feel over his parents destroying themselves with alcohol and partying, especially when he'd needed so badly for them to be there for him. And she couldn't help adding, "It's going to be amazing fun to break plates against the wall, venting all our frustrations in a good cause."

"I like it. And you." He reached for her, brushed his fingertips over her lower lip. "I like you too, Charlie. So very much."

Her heart stilled for a moment as she basked in the way his eyes mapped the lines of her face. This time when they kissed, she wouldn't be able to stop at that. Not with this reckless need pounding through her veins. Just as she was about to put her hands on both sides of his gorgeous face, a horn honked, startling her and breaking the moment.

Sebastian made a frustrated growl. It was the first time she'd seen him fail to get his way, and she was just as frustrated as he levered himself away from the bench, his muscles rippling.

A white van idled on the drive as a uniformed driver jumped out and handed Sebastian a box. A few seconds later, she was surprised when he held it out to her.

"I don't need gifts." He'd already given her so much.

"It's not for you. But you can open it. Don't shake it, though. It's fragile."

What could it be? On the workbench, she grabbed an X-Acto knife and carefully cut through the tape. Inside were six smaller boxes—three flat, three square. She opened a flat box first.

"Oh, my gosh." She gaped at the utterly beautiful china plate. Monarch butterflies floated across the white porcelain, their wings trimmed in gold. The plate's scalloped edge was lined in a dusty pink and outlined with gold. "It's exquisite." The butterflies flew around leaves and ornately painted flowers with swirls of gold between them. "You don't expect me to break this for the mosaic, do you?"

He grinned, shaking his head. "No, these are for your mom."

"My mom?"

"Apart from your visits, the china is her only luxury, isn't it?" When she nodded, he smiled and said, "Open the rest."

Her hands weren't quite steady as she unearthed two more plates and three delicate matching mugs, with yellow butterflies, blue butterflies, all edged in gold. She didn't have to ask to know the gold was real. Sebastian was a man who insisted on nothing but the best.

"They're beautiful. Mom will adore them." Her mother had never owned anything so elegant. *Or so expensive,* she thought before she could stuff the thought away to join all her other conflicted emotions about Sebastian's money—and how free he was with it when it came to her.

"My friend Will imports these from England." He flipped the plate over. "They're signed by the artist who paints them. This is by Rose." He pointed to a small rose under the maker's name.

Charlie was overwhelmed. All she had to do was make one offhand remark about forgetting a plate and a cup, and he miraculously conjured them for her from England. But not just two. Three. Because he clearly planned to join them again.

"I'm going to visit my mom again on Wednesday. I know you're busy, but if you can carve out a little more time, will you come with me?"

"I wouldn't miss it."

Her eyes stung with tears of gratitude. She'd been pissy about his offer to help her mother, making it about her and her guilt. Yet everything he'd done had been kind and thoughtful. He always praised, never criticized.

He built people up, never dragged them down. Right from the beginning, even when she'd expected the rich, take-what-he-wants, stomp-on-whomever celebrity, he'd been different. She'd looked for chinks, but everything he'd done defined him as a flesh-and-blood man who actually cared.

In that moment, Charlie put aside every reservation about his research into her mother's illness. He wanted to give, so she would accept without automatically assuming there were strings attached.

She carefully put the plate back in its box. "Thank you." Reaching up, she framed his face in her hands, then rose on her toes and kissed him. Soft and sweet, still trembling with emotion. "For everything."

* * *

Maybe a better man would have looked at Charlie's kiss as nothing more than a sweet thank-you. But Sebastian didn't have it in him, not after the hours he'd spent watching those lithe curves move, her strong yet elegant hands performing miracles in metal. Hell, the way her mind worked was the sexiest thing of all.

Being with Charlie, especially when they were in her workshop, reminded him that there was a life beyond work and society events. Reminded him of the simple pleasures of working with your hands. Of getting hot and sweaty. She'd brought that joy of art and creativity back into his life, right there in front of him. She'd let him watch, had even let him be a part of it when she'd run with his mosaic suggestion. She was right that he didn't have any spare time to be there with her in her workshop, but Sebastian was inexorably drawn both to being a part of the creative process and being with her.

He'd always craved creating. Now he craved her too. Which meant resisting the irresistible wasn't an option.

His arms around her, he lifted her off her feet, taking her mouth as roughly as she had taken his so sweetly just moments before, steeping himself in her taste. He would have sung a chorus of *Hallelujah* when she opened fully, giving him everything, if it hadn't meant lifting his lips from hers to do so. Holding her tight, he possessed her mouth while she tangled her fingers in his hair.

Her tongue licked out against his, her curves pressed into his muscles, the pulse at her neck throbbed against his thumb, and he was lost in need. Desperate to have more of her. *All* of her. Every gasp of pleasure. Every moan of desire.

She mesmerized him, and his body took over, raging hard and tight. He consumed and was consumed. Never before had anyone made him forget time or place. There was only the feel of her, the taste, the scent, the moan in her throat. He wanted her with every cell, every organ.

And he knew she wanted him just as badly. His hands molded her bottom to shift her, and he felt her heat, hotter than her welding torch. Every instinct told him to shove her up on the bench, to take, grab, own, possess. Need clamored inside him. He wanted his mouth on her everywhere.

He might have taken everything he wanted if a cloud hadn't passed over the sun, if the light hadn't changed and woken him up for an instant. Lord knew he wanted to jump into the deep end with her. Wanted to take her hand and fly out over the edge. Wanted to risk everything on the hope that they were the perfect fit.

But only last night, he'd drawn more pictures of his parents. Sketches that reminded him of how brutal toxic love could be. That it could destroy absolutely everything.

Nothing about Charlie seemed toxic. On the contrary, she seemed to be his ideal match. And yet...he still hadn't been able to completely figure her out, still didn't understand why she hadn't been reaching for her full potential until he'd found her in the middle of her junkyard. He'd never felt this strongly about another woman, never felt like he was falling in love before.

And that very fact made him recognize that if toxic love was going to hit him, it would be now, when Charlie already mattered so much to him. He couldn't imagine how hard it would be to fall completely for her, only to have to give her up. When they finally did dive into the deep end together, he wanted them both to truly know enough about each other to take the risk not just with their bodies.

But with their hearts.

Though it was even harder to pull back today than it had been two nights ago, he forced a breath of space between them. Her chest rose against him, as she gasped for the air they'd both lost in their sweet, desperate kiss.

"You..." The word came out raw. Ragged. "I want..." Damn it, he was never at a loss for words. Hell, his job was always having the right words for everything. But he'd never felt this way about anyone, never had to stop himself from moving too fast because his heart was tied so closely to his desires.

She put her hand on his face. The same strong, elegant hand that could create such majestic art. "I want you too." She sucked in another shaky breath. "Just as badly. But—" She lifted her beautiful eyes to his. "I want to be sure."

Trust Charlie to find the words. Exactly the right ones. Exactly the ones he was feeling.

"Soon," he said again, just as he had after their first kiss two nights earlier. "We'll know soon."

She echoed the word *"Soon,"* in a whisper of a kiss against his lips. Even before the day arrived when they finally stripped away each other's walls and became one, for him every other woman had already been erased. Because all along, something told him he'd been waiting for Charlie.

He hoped like hell she'd eventually realize she'd been waiting for him too.

CHAPTER ELEVEN

For the next handful of days, Charlie alternately worked on the chariot...and daydreamed about Sebastian's kisses. Once or twice she did both at the same time, but that was a surefire way to cut right through a finger, so she forced herself to focus one hundred percent while she was in her studio. When she was back in her bungalow at night, however, all bets were off.

She'd been right about his incredibly busy schedule. More than once, she heard the helicopter taking off, and at one point she was pretty sure there was a film crew on the property up by the main house. But though they were both so busy, Sebastian always made sure to find her each day to give her a kiss. Just one perfect kiss each time. So perfect that he'd left her with her head spinning and her lips tingling. And every single time, as he drew back, he said one word.

"Soon."

It had become both her favorite word...and her most hated.

After working on some of her creations for up to a year or two at a time, Charlie thought she had patience down to an art form. But her need for Sebastian was eating through it faster than a plasma cutter.

But for as much as she desired him, she found herself liking him even more. His thoughtfulness knew no bounds. When Wednesday morning came, he had his driver waiting right on time to take them both to Shady Lane for a visit with her mother. She'd hoped Sebastian would steal his kiss in the limo, but he seemed happy just to hold her hand, stroking his thumb over her palm in seductive circles that made her almost mindless with need. And if they hadn't been on their way to see her mother—who would notice absolutely everything, the way she always had when Charlie was a teenager—Charlie might have given in to the reckless urges pumping through her veins and jumped him right then and there on the black leather seat, with the driver only feet away.

Once they were inside the building, Charlie handed the box of beautiful china to Sebastian. "You should give your gorgeous present to her." He didn't have a mother anymore, but he was a man with so much love to give. Charlie was happy to share hers, especially when she knew how much her mother enjoyed his company and attention.

Despite the dingy room, he was almost ceremonial in his presentation of the cups and plates. Sebastian, it seemed, could transcend anything. Two alcoholic parents. A childhood of poverty. Even the less than stellar surroundings of an elder-care center.

Her mother gasped with joy. A joy that, amazingly, seemed to replace the pain for a little while. "Oh, Sebastian." She pressed his hand. "I've never seen anything so lovely."

"I have," he murmured so softly that only Charlie could hear. He looked straight into her eyes and her heart thumped even faster in her chest.

He suggested they drive Francine out to Lake Elizabeth and share their tea and bear claws as an outdoor picnic. The park was only a mile from Shady Lane, and her mother seemed to enjoy the ride in the limo as much as she soaked up the dappled sunlight streaming through the trees on the comfortable portable chairs he'd stashed in the trunk.

"I'd like to bring a doctor by to see you, Francine." Sebastian had thoroughly discussed the Stanford hand surgeon with Charlie and she'd agreed to his intervention if it had any chance of helping her mother. "Would that be all right with you?"

"You're such a dear, but it's too late now. All the doctors have told me that."

"If you don't mind seeing one more, I know my friend would be very interested in coming to meet with you." Sebastian poured tea from a Thermos he'd brought, having naturally thought of absolutely everything.

Her mother nibbled her bear claw. "It tastes even better on this beautiful china." She added a sip of tea to her delight. "I've never heard of a doctor doing house calls, at least not in this century."

"It's a personal favor. Unfortunately, he's out of the country right now, so he'll see you in a couple of weeks."

Charlie shuddered to think that Sebastian had probably promised to fund a new wing at the hospital in return. She'd worked to get past her hang-up about his spending so much money on her and her mother...but it was difficult when he only grew more generous by the second.

Her mother squeezed Sebastian's hand. "You're going to spoil me," she said in a singsong.

"You deserve to be spoiled."

"I know what a busy man you must be."

"I'm not too busy to see you."

"We both know that isn't true," her mother said in a soft voice. "You're very special to carve out time we all know you don't have to visit an old woman you've just met. Very special, indeed."

Charlie's heart turned over at the glow on her mom's face—and how moved she could see that Sebastian was by the bond he was forming with her mother. She knew how badly he'd wanted to help his parents, and it wasn't hard to see that he'd channeled that need into helping others.

So despite her lingering guilt at accepting his help, she was doubly glad she'd consented. The look on both their faces was worth everything. If the doctor could find a way to help her mother experience even a tiny bit less pain, it would be all Charlie could ask for.

Sebastian was good for her mother.

And, she thought, as he snuck in his one perfect kiss while her mother's head was turned toward the sun, she couldn't deny that he was good for her too.

* * *

"Do you need to head straight back to the workshop?"

The limo had just dropped them off at his house, and even though she should have gone right back to work, how could she resist more time with Sebastian? And if she could actually work on the sculpture while spending time with him? Well, that would be absolute perfection.

"Actually, I was thinking about doing a little shopping this afternoon." At his surprised look—he'd obviously noticed she wasn't particularly into fashion—she laughed and clarified. "For parts to use on the chariot." She'd formed the body and haunch of one horse, but she was working on the legs and head, and the chariot still needed its base. He'd already taken off a ton of time and it was a long shot, but she decided to say, "There's both an estate sale and a construction sale this afternoon, if you'd like to come with me."

"Isn't an estate sale basically just a glorified garage sale?"

It was kind of adorable how his nose crinkled at the words *garage sale.* Clearly, he'd been living in the lap of luxury for a while. Either that, she found herself thinking on a more sober note, or garage sales had been the only "stores" his parents could afford to shop at when he was a kid.

"One person's junk is another's treasure. It can be a goldmine. I adore junk shopping."

"*You* adore junk shopping?" He gave her his best innocent look as they headed for his garage. "Could have fooled me."

She playfully swiped at his chest. He grabbed her fingers, and lifted them to his lips for a quick kiss that left her skin tingling and her heart racing as they stepped into his enormous, and well-stocked, garage. Not that she could make fun of him for his collection of classic cars, however, considering her personal collection of broken shovels and pipes.

She insisted on taking the truck, but he insisted on driving. It made her hot and bothered to watch him behind the wheel. A man with a truck was just plain sexy, but Sebastian dressed in black jeans and a black shirt behind the wheel of a half-ton pickup was downright meltingly hot.

The day had been absolutely perfect so far, so when they uncovered an array of crockery, including chipped and mismatched china, not five minutes after arriving at the estate sale, she honestly wasn't surprised. Everything Sebastian touched seemed to turn to gold.

There was no reason for the thought to send a shiver running down her spine. No reason to be anything but thrilled at connecting with him the way she had. And yet, if everything he touched turned to gold...then did that mean she would too?

It didn't make sense that she should be so uncomfortable with the idea of breaking out as an artist, as Sebastian had told her time and time again was his plan. Especially when she so badly needed the money for her mother's care. Still, it took some work to remember to smile when she caught Sebastian looking at her strangely.

"Is everything okay?"

His hand was on her face and when she felt his warm touch and looked into his eyes, she knew she must be crazy for having any reservations at all. "Everything's perfect."

His gaze dropped to her lips for one heady, heated moment, before he simply brushed his thumb over her lower lip and said, "Are you thinking what I'm thinking?"

Yes. I want you. Badly.

His grin stole her breath, even before he lowered his voice and said, "God, how you tempt me, Charlie." She could see how much self-control it took to add, "The *other* thing I'm thinking."

Her breathed whooshed out in a half-laugh, half-sigh. "The mosaic," she whispered. "The china was meant for us." And truly, her heart was fluttering at both the excitement of the find, and from being with Sebastian.

They picked out every piece. Turning them over, she read names like Royal Albert, Rosina, Coalport, Adderley, Rockingham. "This one says, *By appointment to Her Majesty the Queen.* We should try to break out that part to use. And since they're all broken, I'll offer ten dollars."

"Big spender." He stood close enough to nuzzle her hair.

Her eyes closed for a moment as she savored him. "They're going to end up in the trash anyway. It's ten dollars no one else would pay."

Ten dollars was accepted, and they loaded the box in the bed of the truck. "If they break in transit, who cares?" She was, however, relishing the pleasure of breaking them herself. And she couldn't wait to hand over a stack to Sebastian too, so he could work off some of the latent anger she knew had to be simmering just beneath his calm surface.

"Off to the construction sale?" He handed her up into the truck, his touch doing crazy things to her. This was her world, one that no other man had ever wanted to be a part of. But just having him in it with her made the day extra special.

"Yup." She keyed the address into the GPS.

Fifteen minutes later, the contractor trailed them through the lot until Sebastian gave him the stinkeye. The old house had once been a Victorian, but it was stripped down to bare walls and floors. The sun was high in the sky now, and Charlie was glad she'd slathered sunscreen on her shoulders, arms, and neck bared by the sundress. Sebastian didn't even seem to break a sweat.

They found brass pipes that could work for the sinews of a horse's legs, and several different configurations of pipe fittings for the joints. Then she discovered the spools of copper wire, holding one up for Sebastian's inspection.

"The reins," she said, unable to stem the awe from the clear vision she'd just had.

"From copper wire?" He looked more than a little surprised. "I'm going to have to see it to believe it."

Oh, she'd make him believe all right. She already saw the reins flowing out from the horses' bridles as if they were flying. She'd braid several pieces of wire to give it strength and width.

"It could work for the horses' tails too," he said, his tone offhand.

She sucked in a breath on a gasp. "Oh, my God. Single copper strands bunched together." It would seem as though they were blowing in the wind. "The tails will appear to be on fire when the sun hits them." She kissed him soundly on the mouth. "You're a genius."

He took the opportunity to put his hands on her waist before she could draw back. She felt his utter focus and concentration on her. He tucked away a lock of hair, trailing his finger along the shell of her ear.

When she shivered and fell into his gaze, she felt as if she were falling out of her normal life...and into a magical place where there was only his touch. Only his kiss.

Only Sebastian.

CHAPTER TWELVE

Charlie's ability to amaze him never ceased. She found fantastical mysteries in other people's cast-offs. A dirt-encrusted gate could open the door to another world. A length of copper wire transmuted itself into the flapping reins of runaway stallions. He had no doubt she could do it. She saw inspiration in everything.

And Sebastian found inspiration in *her*.

She came alive when she was working, planning, visualizing. He'd given up on the drawing app and had continued to fill sketchbooks with images of her just like this— her eyes bright, her face shining, her lips smiling. Yet none of the drawings brought him closer to discovering why her work wasn't already world famous. Why she wasn't already a huge, glittering star in the art world. With her talent, beauty, and charm, she could easily command that world, the shining star on top of it all. By now anyone else would have been using his contacts to network, taking anything she could from him to advance her career. But not Charlie. No matter how many sketches he drew of her, he couldn't put his finger on the reason. But he would. *Soon.* Because Sebastian had long ago vowed never to give up on somebody with potential. Especially when that somebody had come to mean as much to him as Charlie already did.

Since she wouldn't take the money for her mother's care from him—he'd gently offered a few times more to help pay for Magnolia Gardens and she'd just as gently turned him down—that meant the only other way to help her pay for her mother's needs was to find buyers for the rest of her sculptures. He'd already made several phone calls to that end, but he wouldn't say anything to Charlie until he had a solid bite from a prospect.

"We didn't even spend a hundred dollars," he said as he pulled the truck in front of the workshop and began to unload the full bed. Even lunch had been a quick but excellent burrito off a taco truck. He'd never eaten from a food truck before—why would he, when he had the best private chefs in the world on speed dial?—but with her it had been both fun and delicious.

Charlie laughed as she set the gate she'd found against the studio wall. Admiring her strength—and knowing that she prided herself on her independence—he'd made himself stop offering to carry the heavy stuff all the time. "Why do you think I chose to work in the junk medium rather than expensive canvases or paints or marble statues?"

"Smart woman." He put the delicate and considerably lighter box of china cups and saucers on the workbench. *Beautiful woman too.*

She'd worn her steel-toed boots in deference to the junkyard terrain and a sexy sundress with minuscule straps in deference to the heat. He'd driven himself nuts the whole day, touching her hair, her face, her shoulders, her neck, anything he could flutter his fingertips across. He hoped he'd driven her nuts too.

"Guess what it's time for?" she asked, with a wicked arch of her brow.

He had a good dozen ideas of his own...all of which involved Charlie naked and gasping with pleasure beneath him. But she wasn't taking off her clothes; she was flicking the lid of the box with her fingernail.

"Smashing up the china for the base of the chariot. It'll be like aggression therapy," she said, a sexy come-hither sparkle in her eye.

"I don't need aggression therapy." No, he needed therapy of a completely different nature, on satin sheets with the night breeze cooling their sweaty, naked bodies. He wanted her badly enough by now to throw all his caution against the wall.

"Sure you do," she murmured in a slightly husky voice as she took a step closer. The spicy, sexy scent of her skin beckoned him, and his fingers flexed, his muscles bunched, ready to pounce like a mountain lion. "Everyone has some anger they need to let out."

"Even you?"

"I'm angry as hell that my mother is always in pain. What are you angry about?"

My father for being a selfish asshole. The words landed in his brain before he even knew they were coming.

As if she knew he wasn't able to say the words aloud, she simply handed him a cup and whispered, "Toss it."

Her words were so low, so seductive, that she could have been begging him to touch her, taste her, take her. He leaned into an overhand throw against the far wall. And the cup shattered.

"What an arm," she cheered, punching the air. "But we might need a little less exuberance. Or we won't get any *pieces* at all."

"Your turn." He shoved a saucer into her hand. She'd been right—the act of smashing the cup felt like it had smashed some of the anger boiling away in places he'd thought had gone cold a long time ago.

She narrowed her gaze and he could see her focusing on her anger about her mother's illness a beat before she executed an underhand toss like a dancer, arm out, up, rising on her toes, letting the delicate porcelain sail and drop.

It broke into solid lines on the concrete. One half remained intact, lying upside down.

"Your turn again," she drawled, then gave him a flirty smile that crinkled the corners of her eyes. He felt the heat of her skin, caught the breathy exhalation. And suddenly this wasn't only about unleashing anger.

It was also about seduction.

He tossed the cup. She chose another saucer and threw it right after his. Everything broke with a tinkle of china. The intact half of the saucer snapped as they piled on.

"More," she said, grabbing, tossing, breaking, faster, one on top of the other.

Her breath came harder, her cheeks were flushed, her lips red, wet, inviting. He wanted to sink into her while he stroked her tongue with his, tasted her lips, feasted on her, the breaking glass ringing in their ears.

"Another," she urged him. One after the other, saucers and cups sailed through the air, crashing hard against the wall, until the box was empty and the concrete in the center of the barn was a rainbow of colored chips. Her skin was covered in a light sheen of perspiration, and all he could think about was licking off the salt, reveling in it.

He didn't think, didn't blink, before hauling her up against him and taking her mouth. She was all spice, sweet and hot. As strong as she was, in his arms she felt as petite and delicate as the china. She devoured him even as he consumed her. Her body heat singed his fingertips as he molded his hands to her waist.

No other woman made him lose himself so completely. The workshop doors stood wide, yet he didn't care. And he couldn't bring himself to heed the cautionary thought that it would be better to wait, to make sure that they weren't toxic to each other before they took this next step. There was only a hard ache inside him, an overwhelming desire to fit himself inside her.

He yanked a spaghetti strap down her arm, then molded her breast in his hand, roughly teasing the tip to a hard peak. She moaned into his mouth, a heady sound that played every chord in his body, vibrating through him.

Until today, he'd made himself take it slow. Made himself take care not to fall too far, too fast, too hard before he was totally sure their feelings for each other wouldn't be their mutual destruction.

But slow was completely impossible now.

His hand slid over her hip, his fingers tugged up the thin material of her dress, and her bare thigh singed his palm. Her kisses stole his breath and fogged his mind, while the heat of her skin made him completely crazy.

"Sebastian." Her eyes were drugged, her lips swollen, her hair framing her gorgeous face. If she'd stepped out of his arms, he'd have made himself let her go. But she molded her hand tightly over his on her breast, then dragged his head down for another intoxicating kiss. He stroked her tongue with his, caressed the hard nub beneath his fingers, and tested the flesh along the line of her barely-there thong, the temperature rising to steamy.

He needed more. *More.* And he couldn't wait for it, knew he'd die if he didn't touch her. When she pushed the back of his head until his lips found her nipple, he knew she felt exactly the same way.

He kissed her, licked, sucked, savored. Her body vibrated with hot, sweaty need, and she moaned, her legs tight around him, her body arching along the ridge of his erection. One after the other, his brain fired off orders he was beyond desperate to obey.

Touch her.

Taste her.

Pleasure her.

He flipped up the hem of her enticing sundress and put his palm on her center, letting her heat seep into him. "Here." The one word was a whisper of need, a rasp of desire. "Now. I need to touch you, Charlie."

He had never *needed* before, not like this, beyond the physical, deep into emotional territory. He truly felt as though he would die if he lost her. He'd never had such a thought about another woman, only Charlie. She was *to die for.*

Before the semi-destructive thought could paralyze him, she put her lips to his and hummed a hot little pleasure sound deep in her throat. "Here. Now. *Touch me.*"

Less than a heartbeat later, he was sinking his finger into her wet heat. She was so ready, her body quivering. He took her lips again, kissing her hard, delving deep, while he played over her arousal. Her hands roamed up and down his arms, cupping his face, into his hair, while her boots scraped the backs of his thighs restlessly. Panting, biting her lip, she looked up at him and he saw that a flush had turned her cheeks pink and her pupils were dilated.

He leaned closer, his reflection in her gaze, and filled her with his fingers. Hard, fast, he took her until her head fell back, her hair cascading across the bench. She gasped twice, then cried out, her body tightening, releasing. The perfume of her climax enveloped him as a full body flush turned her skin hot.

"Oh, God. *Sebastian.*"

Sweet Lord, he wanted to thrust so deep and high inside her that they became a part of each other. Wanted to wrap himself all around her and never let go.

Yet he knew he couldn't. Not yet. Not when making love to her would only bring them closer...and he still didn't understand what made her tick at her very core. And while Charlie had made it clear that she *wanted* him, it was obvious that she was still afraid to trust him, still afraid that any help he offered had strings attached.

Though he ached with unrelenting need, all he could do now was hold her close for another few precious seconds and allow himself the pleasure of breathing in her luscious scent.

"*Soon.*"

She reached out, her hand fluttering, lighting on his arm, his throat, his cheek, and finally her fingers on his lips. He knew he was right to draw back when she nodded and echoed the word back to him. "*Soon.* Although," she said as she licked her lips, "I'm dying to touch you too. Here. *Now.*"

He couldn't hold back his groan of need, even as he said, "If you put your hands on me—" He closed his eyes a moment to let himself soak in the sexy vision before brutally shoving it away. "I won't be able to stop."

She stared at him for a long moment, one that had him wondering if she was going to reach for his belt despite all their well-intentioned reasons for waiting. But in the end, she simply sat up and said, "If you're not going to let me touch you—" She huffed out a long breath of regret that he felt down to his very marrow. "—then we should get back to finding the best pieces for our mosaic."

We. Our. He loved that, how even after he'd worked like hell to put the brakes on, she was not only in agreement, but wasn't holding anything against him out of sheer frustration.

Oh yeah, every sign pointed to Charlie Ballard being special. Being *the one.* Soon he would know for sure—whether it was through his sketches or simply by spending more time with her. Once he was absolutely convinced they wouldn't hurt each other the way his parents had, he'd make damn sure they got their fill of each other, morning, noon and night, with no brakes anywhere in sight.

CHAPTER THIRTEEN

A few days later, Sebastian needed to fly back East. He usually enjoyed his business trips, different sights, a change of pace—but this time, he didn't want to leave Charlie. This meeting had been scheduled a month ago, before everything started changing inside him. He'd invited her to come, but just as he'd expected, she wouldn't desert the chariot.

So he went alone to New York and had a good meeting with the TV network that wanted to carry his series of motivational programs on creating success in everyday life. Even better, over drinks he met with a friend who mentioned a new hotel back in Northern California where they were looking for a big, impressive garden centerpiece. In an instant, Sebastian knew that Charlie's work was meant to be there. One quick phone call got Sebastian an appointment for the day he returned.

He would have headed home that night, but he'd promised Susan and Bob he'd stop in to see them in Chicago. If not for them, he'd never go back there. None of the Mavericks would. The bad memories of Chicago overshadowed the good, even though they'd long since moved Susan and Bob out of the seedy neighborhood and into a big house on a tree-lined street.

"Honey, we're so glad you came."

Susan had prepared his favorite dish, beef bourguignon, which had been simmering all day in the slow cooker despite the Illinois summer heat. The house smelled like ambrosia, and now they were sitting outside on the deck enjoying a slightly cooler evening. A light breeze washed over him, reminding him of Charlie's fingers in his hair.

Susan looked younger every day, if that could be believed. Life was treating her well. She was slender and healthy, walking five miles every day, at least in summer. "You look great. Have you done something new with your hair?"

She patted her silver locks and smiled. "Just a different rinse."

She was only fifty-five, but most of those years hadn't been kind. She'd been a waitress at a diner, and Bob had been a baggage handler at O'Hare. They'd started their family young, Daniel coming along when they were only twenty, and their daughter Lyssa ten years later.

Then there were the Mavericks, the rough-and-tumble teenage boys they'd taken in and raised. Bob and Susan were givers, even when they hadn't had enough to give. Sebastian was inspired by them every day.

Bob pointed to the top of his bald head. "Hey, what about me?"

"Oh, honey, I love your bald head." Susan reached over to stroke the shiny skin.

Sebastian loved the way they were with each other. He couldn't remember them fighting, not like his parents. His parents had loved hard, drunk hard, fought hard. Whereas Susan had always told Sebastian that in any argument, you had to stop, think, and then speak. It was advice that had served him well in business negotiations over the years.

Bob rose from his chair. "I'm going to water the rose bushes. They look a little parched."

"Thanks, honey." She gave him an affectionate swat on the behind as he passed, then he practically jogged down the steps. "He's got a whole new lease on life after his back surgery. I'm so glad you boys talked him into it."

No matter how much money the Mavericks earned, Bob and Susan never took anything for granted. It was only when the pain from an old work injury had become debilitating that Bob allowed Daniel and the rest of them to pay for the surgery. Of course they'd gotten him the best, flying in a surgeon from London.

He could do the same for Charlie's mom. She might not ever jog down a flight of stairs, but if she could live without pain, it would be worth it.

Susan put her hand over his on the arm of his chair. "You've got a different look about you too. Let me guess...you've found someone special, haven't you?"

He didn't even try to play it cool, not when Susan was the heart-and-soul guru for all the Mavericks. She saw all, knew all, understood all.

"Her name's Charlie."

"Charlie." There was a smile in Susan's voice. "I like her name."

"It's short for Charlotte. But Charlie suits her so much better." Anticipating her next question, he said, "I hired her to create the sculpture for the lobby." He didn't have to explain which lobby. He talked with Susan at least once a week, but he hadn't yet mentioned Charlie because he'd hoped to have her figured out before being peppered with questions.

"An artist. Like you. That's wonderful." Susan was always so generous with her praise, even though she knew he'd never think of himself as an artist. "She's made her way into your sketchbook already, hasn't she?"

"You always know way too much."

She squeezed his hand. "You're my boys."

He'd always been amazed that Susan had never made a distinction between the children she'd given birth to and the rest of the Mavericks. She loved them all equally. In many ways, he believed the Mavericks had needed her more even than the children she had carried inside her.

Daniel and Lyssa understood from the beginning that they were loved. Whereas the rest of them had to learn to believe in it.

Sebastian knew his parents had loved each other—and him too, as much as they were able. But that love had destroyed them. And it might have destroyed him too, if he hadn't found Susan and Bob and the Mavericks.

"I've filled a couple of pads so far."

"That tells me she must be very special." She pinned him with an undodgeable look. "And also that you're still trying to figure out something about her."

Yep, Susan knew him through and through. "She's gorgeous, she's talented, she's smart. She teaches classes at the local college in addition to making her own art."

"She sounds fascinating. So where's the *but*?"

"She's gotten nowhere with her career even though her work is amazing." He shook his head. "I don't get it."

"Maybe there's nothing to get."

He didn't get that either. "What do you mean?"

"Maybe she's already happy with her life."

Susan said it as though it were the simplest thing in the world. But Sebastian had spent his life motivating people to embrace their greatness and fulfill their potential to the utmost, so he knew there had to be more going on for Charlie. "She's certainly not unhappy, but she's told me she'd love to see her pieces displayed for everyone to enjoy."

"Still, I wonder if you should be careful how hard you push her."

"Push?" He frowned. "I'm helping her." Though he had to admit he *was* pushing about Francine. "Her mom's got arthritis. Really bad stuff. Charlie's letting me bring in a new doctor, but she won't allow me to pay for a better home for her mother to live in."

"Charlie sounds independent. That's a big part of what you like about her, isn't it?"

"It is." He loved Charlie's strength, her ability to take care of herself, her loyalty to her mother, and her passion for her art, for life itself. He also loved the femininity she usually hid under her face shield and safety apron, and couldn't wait to keep drawing it out of her. "She's starting to be okay with me helping her mother, which is great. But I'm still determined to work out what's holding her back."

"Her? Or you?" At his raised eyebrows, she said, "You've made your life about helping other people let go of their walls, their barriers. But what about *your* walls? *Your* barriers?"

No one but Bob, Susan, and the other Mavericks ever talked this straight to him. And Charlie too, who never couched her thoughts in smoke and mirrors.

Still, it was reflex to say, "I don't have walls."

Susan had the grace not to laugh out loud at his lame protest. But she did shake her head. And perhaps give a small eyeroll.

"Okay," he said in a grudging voice, "I might have a wall or two."

This time she did laugh, but she also reached for his hand. "All of you have done a marvelous job of transcending your childhoods. But some things are hard to shake, Sebastian. You watched two people who loved each other destroy the very person they loved most." Susan had spent twenty years trying to get him to accept that he couldn't have fixed his parents, but now her mouth turned down at the corners. "Love doesn't have to be like that."

"I see you and Bob. Will and Harper. I get that love can work. But for me..." He looked into the garden, where Bob was still spraying the roses. "Charlie's different. Special. I don't want things to go wrong, to turn toxic. That's why I'm being careful. Taking things slow." And working like hell to try to figure her out through his sketches.

"The thing is, honey, you don't always know when it's safe to take a risk until you've already taken it. Until you're already all in. Even if you haven't figured everything out yet." She paused as if to get the rest of her thoughts completely in order before she spoke. "It's nice to think that we can control whether or not we fall in love with someone, but when love is big enough—when it's truly meant to be—it happens whether you're ready for it or not, even if you haven't yet switched from red to green."

He was trying to take in what Susan was saying, knew she and Bob and Will were the lucky ones and that he should listen to their advice. But he couldn't stop himself from saying, "What about Evan and Whitney?" Now there was a marriage *not* made in heaven. Hell, if you looked up the term *toxic relationship*, you'd find a picture of Whitney right beside it. "Evan took a risk with her, but wouldn't it have been better if he had taken things slow and looked at her personality and their relationship from every angle first before marrying her?"

"Honey," Susan chided, "she's had three miscarriages."

Sebastian turned fully in his seat. "I feel sorry for her and Evan. Of course I do. But that doesn't give her a license to be a horrible person the rest of the time. She's a lost cause and Evan should get out. Now."

"He's caring for her for the sake of the baby that could be—and the mother that he believes she'll turn into."

He filled his lungs, then let the breath out on a deep sigh. "I just hope he can figure things out. And be happy. Because we all know she isn't making him happy, no matter how hard he tries to make *her* happy."

"It will work out for him. I know it will." Susan gave him a big smile, which lit up her whole face. "And I can't tell you how happy I am to know you've met someone special."

He leaned over and was kissing her soft cheek, when Bob stepped back on the porch and asked, "What am I missing?"

"We're talking about true love," Susan told her husband.

"Don't push," Sebastian said in an undertone.

"I meant Will and Harper."

"Liar."

She laughed. "Now, how can you say that about an old lady?"

"Because you're not old."

"He's right," Bob said with a grin. "You're my spring chicken."

Bob and Susan were meant for each other. So were Will and Harper.

Was it possible that he and Charlie were too?

Or was he doomed to follow his parents' and Evan and Whitney's examples?

All Sebastian knew for sure was that he'd never felt like this about anyone or anything. Only Charlie. And that had to mean something.

Something big.

CHAPTER FOURTEEN

"Sebastian." Charlie hugged the cell phone to her ear and tried to pretend she was hugging him instead as she curled up on the sofa in the bungalow. "How are Bob and Susan?"

"They're doing great and I'm glad I got a chance to visit." Affection laced his voice. "But I miss you."

"I miss you too." She'd never played coy with him, and she wouldn't start now. He'd been gone only three days, but it had felt like much longer. And even though they'd both been so busy this past week that they hadn't actually managed to see much of each other, when they did, it was absolutely explosive. She definitely wouldn't mind a little more *exploding* soon. "Was your business successful?"

"Yeah. A good deal all around. I'm heading out first thing tomorrow morning."

She felt lightheaded with happiness at the prospect of his return. Sebastian was a different kind of man. She liked hot, fast, and all-consuming. But what he'd done to her was so much more—because he didn't even need to take her clothes off or put his hands on her to make her feel that way. With Sebastian, she could want, need, and feel half crazy while they were simply hunkered on the floor sifting out the best bits of broken china and discussing their placement in the mosaic.

She'd always believed she worked better alone, but today she'd realized how much Sebastian had been feeding her creativity these past weeks. Between the zillion daily meetings that were an integral part of running his billion-dollar empire, he often called from the office to ask about her progress. Recently, she'd even punched his number on her cell a couple of times to bounce an idea off him. He always answered, no matter what he was doing—and his ideas were always so good that she'd continued to wonder if he had a secret background in art. In the evenings, he marveled at her day's work. She'd come to crave his visits to her studio. Just as much as she'd come to crave his kisses, his touch. *Him*.

"What are you wearing?" he asked, as if she'd voiced her thoughts.

She gave a mock gasp. "Don't tell me you want phone sex?"

His lascivious chuckle vibrated across the airwaves and started her engine revving. "It depends on what you're wearing."

"Well," she drawled, "I'm getting into the hot tub soon. And I don't have a swimsuit."

"Lord." She loved the passionate growl in his voice. "I wish I were there."

"I do too." Last week, when they'd broken the dishes, then fallen together onto the workbench as he'd kissed her senseless, put his hand up her skirt, and made her scream with pleasure—it had been perfect. "Which is why you should go to bed now, so you can get up early to come home."

"As soon as my meeting in San Jose is done, I'm coming straight to you, Charlie."

"Good, because I've got so much to show you."

"Don't tempt me, or I'll wake up my pilot right now and we'll fly all night."

"Not *that*." She laughed, a throaty sound that spoke directly to how much she wanted him. "Okay, that *and* the mosaic."

"I've been thinking—instead of waiting for the chariot and horses to be finished, I'd like to take pictures of the lion, the elephant, and all the works in your yard to see if we can find interested buyers." He was matter-of-fact, as if it were going to be the easiest thing in the world to find other people who would love her work. "I know you've probably been looking for buyers for years, but I have a new pool of patrons you might not have met before."

That was certainly true. He had a pool of billionaires. She had a pool of...no one. The idea of Sebastian thumbing through his list of high-powered contacts in search of buyers for her art shouldn't make her frown.

After all, he was all she could ever hope for. A wealthy patron sweeping into her life to make her a big star. And he was right that it didn't have to wait until the chariot's unveiling. It could happen today. If she was lucky, she'd never again have to worry about where her mother was living. And she'd actually be able to make a full-time living from her art.

Ever since she'd met him, she'd felt dreamy and sexy and desired. Sebastian wanted her talent, and he wanted her. So then what could possibly be making her stomach twist like this?

What the heck is wrong with me?

Forcefully pushing aside the dark cloud threatening to storm above her, she said, "Pictures are a good idea." One she'd never thought of for some reason. And even though phone sex was a good idea too, she felt unsettled enough by the idea of Sebastian showing pictures of her sculptures to potential buyers that she simply said, "Sleep well, Sebastian. I'll see you soon."

The low, sexy rumble of his echoing *"Soon,"* was the last thing she heard before she put down the phone.

Her mail had been forwarded and even though flyers, car insurance quotes, and credit card advertisements seemed utterly unimportant—and she'd much rather daydream about Sebastian's mouth and hands on her—she made herself go through it all just in case there was an important bill or letter for her mother's care to attend to.

There was nothing concerning her mother, but there was an envelope from the college. Her heart started pounding hard as she opened the letter asking which sessions she'd like to teach in the fall quarter. She stared at the page. She'd known it was coming eventually, but that was before she realized how different everything would feel here in Sebastian's world. Inside his workshop while working on his commission. The truth of the matter was that if Sebastian's plans for her came to fruition, she might not be able to fit in classes. Because she'd be too busy *creating.*

Honestly, though she wasn't sure she would ever be a fan of the spotlight—she'd never been in one, so there was no way to know for sure—Sebastian's belief in her and the excitement of what she was creating were certainly addictive. When he told her she was a genius, when he marveled at some new piece of the sculpture that she revealed to him, it was as thrilling as the touch of his lips on her mouth or his hands on her body.

As much as she loved teaching, in a way it seemed like an old life calling her back. A life that was a million miles removed from Sebastian. A world apart from everything he was offering—an art career that could be so much bigger than this one project, so much bigger than teaching twenty students two nights a week in a crowded garage where the fuses sometimes blew if too many of them used their tools at once.

She shoved the letter out of sight in a kitchen drawer. She didn't usually put things off, and she'd always loved teaching. But there was so much on her plate right now. If she didn't want to end up with her head exploding, she really only had room for two things.

The chariot.

And Sebastian.

* * *

Charlie always thought better when she was using her hands to create something. But by early evening, her arms and hands were starting to ache from lifting and positioning all the heavy metals for her sculpture, and she didn't want to risk injuring herself. Besides, she wanted to celebrate Sebastian's homecoming in a personal way. Though her mother had done her best to pass on her fabulous cooking talents to Charlie to no avail, she decided she could successfully pull off a Mexican dinner for them both—rice, beans, tortillas, salsa, and grilled fajitas. She lit candles and gave the margaritas a burst in the blender to fluff them up. Even if her meal wasn't amazing, at least her drinks would be.

As she punched off the blender, she heard the helicopter. Her heart tripped over itself and a swarm of butterflies fluttered in her stomach. And when he knocked, then opened the door, she threw herself at him. His kiss was the sweetest thing she'd ever tasted, and his arms around her made her feel like she'd come home.

He framed her face. "You were supposed be waiting for me in the hot tub."

Her feelings suddenly seemed too immense to voice. "And here I slaved over a hot stove for you," she said in a teasing voice.

"You cooked?" He would have done a good job of looking touched if a smile hadn't sneaked through.

She nuzzled her forehead against his chest. "Come on, we should eat the fajitas while they're still sizzling."

He let her drag him to the table. "How did you know I was craving Mexican food?"

"I can read you like a book, Sebastian." She was joking, but the look he gave her made her pause in her tracks.

"Can you really?"

She licked her lips, surprised by how serious their conversation had become in the blink of an eye. "Sometimes I think I can. But other times..." She bit her lip, not wanting to say that she sometimes felt he was holding back. "Other times I think it's just that we're still getting to know each other better."

"I'd very much like to know you better, Charlie. So much better."

"Well," she said as she turned to grab the margarita pitcher and tried to lighten the tone, "we can both learn something more about each other tonight. Do you prefer blended? Or should I make you one on the rocks?" She already knew that despite his parents' disease, he didn't have a problem with alcohol himself.

"Blended is perfect tonight." Even though it struck her that he hadn't actually told her which he preferred, he was already raising his glass to toast. "We have something to celebrate."

She had something to celebrate, all right: Sebastian, close enough to touch and breathe in. He was completely scrumptious in a tailored suit so deeply navy it was almost black. "Your fajita is losing its sizzle." She wanted to relish his surprise, whatever it was, so she quickly put caramelized onions; red, yellow, and orange peppers; mushrooms; and grilled meat onto a spinach tortilla, then topped it all with rice, pintos, and guacamole.

He watched her as if he'd never seen a fajita assembled, with nearly as much awe as he watched her work on the chariot in her workshop. "You sure are good with your hands, Charlie."

She flushed all over under his sensual gaze, as if he'd stripped her down and had his hands everywhere. "So. Your surprise."

"I found a buyer for your rams."

"You did?"

"I did." And he looked positively thrilled, as thrilled as she knew she should be. It was just that she was so shocked, all the way down to her toes. "Walter Braedon owns the new Regent Hotel in downtown San Jose. He wants the rams in the central garden at the entrance."

"Wait," she said, still trying to process the news. "How could he know about my rams?"

"I went over to your place to take pictures this morning after my plane arrived. Before my meeting with him." He pulled a photo from his inside breast pocket and slid it across the table.

Her head was spinning as she said, "I've never heard of the hotel."

"It's almost completed. And it's going to be a palace. Everyone pulling into the circular drive and heading to registration will see your rams battling for supremacy of the garden."

Her head felt as though she were on a Tilt-a-Whirl at the thought that her sculpture would be seen from the road, not only by visitors to the hotel. "But how is that even possible? Especially if you only just took the pictures this morning?"

"I've been keeping my ears open. And visualizing what I want for you. I can see your whole path already, just how acclaimed you're going to be."

"I know you keep saying that, but—"

"You saw your dragon outside the church in Chinatown, from the minute you walked by and the vision came to you. And then you went into the parish office and sold it to them because you *knew* it had to be there. So you made *them* see it too."

"That was your meeting today?" He was probably expecting her to jump up and down with happiness. And she would. After the shock had worn off. Because she'd never honestly thought her rams would ever leave her property, especially not to grace the entrance of a fancy hotel. Reminding herself that it was great news, she added, "The one you mentioned on the phone last night."

"Should I have brought you, Charlie?" He looked worried, obviously having noticed that she wasn't jumping for joy just yet. "Should I have told you that I was meeting with a big hotel about your art?"

She wasn't at all upset that he hadn't included her when she'd have been a nervous wreck. It was tough selling herself. The only time she'd ever done it was with the dragon, and even then she'd known she wasn't going to charge them a thing for it.

"Maybe next time I should go, just to try to get more comfortable with it all." Even the idea of it made her feel more than a little nauseous, but if she was going to swim in the big pond, she'd have to get used to fancy meetings with fancy people, wouldn't she? She held back a shudder at the thought and finally made herself smile. "But today, I'm glad you simply showed up with good news. Thank you. For everything."

He covered her hand, his heat streaking through her, deep inside and all the way to her heart. "I believe in what you create. I want everyone to see it." He gave her a wry grin. "You haven't even asked how much."

"I'm afraid to." She was half serious about that. More than half.

"Don't be." He grinned again as he reached into the inside pocket of his jacket and pulled out a check. "Fifty thousand."

The bottom dropped out of her stomach and she felt herself plunging fifty thousand feet as she took the check from him. The work had been done months ago. It was almost like free money. Free money she tried to tell herself her work deserved—and that it hadn't all just come about because Walter Braedon wanted to impress Sebastian with his purchase. She'd never been insecure before, and Sebastian was endlessly telling her how great her work was. But she'd never envisioned truly wealthy people ever liking sculptures made from transformed junk.

"I figured the rams were a less complicated project than the chariot and horses," he explained. "But the decision is up to you. We can still negotiate for more money."

"No," she said almost sharply. "I'll take it." And all the extra months at Magnolia Gardens that she could give her mother. Because in the end, that was what it was all about, wasn't it? Having the resources to take care of her mother in the best possible way. But it was also about Sebastian's incredible support for her and her art. "Thank you. For believing in me."

"You're worth more than you could ever imagine, Charlie, and soon everyone's going to know it."

The next step was obvious, even for someone as non-commercially minded as she was: The more she created, the more Sebastian could sell for her. Sometimes she needed a break from one project when the juices weren't flowing right, and she let her subconscious mull over the problem while she turned her hand to something else, which meant that even while she was building the chariot and horses, she'd still be able to work on a few smaller projects.

She had a moment of hesitation at the thought of becoming a mass production line. But she already knew what Sebastian would say to that—that she was being self-defeating, letting fear of success and the unknown get the better of her. Besides, she would never let herself turn into a sculpture factory. So why was she still borrowing trouble? She needed to shoo away all these storm clouds that kept gathering over her, when from anyone's vantage point her life was getting better and better by the second.

"Braedon's staging a grand opening gala in three weeks. He wants us there, and you'll be the celebrated artist."

"Me?" For all her self-talk about not letting fear get the better of her, the fear came roaring back in an instant.

"I want to show you off."

"I thought you wanted to show off the rams?"

"You're a package deal. You created magnificence and you *are* magnificent."

For a moment, it felt as though the reflection in his gaze belonged to the woman he wanted to see, not necessarily the woman she was. She liked simple things, and while she stood up in front of others all the time as a teacher, she definitely wasn't used to the kind of attention he was talking about. She'd seen pictures of him on the Internet, the glittery world he walked in, the beautiful women dressed to the nines with sculpted figures and salon-bred features.

Whereas she was just Charlie, a tomboy.

But Sebastian was now her patron and he walked in a world she wasn't prepared for. Which meant she'd better start preparing *now.*

Because Lord knew she didn't have a single thing to wear.

And after everything he'd already done for her and her mother, the last thing she wanted was to disappoint him in any way.

* * *

As Charlie took the time to read carefully through the contract for her rams, Sebastian could easily visualize her dressed in haute couture and covered in jewels. She would outshine anyone in San Francisco society circles.

"It looks good," she said when she finished reading, then took the pen he handed her.

He appreciated that she hadn't just scribbled her signature without reading it the way most people would have. Still, he couldn't help but notice that her normally steady hand shook slightly as she signed. Susan's words suddenly came back to him: *I wonder if you should be careful how hard you push her.*

But making a sale for Charlie wasn't pushing, it was helping. He knew the difference. After all, hadn't he helped hundreds of thousands of people in the past twenty years? Then again, Charlie was more important than anyone else had ever been.

When he looked up at her again, he realized she'd finished signing the contract, slipped the $50,000 check into her bag, and was staring at him. "Is everything okay, Sebastian?"

"Now it is." Pushing away the doubts that had no business hanging over them tonight, he stood, took her hand, and pulled her to her feet—wanting to sweep her away. She was as spicy as the fajitas, her bare shoulders shimmering in the sundress. "I missed you," he whispered. He took her mouth with a long, sweet kiss, then pulled back and raised a wicked eyebrow. "You made a lot of innuendoes on the phone last night, about hot tubs and no swimsuit."

"Mmm," she purred. "I checked the tub earlier, and the temperature is perfect. I like it hot." The *t* sizzled on her tongue.

She pivoted out of his arms and headed to the sliding glass door. On the deck, she slipped out of her sandals. He balanced himself in the doorway, hands on either side of the frame, his heart beating like native drums pounding out the rhythm of a sensual dance. Though they'd been taking it slow, she had to know how badly he wanted to feel every inch of her skin against his, to sink inside her, to hold her as he fell asleep and wake up clutching her tightly against him.

She flipped on the timer and bubbles rumbled up from the tub's jets. Grabbing a clip off the poolside table, she raised her arms to wind her hair into a knot that she secured in back. Sebastian found everything about her utterly erotic. Her dress still on, she stepped down into the water. "Perfect."

His suit jacket was way too hot against his skin. He'd kept it on because he'd had Braedon's check in his pocket, and he'd wanted to present it to her as if he were a hunter arriving home with a kill for his queen.

"Are you coming in?" Water frothed at the hem of her dress. Leaning over, she wet her fingers, then flicked them at him. Her playful smile tucked itself close to his heart.

"You first," he said, his voice harsh in his throat.

He silently willed her to strip off her dress. He'd never wanted anything so badly in his life—to see her glistening skin, her round breasts, smooth abdomen, and every treasure he'd dreamed of night after night.

Her smile was as seductive as Cleopatra enslaving Mark Antony. She curled her fingers into the dress's hem and teased it up even as she took another step down. She pulled it up, up, up and over her head as she sank into the swirling tub. He had a glimpse of pearled nipples and creamy skin before she tossed the dress on the deck and covered herself to the neck in bubbling water.

"Cheat," he said.

She laughed, the husky sound that drove him nuts. God, he wanted her. Her sweetness, her laughter, her heat. She was gorgeously naked in all that bubbling water. He didn't know if he had the capacity to join her without simply falling on her and taking everything he'd tortured himself with in the dark of the night. He almost couldn't remember why he hadn't already taken her to heaven. Could almost forget about his past, about needing to avoid toxic love at all costs. On top of that, he didn't want the sale of the rams to have anything to do with this moment.

Yet none of those reasons could stop him from kicking off his shoes and socks and tugging off his jacket. Buttons popped, skittered across the deck, and fell through the slats as he tossed his shirt. His pants came next and he kicked them aside before walking down into the water to join her, still wearing his boxers.

"Now who's the cheat?" she murmured softly above the churning water.

"Two can play that game." His hand reached out to her as if something else controlled him.

She floated to him. Then she was straddling him. The water was hot, steam rising, the stars overhead bright and shining down on her, turning her eyes a deep glittering green.

"Sebastian," she whispered, all the teasing suddenly gone.

She framed his face in her hands and lowered her mouth to his. His fingers flexed on the smooth skin of her hips, pulling her tightly against him. She rocked as she kissed him, sent him out of his mind with her lips, her tongue, the core of her body. Then he roamed, the pads of his fingers all over her pliable flesh. He caressed from her hips, down her thighs, and back up, close to her center, then traced her belly, her breasts, her shoulders, and back to her nipples. She moaned into his mouth as he played with the tips, teasing, flicking, pinching lightly.

She was hotter than the water, burning him straight through his boxers, her arms tight as she devoured his very essence. He took her hot nipple between his lips and she threw her head back, breathing out his name again. Hands molded to her torso, he sucked the sweet fruit as she quivered and quaked over him. He bit her gently, and she cried out, her fingernails deliciously scoring his shoulders. He wanted to make her come just like this, to bring her over with only his mouth and hands on her breasts.

"Sebastian, please."

He knew she was close, almost there, her breath puffing from her lips, then a gasp. In one swift move, he trailed a finger between her legs. Her eyes fluttered open as she looked at him in luscious surprise at the exact moment that the tremors began to roll through her, her eyes closing as her hips rolled in a perfect rhythm of pleasure over his hand again and again.

God, she was beautiful.

Finally, she opened her eyes. He was so mesmerized by her sexy smile and the hot light in her eyes that when she slid her hand inside his boxers and engulfed him with her palm, he nearly came undone.

"Let me taste you," she whispered. "I can't wait any longer to taste you."

He wanted her hands and mouth on him so badly that he surged out of the water and sat on the side of the tub before he could get his brain to start working again. Right then he didn't care whether the time was right, whether the sale of the rams had anything to do with it, or whether the two of them might emotionally destroy each other down the road. All he cared about was having her mouth on him before he went mad with desire for her and took her right here, right now, in the hot tub, with her naked creamy skin against his and no protection anywhere in sight.

* * *

Sebastian's torso was pure rippling muscle, so beautiful that Charlie's chest tightened simply looking at him. Proud, hard, magnificent. And begging for her.

Or maybe she was the one begging for him?

Of course, when pleasure came this sweet, it didn't matter who was begging, did it? She was smiling at the thought as she lowered her lips to him. His groan echoed into the night air as she tested, tasted, savored with her tongue.

His thigh muscles grew taut and his breath came out harshly, as if he'd been sprinting to get to her. She looked up into his beautiful tight features and reveled in the way she could make him feel, make him forget, make him want. And he wasn't the only one panting—she was too, as she gave him what they both needed, taking him deep. Then deeper still.

She had done this before, but it had never been so right. Because the truth was that being with Sebastian was unlike any other relationship she'd ever had. So good that she wanted to drink in every ripple of power coursing through his body, every harsh intake of breath, every rumble and groan. She loved tasting him on her tongue, loved grasping his hard flesh in her palm, loved knowing that she was giving him so much pleasure with her intimate kisses—just as much as he'd given her. She was utterly lost to the joy of loving Sebastian when his body arched and his hips moved in rhythm with her as he shouted out her name to the night sky above him.

Moments later, he was sliding back into the water and reeling her in with his arm around her shoulders, pulling her face into his deliciously salty skin. She licked him, adding the new taste to the heady ambrosia.

"You're incredible."

She smiled at him from within the circle of his arms, her body sated from his touch, the hot water turning her languid, his arm around her both comforting and sensual. "So are you."

Tonight had been perfect. Yes, she'd had a gut-twisting moment when she'd read through the contract, and another even bigger one when she'd signed it. And perhaps she was still more than a little worried about having to transform herself for the party at the hotel where they'd unveil her rams. But she wouldn't think about any of that now, would just keep telling herself it was completely natural to feel twinges of terror here and there as her art began to find its home outside of her yard.

Right now, all she wanted was to focus on the incredible pleasure that she and Sebastian had just found in each other's arms. Pleasure so sweet that her insides were still spinning from it. And there was so much more waiting for them the moment they were both ready to take the next step. They wanted the same thing—that when they finally made love, it would be exactly that.

Love.

She was so close to that already. Almost to the point of fully trusting Sebastian with her entire heart...just as she hoped he'd trust her with his.

When he tightened his arms around her in the hot tub and they said the word at the same time—*"Soon"*—she knew it wouldn't be long before she trusted Sebastian with so much more than just her art and her career.

With absolutely *everything*.

CHAPTER FIFTEEN

The following morning, Charlie bypassed her workshop and headed straight for Sebastian's waiting car. Though they were going to Shady Lane to see her mom, she couldn't help the delighted, slightly wicked smile at the memory of last night—his touch, his taste, his splendor, and everything that was growing between them moment by moment.

"I'm happy to see you too, Charlie." He followed up his sweet words with a kiss that left her as breathless as if she'd just gone for a morning run.

A large box sat on the seat beside him. "Another gift for my mother?"

He grinned. "I enjoy giving her gifts. I hope she likes it."

"I can't imagine you doing or giving her anything she wouldn't love." Like mother, like daughter. It was enough that he gave her mother his time, but of course Sebastian always wanted to do more. "You're going to spoil her at this rate."

"Good. She deserves it."

She tried not to take his words as a condemnation of the little she'd been able to do for her mother, especially when he tucked her hand into his in the front seat of the car. Guilt, however, immediately reared its ugly little head, adding to her tension over today's meeting with the doctor Sebastian had brought in. She didn't want to make the mistake of getting her hopes up, but it was hard not to. Especially when she knew just how badly Sebastian wanted to make a difference in her mother's life. She hoped he would soon realize he already had, simply by offering his time so willingly.

She was actually quite nervous by the time they entered the nursing home. A tall, white-haired gentleman she knew didn't belong at Shady Lane strode toward them with a confident gait.

"Dr. Hillman." Sebastian shook the other man's hand. "I'm Sebastian Montgomery, and this is Charlie Ballard, Francine's daughter."

The doctor turned, then held her hand in both of his. "It's so good to meet you. I've just left your mother in the lounge. She's an absolute delight."

"She certainly is," Charlie agreed.

The white hair made the doctor appear older, though his features were unlined and his strong hands lacked even a hint of age spots. Rather than speaking to Sebastian, who'd called him, Dr. Hillman focused on Charlie. He cleared his throat, as though switching to professional mode. "I arrived early, so we've been getting acquainted. I did a cursory examination and I'm pleased to be able to tell you that her original surgeon was quite competent."

"I'm glad to hear that." More than glad, actually, both for her mother's sake...and because it was one less thing Charlie had to feel guilty about.

"Her pinkies are very elastic, but I wouldn't recommend putting in a new joint. She wouldn't see a quantifiable increase in usage. I'm afraid there's not much to be done with her other fingers, either. Even with another operation, she wouldn't gain any strength in her hands. I'm sorry, Ms. Ballard, but everything's been done for your mother that can be done."

"What about pain medication?" Sebastian had set his box on the counter, his face grave, the line of his lips flat. "Can we alleviate her pain?"

"She's already on pain management. There are other meds, but the results will be about the same. I'm afraid the pain will never be completely eradicated."

"But there has to be something." Sebastian's jaw flexed, and Charlie knew that the doctor's analysis was hitting him harder than it was her, because her expectations were so much lower.

She reached for Sebastian's hand and held on tight as Dr. Hillman said, "She's quite resilient. Many patients at her stage are confined to a wheelchair. She's good with a walker, and her pain level isn't debilitating. She has admirable tolerance."

"Admirable tolerance?" Sebastian's fingers squeezed Charlie's almost painfully, and an edge grated in his voice. Clearly, he wasn't used to not being able to fix something.

"I'm sorry I don't have better news for either of you."

"Thank you for coming to meet with her," Charlie said. A house call from a renowned surgeon was more than could be expected. But Sebastian had managed it. "It means a lot to us."

Sebastian finally seemed to shake himself, an actual tremor she felt through their clasped hands. "I appreciate your dropping everything to come by."

Dr. Hillman nodded. "I was happy to do it." The doctor shook their hands again before striding out the front door.

A nurse trundled the meds trolley past them, smiling politely. Charlie nodded in return.

"We'll get a second opinion," Sebastian said through gritted teeth when the nurse was out of earshot. "Something has to be done. Dr. Hillman's record said he was the best, but we can't leave it at that. Tell me more about the pain meds, Charlie."

"Mom could take stronger drugs, but they're highly addictive and the body builds up a tolerance to them eventually. The side effects can be worse than the pain, and she doesn't want to start down that road."

He closed his eyes briefly, then nodded once, a muscle still flexing in his jaw. "I understand." But as he picked up the box, she wasn't sure he truly did. Helping people make their lives better was Sebastian's calling. Not being able to help her mother—just as he'd been unable to help his parents—had the potential to hurt him. Badly. "Let's go see your mom."

She held on to him one moment longer. "Thank you for everything. Even if we can't find any other ways to make her feel better, you've already made such a big difference for her." *And for me too.*

"We'll find something." His face was determined. "For all we know, the ankle guy I've contacted might come to a different conclusion."

Charlie already knew how deeply Sebastian cared for the people who mattered to him. His friends, his foster parents. And now her mother. Though she was worried he was going to end up disappointed by the doctors he was bringing in, she couldn't dim his hope.

"So," she said as they headed down the hall toward the lounge, hoping to shift his mood back to the smiles he'd been giving her earlier, "what's in the box?"

She'd asked him the same question a half-dozen times since getting in the car. And he hadn't so much as cracked. "Are you this impatient with your own presents?"

"I'm killer at Christmas. Mom and I have a deal that we only spend twenty dollars, but if you get freebies, like buy-one-get-one-free, then the free one doesn't count against the twenty bucks. Something from a thrift store like Goodwill is okay too. We don't care if it's used."

His mouth was still tight, as if he couldn't let go of the failure with the doctor, but she could tell that he was trying to shake it off. "Sounds like a lot of fun."

"It can take an hour to open all the little gifts we buy each other."

"What about birthdays?"

"Same thing. Twenty dollars." With his hand in hers, she led him down the hall.

"When's your birthday?"

She sidestepped a man in a wheelchair, giving him a brief pat on the shoulder. "Hi, Kurt." Then she answered Sebastian's question. "December. I'm a Sagittarius. What about you?"

"April. Aries."

She couldn't remember whether Sagittarius and Aries were complete opposites or a perfect match. She'd never been into astrology. And no matter what the stars said, nothing was going to ruin the beautiful connection she and Sebastian were building.

"And your mom?"

"January." She could almost see him planning ahead. But December and January were long past her deadline for the sculpture, long past the point when she would be moving out of his guesthouse and back into her own home.

But she didn't want to think about the end.

Not when every new day gave her hope that there wouldn't be one.

* * *

Frustration simmered through Sebastian's veins as they entered the lounge. Francine, wearing a pretty flowered dress, was seated in her usual spot on the sofa.

He felt helpless, just like every time he'd walked into his parents' home only to find them totally blitzed. Again. For five long years after he'd moved into Susan and Bob's crowded but caring household, he kept returning in an effort to get help for his parents. And it had torn him up every single time, especially when nothing he tried to do to help them worked.

Damn it, Dr. Hillman should have been able to fix Francine's hands, do surgery, prescribe a treatment—at least give her some damn pain medication that worked without getting her hooked or having terrible side effects.

"Charlie, Sebastian." Francine held out her gnarled fingers, her smile so big and sweet, despite the lines of age and pain on her face.

"Sebastian brought you a present, but even though I've been pestering him, he won't tell me what it is." Charlie slid into the chair next to her mother and pressed a kiss to her cheek.

"You're such a little girl when it comes to presents." Francine's wrinkled face glowed with fondness. "I am too." She grinned up at Sebastian. "What did you bring?"

Sitting next to her, he also kissed the soft, paper-thin skin of her cheek. "You're as bad as your daughter," he said, keeping his tone light. He wouldn't take his frustrations out on either of them. Instead, he'd do more research. He'd find another doctor.

He'd do *something*.

For now, he simply pulled a penknife from his pocket and slit the tape along the top, then pulled out a second box.

As soon as Francine saw the picture on the outside, she put her hands over her mouth. "Oh my."

"What is it?" Charlie moved the bigger box out of the way so that she could see the picture too.

"A paraffin bath," her mother said, tears glistening in her eyes. "This is the sweetest gift a man has ever brought me. Thank you. You're such a darling man."

Her glow did his heart good after Hillman's disappointment. "I did some research, and the heat of the paraffin wax sounds like it might help ease some of the pain. It comes with gloves you put on after you dunk. Then you start to feel the heat transfer from the wax into your hands. There's a temperature control, and paraffin has a lower melting point than candle wax, so it doesn't burn your skin."

Francine put a hand on his arm, her touch as delicate as a hummingbird's. "Sebastian, you are sweet as the dickens."

Charlie didn't say anything at all, but the look in her eyes said she thought he'd just moved mountains for her mother. He wished he could do more than this one small thing. What the hell use was his money if he couldn't make Francine feel better?

"It takes the wax four hours to melt the first time. And you should toss the used wax from your hands after it cools instead of reusing it. I'll make sure more wax is delivered on a regular basis." He'd read all the instructions. "Would you like to set it up in your room?"

"Oh yes, please. I'll get one of the aides to help me this afternoon."

After filling the paraffin wax, he and Charlie took Francine to lunch, then a drive, along with a stop for coffee and a bit of cake. By the time they returned, the wax had melted.

They helped her dip, put on the plastic gloves, then add the mittens that would help retain the heat.

The bliss on Francine's face was worth every moment he'd spent scouring the internet, and the kiss Charlie gave him melted his bones like the paraffin. He would do anything to make things better for them. He hadn't been able to save his parents, but he would for damn sure make life easier for Charlie and her mother.

CHAPTER SIXTEEN

With Sebastian, Charlie had quickly learned, everything moved fast. The following Monday, though he'd already been out of town for the past several days, he told her, "I've got a gig down in Los Angeles and I'd like you to come with me." He'd held her hand and looked at her with his dark, hot eyes. "I knows it's time away from your work on the chariot and horses, but I miss you and don't want to leave you again so soon."

If a heart could have turned over, that's what hers did, just as it had every time he surprised her with yet another of his sweet thoughts or actions. His consideration was innate, bred into him with years of caring for his parents even when they hadn't wanted it.

Now that she knew exactly what selling more pieces could do for her mother's way of life, Charlie had been toiling maniacally since Sebastian had sold the rams. She couldn't work on the chariot twenty-four seven without the risk of making both creative and technical mistakes that would be difficult to correct. So, during what she called her *creative breaks*, she'd started a couple of new projects, mostly animals for the menagerie she now believed someone might actually want. Sebastian had also arranged for the T-Rex to be brought over to the new studio and she was working on finishing that too.

The truth was that by the time he'd asked her to come to L.A. with him, she'd been feeling tired and a little burned out—a rare thing for her, when she'd always worked at a steady but reasonable pace. A day watching Sebastian do his thing would be pure pleasure.

So now here she was, occupying a special reserved seat in the front row of a sold-out fifty-thousand-seat auditorium. They were all here for Sebastian. People chattered and programs fluttered as the audience began taking their seats for his grand entrance. She'd left him backstage with a kiss—a really hot one that she could still feel tingling on her lips. As an usher escorted her to her seat, her heart was pounding and her palms were sweaty, as though she were the one about to stand up in front of all these people. Whereas Sebastian had been as calm as if they were having a quiet dinner on his terrace.

Charlie couldn't say what she'd imagined one of his presentations would be like, but this was mind-boggling. The stage stood in the middle of the arena. Cameras were trained on the center, with its single stand for a glass and a carafe of water, while special lighting beamed down. Sebastian told her the workshop would be filmed for later syndication to TV stations, as well as DVDs and audio downloads.

He'd called it a *workshop*, but this was like a rock star's performance. Since Sebastian had slowed down to just a handful of appearances a year, the place was packed. Everyone clearly wanted a piece of him.

The lights dimmed, voices hushed, and that was when she realized she'd gotten it wrong. This wasn't a rock concert, where fans shrieked and screamed. It was the symphony, where a reverent silence fell and everyone in the audience waited, breaths held, to be swept away by the magic. Just as Sebastian had swept her away so many times since she'd first met him.

A spotlight snapped on, illuminating Sebastian, who was halfway down an aisle to the stage. The clapping started then, rising until it was deafening. Charlie jumped to her feet too, beating her hands together. She'd understood that he was a celebrity with *beaucoup* bucks, but she hadn't understood *this*, the adulation, the way people reached out to touch him as he passed.

Then he was in front of her, leaning in for a quick kiss and flashing that killer smile, leaving her dazed, until she blinked and realized he was now on stage. His dark suit and white shirt were beacons in all the lights shining on him. His sable hair gleamed, and he was utterly gorgeous.

Who wouldn't listen to a man like him?

He raised his hands and waved people back to their seats. "Welcome." His voice boomed out of the microphone clipped to his lapel. There were indistinguishable shouts in return.

"Today is all about you. About your life and what you want it to be. I don't have guiding principles to give you, just a little common sense. But here's the thing about common sense. Sometimes we're just too close to see it. And sometimes we need help from outside ourselves to understand it."

He moved around the stage, circling slowly so that he could address the full audience. The lights were blinding, and Charlie wasn't sure how much he could see. Until he paused in front of her and smiled. That was when she knew he saw everything. Absolutely *everything.*

"So let me ask you. Do you believe in yourself? Do you believe you deserve happiness and prosperity? Because that's where you have to start."

Four big-screen TVs were mounted above the stadium seating. He was up there in brilliant Technicolor, and she watched his larger-than-life image as he moved around the stage. Most people would have been dwarfed by the huge screens, but Sebastian looked stronger than ever. Charlie couldn't help a fleeting wish that his parents had lived to see him on stage, just once, to see that he'd made something amazing of himself. And that he hadn't given up, even though they'd disappointed him time and time again.

"Opportunity doesn't suddenly come your way once you start believing in yourself," he continued. "It's that you finally recognize the opportunities already there because *you* believe they deserve to be there."

He'd walked into her yard full of scraps and sculptures and offered her the world. But he was right—he'd been there because she'd had the guts to stomp up the parish steps of that Chinatown church and tell them they needed her dragon. One opportunity had brought her another. And another.

Best of all, it had brought Sebastian.

She read the same thoughts in the people around her, the way they were all looking inward, acknowledging the things they'd done right, considering the changes they needed to make.

"Some of you probably know about my childhood. About where I came from. It wasn't pretty. Wasn't fun. Wasn't happy. So if I could do it, if I could learn how to *believe* that I deserved happiness, then you can too." He spoke to her. He spoke to everyone. Fifty thousand people were completely silent, no whispering, no chattering. No one left for a soda or a hotdog or to use the restroom. They couldn't bear to miss a thing, drinking in his every word.

Wanting to believe.

Listening to Sebastian, watching him, *feeling* him, Charlie wanted to believe too. In this moment, he made her feel as though she truly could do anything. Better yet, he made her feel that she *wanted* it all too. That she should ignore her hesitation to reach out and grab the glittering brass and diamond rings, and go for it with all she had. Maybe the thought of being a huge star in the art world still didn't sit quite right with her, but she could learn to be comfortable with the thought of being successful. She could do it. Sebastian helped her believe.

"It's not about the money." He laughed, holding up a hand. "I know what you're thinking. *Yeah, right.*" He brushed his palms down his expensive suit. "Seriously, though," he said with a twinkle in his eyes, "money is great, and I hope all of you make a lot of it doing what you love, but in the end it's not about the money. Not if you get rich but hate your job while you're doing it. You know what I'm talking about, don't you?" He was greeted with shouts of agreement. "You deserve to enjoy what you do. You deserve to have a job that's a vocation, that has meaning, that gives you satisfaction, and makes you feel like you're giving something back." He paused again with impeccable timing, letting the audience ponder. "Let's talk about how to figure that out."

An hour and a half seemed like mere minutes as he offered up a clear-cut pathway to opportunity and success. But Sebastian went a step further—he made it personal too, by telling everyone more about his parents, his struggles, about never feeling he was good enough. Then he told them how he'd had people who believed in him, like his adopted mom and dad, Susan and Bob, and his friends. He explained that they'd helped him learn how to believe in himself.

"You don't have to do this all alone. But you can make changes." His voice rang out. "You can do anything. Absolutely *anything*." He stepped back, drank from his water glass, and for a long moment, he held the big tumbler in front of him, staring, until he turned back to his audience, his fans, his devotees. "We're almost done, but before I leave, I want to tell you about a lovely lady I met a few weeks ago."

Charlie's heart did a somersault as his eyes found and held hers for a split second.

"Francine is the sweetest thing. Tiny." He held out his palm to demonstrate her height against his chest. "She's friendly, upbeat, always with a smile or a laugh even though she has severe arthritis and uses a walker to get around. Most people would be in a wheelchair or bedridden. All her finger joints have been replaced." He held up the tumbler. "Imagine not being able to hold this glass in one hand. Imagine that even two-handed, this glass would slip out of your fingers." He let it slide until it almost fell, catching it at the last second. "Imagine you couldn't jog down the stairs, that your ankle bones had disintegrated and the only thing holding each foot together was a steel bolt and some staples. Imagine your vertebrae had to be fused just so you could hold your head up. Imagine the shocking pain. And yet—" He held up the glass again, pausing. There was complete silence, unbroken by even the whisper of fifty thousand breaths. "And yet, every single day you get up and you walk a mile. No matter what." As Sebastian set down the glass, he said, "Do you know how much farther a mile is for her than for you and me?"

Charlie knew. Sebastian obviously did as well. Though he was a good thirty feet away on the stage, she could feel his anguish at not being able to help as if it were her own. Which it always had been. Until he walked into their lives and tried to help in any way he could.

"Francine tells me that if she didn't walk, she'd be in a wheelchair or a bed. *Use it or lose it.*" He made air quotes to show that they were Francine's words. "There are days she doesn't want to. Days when she can barely move because the pain is too great." His voice dropped almost to a whisper that echoed in the auditorium. "But then she gets up, aims her walker, and starts that mile."

Emotion squeezed Charlie's chest as he said, "So I ask you, can you walk a mile? Every day, rain or shine, pain or gain, because you know you *have* to just to stay alive, just to breathe. Can you walk that mile?"

And Charlie began to cry.

CHAPTER SEVENTEEN

Charlie couldn't hear Sebastian's closing words as everyone in the auditorium rose to their feet with thunderous applause, their unspoken answer to his question perfectly clear: Yes, they would all walk that mile. Simply because Sebastian Montgomery believed they could.

On the way out, he grabbed Charlie's hand and they were propelled down the aisle to a small reception in the green room. Everyone wanted to touch him, as though something magical might rub off. He was polite, friendly, and accepted compliments with humility.

The most amazing thing of all was that he acted no differently at the reception than he had on stage. He was the same man who'd walked into her studio and said her art was magnificent.

The same man who'd told her all about his parents and upbringing after dinner at his house. The same man who'd driven her wild with need every second of every day since they'd met.

He had power no matter where he was, but it didn't come from arrogance. It had come from walking many long miles, the way her mother continued to do every single day.

Two hours later they were ushered out and into a waiting helicopter that flew them to the airport. In the VIP lounge, finally alone with Sebastian for a few moments, she said, "Thank you for letting me see you in action."

"It was my pleasure." He reached out to stroke her cheek. "I've been privileged to see what you do. I was hoping you would enjoy this."

She shook her head, knowing he shouldn't be comparing the two of them. "I make art. But you—" There was no other way to put it. "You inspire the world."

"You inspire too, Charlie. More than you know. Especially now that everyone will see your sculptures once you take your rightful place at the top of the field."

As always, when he talked about her impending ascent to the top of the art world, her stomach twisted. Frustration bubbled up in her for a split second before she could shove it away, along with the question she'd been asking herself for weeks: *Why do I keep having these doubts?*

But today of all days wasn't a time for doubts. Not when Sebastian's tribute to her mother had been beyond beautiful. It had never been clearer that compared to the struggles other people went through, Charlie had absolutely nothing to complain about. So what if she was worried about her life changing—and about whether or not she could fit into Sebastian's world the way he obviously wanted her to? She'd have to get over her doubts.

"My mother will love that you told her story." She touched his arm, admiring the play of strong muscles beneath her fingers nearly as much as she'd admired him on that stage. "It means a lot to me to know you understand."

"I didn't plan what I said, but with you watching me, all I could think about was how much you give to her, and how completely deserving she is. Both of you possess an indomitable spirit."

"If I'm *indomitable,* then why am I so nervous about the grand opening gala at the hotel?" The words were out of her mouth, with more already falling before she could stop them. "Why am I so terrified that everyone will see my rams, and then they'll look at me and I'll be cursing myself for not wearing the right dress?"

Pulling her to her feet, he said, "You're gorgeous just the way you are."

His words made her belly flutter. They both knew better. "I can't wear jeans to a gala."

"Then we'll go shopping."

He was sweet, but like a typical guy, he still clearly didn't get it. "The other women will all be salon-prepped and wearing designer outfits that cost as much as a condo on Maui."

"I have a condo on Maui," he said as the corners of his lips twitched, "and I can confirm that some of those dresses cost even more." She was glad that the laughter bubbling up helped to untwist the knots in her stomach. "So let me take you shopping," he said softly, as persuasive as he'd been on stage.

"You've already paid for the chariot." For an amount she still had trouble wrapping her mind around. When she threw in the money he'd negotiated for her rams... Honestly, her head was still spinning. "A dress isn't part of the deal."

He circled her slowly, trailing his fingers across her neck until he'd pulled her hair back at her nape. "Think of dressing up as part of your job. Showmanship. Salesmanship." His warm breath in her hair made her legs weak. The kiss on the tender flesh of her neck made her knees tremble. "You'll amaze them," he whispered as he pushed her hair to the other side and kissed her just below her ear, then licked her. "Soft velvet," he murmured, circling her waist with his arms. "Silky lace."

Suddenly, she couldn't think straight, especially when he drew her back against him and all she could feel was hard, sexy male.

"Let them see you in all your glory, Charlie."

His hands skimmed her flesh, his mouth crumbling her will and his honeyed words seducing her. She succumbed to the reckless urge, spinning around to kiss him breathless, not breaking apart until Sebastian's private pilot cleared his throat and let them know he was ready for them to board the plane.

* * *

"I've got so much work to do on the chariot. But you seem to be able to talk me into anything." Charlie mock-scowled as she stood in front of him in the designer showroom wearing a red floor-length gown with a slit up the leg. "Except this dress. It clashes with my hair."

Sweet Lord, Sebastian was hot for her. He'd watched her dress and undress for forty-five minutes, zipped her into six different outfits, four of which he'd liked, none of which Charlie would consider. Now he was a heartbeat from throwing her over his shoulder, locking them together inside the nearest storeroom, and ripping the dress off her so he could finally do everything he'd been fantasizing about for weeks. Touching her, Tasting her. Taking her.

It had taken him four days since their L.A. trip to arrange a shopping expedition. Not because of his crazy schedule, but because Charlie had thrown herself back into the chariot and horses, working with total focus around the clock. What amazed him wasn't her work ethic, but the way she dealt with screwups. When something wasn't going right, she simply laughed at herself, then moved to another piece to clear her head. Whereas Sebastian had never been able to go back to a drawing once it had gone wrong. To date, he had four sketchbooks stocked with the woman he still couldn't bring into complete focus or total understanding.

He hated that she wouldn't accept just how extraordinary she was. Up on that stage, he'd spoken directly to her, told her everything he believed she was capable of, that she could do anything.

But he wasn't sure she'd heard him.

Right now, however, he had to agree that despite the display of elegant leg, the red dress just wasn't Charlie. "Try something short and sexy." He gave in to the urge to run his hand down the outside of her thigh. "To show off your incredible legs."

Charlie raised an eyebrow as she sauntered to the rack of designer dresses. "Now I know why you brought me here," she teased before riffling through the dresses.

Because you mean everything to me.

The words knocked around in his head. His heart too. And they might have spilled from his lips if she hadn't said, "How about this one?" She held up a black silk-velvet dress with three-quarter sleeves and a short, flared skirt. "It has pearls across the front. No, wait, that's the back." She frowned. "How the heck do you get into this thing?"

"I'd be more than happy to help you figure it out," Sebastian said in a low tone ripe with desire as he rose from his chair. "Got to get you out of this one first, though."

He trailed his fingers across her back, and nuzzled her hair, impossibly hungry for her. The zipper slid down, and he followed its path with his mouth, the taste of her skin filling him up. The dress slid to Charlie's feet and she stepped out of it, leaning down, clad only in minuscule panties, to swipe it up and place it on a hanger. Then she looked at him over her shoulder, a sexy, flirty smile on her lips and her brilliant green eyes traveling his length.

His heart stuttered at her elegance and beauty. She wasn't a model or a celebrity. She had no artifice. She was simply real, utterly perfect without any help from makeup or fancy clothes, and she made him crazy hot, hard, and reckless. When they finally came together, he knew worlds would collide. Oceans would overflow. Hell, volcanoes would probably erupt.

His mind whirling with images of her, he couldn't find the clasp on the pearls slung across the plunging back of the black dress.

"I see how it works now." She took the dress from him, standing so close that her all-Charlie, all-woman scent short-circuited his brain. "It unzips down here, then goes over my head."

His heart started again, beating harder, faster as she pulled it on, all that beautiful, creamy skin disappearing from view. She presented her back for him to do up the short zipper until the velvet material hugged her figure, and his fingers trembled. When she stepped up on the dais again and slowly spun in a circle for him, he was unable to tear his eyes away from her.

She was dazzling, as if the dress had been made for her and no one else. The neckline scooped down to edge her cleavage and almost bared her shoulders. The bodice hugged her breasts, her waist, and the skirt flared gracefully as she twirled for him. But it was the rear view that did him in. Three strands of pearls draped the flawless skin of her back and the velvet plunged low, making him ache to put his hands and his mouth all over her.

"That's the one." He wanted her, needed her, in that dress, then out of it, the velvet lying on the plush carpet of his bedroom with Charlie spread out on his bed as the delicious main course.

She smoothed her fingers down the fabric, surveying herself in the mirror. Did she have any idea how badly he wanted the hands running over her body to be his? He might go completely insane if he had to wait another moment. He was certifiable for her.

And yet the waiting made his desire for her electric. It sizzled in the air around them.

"I like it too," she said softly.

"Then it's done." He pushed a buzzer on the side table and the designer appeared so quickly she must have been standing right outside the dressing room. Her momentum swung her reading glasses on the end of their lanyard across her ample breasts.

"We'll take it." He needed to move quickly before the woman said anything about the price. "Can you wrap it up?"

"Certainly. Would you like an accompanying wrap or—"

"Wait." Charlie cut her off. "How much is the dress?"

"Twenty-five."

Charlie's eyes bugged. "Twenty-five hundred?"

"Thousand," the woman answered.

Charlie fumbled with the back zip, unable to get the dress off fast enough. "No. I'm sorry. I can't buy this," she said emphatically. "And *you* can't buy this for me, Sebastian."

"Charlie." He had to have her in that dress. In every single possible meaning that statement contained. "Please, it was made for you and you alone."

But she was already stepping off the dais, tugging the dress up and over. Women had never said no to Sebastian. Hell, *no one* said no to Sebastian for any reason. They always happily took whatever he wanted to give them.

"I can't." She put the dress back on the hanger. "I'll come up with something else." She fastened her jeans, pulled on her T-shirt.

He would have continued to argue his point about the dress, but just as he opened his mouth, Susan's words rang in his head. *Don't push* was what she'd said. But he knew her real meaning: *Be careful not to push Charlie away*.

"I promise I won't embarrass you," she said softly.

He couldn't keep his hands off her, holding her shoulders, forcing her to look up at him. "You could never embarrass me. No matter what you do. Do you understand that?"

He counted five beats before she nodded. Before he could give her a kiss, before he could do one single thing to fix whatever it was he'd just broken, she said, "I need to get back to the workshop. Have a good meeting." And then she was gone.

* * *

"I just couldn't take the dress, Mom." Charlie threaded the needle and stuck it into the pincushion.

"I understand, dear. But you do realize he probably earns that much in half an hour?"

"I know." She'd wanted to wear the velvet and pearls for him so badly, wanted him to tear it off her too. But even as she'd felt the gorgeous fabric like a caress against her skin and his gaze heating her from the inside out, she couldn't let him spend that much money on it. On *her*. Even if she could look beyond the price of the dress, the woman who'd gazed back at her from the mirror hadn't been anyone she recognized.

All these years of dating, she'd been so determined to remain true to herself, even when the men had hoped she'd change to please them. Sebastian had repeatedly told her how much he loved the way she looked in jeans and boots, but at the same time, it was clear he wanted her to shine in his social circles.

Was there a way for Charlie to shine while remaining true to herself? She didn't know the answer, but she could only hope that it would end up being yes. The thought of things falling apart with Sebastian made her stomach twist even tighter than hearing the price of that dress.

She and her mom sat in Shady Lane's lounge, as usual, but only for another two weeks. Magnolia Gardens had called yesterday. They finally had a room available. It needed fresh paint, new carpet, and new furniture, and then it would be Mom's. Charlie's fingers had trembled as she'd written the check for the remainder of the entry fee. She still felt slightly sick about it, especially with the monthly charges looming. She hadn't even told Sebastian the news yet, as though not saying the words aloud meant she wouldn't be on the hook for such a huge amount every single month from now on.

"This dress is lovely," her mother said, blissfully unaware of all the thoughts making Charlie's stomach roil. Charlie had taken a short break from working on the chariot yesterday and had been lucky enough to find a dress she thought might work. Her mother held up the garment in her gnarled fingers. "We can certainly do something with it."

But it wouldn't be *we*. Mom's fingers had flown with a needle and thread, creating beauty from scraps, but she'd had to give up sewing long ago. Fortunately, she'd taught Charlie to sew, both by hand and by machine.

"What we're going to do," her mother said in her usual upbeat way—*indomitable* was the word Sebastian had used, "is take in a couple of darts to mold the bodice of the camisole to your chest." She pinched the material, demonstrating. "Think an Anne Boleyn style. Almost a bustier."

"I like that."

Her mom pointed to the matching skirt. "We'll take a little nip here, a little tuck there, and size the waistband down."

Charlie tried not to wince that it had come to this, her mother verbally directing her on how *not* to screw up the inexpensive outfit she'd bought at a consignment store. She'd found a pair of high-heeled sandals too, and a clutch with some of its beads ready to fall off. She'd told Sebastian she wouldn't embarrass him. Her mother was her only hope of keeping that promise.

"Put the camisole on over your T-shirt and pin it." Mom held up the pincushion. Her fingers were no longer nimble enough to hold a pin without dropping it.

Charlie finished pinning. "What do you think?"

"Perfect." The smile on her mother's face was as big as if she were viewing a model at a fashion show rather than the daughter who had always been far more comfortable in steel-toed boots than she would ever be in heels and dresses.

Her mother had adored sewing. She'd loved baking. There were so many things she'd had to give up. It was like losing a piece of herself every time another thing she loved was taken away.

But she still walked that mile every day. And she always did it with a smile.

Charlie undid the short zipper at the back and shrugged out of the camisole. "Sebastian made you famous the other day."

"He did?" Her mother sipped her tea.

"He gave a talk in Los Angeles to thousands of people, and he told them about your arthritis and how you force yourself to walk a mile a day. Then he challenged the entire audience to walk their own mile every day."

Charlie started the dart, using a backstitch to secure it. She poked a finger, then sucked on it so the material wouldn't stain.

"That's sweet of him. But a mile isn't very much." Mom pointed at the dart. "Go over it once more with a backstitch."

Charlie switched directions, rolling the material over her index finger. "It depends on how far your mile is, doesn't it? And how hard it is."

"I suppose." Her mother was quiet for a long moment. "How long is your mile, Charlie?"

She tied off the thread and snipped the ends, laughing a little as she admitted, "I'm not even sure *what* my mile is."

Was it the chariot? All her art? The commissions? A big-money art career? Was it Magnolia Gardens for her mother? Maybe it was the pleasure she got from teaching. Despite yet another letter from the school she'd shoved into the drawer just yesterday without making a firm decision, teaching her students how to create art from what everyone else thought was junk had always made Charlie feel good.

But was that it? Or could her mile be falling recklessly for Sebastian? Not part of the way, but risking it all, every ounce of her heart and soul.

"It's all right, dear," her mother said as though she could read Charlie's confusion in the frown on her face. "You've got all the time in the world to figure it out."

But she didn't. She only had a little over a month until the chariot had to be completed. After that, she wouldn't see Sebastian day in and day out, wouldn't have dinner with him, discuss her day with him. Wouldn't have the pleasure of knowing he might drop by for a kiss at any moment, when just the sight of him would brighten her entire world.

"Let's finish the sewing," her mother said, "and think about the rest later. I have an idea for fixing the beads on the purse too."

Yes, Charlie thought. Finish the sewing. Worry later.

Or, better yet, she could try to make herself believe what Sebastian had told her dozens of times since they'd first met—that everything was going to work out beyond her wildest dreams. In which case, there would be more parties like this one to deal with, more dresses to find and fix, more hours of work to squeeze in—

Stop. She was borrowing trouble again. Especially since she was only a fraction of the seamstress her mother was and needed one hundred percent focus to get it right.

Putting her head down, she began to sew as though her life depended on it. And right then, if it meant managing to make Sebastian proud of her at the big hotel gala, it felt as though her life and her future actually did depend on this one dress.

CHAPTER EIGHTEEN

For the night of the gala at the Regent Hotel, Walter Braedon had comped Charlie and Sebastian the penthouse suite, so they headed over early that afternoon to dress for the evening.

It had been nearly a week since they'd seen each other. With business to take care of in England, Sebastian had literally ached by the time he'd finally pulled her into his arms again. All he wanted, all he'd been able to think about for a week—hell, ever since the moment he'd met her—was her lips beneath his, her body quaking in bliss against him as he buried himself as deeply inside her as he possibly could. But though the sparks between them blew as hot as ever, he knew she was nervous about tonight. It had been tempting to take her mind off it in every sexy, delectable way he could think of, but his arrival at the airport had run late, and they'd had to head straight to the Regent.

Sebastian approached the hotel slowly, coasting past the rams in the center of the circular drive so that Charlie would get the full effect of her incredible creations. She gasped with sheer awe, one hand squeezing his arm, the other covering her mouth.

"Oh, my God."

"I agree. They're pretty damned spectacular."

The animals reared against each other so that you could almost hear the clash of their horns. They battled on a splendid pedestal of mountain boulders surrounded by a garden of rock and exotic cacti, as though they were out in the wild rather than in the center of downtown San Jose. He pulled up beneath the portico. The Regent was grand, its gold front doors framed by huge columns and a flagstone entryway containing ferns, water lilies, and rippling fountains that sounded like music. Braedon had created a flawless setting.

"My rams." Her voice trembled. "Here, in the middle of a palace. I can hardly believe it."

When she turned to him, tears sparkled in her eyes, and his heart bubbled over with joy. He'd done right by her in finding the Regent and Walter Braedon. This was what he'd hoped for her, to see her work displayed for thousands. He hated the huge stumble he'd made with her over the cost of the velvet dress, but all of that was forgotten in the wonder on her beautiful face.

Under the portico, after the valet took his car, Sebastian hugged her tightly. "Believe, Charlie." He took her hands in his and held them to his chest. "I always have."

"Somehow it's even better than seeing the dragon outside the church. I'm not even sure why."

But he was. Just as he'd said on stage in Los Angeles, sometimes people were too close to things to see them clearly. She'd seen her rams only in her yard, and the dragon in front of a modest church. For the first time, she was viewing her work as it was meant to be: the centerpiece for all to marvel at.

Once inside, Sebastian checked them in while Charlie gazed raptly at replicas of Rodin's famous thinking man and his embracing lovers at the foot of the stairs. One day people would study her work with that same rapt attention. He would make it happen for her. He would give her everything.

She pivoted suddenly and caught him watching her, their eyes locking across the expanse of marble, the lovers kissing behind her.

He wanted her just that way, naked and in his arms. But they hadn't even shared a bed yet. That thought consumed him as they rode the elevator to the top floor. The penthouse had two bedrooms, each with an ensuite bathroom.

But they never got a chance to think about keeping one of those bedrooms locked, because a call from Europe came just as they entered the suite.

He'd had to take it, chafing the whole time at business coming between them for nearly two hours. Charlie had long since excused herself, taking the second bedroom. Now, as Sebastian finished dressing for the gala, he silently cursed the unused beds in the two rooms. The unrumpled coverlet mocked him as he padded over the plush carpet to her bathroom door and knocked.

"Ready, Charlie?" It took another rap on the wood before she answered.

"No." There were muffled sounds he couldn't identify, then she called out, "Go ahead without me. I'll be down in a minute."

He'd planned to make an entrance with her hand on his arm, but on second thought, it was better that she come down on her own. She shouldn't be the woman on Sebastian Montgomery's arm, but the magnificent artist who'd created the astonishing sculpture in the front garden. He would be just a footnote to the night. This evening was her turn to shine at last. And yet he still wished he could experience every moment of the night right along with her.

"Okay," he said, working hard to erase the reluctance from his voice. "I'll see you there."

Downstairs, between the alcoves of Roman statues, the curved wall of the enormous lobby was lined with buffet tables. Tuxedo-clad waiters and waitresses passed around trays of champagne. More than two hundred guests were already milling, their voices rising up to the mezzanine level. Later, there would be dancing upstairs. At the foot of the grand staircase, Rodin's masterpiece was still thinking and his lovers were still kissing.

But thirty minutes later, Charlie had yet to put in an appearance.

"Sebastian."

The voice jolted him. His focus on the elevators down the hall to his right—and Charlie's impending entrance—had excluded everything else.

Will Franconi clapped him on the shoulder. "Where's your artist?"

"Still getting ready." And Sebastian, who had mastered patience early on in his career, was nearly out of it.

Decked out in a black tux, Will had his arm around his fiancée, Harper Newman, who wore a floor-length gown with a cropped jacket. She glowed as brightly as the gold of her dress, her cheeks pink with adoration as she gazed up at Will. The same love gleamed in Will's eyes, making them a shade bluer than seemed possible.

As Sebastian gave Harper a kiss on the cheek, he silently noted that he'd never seen his friend truly happy until he'd met Harper a few months ago. Will had battled his demons and won. Considering how bad Will's childhood had been, it was a hell of a feat.

"Saw the rams out there." Judging by his intense expression, Will was impressed. "They're powerful. Unique. Superb."

"Especially with the lights coming up from below," Harper agreed. "The rams could be real, actually fighting."

Sebastian's heart swelled for Charlie. "Make sure you tell Charlie that when she comes down. She needs to hear how her work affects people." Maybe she'd start to believe she deserved all the success he felt should be hers. He glanced at the bank of elevators, barely able to tamp down his impatience. "What's Jeremy up to tonight?"

"He's staying with Mrs. Taylor," Harper said. "He's going to watch Steve McQueen in a special version of *Bullitt* with scenes deleted from the original car chase."

When Harper smiled, Sebastian saw the light Will had fallen head over heels for. Yet for Sebastian, Charlie's light was even brighter. So bright and so beautiful that he had to wonder who was really helping whom? Long before he'd come into her life, she had been creating magnificent works of art and taking care of her mom. Yet for him, it seemed as though he'd merely been marking time until he found her.

Before Will could launch into an account of how he'd acquired the prized *Bullitt* DVD, Matt Tremont joined their group. Once the runt of their Maverick litter, no one would ever have guessed it by the breadth of Matt's shoulders and the width of his chest. Still the brainiac who'd built a robotics empire, he'd bulked up somewhere along the way until he was a force all on his own.

"Hey, Harper." Matt leaned down to kiss her cheek. "You're looking fabulous."

"She always does," Will agreed, playing his fingers through her hair in an unconscious gesture of possession, desire, and most of all, love.

"Thank you, Matt." Harper's smile was a mile wide as she asked, "How's Noah?"

"He's great. He can't stop talking about the last time he saw Jeremy. No one makes him laugh harder than your brother."

Everyone adored Matt's five-year-old son. Susan especially, who'd made it clear more than once that she couldn't wait to have more grandchildren to spoil rotten. And that her boys were taking far too long to get the job done.

"Nice gig," Matt said to Sebastian. "Food looks good too. Looking forward to meeting the artist. Her rams are mind-blowing."

"Glad you think so, but we know you're really here for the free food." It didn't matter how far they'd come, some things were ingrained—no matter how much food you had, it was hard to forget what it was like to be hungry and all out of options.

Sebastian glanced past Matt's shoulder to the elevator bank. Still no Charlie. "You see Evan or Daniel yet?"

"Whitney corralled Walter Braedon, so Evan's with them."

Will scowled. "Whitney always goes for the major players first. Especially if photographers are nearby." Men and women with cameras were everywhere, snapping pictures at the front entrance as celebrities and the who's who of the Silicon Valley elite arrived, dripping with jewels and designer gowns.

"And Daniel's right over—" Matt waved his hand like a snake charmer. "—there."

The fifth Maverick was making his way toward them, a plate of appetizers in his hand. Running a conglomerate of home improvement stores and producing his own do-it-yourself TV show, Daniel was dressed for the part as always, in khaki pants and a camel-colored jacket with leather patches on the elbows, his hair overly long. Sebastian wondered if he would manage to unearth a tux for Will and Harper's winter wedding in Chicago, or if he'd just show up grinning in a plaid work shirt and boots. Truth was, none of the Mavericks would care if he did. Each of them wanted only happiness and a good life for the others.

In addition to taking over the world together, of course.

"Harper." Holding her hand, Daniel kissed her cheek. She was one of them now, a Maverick, as was Jeremy. "You're as lovely as a Tahoe sunrise." Daniel was building a cabin up at Lake Tahoe, so he clearly had the big blue lake on the brain. He was also right that Harper, with all the love shining out of her, was just as beautiful.

Then Daniel was looking past them all, up the stairs. "Holy hell. Will you look at that vision coming down the stairs."

As everyone turned, Sebastian suddenly couldn't breathe...and his heart all but shut down in his chest. Tonight, the woman he'd fallen head over heels for wasn't Charlie the strong, pretty tomboy. She was Charlotte.

But no, he realized, as his heart—and brain—slowly stuttered back into action. She was *both* Charlie and Charlotte. Radiant and alluring. Intelligent and creative. Brilliant and beautiful.

And he'd never wanted any woman more.

"She's coming over to us," Matt said, his voice sounding very far away.

All Sebastian could see or hear or feel was *Charlie* as she descended the stairs with elegance and style. She'd piled her hair on top of her head, a few locks falling carelessly free, brushing her shoulders. Gold drop earrings dangled from her lobes, glittering in the light of all the chandeliers.

"Her dress," Harper said. "It's stunning."

As far as Sebastian was concerned, *stunning* barely scratched the surface. The corset-style top fitted her like the fingers of a tight glove, the thin straps holding it up nothing more than decoration. A teardrop necklace nestled seductively in her cleavage. The strip of bare midriff below the top dried up his mouth. The waist cinched and the skirt flared over her hips, then fell in graceful, swishing folds to her calves, the scalloped hem longer in the back than the front. Even her ankles in the strappy high-heeled sandals were perfection.

"Is that—" someone, maybe Harper, started to ask.

Sebastian could only nod, unable to do more than stare in awe at the woman who had stolen his heart.

The outfit she'd chosen was as striking as anything she'd tried on in the designer shop, even the pearl dress, as much as he'd loved her in it. But it wasn't the outfit that stunned her audience.

It was all Charlie.

The lobby had fallen into complete silence. No one had ever seen anything like her. In the span of sixty glorious seconds, Charlie Ballard had completely transcended the surgically enhanced society mob. To top it all, every single thing about her was real, inside and out.

He'd cherished her beauty all along, beneath the jeans and the T-shirts and the glorious never-seen-a-salon hair, but now he realized there were more sides to her than he could have imagined. Everyone had different facets, some they kept locked away. Sebastian had those hidden features too, like the part of him that needed to draw. He'd never been brave enough to let any but his closest friends see his sketches, but tonight Charlie was bravely letting all her hidden qualities and talents shine.

He was dying to show her off, to drink in the sweet seductive sound of her voice, to learn everything he could about her. He couldn't wait to get his hands on her, to touch her, inhale her scent, kiss her.

And—finally—make her completely his.

CHAPTER NINETEEN

Charlie had spent way too much time on her hair, but she wasn't used to the curling iron, let alone piling the mass of hair on top of her head. She'd had to watch several YouTube how-to videos to figure it out. But the time and effort had been more than worth it for the look on Sebastian's face as she walked down the stairs.

She felt gloriously happy—every cell in her body yearning for Sebastian. At least, until she realized that the lobby had gone silent and absolutely everyone was staring at her. The pounding of her heart spiked higher as she gripped the rail and froze in place for a few moments.

Oh God, what was I thinking, trying to pull this off?

Feeling more than a little desperate, she looked back at Sebastian again. And suddenly everything was *right*. The admiration and pleasure in his eyes told her in no uncertain terms that she actually *had* pulled it off. As she'd fussed with her hair, her makeup, and her dress, she'd decided not only to play the siren for one night, but also to *enjoy* it. Now, with Sebastian's gaze fortifying her and giving her the strength she'd momentarily lost in the face of this huge crowd, it was time to make good on that decision. No matter how difficult she found it to be at the center of all those assessing, judging gazes.

She was going to have fun, damn it! Even if it killed her.

As she descended the final step, Sebastian drew her against him. His murmured, "You take my breath away," sent shivers through her body. She wished she could wear this dress only for him, and that he would sweep her away to their penthouse suite before she had to deal with the throng, all of them staring avidly.

At least she was lucky enough to meet his closest friends first. Sebastian had given Charlie the lowdown on the Mavericks during the drive over. Still, there were an awful lot of names and faces to keep straight. It didn't help that his strong, protective hand was caressing the bare flesh of her back below the corset, making it difficult to focus on anything but the urge to drag him back upstairs and let him strip off her dress the way they both so desperately wanted.

Okay, Charlie, focus, she told herself with the first introduction.

Daniel Spencer, owner of the Top-Notch DIY chain of home improvement stores, was a dark-haired Tahoe mountain guy. He shook her hand, his grip warm and his tone sincere. "You have an incredible talent."

"Thank you." She'd seen how good the rams looked in front of the hotel, but it was still fabulous to hear that someone besides Sebastian agreed with her.

Next, Sebastian introduced her to Will Franconi and she immediately said, "Thank you so much for the china you sent over for my mother. She loved it. It was so kind of you."

A dark Italian type as befitting his name, Will smiled with twinkling blue eyes. "You're welcome. Although Harper picked them out."

Charlie turned to the pretty blond woman on his arm. "Drinking out of those china mugs is one of my mother's favorite parts of the day. Thank you for choosing such a lovely set."

Harper smiled sweetly. "Sipping tea out of hand-painted bone china has now become a favorite part of my day too."

Charlie made what she hoped was a normal sound in response. That, however, was becoming harder to do as Sebastian trailed a hand over her shoulder blade and twirled a lock of her hair around his finger.

"Those cups are probably too fragile for Noah to use for an imaginary party, aren't they?" asked a big, handsome man who she easily guessed was Matt Tremont, the father of five-year-old Noah.

Boy, the Mavericks were definitely a good-looking lot, though she couldn't help but think that Sebastian was the best of an incredible bunch. Whether he was running his hands over her body or not. Right now, given that he was turning her positively liquid inside, all she wanted to do was turn around in his arms and press her lips to—

Concentrate, Charlie.

"Tea party?" Daniel said. "Didn't I give him a kid-size tool belt for his last birthday?"

Matt laughed, his mouth wide, his eyes probably as bright as Noah's would be. "He lost the hammer and the screwdriver and the—"

Daniel cut him off with an eye roll, and Sebastian said, "Maybe he needs a Zanti Misfit."

Charlie thought of the pruning-shear claws and put her hand on his arm. "We probably need to make something else for your son," she told Matt. "How about a lizard? Or better yet, a T-Rex."

"*The* T-Rex?" Sebastian looked mildly horrified at the thought of her dinosaur sculpture becoming a five-year-old's toy.

"I could make a scaled-down version. Or maybe a stegosaurus would be even better for him?"

"That sounds awesome. Just as long as it's not a velociraptor." Matt made a rueful face. "I made the mistake of taking him to see *Jurassic World.* What was I thinking?"

"Your son definitely needs a kinder, gentler dinosaur." She immediately began to envision a child-friendly dinosaur garden filled with plant-eating dinos. What if she used rocks to build the smaller set of dinosaurs? She could encircle different sized stones in metal and weld the individual pieces together like Legos.

"Earth to Charlie," Sebastian whispered in her ear, sending another delicious shiver through her.

"Sorry, I was thinking about little dinosaurs. Lots and lots of them." Was it bad that she wished she were back in her workshop already, getting started on those dinosaurs? Not that she didn't enjoy meeting Sebastian's closest friends. They alone made the party worth it.

In the midst of all the dinosaur planning, an older gentleman entered their circle and Sebastian put his hand on the small of Charlie's back as if to move her closer. "Walter, this is Charlie Ballard."

Walter Braedon could have been fifty, or five years either way. Though he was surrounded by Mavericks he could never overshadow, he had the presence of an older man who was completely comfortable in his own skin. His dark blond hair was thick and going white at the temples, his features strong, and his waistline as trim as that of someone twenty years younger.

She might have felt slightly nervous if Sebastian hadn't still been at her side. With his hand warming her through the fabric of her dress, he made her feel as if he'd battle anything for her. Even her own fear.

"Your rams are a hit, Miss Ballard," Walter said, vigorously pumping her hand. "Everyone's been asking for you."

"Thank you, I'm so glad to hear that. And please, call me Charlie. Even though I teach over at the college, *Miss Ballard* makes me feel like a little old lady schoolteacher."

"You're certainly not that." Dimples appeared when he smiled. "Charlie it is. And you all must call me Walt. I trust the suite is to your liking?"

"It's fabulous, thank you."

"We appreciate not having to make the trek back across the Bay, Walt," Sebastian added.

She didn't want to stiffen at Sebastian's gracious words—and would have stopped herself if she could. But a fairly large crowd had gathered around the Mavericks and Walter Braedon, and she was well aware of the assumptions that the gossipmongers were bound to make about the artist who was not only living on Sebastian's property, but also staying in a suite with him right here at the hotel.

Everyone would assume they were sleeping together.

Charlie had never given a hoot about anyone pondering her sex life. What she and Sebastian did was their own business, and while she'd never regret being with him, she couldn't stand the thought of anyone assuming she'd traded her art for sex.

Her gaze flew to Walt. *Was that what he thought?*

Clearly able to read her inside and out, Sebastian curled his arm around her waist, but that only made her spiral down. Everyone would see the blush he brought to her cheeks, the way he made her bones melt, how he put stars in her eyes...and they'd know she was completely, recklessly smitten with the beautiful billionaire. It had nothing to do with being in his league. Charlie didn't believe in that kind of stuff, but she did recognize that they were from different worlds. Until tonight, she and Sebastian had been together only in her world, full of junk and metal and welding tools. Now, she was smack in the middle of his glittering world.

She pulled off that feat with her own brand of glitter, but she couldn't help feeling like an impostor, because in the morning, all her glitter would wash down the drain.

"Come, we must introduce you around." Walt turned to the side and waved a hand. "Have you met Evan and Whitney Collins?"

Evan Collins was the fifth Maverick. As handsome and fit as the rest, he was their finance guy and the only married Maverick. "It's great to meet you, Charlie. This is my wife, Whitney."

Draped in a floor-length red dress with a slit up the side—one of the dresses that Charlie had rejected, in fact—Whitney Collins had a figure that made men drool. With auburn hair, she was polished, perfect, and obviously bored out of her mind by everyone and everything around her. Her handshake was limp, and the once-over she gave Charlie clearly rated the brocade skirt, camisole, shoes, and beaded clutch as horribly unfashionable.

"Hmm," was all she said, the taut skin on her face hardly moving around the small sound.

Thankfully, Walt quickly moved them on through the sea of faces. It was more than a little exhausting for Charlie to chitchat with so many new people, trying to remember as many names as possible, but Sebastian was clearly in his element. What's more, he seemed to know everyone, asking about their latest project or triumph, about their kids. She was continually amazed at his skill in turning people's compliments back around to their achievements rather than his own.

Even more amazing? Between Sebastian and Walt talking up her artwork, people were literally throwing commissions at her. A garden in Woodside, a fountain in Atherton, a gazebo on

Nob Hill, a condo in Palm Springs, all of which desperately needed a piece by Charlie Ballard.

It was thrilling. At least, it should have been, because taking all these jobs meant she'd never have to worry about her mother again. But twenty-four hours a day wouldn't be enough time to create all of these designs. Already she was doing rapid-fire calculations in her head to figure out what she could give up to make it work.

Worse, she couldn't shake the thought that Sebastian's peers were offering her commissions simply to make points with him.

"Are you okay?" Sebastian asked when they finally had a few seconds to themselves.

She couldn't admit she was panicking again. Not when he'd handed her everything on a silver platter. She couldn't fathom how he did it—be *on* like this for hours, schmoozing, prowling, moving, talking, constantly at attention. It seemed to energize him. But it would drive her insane.

"Everyone is being so complimentary and friendly." She lifted one foot to take the pressure off for one precious moment. "I'm just not used to wearing heels."

He tangled his fingers in the hair at her nape. "I should have been paying better attention to you."

"You have been." She smiled at him. "No one has *ever* been so attentive."

"I can do even better," he promised as he slid a finger seductively along the waist of her skirt, sliding down to caress the sensitive skin of her lower back as they slipped away from the group. "Let's start by getting you another glass of champagne and some food." Sebastian picked up a plate, his lips close to her ear as he whispered, "Tell me what you want."

His arms molded her tightly to his body, and she felt every muscle, every ridge against her more delicate frame. She was hot, liquid, and crazy for him. And one desire after another whizzed through her head.

A great big bite of you.
A long sip of your lips.
Your heat against me.
Inside of me.

She'd worried earlier about people thinking their attraction was the reason Sebastian supported her art. Now, though she heard voices, the clink of plates, the splash of drinks into glasses, she simply didn't care what anyone else thought. In this moment, there was only Sebastian's arms around her, his sweet breath in her ear, his soft hair beneath her fingers.

She knew him in ways the people at this party never would, saw things in him other people could never understand. They felt his charisma, but she recognized his inner beauty, the man who cared, the little boy who still needed to help in any way he could.

Charlie had never wanted anything as badly as she wanted Sebastian. More than teaching. More than the money for her mother. More than her art. She wanted all of him. Now. Tonight. No matter what happened after she finished work on the chariot and they went back to their normal lives. Even if it turned out that he preferred the shiny, glittering Charlie she'd unearthed tonight to the dusty, junkyard woman she'd been until this moment.

Tonight, it was time to give in to the recklessness. Time to finally look into his eyes and say, "You. All I want is *you*."

CHAPTER TWENTY

Sebastian grabbed Charlie's hand and all but dragged her to the elevators. The moment the doors closed behind them, he pushed her up against the wall. Imprisoning her wrists above her head in one hand, he took her lips hungrily, devouring her until she moaned and wrapped her leg around his calf.

"I've been dreaming about doing this all night." He roamed her body with his free hand, stroking her smooth, warm skin. Then he dipped his head to lick along her collarbone. "Tasting you. Touching you."

"Kiss me again. I love how you kiss me."

God, he was dying to kiss her. Every inch of her skin. But first he needed to know— "Do you believe?" His mouth was drawn to hers like a magnet and he had to taste her even though he hadn't finished his question. "Do you believe I want you as much—no, a hell of a lot *more* than I want your art?"

"Yes." The word came out more breath than sound. "Yes."

Then her mouth crushed his and, sweet Lord, how he loved the taste of her and the soft purr in her throat as she consumed him with a ferocity equaling his own.

Love. The word he'd always been so wary of. Now it rolled around in his mind as though it belonged. Charlie made him believe that love didn't have to be the way it had been for his parents.

Love could be like *this.* Love could fill him up from the inside out. Love could make him crazy with need *and* crazy with awe.

Tonight had been everything he'd wanted for Charlie—the crowd fawning over her, acknowledging her work as brilliant. She'd stepped into his world, conquered it completely, and was the toast of Silicon Valley.

Best of all? Now she would finally be *his*.

The elevator doors opened to the penthouse and they spilled out together, lips locked, arms tangled.

Charlie fumbled with the buttons of his tux jacket. "I want you, Sebastian. All of you. I don't want to wait anymore."

"No more waiting," he agreed in a voice made raw with both need and emotion. "Considering that I wanted you from the first moment I saw you in your face shield...it's been a hell of a wait."

She laughed, and he drank in the sexy, throaty sound. He loved her humor. Loved her independence. Loved her art. Hell, he loved her *everything*.

"My face shield and those thick welding gloves weren't sexy," she scoffed.

He framed her face in his hands. "Whatever you've got on, it all drives me crazy. Especially—" He reached behind to undo the slippery zipper on her top. "—this dress."

He pulled the spaghetti straps of her bodice down her arms at the same time as she tugged off his cummerbund and tore at the fastenings of his shirt. Buttons popped and rolled across the marble entry floor. Then she twined her arms around his neck, and he hauled her up, his hands cupping her hips as she locked her ankles behind him. Bare chest to bare chest, her lips on his, her mouth, her tongue, he held her tightly as he strode across the suite's thick carpet to the bedroom, and fell onto the bed with her.

Her hair lay in ringlets on the gold comforter, red and gold like the sun. Her lips were swollen from his kisses, and her nipples were a dusky rose that beckoned to him. He drank in her beauty, his heart beating hard. Beating true. Beating as if it were finally full for the very first time in his life.

"I've never seen anything as magnificent as you, Charlie."

She flushed beneath him, her skin drawing his mouth and hands to her body's beautiful contours. "I thought you said my dragon was magnificent," she teased.

"There are levels of magnificence," he murmured as he lowered his lips to the curve of one breast. "And you are *way* above the dragon."

Her laughter got lost in a pleasured gasp as he laved one taut peak slowly with his tongue. *"Sebastian."*

The sound of his name falling from her lips notched up his need to an epic ache. "I've waited so long for you, Charlie."

It wasn't just the weeks since he'd first walked into her yard. It wasn't even since the moment he'd seen her dragon and felt a kinship with her as an artist.

No, the truth was that he'd been waiting forever to find her. He'd never thought there would be someone like Charlie—a woman he wanted so badly that his insides felt like they were coming apart even as he was filled with pure emotion for her.

"I've waited for you too." She put her hand to the back of his head and pulled his lips to hers. "Kiss me again. Kiss me everywhere," she whispered before she took him to heaven with her mouth.

She toyed with him, sipped his lips, took his tongue, kissed him hard, then soft, twisted her head to come at him from a different angle. Playing. Tormenting. Seducing. They rolled together until she drew up her knees and straddled him. Leaning over, she licked his skin, ran her fingers through the hair on his chest, tugged gently. Then she sucked his nipple between her lips. She licked, suckled, teased, and finally bit him, just enough to send a shaft of pleasure-pain straight to his core.

He grabbed her hips as his body surged against hers. He was hard enough to burst, desperate to possess. He shoved his hands beneath the folds of her skirt and along her thighs until he found the elastic of her thong, and ripped it off her. She tore at his pants the way she'd gone at his shirt, and when they were both naked, he pinned her to the bed and took her mouth again. The kiss was primitive. Insatiable. Not just for him, but for both of them. And though he already knew he'd never have enough of her, never be able to get his fill, all the weeks of waiting had made him greedy for more than just a taste.

Tonight he needed absolutely everything, wouldn't stop until he'd kissed her *everywhere.*

His face at her apex, he breathed in the heady scent of her arousal. He tested her with the tip of his tongue, finding her sweetness, then slid off the bed to his knees in front of her, and nuzzled her. "You're so pretty down here too. Everywhere." He took his first erotic taste, delving with his tongue.

"Oh." It was a gasp. "Oh, God."

She clung to his shoulders, her fingernails pricking his flesh, and it was so damned good. She was like a sweet wine whose grapes had stayed on the vine until they exploded with flavor. Her hot little sounds—a cry, a moan, a hoarse groan—drove him deeper. Flicking his tongue over her, he had to have more of her, had to slide one finger inside.

"Please, please, please," she begged.

She quivered and quaked, and he forced her higher. There was only one thing he wanted, needed, and craved in this moment—her sweet release against his tongue.

Her breath hitched, her fingers tangled in his hair, pulled at the roots, until her body clenched around his fingers, released, tightened again. Then she cried out, shaking as she rode out her pleasure.

He didn't let her senses quiet. Instead he moved back over her so that his chest was flush with hers. "Can you feel how much I want you?" he said against her throat, layering her skin with kisses, licks, little bites as she wrapped her fingers around his erection.

She finally opened her eyes and, instead of answering his question, said, "You should have done that to me weeks ago."

He laughed—she would always be able to make him laugh, even when they were making love—and he swelled even bigger in her hand. "I should have done this to you the very first day."

He nudged her legs apart and rolled between them. "Taken you in the sunlight." Her fingers tightened around him, stroking him, and he shuddered, pushing hard into her palm. "No, on your workbench. The first time I had my hands on you." The first time he'd made her tremble. The first time he'd felt her come and fantasized about how much more she had to give—and how he wanted every last ounce of her pleasure to be his.

"All those times I could have had you." She pushed her head back, closed her eyes, smiled in bliss. Then she cupped the base of his manhood, squeezed with an ideal touch until he thought he'd lose it all right then. "All those times we could have had each other."

"Inside you," he managed. "I need inside."

He'd never been crazy or out of control before. Not until Charlie became a recklessness in his blood. He rolled, opened the side table drawer, and withdrew a foil packet. She took it from him, leaving his hands free to run over her gorgeous curves until she straddled his legs, ripped the packet, and took him in her hand.

"So beautiful," she whispered, leaning close as if she were speaking only to that part of him. "So thick. And hard." She swiped her tongue over the crest, and a tremor surged through him. "You taste so good."

And then—*finally*—she slid down to take him inside.

The feel of her around him, over him, sent him to a place beyond words. He could only groan, arch his head into the mattress, and grab the pillow between his hands, squeezing tight, fingers aching with the effort to stave off his climax.

"Take me, Charlie. Take all of me." It was part plea, part wild, reckless need that wouldn't wait for anything. Not one more second.

She enveloped him even deeper with her body, sliding only so far before rising again, squeezing him tight inside her as he held her hips, played her flesh, testing the suppleness of her skin. Desperate for as much of her as he could get, he took her sweet, succulent nipple in his mouth. She let out a breath laced with a little hum of pleasure and took him deeper. But it wasn't far enough. Wasn't anywhere near enough.

He wanted to fill her all the way to her heart, giving over everything that was in him. "More." He rolled, pinning her body beneath him. "I need all of you."

And when she echoed *more* against his lips, he thrust home, high and deep inside her. His muscles bunched and flexed against hers, their bodies pressed tightly together as though they were welded into one part. One body. One soul. His hands gripping her hips tightly, he rocked with her, taking her higher and higher as he moved deeper. Faster. Harder.

He lifted his head from the crook of her neck. "Kiss me, Charlie. I need you."

Their lips melded, their tongues twined, and their bodies shuddered as their worlds crashed. They rode the tsunami together as she cried his name against his mouth and endless waves of pleasure rolled through them both, head to toe.

She was what he'd been searching for without even knowing it. And now he knew that no matter what happened between them in the future, even if things somehow turned toxic, he would never be able to walk away from her. Because she was *his.* And he was *hers.* Forever.

When it came to Charlie Ballard, Sebastian knew to expect the unexpected. Even the most unexpected thing of all: Falling head over heels in love.

CHAPTER TWENTY-ONE

Take all of me.

As Charlie wrapped herself around Sebastian, it felt like so much more than the simple act of two bodies coming together. It felt like his soul speaking to hers.

It felt like a promise.

All she'd ever had before was the physical side. Never a connection like this. Never such bliss. Never pure, sweet *heaven*.

After the last tremors subsided, he'd left her just long enough to dispose of the protection, then returned to pull the covers over them. They'd lain bonelessly in each other's arms for several long minutes. She loved the feeling of being cocooned with him. So safe. So warm. So full of lingering pleasure.

"Mmm." She wasn't ready to speak yet, but she needed to make at least a small sound to let him know how divine making love with him had been.

He stroked his hand over her bare skin, and she shivered with pleasure at how good it felt. "Now that was worth waiting for." He might have sounded cocky—and she knew he could be darned cocky when he wanted to be—but his voice was soft, reverent.

"More than worth it," she agreed, loving the feel of his strong and steady heartbeat beneath her palm. She wanted to snuggle up to him, sleep in his arms, then make love with him again in the deepest, darkest hours of the night.

She would have done all that if the sound of the doorbell hadn't pealed through the penthouse. "Who could that be at this hour?" she grumbled, her delicious dream going down the tubes.

"I'll get it." He kissed her forehead before he got out of bed, and she pulled the covers over her head, but he peeled a corner back a minute later to let her know, "Walter sent us a little gift."

She wrapped herself in the thick terrycloth robe the hotel had provided and followed him out to the sitting room. In front of the sofa, on a trolley draped elegantly with a gold cloth, sat a champagne bucket, two flutes, and a plate of chocolate-covered strawberries the size of plums. "Walter is so sweet. He didn't have to do this." Her mouth watered not only for the chocolate, but for Sebastian, his legs bare beneath his own matching robe, the sleeves rolled up to showcase his muscled forearms.

He popped the cork, expertly catching the champagne in a crystal flute. Handing her the glass, he poured another for himself.

"My God, you're beautiful." He toasted her, his eyes dark with a desire that made her tremble. "The moment I saw you walking down those stairs in that gorgeous dress, I swear my heart stopped beating. I couldn't remember how to breathe. No other woman has ever made me feel like that, Charlie." He set his glass on the trolley and laid his hands on either side of her face. "Only you."

He pressed his mouth to hers, still sizzling with champagne, and she lost herself in his kiss. Their bodies melted together, their lips almost one, their hearts connected.

When he finally drew back, she realized she couldn't let him think she'd bought a designer dress after she'd turned down his offer to buy one for her. "I bought the dress at a consignment store, and my mom designed the alterations."

"You're kidding." She couldn't quite read his tone, whether he was impressed or upset that she'd bought consignment rather than letting him give her the designer dress.

"Mom loves to sew and is great at giving direction. And I only stabbed myself a half-dozen times with the needle," she joked.

He pulled her down onto the buttery-soft leather sofa in front of Walter's extravagant gift. Then he lifted her hands, kissing each fingertip, one after the other. "The dress was exquisite and you were brilliant tonight. Everyone loved you and you were absolutely gorgeous."

Yes, she'd felt beautiful tonight. And she'd loved hearing that he'd lost his breath over her. But at the same time there was a part of her—a really big part—that wanted Sebastian to prefer the real Charlie in overalls and steel-toed boots.

He'd been able to resist her until tonight. *Was she irresistible only when she was dressed to fit into his world?*

"You outshone every other woman there." He raised an eyebrow. "Which clearly upset Whitney. Sorry she was her usual self when you met her. And you certainly deserve a treat for putting up with her." He plucked a succulent strawberry off the plate and held it up.

Working hard to push away the dark—and surely crazy—thought she'd just had, she bit into the dark chocolate and sweet fruit right from his fingers. It was as delicious and tempting as Sebastian.

But she wanted to know about the Maverick dynamic. "You don't seem to be much of a fan of Evan's wife." Charlie had quickly picked up on the fact that none of the Mavericks felt particularly relaxed around Whitney.

"She treats Evan like crap. He's worth way more than that. Deserves way more." He finished the other half of the strawberry, licking a dab of chocolate from his thumb.

Her mouth watered, wanting to lick him clean herself. She sipped her champagne. Such luxury. She could really love being spoiled. But she'd never take it for granted the way Whitney Collins seemed to. "I can't say I felt drawn to her." Harper Newman—yes. Whitney Collins—absolutely not.

"The woman's toxic. Everything she touches turns bad. No one deserves to live in a toxic, soul-destroying relationship like that. I just wish Evan could figure a way out. To get away from her."

"Whoa." The fervor in his voice as he talked about toxic relationships reverberated through her. "She really upsets you, doesn't she?" Charlie curled her feet onto the sofa, tucking them under the robe.

"Sorry." His tension seemed to ease slightly as he puffed out a sigh. "Got carried away. It's just stuff like that..."

"Reminds you of your parents?" she said softly, finishing for him when he trailed off. She wanted to touch him, to wrap her fluffy white robe around them both.

"Unfortunately, it does. I couldn't help my parents, but I wish I could help Evan."

"You help so many people every day. Thousands of lives have changed for the better because of you." She smiled at him. "Look at me and my mom, for instance. Everything is different for us now."

"Better too, I hope? Especially now that you have so many commissions falling into your lap."

She wasn't used to being the center of attention, but really, who wouldn't be thrilled to be handpicked for greatness by Sebastian Montgomery?

Only her.

She must be crazy, and when she saw his frown, she rushed to say, "I can't wait to start the dinosaurs for Noah. Next time I need a break from the horses, that's what I'll build." She hoped it escaped his notice that she didn't actually say her creative life was better. She was sure she'd feel that way once she got over her weird reticence.

"We should figure out a price tag for the works you've already got in stock. And then—"

She broke in, almost sharply, without thinking through her words. "I'm not charging for the dino. Or for anything else one of your friends might want." She tried to temper her tone with a smile, adding, "They were all so welcoming. So nice."

"That's the Mavericks for you." Though he seemed a little taken aback by her strong reaction to the idea of putting a price on her work, his voice was gentle. "I could tell they loved you."

"I know your childhood was really hard, but the family you created as an adult is amazing. You're very lucky, Sebastian."

"Luckier than I ever thought I'd be." With the softening of his voice and the way he looked so deeply into her eyes, it felt as if he was saying how lucky he'd been to find her too. "Speaking of family, after you told me your mom finally got a spot at the new facility, I looked at the website and made a few calls. You've said the place will be great for her, and from everything I've seen and everyone I've spoken to, I think you're right. But the start-up cost and the monthly fees are astronomical."

She'd given him the good news about her mother's move-in date during one of their calls while he was in England. She'd chosen that moment so he wouldn't see how green at the gills she'd turned at the thought of paying those monthly bills. Making love with him tonight had been so good, and she'd felt so loose, so free and happy, but between talk of all her possible future commissions and the money for her mother's care, her stomach was quickly knotting around the chocolate, strawberries, and champagne.

She struggled to keep her voice even. "Between your commission and the rams, I've already earned enough to take care of it."

But now that he knew exactly how much those monthly fees were, he was easily able to counter her statement. "That will last a year at most."

She pulled the robe more tightly around herself, as though somehow she was too naked, too exposed. She hated feeling that way with him, after what they'd shared only minutes before. "You just mentioned how the commissions are falling into my lap. I'll work harder. Longer hours. I'll sell everything in my yard. Somehow I'll make it work."

"Charlie." He stroked her cheek. "Let me help you. Please."

She wanted to fall into his touch, to nuzzle against his hand. Instead, she leaned forward to set her champagne on the trolley. "I know you want to help. And that's great. But I can't take anything else from you."

"Why?"

"I told you before that you've already done so much, and nothing has changed."

"How can you say nothing has changed? Everything has changed."

Both her brain and her heart stopped working for a long moment that stretched on and on, the knots in her stomach so tight they felt as though they were cutting her in two. "Because we had sex?"

"We didn't just have sex, damn it. We made love."

It was what she'd thought. What she'd felt. But now it was like a knife slicing her up from the inside, where she was least prepared for it. "So why are you using that to justify giving me more money?"

"That isn't what I'm trying to do." His frustration—and hers—felt like living things in the room, battling against each other. "I'm just concerned that you're killing yourself trying to pay for all your mother's needs." He tilted up her chin with his fingertips to force her to look at him. He was so beautiful. So perfect. So *rich*. "It's the same damn thing that happened with the pearl dress. I don't see why you can't accept that I have money and that nothing would make me happier than to spend it on you and your mother."

"Because everyone here tonight probably thinks I'm just another one of the billionaire's acquisitions, handpicked to live on his property and share the bed in his hotel suite!" The words flew out of her mouth before she could stop them.

"No." Sebastian's response was stone hard. And utterly unyielding. "Everyone here tonight thinks you're a brilliant artist. Everyone here tonight thinks I'm a lucky son of a bitch for even getting to be near you. The only person who could possibly think you're nothing but a billionaire's toy is you. If you think I'd pay you for what we did tonight, that the two things even have anything to do with each other, then you've lost your freaking mind. We're a hell of a lot more than that, Charlie." The look on his face wasn't mere pain. It was devastation. "I thought you felt the same way."

His words hit her like a heavy rock right to her belly. With a hard jolt of pain. One that either knocked you down...or woke you up.

She swallowed hard, as though that same rock were being shoved down her throat. Her eyes had already filled with tears as she whispered, "I'm sorry."

So much had changed so fast. In the wake of their incredible lovemaking, her walls had come down...and she'd been unable to stop herself from freaking out over just about every single thing. The pressure from all those possible future commissions so that she'd have money to pay for her mother's care beyond the first year. Wondering if she could actually fit into his glittering world—and if living in it would ever get easier. Worrying that Sebastian preferred the dolled-up version of her over the woman in boots and jeans. But she hadn't meant to take out her fears on him, or to spin his very kind offer into something dark and twisted.

"I'm not usually this emotional. At least," she said with a shaky little laugh, "I can usually control it better."

He slid his hands down her arms, gathered her fingers in his, and pulled her close to rest his forehead against hers. "I've never felt like this either. You've become the most important person in the world to me, Charlie. I never want to hurt you."

"I know you don't." Her voice, her body— everything—felt soft and rubbery with her tears. "And I promise you that I didn't think the dress was payment for anything. I just couldn't see spending that kind of money on clothes. Not when I could pay for six months at Magnolia Gardens for that amount."

"I'm sorry too, Charlie. I should have understood about the dress. But when it comes to your mom?" He shook his head. "I just want to see her as comfortable as she can be, and in a good place, without either of you having to worry over how long you can keep it up, or that she'll have to go back to Shady Lane."

He was so sweet that she felt another trickle of tears down her face. He kissed them away even as she beat herself up for calling his generosity into question. All because she was scared. About pretty much everything.

She cupped his cheek in her palm. "In a few months, if I have trouble making payments, I will come to you, I promise."

"Thank you." He wrapped his arms around her as if she'd just given him a gift simply by agreeing to accept his help if she ever needed it.

She pressed her mouth against his, stroking the rippling muscles of his chest. She could fix this. She needed to fix it, needed to show him how sorry she was.

"Come with me," she whispered, holding out her hands and leading him back to the bedroom. Wrapping her body around his, she pulled him down to the bed. The delicious scent of their loving still lingered on the sheets. And she wanted more, needed it, had to erase the words that had come between them.

"Charlie." Her name was a whisper of pleasure over her skin as he covered her in kisses.

He pushed aside the robe, baring her body to his lips, his touch. "Your skin is so sweet, so soft." He licked, tasted, and kissed his way over her breasts, finally taking a nipple between his lips, teasing her.

"Sebastian." She cried out his name, arched up, pressing her body hard against him. Begging. She'd never felt so cherished or so possessed. Sebastian didn't just kiss, he savored. He absorbed himself in her pleasure, in every inch of her skin, in her textures and curves, as if she were the only thing that mattered in the world.

How could she have doubted him?

Trailing his hand down her stomach, slipping his fingers over her sensitive flesh, he made her forget all her fears, her worries. Made her forget that she always felt she needed to do everything herself.

"Sebastian, please." She writhed beneath him, his leg thrown over hers to open her body fully to him.

"We have all night," he murmured, sliding a teasing finger inside her. "And I'm going to enjoy every second."

Her desire rose so fast, she couldn't wait. It wasn't enough that he pleasured her. She needed to feel his body connected to hers, completely—inside her, filling her, riding the wave with her.

"Now," she whispered. "I want it all now."

He kissed her hard, consuming her for all-too-brief seconds. "I love it when you're greedy." He arched, retrieved the protection. They hadn't even fully removed the robes, the soft terry caressing her skin along with all his hard muscles.

Then he gave her what she wanted, what she craved, filling her deeply.

And nothing else mattered, not the money, not the things they'd said. There was just this—his beautiful touch, his loving murmurs, and then his mouth on hers as they touched the sky together.

* * *

Sebastian relished every single second with Charlie spooned into his body, her breathing gentle and even. The moment was made even more sublime because he'd almost ruined everything, coming close to losing her by doing the most asinine thing imaginable—

talking about *money* after they'd made love for the first time.

He should have heeded Susan's warning not to push, especially with an independent woman like Charlie...

It was just that making love seemed to tear down all the barriers between them. He couldn't hold back his desire to do everything possible to make her happy and to care for her mother. No formal promises had been made, but they already felt like *his* family. He had no expectations and wanted no payback for anything he did, and he'd believed Charlie would finally understand that he wanted to help because she meant everything to him.

But he'd proven he was as big an idiot when it came to love as any fool had ever been. All night long he'd wanted to say the words, wanted her to know he was crazy in love with her. But he'd been afraid she'd see it as just another ploy to get his way.

I love you, Charlie.

Soon. He'd tell her soon.

And hopefully, he prayed as he pulled her closer in the dark, breathing in her scent, she'd fall in love with him too.

CHAPTER TWENTY-TWO

The weekend with Sebastian had been beautiful. If she closed her eyes, Charlie could still almost feel his touch on her skin, and his scent seemed to linger all over her body. When she breathed, she breathed in Sebastian.

But then there was real life, and the Monday after the gala was not only moving day for Charlie's mother, but Sebastian had also arranged for a new doctor to meet with her. Charlie was thrilled her mother would finally live in a nice home with a garden again, but she was more than a little worried about Sebastian. If his hopes for her mother's health were smashed, would he take it as badly as he had his failure to help his own parents?

Dr. Bengali had kind brown eyes and dark skin that showed nary a wrinkle. In his mid-thirties, he was an eminent surgeon who specialized in ankles. Sebastian had researched the man's career, and though he was relatively young, he was considered brilliant in his field. It still blew Charlie away that Sebastian could convince these prominent surgeons to make house calls. Despite her doubts that anything could be done, she still couldn't help the whisper of an internal mantra: *Please help her. Please.*

First, the doctor observed her mother's ability to walk. Then, since Charlie was still packing two suitcases and a garment bag for the move, they'd convened in her mother's room. Sebastian leaned against the wall a few feet away while her mother sat in her reading chair as the doctor studied her ankles. Gently, Dr. Bengali removed both her shoes and the braces, then delicately turned each ankle in his long fingers to check her range of motion and pain level with every movement. He palpated and squeezed the flesh, carefully examining right down to the toes.

Finally he rose to sit on the edge of the bed. Sebastian had remained quiet, but, just as with Dr. Hillman, his tension was like a live wire pulsing in the room.

"I've looked at your X-rays, Mrs. Ballard, and I want you to know that you've had a very good surgeon. I couldn't have done better by you. I agree with your doctor's instructions to keep walking. All in all, you're doing extremely well."

"Thank you, Doctor." Her mother smiled like a ray of sunshine.

"There's nothing more you can do for her ankles?" Sebastian asked. To anyone else, he might have sounded completely normal, but to Charlie, his words seemed to be strained through too-tight vocal cords. She'd kissed his throat, touched almost every centimeter of skin, felt his hard muscles against her, and she *knew*, even if no one else could even sense it, that his sense of powerlessness hurt him core-deep. Yet she could do nothing for him.

Dr. Bengali turned to him. "Mrs. Ballard's arthritis is severely degenerative. Essentially she has virtually no ankle bones left. Her surgeon has done extensive reconstruction, but I'm still surprised and pleased with how well she walks." He turned back to her mother, then reached for her hand and squeezed it. "You're a remarkable woman. For most people at your stage, walking a mile every day is impossible."

Her mother punched the air like a teenager. "No pain, no gain."

"I agree that Francine is one of the most amazing people I've had the privilege of calling my friend," Sebastian said. "But is there something we can do about her pain level, at the very least?"

"We could send her to a pain clinic, but the narcotics are highly addictive, and over time she would build up a tolerance."

Charlie tried to keep her heart intact as she folded her mother's cotton nightgowns into the case. They'd heard it all before. Yet it still hurt to hear once again that there was nothing more they could do. She glanced at Sebastian, whose face was like granite, and that made the ache so much worse.

"I don't want to start any more meds." Her mother was calm yet firm. "Evie down the hall takes that stuff and though it doesn't do much for her pain anymore, she can't go without it. It's terrible to watch when she tries to wean herself off it. That's not for me."

Dr. Bengali stood. "As I said, ma'am, you are a remarkable woman. I thank you for the opportunity to examine you and wish I had better news."

"Thank you for coming to see me, Dr. Bengali." Charlie's mother held out her crippled hands, and he leaned over to take them in his long, firm, nimble surgeon's fingers. "You're a very nice young man."

He smiled, his teeth gleaming white in the sun falling through the blinds. "You're too kind."

After Charlie shook his hand and thanked him, Sebastian stepped forward. Despite how carefully Sebastian was working to hide his frustration, Charlie felt his pain as much as her mother's, his emotion palpable, his anger undulating tangibly around him. And beneath all of it lay a helplessness that Charlie would give the world to erase, just as she would have given everything she had to take away her mother's pain.

Still, Sebastian took Dr. Bengali's hand in his with a firm shake. "Thank you for answering our call. If you learn of any new techniques, medications, or methods, please let us know."

"Certainly."

The regal man left, and Sebastian turned to the window, studying her mother's spectacular view of the parking lot. "I'm sorry," he said, his throat still constricted. "We'll find someone else." He avoided their eyes, as if he was ashamed they'd see the failure in his gaze. "We'll keep looking, I swear it."

Charlie wanted to enfold him in her arms, draw his ache into her own body, kiss away all his hurt. But her mother held out both hands. "Come here, Sebastian."

He hunkered down in front of her chair, taking her damaged fingers in his. "I'll make this right, Francine."

"I want you to keep searching for me, because you never know, something might pop up. Some big new breakthrough. But I'm not disappointed, and neither should you be."

Charlie's heart broke watching them, this big, beautiful man down on one knee with an old woman who'd been forgotten by everyone except her daughter. And now Sebastian.

"I need to help you," he said, his voice raw with the emotion he'd been trying so hard to hide.

"You are helping me." She put her hand on his cheek. "You take time out of your busy life to visit me. And Charlie told me how you'll help us with Magnolia Gardens if we need it. I can't thank you enough for that. Best of all, you make my daughter happy. How can I ask for anything more?"

"Oh, Francine, I love visiting you." He glanced at Charlie, his eyes brimming with lingering sorrow and what looked like love. A love that had no bounds. "And your daughter makes me very happy too."

Charlie had to go to him then, bending down to press a soft kiss to his lips. As she drew away, he slid his free hand into her hair, held her close, kissing her back for a long, breathless moment.

"Now *that*," her mother said on a delighted laugh, "is a kiss!" Sebastian's answering laugh wrapped around Charlie's heart as Francine added, "What do you say we pack up my old kit bag and blow this popsicle stand?"

The darkness hadn't faded completely and tension still vibrated through him, but at least he was smiling when he said, "We'll make like bananas and peel." He offered both hands to

Francine and slowly drew her to her feet before bending low to plant a kiss on her forehead.

Charlie had started falling for him that very first day, but watching his tender handling of her mother made her love Sebastian with her whole heart and soul. Even if he never touched her again, never took her to heaven in his arms, never sold another piece of art for her, she would keep on loving him.

Her love had nothing to do with his wealth or the success he'd created for himself—and everything to do with the man he was on the inside. The son who'd turned himself inside out for his parents, again and again, even against all hope. The man who steadied an old lady as she grabbed the handles of her walker. The friend who would do anything for the people he loved. The lover who made her feel more pleasure—and more cherished—than she'd ever believed possible.

She'd never been in control of her feelings for him. She'd fallen in love with him the moment he'd stepped into her dusty shop wearing his perfect suit and called her junkyard a garden. Though she couldn't be certain that he wouldn't one day want to change her, she would risk everything for him. Even the parts of herself she knew would never fit in with the fancy society where Sebastian ruled as naturally as breathing.

Her mother wheeled her walker into the hallway ahead of them, saying good-bye to all the friends she'd made at Shady Lane. Charlie put her hand on Sebastian's arm to halt him for a moment before he lifted the suitcases. "I love you."

He went so still she wasn't sure he was even breathing. Then he exhaled. "I...you..."

She put a finger to his lips. "You did a wonderful thing today. Every day. I love you not just for trying so hard with my mother, but for everything. I've learned recently about the power of positive thinking," she said with a grin. "So let's not think about anything bad anymore, only the good stuff to come."

She leaned in to kiss him on the lips. Then, because she didn't want him to feel as though he had to say the words back to her, she grabbed the carryall and turned to follow her mother, knowing he would be right there behind her, behind them.

Always there for them.

* * *

I love you.

Sebastian had just failed Charlie, failed her mother. Even with a billion dollars, he couldn't fix this, couldn't make things better for Francine.

Yet—amazingly—Charlie loved him anyway.

No one had ever loved him for his failures and it left him speechless. All he could do was follow the woman of his dreams out of the nursing home, her words playing like a musical refrain in his head.

I love you. I love you. I love you.

He wanted to grab Charlie, ask her if she really meant it. Ask her how she could love him when he hadn't come through for her mother. But with Francine watching them, a knowing smile on her face, he simply stowed her belongings in the spacious trunk of his luxury vehicle and helped her into the front seat like a queen.

Once they arrived at Magnolia Gardens, she *ooh*ed and *aah*ed over the front entry, the carpeted lobby lined with cushioned chairs, the lounge with sofas, card tables, and two big-screen TVs for movie nights, the dining room with white tablecloths and colored cloth napkins. "It's just like a real restaurant," Francine enthused.

Sebastian barely noticed the details at first, given that his entire world had just shifted on its axis with three little words. Momentous words. Unbelievable words. When he finally focused on Francine's new nursing home, he had to admit it was far better than Shady Lane. Magnolia Gardens was more like a large hotel complex than a nursing home. But it still wasn't the Ritz. Francine didn't seem to mind at all, however. She gasped at the beautiful flowers in the gardens and was near tears at the bouquet of roses he'd sent to her room.

"You are *such* a dear boy, Sebastian."

Her living room featured a postage-stamp sized flat-panel TV and utilitarian furniture. The chairs seemed comfortable enough, though still institutional. French doors opened onto a balcony with a small table and a plastic chair.

"I'll bring you a nice new comforter for the bed, Mom. Something with a flower print." Charlie unpacked the porcelain cups and plates, stowing them in a cabinet over a counter with a wet-bar sized sink and a dorm-room fridge. "And we'll get an electric kettle for your tea."

Every time Charlie spoke, he could hear her saying it again. The very best thing anyone had ever said to him. *I love you.* And also, in many ways, the most unbelievable. It would be one thing if she'd said it when he'd landed her a new commission. But to say the words after he'd come up with nothing but blanks for her mother?

Belatedly realizing that Francine was trying to sit in the chair, he hurried to help her into it. "Oh my. This is so wonderful." She picked up a card that said they had free Wi-Fi for the residents and shook her head. "I'm overwhelmed."

Yet Sebastian still wanted more for her. So much more.

"Are you going to stay for dinner?" she asked brightly.

"I would love to." He wanted to see if the food was up to snuff. If it wasn't, he'd have to consider how to break it to Charlie.

After her meager belongings had been put away, they headed to the dining room. Francine stared goggle-eyed at the posted dining menu as though she'd never had a choice between grilled tilapia and Irish stew before. They parked her walker outside the dining room in a long line of wheeled conveyances, and Sebastian ushered her in on his arm. At the buffet, Charlie put a little of everything on Francine's plate. In addition to hot food in warming trays, the salad bar sported an impressive array of cut vegetables, and along the back wall, various desserts decorated the countertop. When Charlie wasn't visiting, a waiter would assemble Francine's meal for her.

"If you don't feel like eating the buffet," Charlie said once she returned to the table, "you can order off this standard menu." She held up a small display stand. "Fish and chips. Crab cakes. Grilled ham and cheese. Hamburger. Garden burger. And steamed broccoli."

"Oh, I love broccoli." Francine daintily attacked the Irish stew. "*Mmm.* Very good."

It wasn't filet mignon. It wasn't even gourmet. But thankfully, it wasn't plastic cafeteria food either.

"Isn't this marvelous, Sebastian?"

Francine damn near glowed, and it really hit home what her life had been like at Shady

Lane. Both Francine and Charlie were so delighted and excited. Was he jaded by five-star hotels and first-rate service? Or was he just trying to make up for not being able to cure Francine of her illness?

Under the table, he put his hand on Charlie's thigh. Though he'd tried to hold back while they were with Francine—he didn't want the dear lady to think he was always pawing her daughter—he had to touch Charlie, craving the connection, brief as it was. She laid her fingers over his, keeping him close for a moment. Nowhere near long enough. Forever wouldn't be long enough.

They were on to dessert when Francine asked Charlie, "How are your class plans coming together for the fall? Any new, exciting projects on tap?"

Charlie suddenly became engrossed in stirring her coffee. But he was glad Francine had asked. He'd been wondering the same thing. Charlie hadn't mentioned her classes in a while. Was she planning to teach again this fall or take a quarter off while she worked on new commissions? The last thing he wanted was for her to wear herself down.

"I've been so busy with the chariot and horses that I haven't really had time to think much about my teaching schedule."

Francine turned her bright gaze to Sebastian. "I've sat in on her classes several times and she's such a gifted teacher. She always describes what her students need to do in such clear terms that even I was tempted to pick up a welding torch. Her students absolutely love her. But I'm sure you understand that, don't you?"

"Yes." He couldn't take his eyes off Charlie, couldn't even begin to hide what he felt for her. "She's very easy to love."

Francine beamed at the two of them while Charlie flushed at the compliments. "She certainly is."

A short while later, they said their good-byes, leaving Francine sitting happily in the lounge meeting other residents and already making new friends. Sebastian and Charlie were still in the middle of the parking lot when he crowded her up against a parked car, cupped her face in his hands, and bent to take her mouth.

She tasted sweet and fresh and perfect. More perfect than anything he'd ever known, anything he'd ever dreamed of. His heart beat in a wild frenzy of need—and love. Endless, boundless love. Her lips parted beneath his on a cry of pleasure, then his gentle kiss turned savage. Possessive. So damned erotic that they could have started a fire right there in public.

When he finally let her up for air, he needed her to know how he felt. "I love you, Charlie Ballard."

"I know you do. I could hear you saying the words when you were holding my mother's hand, telling her all you wanted to do was help her." Her eyes were slightly dilated as she looked up at him, her lips still gorgeously damp from his tongue. "And I could also hear it in your kiss."

"Then get ready to hear me say it all night long," he murmured before he took her mouth again.

CHAPTER TWENTY-THREE

Three little words. They changed everything. Because Charlie had said them. To him.

Sebastian had wanted her right there against the door of the car, was already half crazy with desire and need. Those words. Her kiss.

He was head over heels.

The moment he got her home, he scooped her up in his arms.

She laughed. Her sexy, throaty laughter always turned up the heat inside him. "What are you doing, you crazy man?"

"Crazy for you." He carried her off to his bedroom, her body soft, warm, and yielding against his.

He needed her lips, now, her mouth under his. Her kiss seared him, burning straight to his heart. In the bedroom, he let her feet slip to the carpet as he buried his fingers in her lush curves and steeped his senses in her taste.

"Charlie," he whispered. "I need you." He needed her skin branding his flesh, her taste on his lips, her scent filling his head.

"I'm right here," she promised.

Desperate to get to her skin, he tugged on her blouse and the buttons seemed to pop off. "Too many clothes," he growled.

"Tear them off."

He went wild. Crazy. Totally reckless. The cloth tore, fabric flew across the room, hitting a wall, falling into a corner. Until he could worship her gorgeous, naked skin.

This was what he wanted—to worship her, to give her everything, to be the man who made all her dreams come true.

She wore the laciest of lingerie, her bra almost see-through, her panties a mere wisp. And she stole his breath. He couldn't move. He could only trace her body with his gaze, the sweet pearls of her nipples dusky through the lace, the strong muscles of her arms that could hold him so tightly, the smooth belly he'd kissed.

"You are so beautiful." He felt like a caveman kneeling before a princess.

And she'd said she was his. *I love you.* The beautiful princess was all his. He would never believe it, never truly accept it. He was terrified he'd wake up and find her gone. Terrified he'd screw up with her one too many times. And yet she'd said she loved him right *after* his biggest failure. She'd forgiven him. She was so damned unique and special.

"You have too many clothes on," she whispered. And with seductive sweeps of her hand, she unbuttoned his shirt, his pants. The fleeting touch of her fingers was electric. She stripped him down and set his skin on fire, made his body burn for her.

Saturday at the Regent had been momentous, but this was beyond anything. This was Charlie *loving* him.

"Come here." Taking his hand, she backed up to the bed, pulling him with her.

The balcony doors were open, the evening breeze fluttering like fingers through her hair. Her skin was bathed in the last golden rays of the sun before it fell behind the distant coastal mountains, and her hair was lit by fire, a red-gold halo.

She pushed him down on the cool sheets. Moments before, he'd been desperate with need, dying to be inside her. Now he craved her slow seduction.

"You're the beautiful one." Her lips curved in a sensuous smile. She climbed on top of him, straddling him, the feel of her so sweet, so good, so hot that his body rose, tensed, caressed her. His hands on her hips, he held her tightly to him, exulting in the slip-slide of their bodies. She was so soft, so wet already, and he was so hard, he could have rolled her over and taken everything right now.

The fever in his blood begged for it.

But Charlie bit her lip and smiled. She rocked, driving him mad, then slowly she sidled down his body, leaning to kiss her way over his chest. "Not so fast," she said, licking his nipple, then biting it lightly. "I've got plans before *that.*" She slipped a hand between them, wrapped him in her palm, and squeezed until he groaned.

"Do you like that?"

"Yes." He loved everything she did, loved that she dressed herself up like a princess, held court with her subjects, then brought them all, including him, to their knees. Yet in his bed, she was also the sexy, gorgeous, seductive tomboy, her hands all over him, driving him crazy.

"I want to taste you again," she whispered.

He was seduced. Completely. In love. Irrevocably. There was only Charlie. There would only ever be Charlie. She was his gift. How or why he deserved her, he had no clue. But he would give her anything she wanted.

"Taste me," he begged.

She drove him wild with licks and kisses before she took all of him, so deeply that his body arched and he threw his head back against the mattress, crying out her name.

"Charlie." Always Charlie. Only Charlie. Forever Charlie. There'd never been a woman like her, and there would never be another.

She took his pleasure, took the thick growl in his throat, pushed him higher with her mouth, her lips, her tongue, her hands. She set his blood on fire, a conflagration burning through his veins.

"I need you. Inside you. Please. Love. I love you." The words fell from his lips. He had no control.

The effort was Herculean, but he pulled her up, rolled with her, flattened her to his bed, all her curves a perfect match for his, her skin a fiery brand against his. He held her face framed in his hands for one long moment, her eyes pulling him into their depths, as if he were a part of her and she him.

"I love you." The words were just a breath on her lips and yet they reached up inside him all over again. This beautiful, incredible woman loved him.

He slipped his hand down between the softness of her thighs and she moaned, low and sweet. Her pleasure was all that existed. Her breath fanned his cheek, her gasps and her little moans fueling him. He found every hollow, every sensitive spot, learned her curves inside and out, until finally she cried his name. Her body shivered and shimmied, then she wrapped him tightly with her limbs, riding out her storm.

A heartbeat later he had on protection and entered her before she came out the other side. "God, I love you." His voice was hoarse, his words harsh with his emotion.

One arm around his shoulder, she shoved a hand into his hair and pulled his head down. She kissed him with her heart, with her soul, her cheeks wet with her pleasure.

Then she let him go, just to breathe, to whisper his name. And one little demand. "Don't stop. Don't ever stop."

She drew him in, fit him as though her body had been tailored for him, only him. He'd wanted to keep it slow, drive her crazy with short, sweet strokes over all her special, sensitive places. But with Charlie, there was no holding back.

"Jesus." He moaned into the sweet, hot pleasure of her body around him. "I love you."

He could never say it enough, never hear it enough.

She said his name, and he went deep and high inside her. Harder, faster, deeper, until there was just her skin against his, her sweet and sexy scent floating in the air around him, her luscious taste on his lips, her body convulsing around him, pushing him to the edge right along with her.

All his emotions broke free. All his pleasure. All his love as he tumbled with her right into the eye of the hurricane. "I love you, Charlie. I've never loved anyone the way I love you. Never knew I could love like this."

"I did." Her whispered words came on a gasp of pleasure a beat before bliss took them over completely. "I knew."

* * *

The full moon shining through the balcony doors lit up the room, and a cool wind blew in off the Bay, but Charlie was wrapped in the sweet, warm cocoon of Sebastian's arms in the king-sized bed. She loved curling up next to him, loved falling asleep to the sound of his breathing, loved waking to the feel of his hands doing delicious things to her.

Loved *him*.

And he loved her too.

Sharing those words had been earth-shattering, making her dream of a different future than she'd ever imagined for herself. Especially with the way he'd been so kind to her mother today. Her heart was still touched each time she remembered him at her mother's feet, holding her hands, his emotion spilling over.

She didn't want to move. She wanted to drench herself in his scent, snuggle into all his hard muscles, and sleep beneath the comforting weight of his arm over her. But she hadn't been in her workshop since the morning of the gala, hadn't welded a single horse's joint in three days. If she stayed in Sebastian's house and his bed, she'd never finish anything.

She knew she should go. Work. At least think about work. Or be independent in *some* way about *something*. But, oh, it was difficult to even think of leaving Sebastian's bed, to willingly give up all the pleasure that was only a kiss, only a caress away.

As if he sensed the direction of her thoughts, he stirred, then began to slowly slide his hand over her stomach. So slowly that by the time he reached the vee between her legs, she was arching into his touch.

"I know I've taken you too many times already—"

She rolled to face him, her naked breasts pressed against his broad chest. "There could never be too many times."

He kissed her hard and hot, devouring her. "*Never*," he echoed against her mouth. "I'll never be able to get enough of you."

She wound her arms around his neck and rubbed sinuously against him. "You said you like it when I'm greedy, and right now, I want more." More and more. Sebastian was right—there would never be enough.

He pulled her on top, and she nuzzled his chest as he slid his hand between them.

"I love the way you do that," she said against his salty skin and the light fur of hair.

"What?" he murmured against her ear.

"The way you like to touch me. Always kissing me, putting your hands on me." She sighed out her pleasure, gently rocking on him. "Making me crazy."

"I love the silk of your hair against my skin." Her hair was a mess, its tendrils all over him. And she loved that he loved it. "What do you want?" he whispered.

"You." She rolled her face against his chest, her hips creating a rhythm against his hand. "Now," she added, her voice a breathy plea.

He donned protection, then rolled with her almost lazily until they were wrapped around each other in the most beautiful way possible. "Mmm." It was all she could manage.

He was slow and sweet, building the sensations, his body surrounding her, the covers warm against the chill of the night wind off the Bay. She could almost be dreaming, almost be asleep, her eyes fluttering their pleasure beneath heavy lids. The explosion when it came was pure bliss as they shuddered together, the pulse of their pleasure simultaneous.

And then she fell down into something like sleep, holding him inside a few moments longer. She would always want and need a few moments more, she thought dreamily. She would always want more of him...

* * *

An idea for the horses came to Charlie in the middle of the night. One so vivid that it woke her up.

She used to make the mistake of thinking she'd remember her middle-of-the-night thoughts, but come morning they were always lost to the darkness. Unless she wrote them down.

It had never been *this* difficult to get out of bed at three a.m. before. Given that she was sleeping with the most gorgeous man on the planet, curled in his strong arms, it was no wonder she hadn't been able to rouse herself to do some work earlier. No one would have been able to resist Sebastian's touch, his kisses.

Fully awake now—and he was dead asleep this time—she took care to slip soundlessly from the bed. She had no idea where he'd tossed any of her clothing in their mad rush to tumble into his bed earlier that evening, so she pulled his shirt over her bare skin. It smelled mouthwateringly of him, all male, all sexy, yummy... *Stop dreaming, Charlie.* She needed paper, a pencil. Not seeing any, she followed the moonlit path across the thick Persian rug to a small study. Stepping inside, she found a chair and a side table stacked with books and a bunch of sketchbooks.

She switched on the standing lamp beside the chair. Why would Sebastian have a mound of sketchbooks? Trying to be quiet so she wouldn't wake him, she reached for the top one, but the pile wobbled and several fell to the floor before she could catch them.

Bending to retrieve them, she couldn't help seeing a sketch that had fallen open on the carpet...and her jaw dropped in awe.

It was a pencil drawing of her face, one in which the artist had caught her intensity, as if she were far away in deep thought. He'd captured the frown line between her eyes so effectively that Charlie actually reached up to her face to smooth away the wrinkle. He'd added a beauty to her features that was almost otherworldly, but at the same time the stroke of his pencil made her a little pensive.

Her hands shaking as she picked up the sketchbook, she flipped to another page. Here, she was laughing. The artist had even created the sparkle in her eye.

She knew without a doubt the artist was Sebastian.

My God, he had startling talent. The sketches were so detailed, the drawings could have been black and white photographs. She could almost feel the texture of her hair, her eyelashes, the slope of her cheeks. He'd added the lines of concentration at her eyes, the marks of the face shield after she'd removed it, and caught her nose at that angle she hated, making it look bigger than she liked. Yet in his work, even those things were beautiful. Occasionally there was a line here or there that seemed slightly off, but that only made the drawings more poignant, as if he saw her flaws and didn't care. There were drawings of her laughing, talking, eating, working, even one of her looking up at him from the hot tub's bubbling waters. Sometimes she was frowning, sometimes a secret smile curved her lips.

He'd filled several pads, as if every night after she left, he came here to put her face on paper.

They were unbelievably good, the kind of drawings that should be framed and sold for thousands. Sebastian could have a show of his own, one where everything sold out immediately. He was brilliant.

Utterly *magnificent*.

Why hadn't he told her about his art, his wonderful talent? Why did he hide it away in a room she would never have entered if she hadn't been searching for a piece of paper? All of this was inside of him, and yet he'd only talked about *her* talent, *her* art, *her* commissions.

She'd trusted him enough to tell him about her mother's illness, about Shady Lane and how badly she'd needed the money to pay for a better place. She'd even turned her mother's welfare over to him, letting him bring in doctors. She'd told him she loved him, for God's sake. Yet he hadn't trusted her with his secret.

As an artist, she knew just how vital creation was to her soul. This was clearly a *huge* part of what made Sebastian the man he was, and they could have shared their love of art. No wonder he'd had so many helpful ideas for her chariot and horses. His interest in the drawing program suddenly made sense too. An iPad lay on the floor, as if he'd started playing with that as well. Creation was in his blood.

But he hadn't told her.

Knowing he didn't want to share his work wounded her deeply. It meant he didn't trust her with this special piece of himself.

And yet...

When she looked at the drawings again, she saw all incarnations of herself, from the overalls and steel-toes to her descent of the Regent's staircase in her consignment dress. There was even a sketch of her at the designer shop wearing the velvet and pearl dress.

She'd worried that he hadn't actually *seen* her until the gala when she'd walked down the stairs and into his arms, that he hadn't truly wanted her until she could fit into his glittering Cinderella world. But these drawings showed that he'd seen the real Charlie all along—her independence, her commitment to her vision, even her playfulness.

Most of all, she saw his love for her. And knew that it had been there all along too.

None of that explained why he hadn't shared his talent with her, but in the face of so much love, how could she possibly hold on to her hurt? As she moved her fingers over yet another superb drawing, she vowed to help him bring his art into the open.

He had done so much for her, again and again. Now, she would do the same for him. No matter what.

Perhaps she should have used a blank page to draw the now nearly forgotten vision from her dream, but she couldn't resist looking through more of his sketches. And she saw that she wasn't his only subject. She found sketch after sketch of a couple in their thirties. The similarity in the man's jawline and mouth to Sebastian's features tipped her off to their identities.

His parents.

Her heart raced as she studied the pictures carefully. Though obviously a good-looking man, there was also a weakness in his father's face—a weakness there was no evidence of in Sebastian's. His mother was pretty, but tired and worn. And yet, what came through was Sebastian's love for them. It was in the details, the laugh lines at his mother's mouth, the occasional hint of a smile in his father's eyes and around his mouth despite the slightly slack skin.

"What are you doing?" Sebastian's voice was like a slap out of the dark.

CHAPTER TWENTY-FOUR

Sketchbooks slid off Charlie's lap in her surprise, one falling open to the drawing from the night of the gala. Sebastian marched into the small room, filling it, overwhelming it, his face shadowed and his eyes dark. He'd pulled a pair of sweats over his lean hips, leaving his chest bare and beautiful. Her mouth went dry, from the sight of him as much as from the knowledge that she'd been snooping through his private sketchbooks.

"I woke up with an idea," she explained. "I wanted to get it down before I forgot." It was long forgotten now, and she didn't even care, not when she'd discovered something more precious than diamonds. "I couldn't find any paper in the bedroom, so I came in here."

His features were hard, immobile, like a piece of metal she hadn't yet welded into submission. "How long have you been looking through my things?" His voice was as hard as his face. It could break rocks.

Worse, it could break her. Right in two. Straight through the center of her heart. The heart she'd just given to him.

All the hurt she'd worked to push away rushed back. "I was only planning to take a blank piece to write some notes on, but then..." She waved a hand at the sketch still face-up on the floor. "I saw a drawing of myself. And I was—"

Before she could let him know how moved she was by his talent and the incredible emotion he'd captured in every single sketch, he grabbed the pads off the floor and the side table, then snatched the one she held right out of her hand.

"They're not for public consumption." He tossed the sketchbooks in the drawer of a small bureau against the wall.

"*Public* consumption?" The words burned her throat as they came out in a horrible echo.

"They're private."

It was pure instinct for Charlie to push past him and leave, to run as far and as fast as she could. Far enough for her to figure out how to weld the break in the heart he'd just ripped apart. But how could she forget what he'd said to her as they made love? *I love you, Charlie. I've never loved anyone the way I love you. Never knew I could love like this.* He'd told her he loved her. With his words, his body. Despite the way he'd lashed out at her, she truly believed his drawings revealed how much he loved her, over and over again with every single stroke of his pencil. But now, he was trying to push her away, trying to make sure she never asked him about these drawings.

Well, it was going to take a hell of a lot more than that to make her leave. She wouldn't walk away from him.

But she would get him to tell her why he hid his beautiful art in a tiny room where no one would ever see it.

* * *

"Private." Charlie spoke softly now, but her voice curled around his insides, her hurt tangible. "How would you feel if I never allowed anyone to see my work? If I refused to show it for *public consumption*?"

Sebastian clenched his fists on the dresser into which he'd thrown all his secret thoughts and feelings. He couldn't believe what he'd just said to her. Especially when he knew firsthand how rough, angry words could hurt more than anything else.

"I'm sorry, Charlie." He straightened, turned, feeling like his bones were cracking. "So damned sorry. I didn't mean it. Not any of it."

He'd screwed up *again*, despite the vow he'd made to himself only hours ago to do anything for her.

"I should have asked instead of prying." Her hand on his arm was so soft, so warm, so strong, the faint scent of his loving still clinging to her. "Your sketches are beautiful, Sebastian. I wish you'd shown them to me. You should be proud. They're not just drawings you do in your spare time. They're works of art."

"You're the work of art," he said to the carpet beneath his feet. He couldn't even gaze at the perfection in her face that he hadn't been able to capture.

She pressed her fingers into his arm, urging him to look at her. "Don't shrug me off." She held his gaze for a long moment, her eyes darkly serious. "You're a very talented artist. *Very.*"

He respected her artistic vision more than that of anyone he'd ever met, yet somehow she had a blind spot for him, even after she'd seen all his imperfections. Not only in his drawing skills, but also in the way he'd failed her mother. He'd promised he would fix things and he hadn't. He wanted to shove the thoughts and feelings away, back inside the dark, secret place where he'd kept them for so long. But with Charlie...

Sebastian had never been able to hold back with her.

"I'm not an artist." The truth felt like razor blades on his tongue, but he made himself go on. "There are so many mistakes. I can't capture exactly what I see. I can't figure out how to make the drawings perfect no matter how hard I try."

"You made *me* beautiful even though I'm not perfect." She reached up to touch the tiny frown line between her eyes. "I suppose I could have a doctor stick a needle into me to get rid of this, but if you ask me, perfection doesn't have nearly as much character as *real*."

"God, no, don't ever let a doctor with a needle near your face." He gently slid a finger over the same mark. "I love that line. It shows your concentration, your dedication."

"And your drawings show so much about *you*, Sebastian. How you see people."

"They show the imperfection in my own abilities."

Closer now, her heat shot toward him like the pilot arc of one of her machines. He wanted to bury himself in her warmth.

"Sebastian." She ran her thumb over his lip as she said his name, her voice warm and husky. "Your drawings made me feel beautiful and cared for. And understood."

"Putting my pencil on the paper usually helps me figure people out. I'm simply analyzing people. I'm not an artist. Not like you."

"You are." She paused for a moment before adding, "The drawings of your parents are beautiful too. I feel as though I've met them now. Does drawing them help you remember them?"

He shook his head, fast, almost violently. "No, I'd remember everything, even without the sketches." Especially all his failures with them. "I guess I've never given up trying to figure out what I could have done for them."

An even deeper understanding lit her eyes. Then she pressed against him, rising on her toes to whisper, "Have all your drawings helped you figure me out?" She curled her arms around his neck.

"Not yet." His answer was muffled in her hair. "But I'm working on it."

"Maybe you just need to put a few more hours in, only this time instead of using pencil and paper, you could draw on my skin with your fingers."

His hands were already on her, burrowing beneath the shirt she'd borrowed, shoving it off her shoulders. "I can draw with my tongue as well."

"Draw with everything, Sebastian. Absolutely *everything*."

He picked her up, her body as light as a down pillow in his arms. He needed her love to banish the darkness of his thoughts and the things he'd so stupidly said to her. After laying her carefully on his bed, he stripped off the sweats he'd pulled on.

"Now, let's see," he murmured like a painter studying his canvas. "A line here." His tongue marked a streak from one beautiful, rose-tipped nipple to the other. "Geometric designs, I think."

She laughed, then shivered as he drew tongue circles around her nipple.

"We need more than one paintbrush." And his fingers joined the play. He traced her supple skin, her flesh quivering beneath his strokes.

"You make beautiful art—" She gasped as his touch painted a line straight down between her legs. "—but your work is also highly stimulating."

"It will take hours to cover every inch." Hours of bliss, hours of begging her forgiveness for his lapse into the anger and fear of the past, hours of loving her.

Her body was his sketchbook and he filled every inch until her body shuddered under his tongue, around his fingers. She tangled his hair, arched into him, and as she wrapped herself all around him, he prayed she felt his love for her in every kiss, every caress, every breath.

* * *

Charlie had long since fallen into an exhausted sleep in his arms and the sun was peeking over the horizon. Yet Sebastian still couldn't sleep.

She'd told him how beautiful his drawings were, how talented he was, that his sketches shouldn't be shoved in the back of a drawer like a dirty little secret. But if he truly had talent, then by now he should know how to help her fully realize her potential. He should have figured out how to convince her to step into the light and accept everything the world could give her.

He'd sensed her hesitation at the gala as people all but threw commissions at her, begging her to create sculptures for them. It was the same hesitation he'd felt with her more than a dozen times since then. It was almost as if she didn't *want* to be a huge success.

Sebastian frowned. Could he be reading her wrong? Was it possible she could be the one artist on earth who wasn't looking for acclaim or accolades? Or were all his screwups with her coloring everything else? First he'd blown it big time by offering to pay for her mother's care right after the first time they made love. Then tonight he'd lashed out at her for discovering a secret he shouldn't have kept from her in the first place. The fact that she hadn't walked out on him was a true miracle...and more than he deserved.

He tightened his arms around her, renewing his vow to get things right with her from now on—and to make sure he gave her absolutely everything she deserved. No matter what.

CHAPTER TWENTY-FIVE

Sebastian had made Charlie's body his work of art into the small hours of the morning, bringing her to ecstasy so many times she'd lost count. But even if she'd never had the pleasure of making love with him, she would still think he was a true artist in every sense of the word.

She had to find a way to make him believe that. And she knew where it had to start—with getting him to realize he didn't have to be Mr. Perfect. Was da Vinci perfect? Michelangelo? Of course not. And neither was she, with her dinosaurs built out of bullet-riddled road signs. That didn't mean she wasn't an artist. It didn't mean he wasn't either.

It was obvious his need to be perfect all came down to his parents. He was still broken up over not being able to save them. The drawings of his father, though, revealed so much. The lines on his face exposed not only weakness, but cruelty too. Sebastian had never mentioned a mean streak, but Charlie suspected there was more to the story than he'd admitted on stage—or to her. More, maybe, than Sebastian even wanted to admit to himself.

It was easy to spend all her time thinking about Sebastian. Wanting to give back as much as he'd already given to her. Just plain *wanting* him. But she needed to hustle on building the horses if she ever hoped to start the dinosaur for Noah.

Pulling down her face shield, she sparked up. The horses' legs needed to appear like fine machinery, pumping, working, galloping headlong. They didn't care that their master had been thrown to the ground in a heap or that the chariot was a broken shell they dragged behind them. They simply needed to fly. Just like Sebastian.

The day grew hot as she worked, and the protective gear and torch turned the heat on high, but still she lost track of time. She relished both the physicality of it and the ability to let her creativity run completely free. She'd just finished off a weld, its line clean and smooth, when a feeling struck her, a sense of something not quite right with her lead stallion.

She frowned and walked a wide circle around it. She'd sometimes asked her students to weigh in on a sculpture and had always been pleased by their insights. She still hadn't made a decision about the fall session—whether to keep one leg in her old world or to take the huge and scary step fully into Sebastian's world. And thinking about her students now made her stomach clench.

Pushing the thought away, she refocused on the horse and finally isolated the problem. Her prize stallion was bowlegged. Had she gotten the angle of his knee joints wrong? Or made his chest too wide?

"What's wrong?"

She almost dropped the torch in her surprise. Thank God she'd already turned it off. Laying it down, she flipped up her face mask. Her heart was racing as fast as her galloping stallions, and it wasn't only from the scare. It was Sebastian, all dressed up in a dark business suit and tie, his hair perfect, every-absolutely-freaking-thing perfect about him. She could feel his gaze sketching her body, as if he were running his fingertips over her.

"You scared me." Putting the face shield on the bench, she tugged off her gloves. "What if I'd been using my torch?"

"I wouldn't have said anything if you were," he drawled. "I just thought I'd bring you a refreshing bottle of beer." He set two imports on the workbench.

She wasn't normally a beer drinker, but with the heat of the day, her work, and Sebastian making her feel so temptingly hot...

"God, that sounds good." As good as having him here with her in the studio, close enough to touch, to taste.

"So tell me what's wrong."

She pointed at her horse. "He's bowlegged."

"He looks fine."

She traced the lines of both legs with her hands to show him...and a memory of Sebastian's sleek muscles beneath her fingers sizzled over her skin.

He stepped in close, his male scent surrounding her, making her a tiny bit crazy. "You're right, he's totally bowlegged."

Laughter burst out of her. She wasn't a *tiny* bit crazy for him. She was over-the-top completely crazy.

"But he's good this way." Sebastian threaded his fingers through the tips of her hair. She loved that he couldn't do anything without touching her at the same time. "He's the handicapped horse that Ben-Hur gave a chance."

See? He was making up a story, like all great artists did. "Ben-Hur's kindness would have meant he was gambling with his life."

"That makes it even better. Kindness trumping both the win *and* safety." He was close, so close behind her. She wanted to take him to the floor and tear off all his perfect, polished clothes.

"We should leave the horse like this," he insisted softly.

"Even though he's not perfect?" Desire hummed through her voice, but she kept herself in check.

"He's perfect the way he is." He dropped a kiss on her neck, heating her all the way through despite the two fans blowing over them. "I know what you're doing, by the way. You're saying that art isn't about perfection."

"It's about heart." She leaned back, letting him put his arms around her, then turned her face up to his. She wanted him, but just as badly, she wanted the moment he trusted her enough to share all the things he'd been holding back. "Is my plan working?"

He drew her tightly against him, all hard male muscle and heat. "Oh yeah. It's definitely working."

She wriggled, tantalizing them both. But she knew he hadn't gotten her real message. *Soon*, she promised herself, she'd make sure he understood how amazing he was, *exactly* the way he was, no perfection necessary. "What message am I sending now?"

"That you're hot and I should strip off every last stitch of your clothes."

She had so much to do, and so much she wanted to help him see about himself. But wherever Sebastian was, something delicious and sexy was bound to ensue. And she could never resist him. "Anyone ever tell you how smart you are?"

He was already busy trailing his fingers to the smock's buttons and undoing them. As for her? Despite making love over and over again last night, she ached for him, so desperate and full of desire that her voice was a little breathless. "What are you doing here, anyway? Don't you have important meetings?"

"I couldn't stay away from you."

His simple, sweet words dissolved what was left of rational thought. The horse's bowed legs could stay bowed for another couple of hours. Sebastian's eyes were molten, his body all hard edges against her as he shoved the smock off her shoulders and let it fall. Then he unhooked the buckles of her overalls and flipped back the straps.

Charlie shimmied. Everything fell to her feet, and she kicked it all aside.

"Holy hell." A pulse beat rapidly at his throat.

She wore nothing but panties, bra, and her steel-toed boots. In the heat of his eyes and the flare of his nostrils like a fine racehorse ready to run, she'd never felt sexier.

He dove on her, her face between his hands as he consumed her mouth, deep, hard, fast. She grabbed his lapels before her knees buckled beneath her. Hauling her up, he pulled her legs around his waist, and whispered, "Hang on, baby."

God, yes, she would hang on. And she would make him see that everything he did was perfect simply because he was the one doing it.

Because, oh my, the things he did to her. She couldn't live without them.

She couldn't live without *him.*

* * *

Carrying Charlie to the workbench, Sebastian remembered the day he'd first touched her and all the things he'd been dying to do but hadn't.

"This is crazy," she whispered as he licked the swell of her breasts.

Snap and the flimsy bra fell away. "Completely reckless."

"Any of your employees could walk in."

"They could," he agreed with a wicked grin. "But they won't." It was long past lunchtime and there was no reason for anyone to come down here. Besides, he was too far gone to care if they did.

"How can you be sure?"

Even as she asked the question, she was threading her hands into his hair and arching her breasts closer to his mouth. But he made himself lift his head. "I'll stop if you want me to."

"Don't you dare."

Sweet Lord, she was exquisite. Her hair falling loose from its knot, the face shield leaving dents on her forehead, the adorable lines of concentration between her eyebrows.

"I couldn't get a lick of work done today, Charlie." He emphasized the word *lick* with a long, slow swipe of his tongue across her nipple. "All I could think about was taking you." He trailed his fingers down to her hips, laid his thumbs along the creases of her thighs, so close but not yet touching. "Loving you."

She dragged his head up to take his mouth. Kissing her was heaven. With long, drugged swigs of her, he immersed himself in her taste and her scent as she pulled him tight, her legs trapping him against her center.

She went back on her hands, her breasts rising and falling with gasps of breath. "I want you just like this. In your suit. All your clothes on. And me in nothing at all."

"Except the steel-toes."

"Sure," she agreed with a naughty little smile, "we can keep the boots."

He didn't mean to tear everything she owned, but she flipped all his switches. He couldn't think and before he knew it, there were only shreds of satin in his fist...and the silky-smooth feel of her skin, her thighs urging him on. He'd wanted to taste her, savor her, make this last forever.

But he couldn't wait.

She quickly undid his belt buckle and they unzipped together, he holding the zipper straight, she pulling the tab. A handful of beats later, he'd slid on protection, then he took her hips in his hands.

With one hard move, he thrust into her, so fast and deep she gasped his name. *Sebastian.*

For a few precious moments, he tried to slow it all down, to watch her, memorize her, savor her muscles tightening around him. Her color deepened, and heat rose off her flesh. She bit her lip, and her lids closed, fluttered, opened again, her eyes dazed with pleasure.

He moved, stroking that perfect spot inside her, then added the caress of his finger over her arousal. Then he lost himself completely in the clench of her slick heat around him. There was no holding back. He took her harder. Faster. Deeper. His lips found her mouth, and he swallowed her cries as she swallowed his. And they went up in flames together.

* * *

Charlie wasn't sure how they ended up on the floor, with her straddling Sebastian. It was a good thing he didn't seem to care that his suit pants were getting dirty. Because she couldn't move. She was boneless and sated, wanting nothing more than to stay in his arms, keeping him buried deep inside her.

"*Mmmm.*" She breathed against his neck. "I'm glad you came back early today."

He ran his heated gaze over her naked body. "No more than I am."

As hard as it was to leave him, she pushed off, using his shoulders for leverage, then held out her hand to him. "I still have so much to do."

He wrapped his fingers around hers and rolled to his feet, holding her close a moment, his hands all over her naked curves, his lips against her hair. "You're just too tempting to resist." He smiled down at her devilishly. "But I have to, don't I?"

"Yes, you do." Though a part of her prayed he wouldn't. All she had to do was say the word... But she didn't. They would have tonight, but the bow-legged stallion needed her now.

Sebastian left her to use the bathroom at the back of the workshop while Charlie scrambled into her clothes. The lingerie was toast, but she didn't mind. She loved how wild he got, tearing off the satin. It was so sexy, so erotic...

"I have a brilliant idea." She hadn't heard him come up behind her, but now he trailed his free hand down her waist to the curve of her hip. "You should always work naked."

She laughed. "Tempting." Especially if he came home early to do *that* to her again. "But I play with torches all day, remember?"

"In my bedroom, then," he murmured as he turned her in his arms to brush his lips over hers. "Naked. Just for me." Then he kissed all the sense from her brain, until she couldn't think of a single reason why she shouldn't comply. "I'll leave you alone soon," he said, but he didn't let her go, his hands resting at her hips, a tingling reminder. "But I wanted to talk with you about a couple of things."

"Ah," she teased, "so you did have ulterior motives for coming to see me today. It wasn't just to bring me beer and love me senseless."

"*You* are always my first motive. Everything else places a distant second."

He always knew the perfect words to melt her, but she leaned back against the workbench. The *couple of things* he wanted to talk about were already making her wary, even before she heard what they were. It would be easier to listen if she wasn't pressed tightly against him. Then again, just gazing at his beautiful face was distracting. "Hit me with those other motives."

"I'm glad you and your mother let me help with the move into Magnolia Gardens. It's clearly a much better place than Shady Lane." He paused, as if he needed to let that sink in first. "But I thought we could probably spruce up the furniture in your mom's room. Cushy chairs. A bigger TV. A bookshelf. And something that's not plastic for the balcony."

The topic threw Charlie off—this wasn't what she'd expected at all—but it was clear from the expression on Sebastian's face that he'd wanted to discuss it for some time. She fought back her instinctively defensive response, but ultimately couldn't stop herself. "They recommend that residents bring stuff from home they're comfortable with. But I didn't have room at my place to store everything from the house she shared with my father."

"We'll get her something new, then." He stroked the bare skin of her arm. It should have soothed her, but the subject was pushing her buttons.

Still, she tried not to read any criticism into what he was saying, especially when she'd also thought about sprucing up her mother's new bedroom a bit. "Mom would like that, I'm sure. Some pretty sheets and towels, in addition to the bedspread I was going to pick up for her. So it feels homey." She was totally ready to switch focus to something that would make her less edgy—which she knew was her deal, not his. "What's the other thing you wanted to talk about?"

"Actually," he said, easing into her so he could rest his hands on her waist, "I wondered what you thought of the food at Magnolia Gardens."

She could feel the frown between her brows and resisted the urge to scrub it away. "They had a great salad bar. Some stuff is probably better than others. I read that they have a brunch on Sundays with prime rib or turkey, baked ham or rack of lamb. I think it's good." She waited a beat, letting his hands on her ease her tension. Except that they didn't, and she couldn't help adding, "Didn't you?"

She was working very hard to keep her voice light, but she heard the strain threaded through the question, *Didn't you?* Because what she'd really meant was, *Don't you trust me to take care of my mom?*

He seemed to battle with himself for a long moment, his fingers flexing against her, before he nodded. "You're right. The food was fine, the gardens were great, and the doctors and the care seem good too." He stroked her arm, once, twice, maybe trying to soothe them both this time. "The last thing is good news. Remember the couple at the gala with the house out in Woodside? She had the koi pond."

"Vaguely."

That was a lie. All she remembered about the gala was the way he'd shoved her up against the elevator wall, ravaged her mouth, then stripped her out of her dress in the penthouse. He'd taken her to heights she'd never dreamed possible.

At the same time, she was more than happy to leave behind the topic of her mom's new nursing home. Sure, they might be able to find something better than Magnolia Gardens, but it would also cost even more than the shocking monthly amount she was currently paying. And though Sebastian could easily cover it, Charlie simply wasn't ready to let him take over. Even if he had a miraculous capacity to overwhelm her resistance to whatever he wanted, she wasn't going to bend on that one.

"The couple would like something with an Asian flair to sit by the pond. I said I'd set your creative juices loose on the idea."

"A commission?" Charlie ran her fingertips over his jaw, loving the faint hint of five o'clock shadow bristling against her skin. She'd doubted anyone would call after the hotel gala, but in a matter of days, Sebastian had made things happen.

"Yeah." He reached around her and grabbed one of the beers, popping the top for her. Then he raised his, tapping the bottle rims. "Here's to getting all the commissions you'll ever need."

Need? What had happened to inspiration? She thrust the thought aside because she truly did *need* all this for her mother. And Sebastian was so excited for her.

"They sent me a photo of the pond." He kissed the tip of her nose. "I'll show you later. And there's a party we should attend tomorrow night. We'll make great contacts for you."

Charlie sipped the brew. And it was surprisingly delicious. But another party? These galas could turn into work. And without an ounce of the fun part, like digging through junk shops and combing old worksites for the buried treasure left behind. Besides, she'd rather be working on the stallions. Or better yet, spending tomorrow night alone with Sebastian, making love in the workshop, in the hot tub, and in his bed. She wound her arms around his neck, the cool bottle dangling from her fingers, and pressed sinuously against him in anticipation of all that lovely, sweet sex.

"Charlie." Her name was raw with need as it fell from his tongue. His wickedly talented tongue. "You want the commission?"

"Yes. I want it." At least if the party was tomorrow night, she'd have time to find another dress. Considering his social circle, God forbid she should wear the same outfit twice. As for the koi pond, she'd happily think about a design for it later. "But right now?" She licked his earlobe, loving the growl deep in his throat. "I just want *you.*"

Again. It was so much easier to love Sebastian—with her hands, her mouth, her body, and her heart—than to deal with her emotions about her mom's infirmities or Magnolia Gardens, or even the commissions.

She pulled his mouth down to hers and kissed him until she couldn't think about anything else, until he grabbed both bottles and set them on the bench. Then he lifted her, and everything started all over again.

This was the only place she wanted to be—in Sebastian's arms, thinking about nothing but him.

CHAPTER TWENTY-SIX

Charlie stood in front of the mirror in the ladies' room of the San Francisco War Memorial Opera House, repairing the lipstick Sebastian had just deliciously kissed off her mouth. It was a lovely old building with classic Roman Doric columns—columns behind which they'd escaped for the luscious kisses that made everything worth it.

Since that day in her workshop two weeks ago, all the parties Sebastian had taken her to seemed to blend together. Tonight's benefit was for... Well, she couldn't remember. They were on the tail end of a dozen galas, benefits, and events where Sebastian was hell-bent on making her name as well-known as his.

She left the chattering crowd of women, returning to the grand entrance hall. Voices echoed in the high, vaulted ceiling, and tonight's crowd seemed almost impenetrable. She felt invisible in the crush, and honestly, it wasn't a bad thing. Charlie found herself craving quiet, empty moments more and more.

Just as Sebastian had predicted, the commissions were rolling in. So many, in fact, that she'd had to use the scheduler on her iPad. What's more, she was being written about—not as Sebastian Montgomery's new bit of arm candy, but as an artist. After the Regent Hotel opening, her work had been roundly praised. Even, shockingly, called *genius*. Soon after, Sebastian had convinced a group of reporters to come to her place in Los Altos, and then one newspaper had ended up doing a Sunday spread on Will Franconi's rock garden teeming with her Zantis. After learning he was a fan of *The Outer Limits* as well, she'd sent him a crate full. The commissions were mostly for garden works, smaller pieces than the elephant, rams, and lion. But an eccentric old guy from Palm Springs was fascinated with the T-Rex and was considering it for his desert ranch.

Sebastian was opening all the doors he'd promised. The possibility of a huge art career was deep in her bones now, not to mention a much bigger bank balance that brought her giant steps closer to making sure her mother could stay in the comfort of Magnolia Gardens.

He'd done so much for her. So how could she tell him she was tired right down to the roots of her hair?

What's more, she wanted, needed, *craved* the time to finish the chariot race. It turned her fingers to fire as she worked. The sculpture was her shining vision, and she could visualize the sun pouring through the glass ceiling, her stallions glowing like mythical creatures in flight.

Yet there was always another piece to slip in here or there, projects she hated to admit that she completed on autopilot as quickly as she could. Her only goal was to return to the stallions and their broken chariot. She hadn't even found a moment to start Noah's dinosaur.

Charlie sank down on a bench in an alcove out of direct traffic. She wasn't hiding. Okay, maybe she was. Just for a little while, until Sebastian found her and it was time to start schmoozing again. But her legs—and her soul, if she was being totally honest with herself—felt like they might give out if she didn't take a moment's respite.

She'd always assumed turning her art into a career would be a good thing. But she'd finally learned the downside to success— working on commission meant you weren't always doing what you were *inspired* to do, just what you *had* to do.

Which only made inspiration harder to find.

Take last week, when she'd visited a prospective client—God, now they were *clients!* The woman wanted a cherub or something equally mediocre for her garden. And Charlie had felt absolutely nothing. She couldn't have summoned a vision if the lady had offered a million dollars. But, with big Magnolia Gardens bills to pay, she'd signed up to make a cherub. Somehow she had to find a way to feel like an artist again rather than a worker on an assembly line.

She thought about slipping off her high heels to rub her feet, but, despite being sidelined, she was sure someone would see her. Closing her eyes for a few precious moments, she willed every thought to drain away. *Breathe in, breathe out.* Maybe it was the clearing of her mind that suddenly let in the voice. Or maybe it was Sebastian's name that made her prick up her ears.

"She's just a little nobody Sebastian found in the wilds of Los Altos. One of his *projects.* You know how much he likes to save the underprivileged."

Charlie didn't have to peek around the edge of her alcove to know that voice. Whitney Collins. Evan's wife sucked up to important people with the nicest, sweetest voice. The rest of the time, she was catty and mean.

"Now she's the toast of San Francisco because she's *sleeping with him.* Although what he sees in her is beyond me. I swear, she reminds me of an undomesticated animal. You can dress up the ratty cat, but we all know what's still beneath the sequins and pearls, don't we?" The women laughed. "Don't breathe a word of what I've said, of course. Evan will get his shorts all bunched up, even though I've told him in no uncertain terms that he'd better not bring home one of her *creations*." Her tone suggested Charlie's work was something you'd stuff in a doggie-waste bag.

Charlie slipped off her shoes and curled her feet up on the bench. Really, if she didn't care what Whitney said about her, then she *really* didn't care if anyone caught her massaging her toes. She recognized some of the other voices joining Whitney's, women who had fawned over Charlie earlier, told her how fabulous her art was, begged her to fit them into her schedule. Of course, Sebastian had been at her side. They were the mean-girl clique from every teenage TV movie, their glittery world filled with sycophants and backbiters.

Charlie wanted honesty and reality, and while there were absolutely some very nice people at these parties, too many in this brightly swirling society were on the opposite end of the spectrum. Which was why Charlie didn't care enough to feel hurt by the gossip. She loved the things she found in junkyards, and she'd never stop no matter what they said. Fortunately, there were enough people like Sebastian and Walter Braedon to drown out their catty negativity. As far as Charlie was concerned, all Whitney's comments did was reveal the mean-spirited woman she truly was, with beauty barely skin deep.

More than once, Charlie had wondered why—and how—Sebastian thrived in this world. But whether she understood it or not, the fact was that he did. She loved him, so of course she would fully support him in anything he wanted or needed to do.

And yet...she realized how important it was to him that she love it just as much, that she fit in and glitter as brightly as the rest of the peacocks. Yes, she'd met people she liked—the Mavericks, Walter Braedon, and many others—but there were far too many like Whitney Collins.

The very last thing in the world Charlie wanted was to hurt Sebastian in any way. But this social whirl was becoming harder and harder to live in.

No, she hadn't forgotten why she was doing this. To pay for her mother's care. And, honestly, to finally receive some validation and recognition for her art. But she'd begun to wonder if she wanted this new path of success and endless commissions as much as Sebastian wanted it for her. There were so many things she missed from her life before he'd walked into it and changed everything.

She missed her students, but she kept shoving all the letters from the college into that same drawer in the bungalow. She loved teaching, loved watching her pupils grow and stretch themselves. There were some that were all about gaining a marketable skill, getting a job, and having a career, which was great, but there were others who visualized masterpieces. She missed helping each one find the path he or she was meant to take.

She missed creating just for the sake of creating—following inspiration without a goal or a commission or even a plan.

And, oh, how she missed the quiet. Especially in the evenings, when she used to either curl up with a book or on the couch in Sebastian's arms.

Now, she was constantly on the hunt for appropriate dresses, heels, and hairstyles. She reached up to massage her face with one hand, realizing that even her jaw hurt from the constant smile pasted on her face.

Was it only a few weeks ago that Sebastian had asked her if things were better? It seemed like forever. Early on in their relationship, she'd known that having him in her life was better than any love story she could have dreamed up. But the rest of what came with loving Sebastian was still up for consideration...

"There's the congressman," Whitney's voice grated its way back into her thoughts. "I need a word with him."

Whitney passed Charlie's alcove a moment later without even noticing her. She thought fleetingly of confronting the woman, but Sebastian would probably hear of it and make a huge deal out of Whitney's insults. After his outburst about how toxic Whitney was, Charlie was sure he'd love taking the woman on. But Charlie didn't want a scene. It was just another thing to handle when all she wanted to do was get out of here, finish the chariot, then fall asleep in Sebastian's arms.

"There you are. I've been looking everywhere."

He leaned close for a steamy kiss, and she simply melted into him. When he finally drew back, she whispered, "You have no idea how much I needed that." She laid her hand on his stomach, all his beautiful muscles flexing beneath her fingertips. *This* was what she craved. Sebastian's smile, Sebastian's mouth on hers, Sebastian's arms around her. "Any chance we can head back soon?"

"Of course." Relief nearly swamped her. Until he added, "Ty Calhoun and his wife Julie want to meet you first—they have an excellent commission for you. Then I promise we'll go."

She recognized their names—he was a local pro football player and she was a prominent image consultant. Two more new people to meet. She could do it. If... "Another kiss first, please."

Sebastian gave it to her, hot and sweet but way too short. "There's more where that came from on the way home. Over every inch of your body."

"In the limo?" Oh God...just thinking of the things he could do with his hands and mouth made her want to drag him off to the limo, pro football players and their commissions be damned.

"Why do you think I brought the stretch instead of the helicopter? That way I don't have to wait until we're home to put my hands all over you."

She truly did love everything about him—the way he smelled, the way he tasted, the way his mind worked. Which was why she made herself put her feet down and slip the shoes back on. "Okay, let's do it. But only because you've promised me a very sexy reward when we're done."

He raised a wicked eyebrow and whispered to her, sending a delicious shiver through her. "Oh baby, it's going to be the best damned reward you've ever had."

He was her reward. Not just his touches or his kisses, but simply being with him.

She would keep going, for him, because he wanted so many good things for her. And maybe there would come a day when they wouldn't have to hustle, when they wouldn't have to worry about hoarding every dime for her mother, when she could create for herself instead of for everyone else.

They stood and she looped her arm through his. She'd get through this last introduction. Then he was all hers. Until the next party, at least.

There was no doubt in her mind and heart that she loved *him*.

Loved him so much that somehow, some way, she'd figure out how to endure his glittering celebrity world.

CHAPTER TWENTY-SEVEN

Charlie's scent filled the truck. Sebastian would never get enough of her. "I'm glad you could carve out some time away from your work to help out today."

Glad was the world's biggest understatement as they pulled into a San Jose neighborhood at seven o'clock on Wednesday morning. The community had planned the group home for teens transitioning out of the foster care system to provide a clean, safe, temporary environment while they looked for jobs and permanent housing. Unfortunately, the bond measure to raise the building funds hadn't passed, so Daniel had stepped in. Anyone working at his Bay Area stores was encouraged to lend a hand, and he'd volunteered the Mavericks too. He'd even flown Susan and Bob out from Chicago because they wanted to be involved. Their flight had been delayed, getting in extremely late last night, so they would arrive a little later.

Sebastian had looked forward to working on the community project. But it was all a million times better knowing that he could look up to find Charlie smiling across the room, that she was just a step away, a touch away.

It meant everything to him that she kept giving him the chance to get things right. Every stumble with her killed him—yet he'd done it again when he'd sounded as if he was questioning her judgment about her mother's new nursing home. What the hell was wrong with him? He knew Charlie needed him to believe in more than just her art. She needed him to trust both her choices and her financial independence. He didn't want to take over. He simply wanted the best for Francine. But wasn't he the one who preached to thousands of people that while it was important to support someone, it was equally important to know when to let them be free and be true to themselves? Which meant he had to stop circumventing her decisions when it came to her mother.

If he didn't want to lose Charlie, he had to let her be free to be herself.

And he wanted Charlie's love more than anything in his entire life. So he'd worked extra hard the past couple of weeks to let her do things her way and hadn't stepped in to fix everything for her the way he so badly wanted to.

"I'm excited about helping out." She squeezed his hand as he parked outside the big white shell of a house. The street was packed with work trucks and panel vans. "Even better," she added with a quirk of her lips, "working here today means we won't have time for another big party tonight." She climbed out, smiling as she closed the truck door.

She may have been teasing him, but he also heard the thread of truth in it. Since the benefit at the Opera House, they'd been to four galas in three evenings. Things with her career were progressing beyond his expectations—so well, in fact, that he'd started to worry Charlie was pushing herself too hard. He'd told her people would wait, but it was as if she feared the projects would dry up if she didn't complete them as quickly as possible.

But Charlie was as independent a spirit as he'd ever come across, and he'd sworn not to get in her way, letting her make her own choices. He would *not* screw up with her again.

Still, it was getting harder to keep his mouth shut, especially this morning, when he'd noticed the dark shadows beneath her eyes after they'd made love. Fear had hit him like a knife to the rib cage, fear that she was sick, that she was hurting, that she was burning herself out. He couldn't stand the thought of anything or anyone hurting Charlie. It was why he'd been hustling up so much business for her—if she wouldn't take his money, he had to do *something* to ease her financial concerns. But was he going about things the wrong way?

Could *he* be the one hurting her?

The thought that he might be toxic to Charlie had hit him harder than the mere slice of a knife. He felt completely gutted by the possibility.

For the past hour, he'd mulled over ways to broach his concerns without freaking her out—hell, he knew he had issues, and odds were his fears were nothing more than shadows popping up in the dark—but for a guy who talked for a living, it was pathetic to realize he had no clue how to phrase his thoughts. Just as his sketches were never quite right, now he couldn't find the perfect words to make sure his behavior didn't destroy the person he'd come to love most in the world.

"Sebastian?" Her hand on his arm, she'd moved closer, her expression clearly concerned. "Are you upset with me for saying I prefer this to the big parties?"

"No." He stroked her cheek. "Of course not." He was upset with himself for not paying attention to that fact. Every party they attended should have been balanced by a junkyard visit where she could discover magical pieces to perfect her sculptures. He would try to do that in the future, but it was so hard for Charlie to give up her workshop time during the day.

Except for *this* day. He made himself smile as he added, "I like getting my hands dirty too."

She stared at him a moment longer, as though she thought something lurked beneath the surface of what he'd actually said. Finally she smiled back. "I understand Daniel knowing his way around a tool belt. But you, with your fancy suits—" He was beyond relieved to see the teasing glint in her eyes again. "Do you actually know how to do all this stuff?"

"When we were growing up, everyone had to pitch in at the Spencer household when something needed fixing. Daniel's not the only one who can build a cabin from scratch."

"That," she said as she pressed closer, lifting her mouth to his, "just might be the sexiest thing you've ever said to me. Say it again."

Her lips were only a breath away. "One day, I'll build you a cabin from the ground up with my own two hands."

"*So hot.*" Her tongue licked out against his lips before she gave him a sizzling kiss right there on the sidewalk.

Her taste thoroughly fried his brain. He almost couldn't remember where he'd put his tool belt.

"It's in the back," she drawled, knowing exactly what she'd done to him.

He smacked one last kiss on her beautiful mouth, then grabbed his tool belt from the bed of the truck and called out to a couple of guys in the garage, who were checking off boxed materials on clipboards, "You know where Daniel is?"

An older man, his shirt sporting the Top-Notch DIY logo, hooked a thumb over his shoulder. "Inside."

With Charlie's hand in his, they climbed the wooden crates that had been set up as temporary porch steps. Voices carried from the kitchen and they followed the noise into a room crowded with Mavericks, the contractors Daniel had brought in, and a group of teenage volunteers.

"Glad you could make it." Daniel high-fived Sebastian, then leaned down to give Charlie a hug. When surprise flickered on her face, Sebastian realized she still hadn't accepted the fact that she was now a Maverick.

Standing next to Daniel, Will had his arm around Harper, her brother Jeremy beside them.

"Hey, Sebastian, Will said I could have a day off to come help." Jeremy's voice was big, enthusiastic, bright, and that described him to a T. He'd been hit by a car when he was seven years old and had suffered extensive brain damage. While he would always have the mind of that seven-year-old, he was the sweetest kid. Okay, he wasn't a kid at eighteen, but he was always so damn happy and optimistic. Just as Sebastian had told Francine's story at his last workshop, he'd told Jeremy and Harper's story too. Bad things happened sometimes, but people were capable of overcoming them.

Sebastian introduced Charlie, and Jeremy was immediately bouncing on his toes with excitement. "The Zantis are awesome, Charlie."

"Thank you." She patted his arm. "What do you think about having something of your very own? Maybe a sculpture to look like your favorite car?"

His eyes went wide. "Wow. A Birdcage Maserati sculpture would be way cool."

Matt had brought his son Noah, and the boy was already down on the floor playing with a plastic toolset, aided by a pretty, twentysomething young woman.

"Who's that?" Will asked. "Your new nanny?"

"Ariana works at my San Jose store," Daniel answered for Matt. "She had to rearrange some hours at her second job so she could be here today. Everyone loves her."

"She's great with Noah," Harper noted. "He's laughing as hard as he does when Jeremy gives him an elephant ride on his back."

Noah's laughter was a balm, especially to Matt, whose only desire was to see his son happy. He'd had a rough go of things with Noah's mother. Sebastian felt his pain. All the Mavericks did.

Speaking of pain, thankfully Evan hadn't brought his wife—God forbid Whitney should break a nail. Evan's sister-in-law Paige had come instead. Sebastian had always liked her. Though she was pretty, she wasn't the bombshell her sister was—at least, not until you saw her smile—and mercifully she didn't have her sister's explosive tendencies either.

"Okay, people," Daniel called. "I'll organize everyone into teams and assign your tasks. You're my leaders, and you'll be responsible for your team members. I'm including a list of kids on each task so they can get some experience. We want them to learn, so be patient and explain what you're doing, okay? Materials are in the garage and on the concrete pad out back. John does electrical and Roger is our plumber, so check in with them if you have questions. In addition to remodeling the kitchen, we're painting inside and out, installing double-pane windows and new floors, and redoing all bathroom fixtures, toilets, and showers—three upstairs, two downstairs. With all of us working hard today, we should be ready for the inspectors tomorrow. Here are the assignments." He grinned at everyone. "Let the fun begin."

* * *

Charlie and Sebastian were given kitchen duty and assigned two fresh-faced seventeen-year-olds, a boy named Ezekial (who asked them to call him EZ) and a girl, Stacey. As Sebastian laid out the base cabinet instructions on the floor, Charlie was again glad she'd come. If it turned out that she couldn't squeeze any college classes into her fall schedule, at least she'd have logged in a little teaching time today.

"We'll need screwdrivers." Sebastian pulled one from his belt. "Here's how we put the pieces together." He was fast and efficient, as if he used to install kitchens for a living, and the kids watched with interest, taking in everything he said and did. "And we're done." The cabinet, which would contain drawers, fit perfectly next to the stove, according to Daniel's floor plan. "Now let's do the corner cabinet that'll go beside it."

Instead of letting them try themselves, Sebastian put that one together too. Charlie didn't want to take over, but since teaching was a big part of the exercise, when Sebastian started to take on a third cabinet solo, she had to butt in.

"We probably need to split up and each take a cabinet, or we'll never get them all done." She tried to make it sound like an idea rather than a comment on his training skills.

For just a moment, frustration flashed in his eyes, then it was gone. He nodded and everyone took a carton to start work.

Charlie was usually a pro at this sort of thing, but honestly, today she was having trouble focusing on the job at hand. Sebastian was so damned sexy in his tool belt. And when she started to have visions of him wearing *only* the tool belt and nothing else? Her hands actually trembled, she wanted to reach for him so badly.

As if she'd transmitted her thoughts straight to him, their gazes met over the kids' bent heads. The look of love brimming in his eyes wrapped around her, as though he held her heart carefully in his hand. God, she loved him, falling deeper with every day, every moment.

She'd seen him on stage and at what seemed like a million galas, but it was a whole different level of sweetness to see how kind and patient he was with the kids. When Stacey started screwing in the corner cupboard carousels before they'd mounted the cabinets, he didn't get mad or banish her to the garage to fold cardboard for the trash. He simply said, "We'll hang the cabinets first, and *then* put in the carousels and drawers, okay?"

"Why?"

Sebastian was already moving ahead and said only, "You'll see."

Charlie touched Stacey's arm. "Since the cabinets are actually mounted on the wall, it's easier to hang them and get them straight when they're empty."

Stacey smiled at her. "Thanks, it helps to know that."

Meanwhile, EZ had forgotten to use the level on the cabinet mounting bars, ending up with one side lower than the other—and

Sebastian had already stepped in to fix it while EZ stood back and let him.

Just as Charlie decided to butt in again, suggesting that EZ fix his own mistakes, she was interrupted by a gravelly male voice. "What have we got going on in here?"

A smile a mile wide creased Sebastian's face. In the open garage door, the big, bald, ruddy-faced man enfolded the much taller Sebastian in a bear hug. Then Bob stood aside so that Sebastian could gather Susan into a hug as bearlike as the one Bob had given him.

It was obvious who the couple was given the affection and adoration in Sebastian's eyes and voice. Charlie felt her chest squeeze tight. These people might not be his birth parents, but they meant the world to him.

"I've got someone I want you to meet." Sebastian held out his hand to her. "This is Charlie."

The fact that he didn't say her last name—that she was just Charlie—meant he'd told these special people about her.

Susan took both her hands, giving Charlie's heartstrings another strong tug. "Charlie, I couldn't be happier to meet you. I read that article about your sculpture at the Regent Hotel. I'm so delighted for you."

"Thank you. And it's so nice to meet you too. I've heard such amazing things about you and Bob." She smiled at the lovely, fiftysomething woman. "And Sebastian hasn't exaggerated a bit."

A few inches taller than Charlie, Susan had a trim build, an engaging smile and knowing eyes. When she glanced at Sebastian, then back to Charlie, it was as if she knew everything, approved, and accepted. Charlie warmed all over. The only woman she'd ever felt total acceptance from was her mother. But with one little sideways look, Susan Spencer made her feel as though she could be a Maverick.

"Now, where are the rest of my boys?" Susan called, and Jeremy immediately came running.

"Grandma!"

After fifteen minutes for all the hugs and hellos, Daniel put his parents to work in one of the second-floor bathrooms. They all settled back into their jobs, until twelve-thirty, when Daniel blew a whistle like a drill sergeant and yelled from the front room, "Lunch break, everyone! Pizza in the backyard."

"I didn't notice before," Charlie said to Sebastian after everyone had headed out to the yard, "but now that I know there's pizza, I'm starving,"

"I am too. Starving for this." He grabbed her up in his big arms, right off her feet, and planted a kiss on her mouth before dropping her back down.

One kiss and her heart was galloping like her stallions. "There are youngsters here." Her smile ruined the effect of her teasing admonition.

"They can watch and learn, then." His grin was bigger than hers as he put his arm around her, guiding her to the backyard. She loved the sweetness of it, the ease of his touch, his smile, as if they'd been together forever.

Outside, Daniel had set up canopies for some shade. Thank goodness there was a decent breeze to cool down the warm afternoon. Susan waved an arm at her. "Charlie, I've saved you a seat." There was only one deck chair available next to her.

"You okay with this?" Sebastian asked Charlie softly.

"Why wouldn't I be?"

"Because Susan clearly wants to grill you on everything we've said and done—and probably on when you're going to commit to having my firstborn."

"Trust me, I'm going to grill her right back about you."

He looked a little shell-shocked at her return volley. She grabbed a slice of pizza and a soda, then took the seat Susan offered. Heck, she felt kind of shell-shocked herself. She hadn't thought much about marriage or a family, but having kids with Sebastian sounded so good...as did everything that came with it, including his ring on her finger.

"Lord, that sun is bright," Susan said from behind an oversized pair of sunglasses. "Daniel tells me he's going to build a deck and lay in a drought-resistant garden, front and back, with drip watering." She scuffed her shoe in the dirt and lowered her voice. "I know it's impractical out here, but I do love a nice green lawn."

Still stunned by the vision of herself in a long white dress, walking down a rose-strewn aisle toward Sebastian, the best response Charlie could come up with was, "Me too."

Despite Sebastian's threat, Susan didn't pry at all. She simply asked about Charlie's work and then talked about her boys. Her deep, abiding love for every one of them shone in her voice, her smile, and the softness of her gaze. They were all her sons, not just Daniel, and each of them had special qualities. She clearly loved her daughter no less.

"Lyssa is traveling through Europe on her own." Susan said. "She's so adventurous. I'm not sure I could have done anything like that when I was her age. And I certainly couldn't do it now."

"Of course you could. Just imagine." Charlie closed her eyes dreamily. "You and Bob floating through Venice on a gondola." It was so easy to picture the scene with Sebastian at her side.

Susan laughed. "Bob would get seasick."

"How about drinking wine with fresh bread and cheese at a Tuscan villa?" She could easily while away the hours with that divine daydream.

"I'm lactose and gluten intolerant."

Charlie stared at Susan's straight face for three seconds, then said, "Maybe you shouldn't eat the pizza."

Susan laughed heartily, from deep in her belly all the way to her eyes. "I like you, Charlie—you let me joke around."

"I like you too." *Especially because you took in Sebastian when he badly needed a family to love him. Thank you for being there for him, Susan.*

Just then, little Noah let out a squeal of delight from across the yard. "Isn't he a doll?" Susan's face turned mushy with love.

Matt's son was incredibly cute as he drove a toy dump truck through the dirt. With the help of Paige and Ariana, the young woman who worked for Daniel, Noah loaded his truck, though he appeared to be getting more dirt on himself than in the toy. "You go, Noah," Sebastian called out. "Fill up that truck with all the rocks so your Uncle Daniel doesn't have to move them later on. They're too heavy for him." He scooted quickly out of range of Daniel's elbow.

"Sebastian's going to make a wonderful father someday," Susan said.

"Yes, he will." Sebastian would love any kid he had with everything in him.

"Speaking of family, I'm sorry about your mother's health. Sebastian has mentioned her more than once." Susan's gray eyes were misty with empathy. "Being in pain all the time must be terrible, and so hard for you to watch."

"Thank you for your kindness." Charlie smiled softly, though she stiffened slightly, nervous that Susan might add in her two cents about letting Sebastian do more. "It is hard, but Mom's always upbeat."

"Your mother's new home sounds lovely. You're Sebastian's hero, with your dedication to caring for her. As busy as you are, I'm amazed you still manage to visit twice a week."

Charlie shot a look at Sebastian. He'd told Susan all the good stuff and none of the bad. He hadn't said that Charlie was hesitant about the doctors he'd found or that she wouldn't take his money to help with Magnolia Gardens. Had he really called her his hero?

"Sebastian bought Mom a lovely china tea set," Charlie wanted Susan to know. "Will and Harper picked it out. That's become part of her ritual too."

"He's a good boy." Susan was quiet a moment before looking straight at Charlie. "I'm sure you've noticed that he thrives on helping."

Charlie nodded. "He's amazing with the people at his seminars and he's been so nice to the kids this morning too." Even if he hadn't always stopped to let them learn by doing the work themselves.

"His heart is in the right place. Always. But..." She paused, as if wondering how Charlie would take what she was about to say.

"Sometimes he doesn't know when to step back a bit and stop helping."

"It's only because he thinks everything needs to be perfect." His need for perfection had driven him to hide his sketchbooks from the world. He wanted everything to be perfect for her mother, and for Charlie's career. Somewhere along the way, he'd learned that perfection was crucial. Though as far as Charlie could see, Susan obviously wasn't the person who'd taught him that lesson.

Susan's eyes lit with hope. "You understand him, don't you?"

"I'm trying to." Charlie took a deep breath. "I love him." Once the words spilled out, she couldn't stop the rest. "I love him so much that all I want is to make him happy any way I can."

"He wants the same for you, Charlie." Susan took her hand and held it tightly. "Promise me you won't give up on him."

"He's the most incredible man I've ever met. I'll never give up on him." *Never.*

"You're a strong person. An independent woman who clearly knows her own mind. And Sebastian has never been as happy as he is now, just from being near you. Do you know what else I see, Charlie?" She paused, holding Charlie's gaze. "That he loves you exactly the way you are."

CHAPTER TWENTY-EIGHT

Daniel broke the moment, clapping his hands and announcing that their break was over. Charlie and Susan only had time for a hug before heading back to their posts.

He loves you exactly the way you are.

Charlie still wasn't completely sure about that. Yes, Sebastian loved her—she believed that with everything in her, with his every touch—but he also had a vision of the celebrated artist and socialite he wanted her to be. He'd never say it—maybe wasn't even aware of it. But she didn't know how long she could live up to that vision.

She still had so many more questions for Susan, so many important things she needed to know. What had Sebastian's relationship with his parents been like, particularly with his father? How had he dealt with their passing, given that they hadn't made the changes he'd so hoped for? What had Sebastian been like as a teenager? Had he always been so positive, so sure that everyone was capable of change? And why he was so intent on keeping his artistic talent a secret from everyone? Charlie was almost sure Susan had to know about his drawing.

Unfortunately, she couldn't sneak away when she was in the middle of assembling drawers with Stacey. She would have asked Sebastian all her questions face to face if she could be certain they wouldn't upset him. He'd been almost feral the night she'd found his sketches. She couldn't do that to him again. All she wanted was to support him and his art, not tear him down by forcing him to face a painful past.

Charlie sighed, wishing, not for the first time, that there were easy solutions to everything—from how to move Sebastian past his block about his talent to keeping up her stamina during the endless stream of galas and new commissions. Long days full of hard work, evenings full of sequins and small talk, and moonlit nights wrapped in Sebastian's arms tumbled into one another faster than she could believe. She'd found love, but that didn't mean life suddenly became an effortless walk in the park.

Glorious. Breathtaking. Heart-racing. Yet still completely confusing at times.

She watched him, brimming with all her emotions.

"We'll apply the adhesive to the wall, then press on the tiles," Sebastian explained, and like a typical teenage boy, EZ grunted in response. "We need to get the squares straight along the line I've drawn." Instead of letting EZ try, Sebastian fit the next square, turning it a couple of times before finding the right position and pressing it into place. "We also want to make sure we don't get any black ones side by side." EZ nodded and handed Sebastian another tile set, then another.

Sebastian was doing it again, telling rather than letting EZ do the work.

Stacey was cooking along nicely with the drawers, so Charlie left her to it, sauntering close to lean against the doorjamb next to the empty spot the stove would fit into once the backsplash was done. "Looking good." Before Sebastian could reach for another tile, she added, "Let's see what you can do, EZ."

"Me?" EZ put the fingertips of both hands to his chest, his brown eyes wide.

Charlie laughed. "Yeah, you. You've been watching Sebastian closely enough."

Sebastian glanced at her with an expression she couldn't quite read. Then he nodded. "Sure." He cleared his throat. "Good idea. Lay some in, EZ."

The edge of tension thrumming through Sebastian's voice was subtle enough that EZ wouldn't notice. But Charlie heard. Still, Sebastian was as encouraging as ever, complimenting EZ's technique as he worked.

Once Stacey finished the drawers, she joined them to watch EZ press the next pieces into place on the adhesive. Clearly distracted by the pretty girl, he pushed it a little higher than the straight line Sebastian had drawn.

"You're doing great, especially considering it's your first time," Charlie said, feeling Sebastian tense beside her. She wanted to shake the person who'd taught him there were ugly consequences to imperfection. She not only learned from her mistakes, but sometimes they even led to her best accidental creations. "When you're doing this kind of work, it's good to pause and take the time to check things out," she coached EZ.

"Cool, will do." EZ backed up a couple of steps, then said, "That side's a little high, isn't it?"

"Good catch," Sebastian said, smiling at the boy. "Why don't you look at the info on the bucket of adhesive to see if it's still okay for you to adjust them." While EZ and Stacey both squatted down to read the fine print, he turned to Charlie. "Can I grab you for a second?"

* * *

Leaving EZ and Stacey to work on the tiles, Sebastian took Charlie's hand, leading her outside to a semi-private spot beneath one of the backyard canopies. "Thank you."

"Is that really what you want to say to me?"

He appreciated the fact that she didn't pretend she had no idea what he was thanking her for. "At first," he made himself admit, "I was annoyed when you stepped in. I know you teach, but I do too. I know what I'm doing...at least, I thought I did."

"You're great with the kids—"

"But I was still screwing up. I didn't want the tiles to be laid in crooked so I stopped teaching and started doing it for them instead." Through the window they could see how well the two teens worked together, figuring out a great tile pattern all on their own. "Now they're doing better than I was."

Charlie smiled. "You're welcome." Then she put her hand to his cheek. "Who ever made you feel you had to be perfect?"

He tensed. He didn't want to get into it, not now, as if he were whining about his childhood *again*. "I don't need to be perfect."

She studied him. He thought she'd push, but her gaze roamed his face, then she looked down at his mouth as if suddenly making a decision. And she stepped into his arms.

Her mouth was soft and sweet against his. Yet again, he couldn't believe his luck. From the Opera House last Saturday night to a young adult group home in San Jose was a major difference. He loved watching Charlie wend her way through a ballroom, wearing another of the sexy little numbers she and her mom were so good at putting together. But Charlie in jeans and a work shirt *really* got his engine going.

Every time he looked at her, every time their lips met, a wave of emotion rolled over him, swamping him. It was more than mere desire, more than need. He wanted her in every part of his life, not just his bed. She brought laughter and joy. She brought him meaning and new goals. He needed to help her take her career to the very top, to ease her mother's suffering, even to be her family. While she had only her mother, he had the Mavericks. They weren't his blood; they were so much more than blood. And he wanted to share his family with Charlie as well as her mother.

Susan was probably the only other person in the world who got away with stepping in to guide him when he needed it. Like Susan, Charlie was smart, and even more, she was diplomatic. No wonder she'd chosen to augment her art career by teaching. She was great with people, instinctively knowing when to offer a suggestion and when to back off, letting her students learn for themselves.

Yet he couldn't help but worry how she'd do both once classes started again in the fall. She was already working on the chariot and her new commissions from six in the morning to six at night—not to mention the hours he kept her in his bed, loving every beautiful inch of her, never able to get enough. How much more could she possibly fit in? The number of galas and events would ease up a bit after the grand opening and the sculpture's unveiling, but he couldn't see how adding her teaching into the mix would be a good thing at this point.

"Have you made a decision about your classes yet?" He hadn't pushed her since they'd talked about it with Francine.

"They don't start until the end of September, so I still have a little time to decide." She glanced back at the kitchen. "Now that they've got the tile covered, we should finish the cabinets."

Clearly, she didn't want to talk about it any more than he'd wanted to talk about his father or his past. Because it was *in* the past. But this was Charlie's present, and he was too worried about her budding exhaustion to let it go. "You've got a lot of commissions. I can see what a great teacher you are, but you don't have to go back, you know."

"I know that." She went quiet for a long moment. "Like I said, I'm not sure what I want to do yet." Her voice squeezed with a note of frustration. As if she felt conflicted. As if *he* made her feel that way.

And yet it was his duty to watch out for her. He wasn't pushing. He was simply offering. "Charlie." He ran his hand down her back, her muscles stiff under his touch. "You can talk about it with me."

She looked up, and for once, her beautiful eyes weren't clear. She'd gone inward, shutting him out.

Damn it, *no*. He wouldn't let her shut down, couldn't bear the thought of it. He needed to keep their connection strong, no matter what it took.

"Come with me." He wasn't thinking straight, but he didn't care as he led her to a shed by the back fence.

"Where are we going? We need to get back to the kids."

No one had been in or out of the shed all day. The door wasn't locked and he pulled her into the bare, clean space inside. The lone window was too high in the peak for anyone to see through.

"The drawers can wait." He pushed the latch shut on the shed door. "This can't."

* * *

Charlie had loved everything about today. There'd been no need for all the schmoozing required by the crowded, impersonal galas Sebastian loved. If she fell asleep exhausted tonight, it would be due to a hard day's work using her hands, not because she'd worn herself out with small talk. The Mavericks welcomed and accepted her. It didn't matter that they were all wealthier than Saudi princes. She *fit* with them, like Susan and Bob or Harper and Jeremy, or even Paige.

If only Sebastian hadn't asked her about her classes. But she'd started it by poking at his past, asking about why he had to make everything perfect. She shouldn't have brought that up, because it had only led to his questions. And now her insides were all twisted up. There were all the letters from the college in the drawer at the bungalow. She *had* to make a decision. After Labor Day, the kids would start signing up for classes, and hers would either be in the catalog or they wouldn't. She had to do *something*.

She knew what Sebastian wanted—he'd opened the doors to a bona fide art career and clearly thought she should step through, reaching for the success right at her fingertips. Charlie had never been foolish enough to think she could do everything. She understood you had to make choices about what you could and couldn't do, and that if you took on more than you could handle, you'd fail. Yet her heart wrenched at the thought of telling her dean she wasn't coming back. Lord knew she'd far rather give up all the parties, the endless schmoozing, being on, on, *on* all the time.

Any way she looked at it—and sometimes she felt that was all she did, examine the situation from every possible angle—she couldn't do that to Sebastian. Not when it would be ungrateful, and worse, it would seem as though she'd chosen teaching over him.

Something had to give—either teaching or the parties. But there was one thing she absolutely *would not* give up. Not for anything in the world.

Sebastian.

She wanted him with a need that scared her sometimes. Her fear abated when he touched her, looked at her, when he loved her late at night in his big bed until she was boneless with pleasure. And she knew he was in as deep as she was.

But then a new day dawned, and alone in her workshop all those bigger, heavier storm clouds still gathered above her. If she couldn't figure out how to survive in his world of important parties and even more important people, did she stand to lose everything? She honestly wasn't sure how long she could keep on being that perfect celebrity. One day—and she could feel it coming soon—she'd slip up. She'd snarl instead of smile. She'd snap instead of laugh. She might even scream.

"You want to talk yet?"

Despite the heat in his eyes, he was giving her another chance to open up to him. But she was so knotted inside. Too twisted up to talk anything through right now.

"Not yet." His arms were open and she stepped right into them. "But I need this. I need *you.*"

Thankfully, less than a heartbeat later his mouth crushed hers and he hauled her up to wrap her legs around his waist. Backing her up to the counter, he set her down, so thick and hard between her legs that she whimpered.

He yanked her tank top up, then pushed aside her bra and closed his lips over her nipple.

She writhed against him, holding him tightly in the vee of her thighs. *"Sebastian."* There was such need in her voice, such desperation.

"You make me nuts." He kissed her lips, her neck, the hollow of her throat, while his fingers worked the button and zipper on her jeans. Faster than should have been possible, her pants and boots hit the floor, then her panties. He trailed his lips down her body, licking, tasting, his eyes dark with desire. "I need to taste you." He nipped her thigh, kissed her belly, circling ever closer. "I need to feel you come apart and hear you cry out my name."

He covered her with his lips and there was no more talking. There was just his mouth on her, his fingers inside her. Charlie curled her hand in his hair, holding him close as he took her. There was such sweetness in letting him take over, and the moan in her throat becoming a cry of pure pleasure.

His touch eased all the knots in her stomach, made her forget everything she was supposed to think about. She could only make little sounds, leaning back on her hands, opening herself to him. He was gorgeous, sensual, always needing to please as much as to take his own pleasure.

He held her hips in his hands, forcing her to take everything he had to give. Sensation spiraled up inside her, deep, into her core. Her stomach muscles clenched as the first swell of her climax hit. She panted, then lost it all, falling back on the counter, writhing wildly, crying out his name in broken syllables through wave after wave of ecstasy.

She'd barely come down before he'd rolled on protection and entered her, so deep, so fast, so exquisitely, that she lost what was left of her breath. Holding her tightly, melding their bodies, he forced her higher, pushed her limits. Then he catapulted them over the edge together and she flung her arms around him, kissing him so deeply she tasted pleasure. She tasted reckless abandon.

And, most of all, she tasted love.

CHAPTER TWENTY-NINE

"Isn't the garden lovely?" Francine sighed blissfully a couple of days later.

Sebastian was seated with her at a café table, having just finished a lap around the Magnolia Gardens walkways. "There's some nice shade under this tree."

"Yes, and the breeze truly makes it an idyllic spot."

Francine was radiant. Despite her infirmities, she always looked to the brighter side of things, even if it was just the weather. Sebastian had learned a long time ago that there were two ways to consider life—choosing to see the negative or the positive. Your choice was what defined you, and Francine was a happy person.

Sebastian tried his best to be happy too. Unfortunately, since working on the group home in San Jose, his frustration had been building. All right, it had been building longer than that, for weeks, since Francine had first brought up Charlie's fall classes. Yet Charlie still wouldn't talk to him. If he so much as hinted at her decision about teaching this fall, she completely shut down on him.

For the third time in his life, he had absolutely no idea what to do. First with his parents. Then with Francine's health. And now with the woman he loved—and would do absolutely anything for. But she was too damned independent to let him.

Since their tryst in the shed behind the group home, he'd barely let her take a breath without having his mouth or his hands on her. Even if she still wasn't ready to talk to him, he would damn well make sure they didn't sever any of the threads that connected them. She clearly needed time to decide she could trust fully in him, and he was forcing himself to give her that time. He always wanted her, but now more than ever, making love to her until her limbs were jelly and she was hoarse from crying out his name seemed the only way to keep their connection strong.

He worked to shove away the frustration as Charlie returned with the china plates and mugs, one pastry split with her mother and a whole one for him. Francine truly looked as though she was in heaven as she took a delicate first bite.

"Oh my dear, I'll never tire of these." She closed her eyes in rapture. "Your father, God rest his soul, would have gotten fat, wouldn't he, honey?"

Charlie laughed. "He probably would have."

"So does that mean I'm going to get fat if I eat a whole one every time I come to see you?" Sebastian asked.

Charlie merely smiled at him and said, "You'll work off that bun in no time."

She was right. In fact, he'd already burned plenty of calories in the shower with her that morning...with more plans for tonight.

The same thought simmered in Charlie's eyes and in her secret, sexy smile. "Come to think of it, maybe I should start working out more often too."

Her mother *tsk*ed. "You take after me, honey."

"That's why she's so gorgeous," Sebastian said.

"You're such a shameless flatterer," her mother said with a roll of her eyes and a sweet smile.

When the plates were empty, Charlie put her hand on his arm. "Sebastian, I've got a huge favor to ask."

Her tone was surprisingly serious for the mellow day they'd been having. "Anything for you." They weren't just empty words. It was a promise he planned to keep until the very end. He needed her to know that.

She stared at him for a long moment before rummaging in her enormous bag. Then she pulled out a sketchbook. He glanced from the pad to Charlie's face, his breath tight in his chest. Was she really blindsiding him?

Guilt flickered across her face. But right behind it was determination.

And love.

"It would be great if you'd sketch Mom." She held out the pad and one of his pencils, her hands the slightest bit shaky.

He stared at her offerings for several beats, a hint of anger swirling in his gut. No, not anger. *Fear.* The two emotions could so easily be mistaken for each other—but if he were totally honest with himself, he'd have to admit he wasn't angry at Charlie.

He was simply scared.

"Oh, Sebastian." Francine's voice was warm and comforting. "I didn't know you were an artist."

"His drawings are amazing, Mom."

They weren't. He'd known it since his father had pointed out every flaw, every mistake, and laughed at the crap his kid had drawn, throwing all his sketches into the fire. Knowing Charlie believed in him despite those flaws was the only thing that kept Sebastian in his chair.

Francine put a hand to her cheek, her fingers bent, her skin mottled with age spots. "You can't possibly want to draw an old woman like me. You should draw Charlie, instead."

"I want to see you through Sebastian's eyes, Mom." She touched his arm again, smiling hopefully. "He has very special eyes."

He couldn't possibly decline. There was no choice. Francine needed this drawing, if only to show her that she was worthy of being seen. And he was so damn tired of listening to his father's voice. He would not allow his fears to hurt this lovely woman. He would overcome them, if only for this moment.

And there was no question about it, Charlie was not only a brilliant diplomat—she was a master strategist. Especially when her actions came from pure love. However misguided she was about his talent, she'd never meant to hurt him.

He finally took the pad and pencil from her. Leaning forward, he pressed his mouth to hers, letting her know he wasn't angry with her.

He tasted the relief on her lips, and hoped she could taste his love for her on his. Even if he'd never drawn in front of anyone before, and was honestly scared shitless. He could stand on a stage in front of tens of thousands of people, absolutely calm and in his element. But in this moment...

It felt like he was trying to walk the mile Francine had just walked.

"Drink your coffee," he told them. "Have a chat. Don't mind me."

His voice sounded stronger, and more confident, than he actually felt. Then, with Charlie's warm smile on him, he began to draw. She chatted with her mother about the new friends Francine had already made, told her all about the group home, the Mavericks, Susan, Bob, Noah, the kids working on the tile. She repeated the word *family* and by the fourth time, he was so glad to realize she'd felt like part of his family. Finally, she understood that she was a Maverick.

As the women talked and his pencil flashed across the page, he felt pretty good. For a while. But then...

His tension started to rise, higher by the second. The drawing wasn't right. Wasn't perfect. He could show off Francine's bright eyes, her childlike delight, her enthusiasm, but something about her face didn't hit the mark. He wanted to capture the webbing of fine lines, contrasting it with her sweet smile and illustrating the woman who was strong enough to endure. That was the real Francine, but he couldn't do it. Couldn't master any part of the sketch. Couldn't do Francine justice.

You drew this crap? You drew all these pictures of me looking like shit? His father's voice rang through his head as if Ian Montgomery had risen from the dead and was standing right in front of him. *My stupid, worthless kid thinks he's an artist. But he's nothing. I'll show you where your pictures belong, you little shit.*

Sebastian erased the lines and started over. He would not let his father get the best of him. But when he tried once more, the voice he couldn't get out of his head was even louder now, and he had to erase again.

"May we see?"

Charlie's voice abruptly jolted him back to the present. To the garden at Francine's nursing home—and the sketch he was all but erasing holes in.

He took a breath, silently counting to four before replying. "Let's work on this drawing later." He made himself smile for them both, feeling it stretch too far across his face until it resembled a grimace. "I can sketch your face from memory, Francine."

But Francine was already holding out her hand. "Please, Sebastian," she said with a sweet, appreciative smile, "don't keep me in suspense."

He couldn't hurt Francine's feelings, would never forgive himself if he did. So he handed over the sketch, hiding his reluctance. It was ten brutally long seconds—he counted each and every one of them—before she looked at him again.

"You've made me beautiful."

"Of course I did. You're very beautiful, Francine."

"I'm old, Sebastian. Old people are usually completely invisible. But I'm not anymore. Not when I look at this wonderful picture you just drew. Look how marvelous this is, honey."

He swallowed hard as Francine handed Charlie the sketchbook.

Whereas Francine had taken only ten seconds, Charlie had barely looked down at it when a sheen of tears swelled in her eyes. Her smile trembled. "This is beautiful." She held the sketch to her chest, as if she needed it next to her heart. "The most beautiful drawing I've ever seen."

* * *

Charlie had begged her mother to let her keep the drawing—and Sebastian had promised to do another of her very soon. It lay on Charlie's lap as they drove back up Highway 880 to Sebastian's mansion on the hill. She smoothed the edges with her fingers. "I'm going to frame it and hang it on the wall."

"You're going to frame it?" Sebastian got that panicked look she only ever saw when he was talking about his art—or his parents. "You've got to let me try again. I'll make a better one."

They'd stayed late at Magnolia Gardens and now traffic was gridlocked. But for once, Charlie appreciated it, because it meant Sebastian was her captive audience. "You can draw my mother as many times as you want, but you're not getting this one back. It's mine now."

Sebastian was silent for a long moment. Long enough that she prayed he finally understood just how special his gift was.

"I wanted to convey her strength of character. But I couldn't get it right."

"You *did* get it right," she said, frustration seeping into her voice despite her attempts to hold it in. "This is my mother the way I remember her when I was a child. Before the pain. You've captured her heart as a young woman."

"That's great, but I still didn't draw what I wanted to draw."

Why was it so hard for him to believe in his own art? "You might not have meant to sketch her like this—" She stroked her mother's jubilant face. "—but it turned out to be magic. This drawing makes me remember cookies baking in the kitchen and the dolls she used to knit. Can't you see? That's what art is all about. How you make a person *feel*."

He kept his capable hands on the wheel, switching lanes, eyes on the road. "You love it because you love me."

She almost growled at him. She'd shamelessly tricked him into sketching her mother, but even though she and her mother had been moved to tears, it clearly hadn't proven anything to him.

Why could he see everyone's brilliance but his own?

CHAPTER THIRTY

Early Sunday morning, Charlie had to drag her butt down to the studio. Between working on the house in San Jose, a Saturday afternoon barbecue with the Mavericks, then heading straight to another event that Sebastian was absolutely convinced could be critical to her career—she hadn't even had the energy to make love last night. She was pretty sure he'd carried her in from the car, undressed her, pulled the covers over her, then given her the softest, sweetest kiss on the forehead before whispering, "We'll take tomorrow night off. I promise."

God, she prayed that wasn't a dream. *Please, please, please, not again tonight.*

Utterly exhausted, she dropped down to sit on the bare concrete floor and stared at her magnificent stallions. Once upon a time they'd been so alive to her. Now they were mere skeletons. She just didn't *feel* them anymore, and she was so tired that she couldn't get her brain to focus on the vision she used to have.

But Sebastian was trusting her to create something truly amazing for his building. And she'd had a powerful vision of the two of them working side by side, showing their art together—a vision she would give anything to see come true. With only three weeks to go before the grand opening of his headquarters, she would get through the rest of the work even if it killed her.

At this moment, it felt like it would. Even her teeth were tired. All she could manage was coffee, hot and extra sweet. Just the way she liked Sebastian, she thought, but smiling was beyond her.

"Have you eaten?"

Thinking about him must have been like a psychic telegraph message, because there he was. Big, beautiful, sexy. Perfectly silhouetted in the open barn doorway.

"No." She was starving. But not only was she too tired to make herself something, she was too tired to get up and walk into his arms.

Sebastian approached, a tray balanced on his hand. "Eggs Benedict." He sat down with her so they could eat right there on the floor, bending over the plates on the tray. She managed half of hers, plus a piece of toast and some freshly squeezed orange juice.

"You spoil me." The food helped. She was still tired, but now she might actually be able to get up off the floor at some point today and start her work.

"I love spoiling you." He leaned in for a kiss that was as delicious and sweet as the orange juice.

When he helped her up, she swore her knees creaked as if she were her mother's age. She might be exhausted, but that didn't mean she'd given up her plan to bring Sebastian out of his artistic shell. "I've got a brilliant idea."

"All your ideas are brilliant."

He was so quick to praise her. But so hard on himself. "Draw me while I'm working, Sebastian."

He frowned at her. "Charlie."

"Please."

"I have work up at the house."

She worked to bite back her frustration. Frustration that had grown monumentally with every day that passed, because he simply wouldn't trust her when she told him he was a great artist. "You own the company, which means that while you might have work to do at the house, you can probably shift the timing of it around if you really need to." She pressed into him. Using their attraction to get him to concede might not be fair, but... *All's fair in love,* she decided. "Pretty please."

"You know I prefer to draw when I'm by myself."

She wanted to kick something, not him, just *something*. "It doesn't have to be perfect."

"I know." She could almost hear his teeth grinding when he said it.

Should she push? She knew his past was painful, and she hated bringing it back. But how was she supposed to do anything for him when she didn't know exactly what had happened?

"Who taught you that you had to be perfect?" she asked gently, as though the more softly she spoke, the easier it would be for him to answer.

"No one taught me anything. I just like drawing for myself." His knuckles cracked as his fist bunched. Watching him broke her heart into ragged halves. And she wished she'd kept her mouth shut. He hadn't been ready the last time she'd asked, and he wasn't ready now.

She was afraid he never would be.

She pretended she'd never brought up the subject, adopting a teasing tone. "All right, then I won't look at you while you're sketching. I'll pretend you're not even here." She licked her lips and fluttered her eyelashes. "But you can look at me all you want."

She was surprised by his sudden kiss—rough, raw, and so passionate that her head was spinning by the time he drew back.

"That was *way* better than just looking," she murmured, her voice breathless. She put her hand over his chest, felt his heart pounding hard and fast beneath her palm. And she understood that his kiss was a way of deflecting the question he didn't want to answer. "Is that a yes to sketching me?"

He breathed in, held it, then finally exhaled on a sigh. "We're different. You go into yourself as if you're not even aware of me while you're working. But for me—it's a hell of a lot harder to know you're watching me make one mistake after another." His explanation was actually a concession, giving her a piece of what she so desperately wanted to know.

She wanted to make him see it didn't have to be like that. "Can't it just be for fun? You don't have to figure me out. It doesn't have to be good." Pressing her lips to the side of his neck, she licked his deliciously warm skin. "Come on, for me?"

"I don't have a sketchbook."

He was finally bending. She could feel it, and she nearly shouted with glee, but managed to contain the victory. This was a start. All the rest would come eventually—at least, she prayed it would. "I've got a clipboard with some paper." Instead of getting them, she pushed against him, his scent and his heat wrapping around her. "I'll give you a reward later."

Looking down at her, his eyes were suddenly deep. "What kind of reward?"

"Whatever you want," she whispered.

"Anything?"

"*Anything.*" Heck, she was almost ready to give him the reward right now, before he'd so much as made a mark on the paper.

He lifted her wrists, circling them with his hands. "Have I mentioned that I have some brand new leather wrist ties at the house that I've been thinking about a lot lately?" She was nearly panting as he added, "Looks like they'll be just the right size."

"So it's a deal?"

He sealed his mouth to hers, stealing all her thought, her breath, before he whispered, "It's a deal."

She danced away to get him the clipboard and pencil, suddenly energized from the gourmet breakfast. From Sebastian all predatory and sexual. From knowing he'd sketch her while she worked. And then there'd be lusciously hot nookie afterward.

Turning to her stallions, the vision suddenly burst to the surface, the shot of energy Sebastian had given her starting her creative juices flowing again. All at once, she could see why the horses looked skeletal. Because they *were*—just bare metal rods stuffed into pipe fittings. The rods needed filling out so that they emulated the curve of muscle and the suppleness of sinew. Somehow over the past weeks, she'd forgotten the brass pipes she'd found at the construction sale. They'd be a perfect fit.

She dove in to create the effect she wanted. But she didn't forget Sebastian, not for one single second. Seated in one of the deck chairs he'd brought in weeks ago, he balanced the clipboard on his legs, his hands gliding over the page. After a while, he started asking questions, and she was happy to answer them, especially if it meant he would keep drawing.

"You're doubling up on the rods?"

"I'm going to augment what's there with the pipes. The brass will look like sinew and that will flesh out the muscles."

He drew as he spoke, his fingers flying. He looked up, down, tipped his head one way, then the other. He talked, she answered and explained as she manipulated the metal and tack-soldered the pieces into place.

When she got to the welding itself, however, there was just her, the metal, and her torch for long enough that at some point Sebastian got up to leave. Immersed in her work, she hadn't wanted to shut down and pull off her mask to ask where he was going. Not until he waved a ham sandwich under her nose, the aroma so tantalizing that her stomach growled raucously.

"You're a life saver."

Throwing off her gear, she slid down into the deck chair next to his as a new wave of exhaustion hit her. Hard. The work had sustained the flow of energy through her body until the moment she'd stopped. Now she honestly wasn't sure she could get out of the chair.

Seating himself next to her, Sebastian jutted his chin at the stallions. "You were right, they needed filling out. Now you can see they're racing like the wind."

"Before, they were stick figures." She took a bite of the simple sandwich, then closed her eyes and sighed. Sitting down was as delicious as the honey-roasted ham. "This gives them depth."

"You never cease to amaze me. The way you envision your art and how you work. You try this thing, then that thing, changing it until finally the work perfectly matches your vision."

"Isn't that what every artist does?" She spoke without thinking as she drank thirstily from the frosty mug he'd brought.

"No."

The simple word said it all. By this point she was too tired—literally a million miles past exhausted, all the way down to her bones—to keep pussyfooting around the issue. She was going to help him, damn it, whether he wanted her to or not!

"Can I see the drawings you did of me?"

* * *

Charlie's tone was different. Not harder exactly. Not frustrated, either. But no longer the gentle persuasion she'd used before.

Her love for him still laced every word, but Sebastian instinctively knew that didn't mean she'd back down any time soon. Just as he'd wanted to facilitate her career by finding her all the new commissions, she wanted to return the favor. The difference, however, was huge. She was a brilliant artist who deserved every accolade. He was little more than a hobbyist. Still, he wouldn't hide the sketches from her. He'd made that mistake once, and he wouldn't make it again.

He handed her the clipboard.

"Oh my God, Sebastian." He'd caught her down on her haunches scrutinizing the weld on a horseshoe as if she were a vet examining a hoof for an abscess. "They're fabulous."

Of course she'd say that. She probably even half believed it. "They're okay," he said as mildly as possible. And by *okay* he meant *crap.*

Holding up the clipboard, she tapped the picture. "Tell me what could possibly be wrong with it? You've caught my concentration, even the squint while I'm studying that weld. Your drawings make me actually *feel* how hot it is in the room. And I swear the horses are going to fly off the pages. You really can't see how brilliant your drawings are?"

"You have a vision, Charlie. You pound your work into submission, work and rework metal and parts until it perfectly meets your vision." His gut felt completely wrenched as he admitted, "I don't know what my vision is. I never have."

"You keep talking about this *vision* thing as if it's a big deal. Keep saying it's *perfect.* But half the time I hardly know what I'm going to do with something until I stick it on somewhere and finally see its true purpose. And we both know my work isn't perfect—how can it be, when I'm slapping together disparate pieces of junk all day? It can't be perfect, but it can make people *feel.*"

"You don't think I wish I could make people feel what I want them to feel when they look at my drawings?" A massive wave of frustration rushed through his veins, and he stabbed so hard, his finger nearly sliced through the paper. "All I wanted was to show your concentration, your focus, your drive. But I can't get down what's in my head. I never could."

"Maybe that's it," she said slowly. "Maybe you should stop trying to *make* people feel one way or another. Stop trying to control other people's emotions through your art and just trust that they will feel *something,* whether you intended it or not." Carefully, she smoothed out the drawing. "You might have been trying to show my drive and focus, but I'd much rather you did what's on the page instead—you showed my *heart,* Sebastian. And I've never felt more beautiful or more appreciated than when I look at this drawing."

But if he'd truly drawn her heart, then why couldn't he understand what she really wanted? Half the time he thought she was doing everything for her mother. Sometimes he even thought she was doing it for him. Lord knew she had enough commissions to take her into next year. Her bank account would be full and her mother cared for.

Yet he sensed Charlie wasn't happy—and was becoming less and less happy by the day. He had no clue how to fix that. Was she focusing on his sketches simply as a way to get him to slow down the pace of everything else?

"All I want is to understand you, Charlie. And to make you happy." She'd be done with the sculpture in three weeks. Twenty-one days that felt like a ticking time bomb. Despite knowing that they loved each other, he was beyond frustrated that they hadn't figured out anything else. "Tell me how to do it. Tell me what I can't see or fully understand." Because he didn't want to screw things up again.

"Do you really want to know what would make me happy?" She smoothed a hand over the four sketches in her lap. "That reporter from the big magazine you got in touch with—she's coming next week and she wants to show the artist at work. Your drawings are good enough for that article."

He didn't equivocate, just gave her a flat, "No."

But she was just as stubborn as he. More, maybe. "It would be awesome, Sebastian. Your art and mine on the same page. This is a *perfect* opportunity for us to do something together."

"No," he said again, his voice harsh this time. "Drawing is just for myself. I already have a career."

"I know you do. But I see the way your hand flies over the paper when you draw. And how, despite your fears, you're totally alive in the moment. You have to know you're not alone—every artist who lives a creative life deals with fear and uncertainty. None of us have any idea how things are going to turn out—but that's part of the magic. And that's why I'm here. To tell you that I trust you, that I'll be right here, right beside you every step of the way, believing in you until you can believe in yourself." She balanced on the edge of her seat, gesturing in the air, her sentences a rapid-fire burst. "You just asked me what I want you to see. What I want you to understand. *This* is what you need to know, how amazing your art is. I know it would be exposing yourself, but I do it all the time and I can tell you that—"

"You're not exposing *yourself*, you're exposing your art. It's not the same as what you're asking of me."

"I *am* exposing myself every night." She clenched her hands together, so hard her knuckles turned white. "At those parties we're always going to. I always have to be *on*."

His gut was torqued so tight he could hardly breathe. In the back of his mind, he knew he should pause, take a breath, step back and look at things objectively. But he was already way past any of those choices.

"Those parties are about introducing people to your art. They're about creating massive anticipation for the chariot and stallions. Once you're huge, once you're at the top, you can call all the shots, Charlie." He reached for her hand. "*Soon.* It will happen soon, I know it will, and then it won't all seem so crazy and nonstop."

"If it's all about my art and not about me, then we should just wheel one of my sculptures from party to party." She tugged her hand from his and ran it over her face. "Dressing up, schmoozing every night for endless hours. I'm so tired I can't even create anymore." She looked at him, her eyes suddenly swimming with tears. "I don't even know if I can finish the stallions or the chariot, Sebastian. I'm burned out."

He reached for her, but she almost seemed to shrink from him. *Jesus, what had he done?*

"We'll take the whole week off if you want. Or I can attend the parties by myself and talk you up. I'll stall any other projects you get until after the chariot is done."

But she was no longer focusing on him. She looked at the stallions, then her hands. "And there's my classes. If I want to teach in the fall, I need to put my syllabus together."

God, he was such a fool. Last night she'd fallen asleep in the car on the way back from another event. She hadn't woken even as he carried her into the house, not when he undressed her, not when he whispered to her and kissed her good night.

How could he have done this to her?

"Maybe you should take a few months off school." It was the first thing that sprang to mind, a surefire way to stem the flow of lost hours. "You can go back in the spring."

In an instant, she blinked back into total focus. "That's your solution? I need to give up teaching?"

"Not give it up." He felt as though he were watching himself from a distance, shovel in hand, digging the hole deeper and deeper. And yet, he still couldn't figure out how to drop the handle and call for a time-out. "Just take a quarter or two off while you see how things go and how much time you have in the future. I can't stand the thought of you burning yourself out and losing even an ounce of your brilliant artistic vision. Anything but that. Tell me what I need to do to fix this, Charlie, and I swear I'll do whatever I can to make you happy."

* * *

"You've already done so much. And I appreciate all of it, all the doors you've opened."

"Charlie—"

She held up a hand to stop him, both from saying more or coming closer. She was going to break if he didn't stop. She might break anyway. She was *this close* to crying. To exploding into a million pieces and gushing until she could fall asleep. That's all she wanted to do—sleep. Until she stopped feeling like she was a hundred years old.

"I *am* grateful. But you expect me to slather on all the glitter and let you parade me around among all those people. Night after night, putting on a mask that I'm having trouble fitting over my face. I'm not the glittery celebrity type, and I'm tired of trying to pretend I am." How could he not see how much of herself she'd exposed for him? "Why can't you see that I don't fit into your world?"

"Of course you fit. Everyone loves you. They love your art." He stretched out his hands to her, and the pain on his face and in his beautiful eyes cut her in two. Worse were his two whispered words: "You're perfect."

"No! I'm not perfect." God, she hated that word! "No one and nothing is. Not even the priceless pieces of art hanging on your walls." The last thing she wanted was to hurt him. But she couldn't go on like this. Couldn't keep pretending when it was ripping her to pieces. "I'm just like a Zanti Misfit, Sebastian. I sneaked into your world and pretended I was like all of you." She couldn't bear hurting him, but everything she said was true, and it broke her heart. "The truth is that I don't *want* to fit in anymore. I miss my students. I miss working on whatever I feel like working on without worrying about getting paid for it. I love the stallions, but all the other commissions are just busy work. I never thought it could happen, but I'm losing all my joy in this. And do you know what I miss most of all?" Two tears slid down her cheek. "You. I miss spending time with you. Just the two of us getting closer. Sometimes lately, it feels like you're so far away."

"I'm right here, sweetheart. Right here." Before she could stop him, he cupped her face so gently, so sweetly. "I just wanted to make sure you had the money to take care of your mom. Because you wouldn't take mine. I don't want you to ever have to worry about anything. Why do you think I've done a thousand drawings of you? I needed to figure out a way to get you there, to keep you safe. But I couldn't do it, couldn't figure you out."

It was like the kids at the group home. His heart was in the right place even as he micromanaged, finding solutions instead of letting them make their mistakes and figure it out for themselves. He wanted all the lines straight—was so intent on everything being *perfect,* that he forgot magical things happened all the time if only you just stopped trying so hard.

She folded her hands over his and held them tightly. "Do you remember telling me right after we met that you were keeping your eyes open and visualizing what you wanted for me?" Before he could respond, she went on, "I know all you want is the best for me, because that's exactly what I want for you. But it took me this long to realize that I can't live the life you visualize for me, no matter how good it might be. I'll only be happy, truly happy, if I take care of my mother my own way, not your way. And I have to manage my art my way, not yours. I love teaching too, and I *hate* the thought of not having students to work with this fall."

She'd been trying to make up her mind all these weeks, but suddenly it was crystal clear. Giving up teaching would be losing an important part of herself. One that was a crucial piece of what made her whole.

"If something else has to go, then it will, because I'm not giving up my classes."

"I'm sorry." A tremor ran through him, and she hated feeling as though she'd just ripped his heart to shreds. "I'm so damned sorry," he whispered.

"No," she told him. "Don't be sorry. Not for onc single thing. Not for one single moment. I know I'm not."

He breathed in deeply, flexing his fingers under hers. He was a helper. He fixed things. He took care of people. When he couldn't do that, he was lost. But knowing that didn't make the desolation on his face any easier to take. His pain ground her insides to mincemeat.

But she knew what they both needed. Time. To take a breath. To think clearly again. "I need to see my mom. Alone this time. And I think it would be a good idea if I spent tonight at my place. That way I can focus on my class syllabus."

An ache that came from deep inside threatened to pull her apart...but she still made herself walk away, out of the workshop, on legs that felt like they'd collapse with every step. She wasn't walking away because he'd done anything wrong. On the contrary, when the dark clouds appeared, when the shadows crept closer, she hadn't put the brakes on. Instead, she'd let that first bit of adoration and celebrity turn her head. She'd let the promise of financial security turn her work in a direction in which she should never have let it go.

She had a lot of things to unravel. Maybe she couldn't sort them all out tonight. But she could at least make a start. Tomorrow, she hoped she would be one step closer to being the *real* Charlie Ballard again.

But would Sebastian be able to love that woman, without all the glitter and all the fame to go along with her?

CHAPTER THIRTY-ONE

The workshop was too damned quiet. Too big. All wrong without Charlie.

Sebastian hadn't moved since she'd left him. He'd barely been able to think, to process a damned thing when he already missed her so badly his whole body felt cleaved in two.

The four horses—closer to looking like real, living creatures now, and brilliantly, beautifully executed beyond anything his imagination had conjured—stared at him mercilessly from across the space. And they judged him harshly.

She really loved you. And you screwed it up, hurt her in the worst way possible. The woman who always created from her soul and heart actually stopped enjoying her work. She stopped loving us.

The last word seemed to hiss in the air, condemning him.

All these years, Sebastian had been so sure, so certain, that he'd eradicated his old demons. But he'd been lying to himself. His father's voice still shouted inside him every single day. He wanted to climb onto that chariot and let the wild horses drag him through the streets until all of it was gone. His father's cruel laughter. The pain of his childhood. And worst of all, the hole in his heart where Charlie should have been.

If something else has to go, then it will.

Charlie's words played over and over in Sebastian's head. And he knew. His worst fears had just come true.

Because that *something* was him.

He couldn't blame her for leaving. Everything she said was true. The first night at the Regent might have been fun for her—new, different, exciting. But after that, he'd forced his vision on her, believing it would solve all her problems. All *his* problems. It would make her a star. She'd have the fame, all the work she could possibly want, and all the money to take care of her mom. That was *his* vision. Just as she'd said, he'd tried to make her into a glittering celebrity. But no matter what she thought, she hadn't just fit, she'd conquered. She wasn't the ugly duckling—or a Zanti Misfit—she was the gorgeous swan. She was bright, intelligent, and talented, and she fit his world perfectly in every way.

Except that she didn't want it, didn't love it. And that was the most important thing of all—that she loved what she did with her life.

Charlie wanted a normal life, wanted to build animals out of junk in her workshop just for fun. He'd been pressuring her in directions she didn't want to go. He should have seen it when she didn't want the dress, when she wouldn't accept his money. The signs had all been there.

He'd wanted to make her happy, but she'd been so much happier before he'd pushed her, before he'd run her ragged. He'd brought her to this, had pushed her to the point where she'd said, *I can't even create anymore.*

Charlie's lifeblood, her truest joy, came from her art. If she lost her art, her joy would be gone too. He'd never forgive himself for taking that away from her. Never.

He wanted Charlie happy. He wanted her laughing. Instead, all he'd done was cause her pain.

Susan had tried to tell him he pushed too hard, but he just wouldn't listen. Not when he thought he knew best. Not when he was so busy keeping all the lines straight.

Except that Charlie wasn't a straight line. She was elephants and dragons and dinosaurs and Zanti Misfits. She was magic, his unexpected.

And he was her toxic other half.

Everything inside of Sebastian went still and freezing cold.

He hadn't wanted to imagine a world in which he and Charlie could ever be toxic to each other—or worse, where *he* was toxic to *her*. But that was exactly what he was—the worst thing for Charlie. Just like his dad had been toxic for his mom. Like Whitney was for Evan.

You could love someone to death—and that was what he was doing to Charlie, crushing her spirit and her independence. Crushing her joy.

Just like his mom and dad. On her own, Mom might have gotten clean, but his dad was always the one who said, "Come on, honey, let's have some fun tonight. We can stay home tomorrow if you want."

His father had been drawn like a moth to the party flame...and though Sebastian's parties were shinier and prettier, they were still noise and distraction and the buzz of always being surrounded by people, their voices and laughter drowning out everything else.

Like his father, Sebastian thrived on his events. That's where he made his contacts, did his business, lived his life, all in the public eye. And that had been fine until he'd become driven by the relentless need to sell Charlie's magnificence, to sell her art.

The stark realization that he might be more like his father than he'd ever thought possible made everything painfully clear for Sebastian. He'd vowed he would stop screwing up, and yet he kept on doing it, kept on driving Charlie, deciding what was best for her. And he couldn't stop, despite all his promises, because he didn't know how.

Charlie deserved all the happiness and all the joy in the world. Sebastian couldn't stand the thought of seeing her destroyed by his choices or his desires. And yet that was exactly what he was doing, dragging her into his world and tearing her apart. But it *was* his world, it was how he lived. He didn't know any other way. For her sake, for the sake of her art—because Charlie lived and breathed her art—he had to walk away. He couldn't get down on his knees and beg her to come back to him. He couldn't let her see his heart break open and his guts bleed for her.

He'd thought it had been hard to leave his parents, but this would be light years worse. No wonder his father had never cut his mother loose, though he had to know he was destroying her. Just as Sebastian had come close to destroying Charlie, forcing her from party to party, one after the other, sometimes even on the same day, and supplanting her art in the process.

Cutting Charlie loose was the very last thing he ever wanted to do, and the hardest. But he would not be like his parents, damn it. He would not be like Whitney and Evan. He would own up to the painful truth that he was the worst thing for Charlie, the toxic component of their relationship that drained all her inspiration and her creativity.

She had all the new commissions. She'd do great on her own. When the chariot was unveiled, she would become the talk of the art world. The critics would love her, and art patrons would wallow at her feet. He would die a little more every day without her. But she would thrive, would pick and choose her commissions, take only what she wanted. And she would never again have to worry about Francine.

Don't be sorry. Not for one single thing. Not for one single moment. I know I'm not.

Lord...he was so damned sorry. He'd never wished so badly that he could rewind time and get it right, that he could have torn off the blinders before it was too late, before he'd pushed Charlie so far in directions she'd never wanted to go.

Even if he could do those impossible things, there was only one way he could be absolutely sure to keep Charlie safe and happy, full of her vision and creativity. Though it would kill everything inside him, he would do it.

He would set her free.

CHAPTER THIRTY-TWO

"Honey, what's wrong?" Her mom's face creased with worry, and she held out her hands.

Charlie had barely set foot inside the room, but her mother knew her so well. It had been at least twenty years since Charlie had run into her mom's arms, but she went down on her knees in what felt like the only safe place left in the world.

"Everything's gone terribly wrong." Charlie's words were muffled by the fabric at her mother's chest. She lifted her tearstained face. "I should have told him I didn't want to go to all those parties or take all the commissions, but I didn't mind it at first. All this time I've said I'd never change myself for anyone, but wearing the pretty dresses and making the dumb cherubs for society patrons were all tied into helping y—" She clapped her hand over her mouth. She'd been on a rant, not thinking about what she was saying or how it would make her mother feel.

"Oh, honey." Her mom stroked her hair so gently that tears clouded Charlie's eyes once more. "I know you've been turning yourself inside out for me. A thousand times I've wanted to tell you that you've already done more than enough."

"That...that's what I'm always telling Sebastian."

Her mother smiled. "Does he listen any better than you do?"

"No." Charlie took a shaky breath and let it go. "Neither of us listened." Then she'd woken up this morning and found she simply couldn't breathe anymore. "I didn't even give him a chance to listen today." She'd blasted him with all her frustration, then told him it would be best if she processed everything alone. As though she would be a better, smarter version of herself without him. Only, that could *never* be true.

Her mother held her gaze, her eyes serious and full of deep love. "Then go back. Make sure he hears you. And while you're at it..." Her mother squeezed her fingers with the little strength she had, and yet it seemed so mighty. "Make sure you're always listening to what's in your heart too. Even if it scares you. Even if it doesn't feel like it makes sense. Trust yourself, honey. I always have."

The tears spilled down Charlie's cheeks. Her mother's words seemed to echo what Charlie had tried to make Sebastian understand about his art. *Trust your heart.* Because Sebastian's art came straight from his heart. He just hadn't learned how to trust it yet.

Her mother had asked Charlie what her mile was, the one she needed to walk every day. Now she knew. It was this—committing to Sebastian with no more reservations, no more holding back, no more running away or keeping secrets, no matter what.

Charlie wasn't a quitter.

And Sebastian was worth fighting for.

* * *

Sebastian had been sitting at his computer for the past hour trying to write the damned email that would set Charlie free. An email that would let her know he loved her with every beat of his heart and every breath he took. That was why he had to let her go. Because he was toxic for her. Because he knew she'd be happier without him pushing her into a scene she didn't want to be a part of. Because he knew the art world was her oyster, even if he wasn't there with her. And that he would always be her biggest fan, would always appreciate every single masterpiece she created.

But just like his drawings, the words wouldn't come out right. *Dear Charlie* was as far as he'd gotten. Hell, it felt like he barely had a grasp on the English language, for all the success he'd had stringing together sentences that made sense.

Maybe because his chest was so tight he couldn't get enough oxygen to his brain.

Maybe because nothing made sense without Charlie in his life, without holding her in his arms or waking up to see her beautiful face lit by the first rays of the sun.

Or maybe it was because he'd been lying to himself all these years about knowing the right words, about believing in yourself. *Just believe and all your dreams will come true.* Charlie was his dream, so much more than any dream he'd ever dared to have.

And now...

He shoved his chair away from the desk so hard the whole thing toppled over, crashing to the floor. He didn't care. Didn't care if every piece of priceless art sitting on his shelves fell and shattered into slivers.

He'd never let himself get truly drunk before, not even when he was a teenager. He'd always been so careful not to turn into his father.

It had happened anyway, hadn't it? He'd become toxic to the woman he loved.

His hands shaking, he poured himself a full glass of whiskey. With his gut a coiled mass and his chest so tight he was choking, he raised his glass to the memory of his father, then tossed back the liquid in one harsh gulp. The whiskey seared his throat going down, burned all the way into his heart, setting fire to the image of his father laughing at him.

His grip on the glass tightened until his knuckles turned as white as the ghost of his father. Then, with all his anger, all his fear, all his grief, he threw it against the brick fireplace.

"Sebastian?"

He spun. Charlie, lips parted, eyes wide, stared at the mess in his office, the remaining whiskey in the bottom of the glass still dripping down the brick. He'd never needed to let her go more than he did in this moment. Right now, when she saw it all, saw him at his worst.

But he couldn't get the words out. Couldn't find the strength to tear off the shackles he'd bound her with. Not even when she strode to him through the glass, her steel-toed boots crushing the shards. She was so beautiful, everything he'd ever wanted, everything he could *ever* want. She owned his heart and soul.

"I'm not running again." Her words were quiet but firm. Utterly determined. "No matter what."

"*Charlie.*" It was the only word he could push out of his burning throat. Her name was both a prayer and a desperate plea not to give up on him, even after he'd given up on himself.

"I have so many things I want to ask you. So many things I want to tell you. But first—" She held out the clipboard of sketches he'd worked on this morning, forcing him to look. "I'm going to tell you what I see when I look at this drawing." She traced the lines of the sketch with one fingertip. "I see me. The *real* me."

He had to say, "You're far more beautiful than that." His hands could never bring out her true beauty.

"Maybe I am, but this is my essence," she insisted. "This is when I'm at my best. When I'm working. You show that with every look you give me, with every kiss, and with this too." Another step closer, glass crunching beneath her boots. "Now it's your turn. Tell me what you see, Sebastian," she whispered. "What you *really* see, not just what you're afraid you see."

He *was* afraid. Not only of being an artistic failure, but also of somehow diminishing her in the drawing, as his father had accused him of doing so long ago.

"He threw my sketches into the fire." The words were out before he even realized he'd opened his mouth. Tonight his control had fled, gone after all these years of locking his secrets deep inside, hiding them from the Mavericks, from Bob, even from Susan. "My father found my drawings. When I was twelve. Of him and my mother. He hated the way I'd sketched him. Said I made him look like a weak drunk." Only Charlie's hands over his kept Sebastian from falling back into that night in the filthy living room. "All I wanted was to help him, help my mom. But he and his friends tossed my drawings into the fire, and they all burned while they laughed." Angry, bitter laughter that had echoed inside him with every chink in his walls. So he'd built those barriers higher, thicker, hiding that secret part of himself. Until Charlie. Until he fell so deep, so recklessly in love, that all the walls had shattered like the whiskey glass against the fireplace.

Charlie gently cupped his cheek. "What did your mom do?"

"Passed out," he said as softly as the feel of her skin against him. "She never saw a thing. Never mentioned it. She was almost like a shadow around the house."

"That's why you stopped drawing, isn't it? Why you've been hiding all your sketchbooks ever since. Because your father—" She spat out the word in disgust. "—sent your dreams up in flames." She wrapped her arms around him, holding so tightly it felt as if she could weld the pieces of his shattered heart back together by the sheer force of her will to heal him. "Yet you still tried to do everything you could for them."

"I spent my teenage years trying to fix them. I believed that if I poured enough liquor down the drain or got them into rehab or AA, I could change them. I believed I could find something to replace whatever they were missing." He stared at the whiskey glistening on the bricks. "But maybe there's a part of me that's just like my father," he whispered. "Maybe that's what all the parties and galas are about. He needed his parties too, craved them as much as he craved his next drink."

She drew back, gripping his shoulders to force him to meet her gaze. "Don't you ever say that. You're nothing like him. And those parties were all about helping me. There's *nothing* wrong with you."

"Then why couldn't I fix my parents?" He needed to find a reason.

"It was never your job to find their solution for them." She ran her strong, yet gentle, hands down his arms. "They had to find it for themselves, and they never could. They might never have been capable of it."

He'd never wanted to admit the painful truth that some people simply didn't have the strength to change. People like Bob and Susan had just as many trials in their lives, but they'd never given up. But his parents hadn't even tried.

"They did one thing right, Sebastian. They helped make you who you are. Between them, they raised a man who has the strength, the passion, and the heart of ten men."

"That was Susan and Bob and the rest of the Mavericks." He wanted nothing more than to wrap her tightly in his arms, but he had so much to confess before he could do that. "I tried to do the same with your mother. New doctors, new treatments, as if I had the power to change everything for her."

"I love that you wanted to try. But after we've done everything we can, we have to accept things the way they are and make the most of what we have. I love you for your empathy." As if she'd had a sudden painful thought, she stiffened slightly against him. "I'm so sorry I made it sound like everything was your fault. It isn't. Not even close. I was wrong for fighting you about contributing to Magnolia Gardens."

He ran his fingers through her hair. "I understand your need to take care of that yourself. I pushed all the parties and the commissions because it seemed like the only thing I could do for you."

She rested her hand on his chest, her fingers stroking lightly. "I know. And I was afraid of letting you take over, as if I'd lose my independence." She shrugged. "I've always taken care of my own responsibilities, so it was hard to accept anything from you. But I was wrong. I told you I loved you, but I never turned my whole heart over to you. I was always holding something back, because—" This time she was the one swallowing hard. "It's the same reason I thought I should drop teaching when my art career started to take off—because it's the reasonable, streamlined thing to do. I mean, why would anyone keep a lower-paying job when every hour she spends making sculptures can earn so much more? But I've realized that's who I am. Someone who does things that don't make sense to everyone else, who tosses together those jumbled pieces of life in weird ways no one else could imagine. But it works for me. If I ever tried to change who I am, I'd only be destroying an important part of myself." She trembled in his arms. "Can all those jumbled-up, junkyard pieces of me be good enough for you?"

"*Yes,* damn it." It killed him that she needed to ask. Didn't she know that she was everything to him, exactly the way she was? "You're the best person I've ever met, the most amazing woman I've ever known." He grabbed the clipboard and this time he made *her* look at it.

In the sketch, she wore her face shield, her gloves, her smock, her boots. The sparks of her torch flew out all around her, almost like a halo. The lines of the horse she worked on weren't perfect. They were a work in progress. And he saw something he hadn't known he'd added until she made him look. The face shield's reflection showed lines that weren't there yet, the perfect lines that were still in Charlie's head, lines that would eventually grace the horse itself. Because Charlie could fix anything.

"Do you see?" His whisper was gentle, but firm. Determined. For the first time ever, he could see one of his own drawings with total clarity. "Whatever you set out to do, you truly make the imperfect extraordinary. Not perfect, but amazing all the same." He put his hand under her chin to make her look at him. "How could I not love you? How could you ever think you weren't good enough for me?"

She was silent for a long moment, before she finally said, "I wasn't listening to all the things both of us were too afraid to say to each other. But they were there all along and I'm listening now, Sebastian." Her voice beat inside him, became a part of him the way *she* would always be a part of him. "I wish you'd told me about your drawings, what your father did. It explains so much. He was the one who made you feel you had to be perfect, that your art had to be. And he made you think that the truth you tell in your drawings is bad, when the exact opposite is true."

He nuzzled her hair. "I'm sorry. You asked, and I tried to pretend it wasn't a big deal. But I will always tell you everything. No more secrets. No more hiding. And I'll always listen."

"Then let me tell you what I'm going to do," she pushed on in a low, seductive, mesmerizing tone. "I'm going to teach my classes in the fall. I'm going to put the other commissions on hold while I finish the chariot race for your building's grand opening."

His blood pulsed wildly. "And then?"

"Remember, I'm a Zanti Misfit. With me, you have to expect the unexpected. So after our grand unveiling, I want to wing it." She smiled her gorgeous, beguiling smile. "Being without a plan and letting the unexpected happen won't send our lives down the tubes. In fact, something tells me that's when things are going to become more magical than ever. You see, I've decided to stay for keeps. You're not getting rid of me. And we'll figure out how to make this work. Together."

She leaned close to brush her mouth across his. She couldn't know how he'd longed for that when he believed he'd never feel the sweet caress of her lips again.

Lord, he wanted nothing more than to take everything she was offering—her complete and unconditional love. And yet, beneath everything, there was still that one unavoidable fact. His way of life was toxic to her, and he'd never forgive himself if he continued to hurt her.

So instead of losing himself in her kiss—in her—he forced himself to speak the truth. "What if I do it again? What if I push too hard? What if I hurt you?"

Always doing the unexpected, she smiled. "We're both clear that I don't want to be the glitter girl you want me to be. But I do want *you*. And I get that figuring it all out might be messy. It won't always be easy to decide where I should draw the line on my junk and where you should draw the line on your parties." She pressed a finger to his lips when he began to open his mouth. "And you aren't like your parents, craving the next party. For you, there's a *purpose* for it."

No, he definitely didn't crave it the way he craved Charlie, her touch, her kiss, *her*.

She gave a delicate shrug of her shoulders. "But life and love can be messy and hard. That doesn't mean we chuck it in. We aren't Whitney and Evan. We certainly aren't your parents. We're strong enough to keep at it until we find the right compromise." She barely took a breath as she said, "We won't always be perfect, but we can make this work. We can be *magnificent,* because what we have is the best thing I've ever known. *You* are the best man I'll ever know. And I refuse to give up on you. So are you going to give me up without a fight? Or are you going to walk the mile right beside me every step of the way, no matter how hard it is?"

He felt what she was saying deep in his marrow. *Come on, baby, fight for me like I'm fighting for you.*

His parents had never fought for each other. But he and Charlie weren't his parents, damn it. With her by his side every single step of the way, the ghosts of his past couldn't have power over him. Not when her love for him—and his for her—was a billion times stronger than anything else in the world.

"I told myself I needed to let you go. That it was the only way to keep you safe. To make you happy. But damn it, I could never have done it." He framed her delicate face in his hands. Except that there was nothing delicate about Charlie. She was strong, independent, talented, stubborn. And she was perfectly imperfect. He loved her more than anything in the world. "I'll never stop fighting for you, Charlie. And I'll never stop loving you. Not for one single second. No matter what."

Then he lowered his mouth to hers, sealing his promise with a long, slow, lusciously sweet kiss.

CHAPTER THIRTY-THREE

It was the most decadent kiss Charlie had ever tasted, and overflowing with hope. When he lifted her into his arms to carry her out of his office and into his bedroom, she deepened the kiss until her heart beat recklessly.

Their kiss was gentle and rough all at once, sweet and desperate. They rolled over on the bed until she was straddling him, and he reached up to smooth her hair back as it fell in a curtain over them. "I believe in love," he said softly. "And I've loved you from the very first moment." His gaze roamed her face like a touch. "But I grew up believing love wasn't enough."

She leaned her forehead against his. "It can be."

"You're teaching me that. Teaching me that we aren't my parents and we don't have to drag each other down. We don't have to be toxic to each other even if we're not exactly the same, even if some of our passions and hobbies are different. I should have learned a lot more from Susan and Bob than I did from my parents."

She nuzzled his hair. "It just took longer to understand that you could break the cycle your parents were stuck in."

He nodded so slightly it was barely there.

"Love goes wrong because of the two people involved," she told him. "It doesn't have to be that way for us, not if we're willing to work at it."

He stroked beneath the fall of hair at her nape. "Loving you isn't work. But I don't know if I'll be able to stop trying to help you in any way I can."

She held his face in her palms. "You wouldn't be you if you did. And I wouldn't love you so much if you weren't true to yourself the way I need to be true to who I am. I didn't see us as a partnership before, but now I do. And partners support each other. They share the cost, both physical and emotional."

"I will share anything and everything with you. You tell me what you need. I'll tell you what I need. Then like you said, we'll figure it out." He spread his hands. "All those parties, the people...I like to play there, but you, the Mavericks, Bob and Susan, *that's* my world. So if you want to attend a party with me, then you'll come. If you'd rather stay home to work or catch up on lessons or whatever, then that's what you'll do. I want you to be happy. We're not joined at the hip. I just want to come home to you."

"Home," she whispered. "I like the sound of that."

"You pick and choose your commissions. If it doesn't inspire you, don't do it."

"Or maybe when they ask for a cherub, I'll tell them they need a pterodactyl instead."

He laughed. Truly the most beautiful, wonderful man she'd ever known.

"God, I love you." She threw herself into him, hugging hard and tight, with all her breath, with everything in her.

"Then move in with me for good. Tonight. Now. Share my bed. Fall asleep in my arms every night. Wake up beside me every single morning."

"*Yes,*" she whispered. "*Yes* to tonight. *Yes* to now. *Yes* to every night. *Yes* to every single morning."

Then she kissed him. Tasted his lips, then took his mouth, played with his tongue, and opened herself fully. She was ravenous for him, ripping his shirt off his shoulders, popping the snaps of his jeans. She gasped as he pulled down the top of her sundress and took her nipple in his mouth. She arched, moaned, tangled her fingers in his hair to hold him tight against her as pleasure spiked deep in her center.

His fingers caressed sensuously down her belly, pulling up the dress so he could slip beneath the elastic of her panties. "Marry me, Charlie. Marry me and be mine forever."

"Wait. Stop. What did you just say?"

But Sebastian didn't stop stroking her with sweet, hot patience, pushing her even higher. "Marry me."

"Sebastian." She writhed against him, struggling for breath, panting, everything a blur of sensation, his fingers inside her, his body plastered against her, his words. *Marry me.* She couldn't seem to say anything more than his name.

"Say yes, Charlie. Say you'll marry me."

She cried out then, a full-body explosion, an earthquake shuddering through her, breaking her apart, tearing her down. Then she grabbed Sebastian by the hair and pulled his face to hers. "*Yes,*" she whispered again. "Yes, yes, yes."

And she devoured him with a kiss that said she'd never let him go.

* * *

They tore off the rest of their clothes in a flurry of madness. Sebastian wanted to be inside her, needed it so badly he could barely stop long enough for protection. Charlie's fingers trembled as she helped him. When the deed was done, she pushed him down and took control.

And it was so damn good to give everything he was over to her.

"Marry me," he rasped as she buried him deep inside her.

She rode him, slowly, tantalizingly, then leaned close over him. "I already said yes."

"I thought that was the orgasm talking." It was probably the last coherent thing he could get his mouth to say.

"That was an I-love-you-want-you-need-to-spend-the-rest-of-my-life-with-you yes."

He planted his hands on her hips and moved her, needing so much more than the sensuous slip-slide of their bodies. "God, thank you, yes."

He filled her until she gasped out his name. She filled him just as deeply, claiming his heart. "Take me, Charlie," he begged. "Take *everything*."

They came together, split apart, moving as one, over and over, stealing his sanity, giving him his soul. Her hands on his chest, her eyes so green, glittering like jewels, her lips plump from his kisses.

"I love you," she whispered.

"I'll always love you." There was no other way. "I'd have loved you forever even if you never came back."

"I'll always come back, Sebastian." She made the vow even as her body contracted with pleasure around his. "Always."

He lost it all then, gave her everything, joined her in ecstasy, riding the perfect wave of release with her.

A while later, they lay sweaty and replete in each other's arms. He kissed her forehead softly. "You're my gorgeous Zanti Misfit." She laughed, the throaty sound that never failed to make him tremble with desire. He tipped up her chin with a finger. "I'm serious. You're my unexpected."

"Don't make me cry," she said, her voice already full of tears. Then she gasped and sat up, her eyes sparkling with that vision he so loved to see. "Oh my God, that's it."

"What?" He loved her gasps. They were either pleasure or inspiration.

"The gate!"

"The crusty old thing you found at the construction sale?"

"Yes." She bit her lip, her eyes sparkling. "I know what to do. We need to put it on the slope below the terrace with all the Zanti Misfits behind it. Whenever we need something unexpected, we'll let one out."

"Brilliant. That's what the Zantis are—all the unexpected things to come."

"I love you." Her smile lit the room like a moonbeam.

"And I love you." He disentangled their limbs. "So here's the first test of our new plan."

She sat up as he climbed off the bed, reaching over to turn on the lamp. They'd never slipped beneath the covers, and the light falling across her set her radiant skin glowing.

"What kind of test?" She narrowed her eyes playfully.

"You'll see." He retrieved the box from the closet and laid it on the bed. He'd had it wrapped in blue, with a dark blue ribbon around it. "A present."

Charlie tore into the paper with gusto, the way she did everything, from making love to welding her stallions to loving him. Then she pulled off the lid of the box.

After a long moment, she reached out to stroke the silk velvet. "The pearl dress."

"I bought it the same day you tried it on. I wanted you to wear it when we unveiled the stallions."

"Sebastian."

He put his finger over her lips the way she always did with him. "You know exactly how much it cost. I have money, and I'll always want to buy you pretty things without looking at the price tag. I'll want to spoil you. You just have to decide whether you want to take it."

She pulled the dress from its box, holding it up, touching the strands of real pearls. "It's so beautiful."

"You're what makes it beautiful."

She held it against herself, then gave him the gentlest of smiles. "Thank you. I love the dress. I want to wear it for you. Especially when we show everyone the chariot race."

"The chariot race?"

"It needs a name. Like a Rodin statue. *The Chariot Race.*"

He pulled her close to kiss her. "It's perfect."

"And actually," she said when he finally let her up for air, "our first test has two parts."

"Anything, Charlie."

She let out her breath in a sigh as if she were preparing herself. "I'd like to frame your drawings of me working on *The Chariot Race* and hang them on the lobby walls for the grand opening. I want your work to complement mine." She dropped her voice to a plea. "To *complete* mine." She waited three beats of his heart. "And I want the world to know we're a team."

His body felt hot and cold, but he'd said he could change. He thought of all the nights she'd exposed herself for him, all the nights he'd paraded her through crowds of people. And the truth was that she'd shown him something special in his own work. She'd shown him the magic with that reflection in her face shield and the halo of sparks around her head.

"We're a team," he said. "How many drawings do we need?"

Charlie threw herself at him, crushing the dress, the box, and him. Giving him everything he'd ever wanted, all the love he would ever need.

EPILOGUE

Sebastian's sketches of Charlie were nothing short of genius.

Matt leaned in for a closer look. Sebastian had captured the fully completed sculpture in the reflection of Charlie's face shield. That small detail turned the drawing into a masterpiece.

Next to him, Daniel was grinning. "I'm glad Sebastian finally came out of the closet."

Matt laughed. "Don't let the press hear you say that or they'll be starting rumors it'll take years to put down."

"Sebastian wouldn't care. Hell, he'd probably love it."

Matt laughed his agreement.

Everyone had arrived for the big unveiling at noon, and the lobby of Sebastian's new building was a crush. The *crème de la crème* of San Francisco society had turned out for the grand event—and so had all of Charlie's students from over the years. Her mother too. The champagne flowed, white-coated waiters circulated with trays of hors d'oeuvres, and at twelve-thirty, there would be a buffet on the mezzanine level above.

The sun edged toward the fountain. *The Chariot Race* was covered with a drape of silk attached to a pulley by nearly invisible wires that would sweep it away at the appropriate moment. The building itself was incredible, the glass setting off an astonishing view of San Francisco's financial district, and the bright, cloudless sky above. The supporting columns were gleaming chrome, and even the polished marble floor could be considered a work of art.

"How the hell did Charlie get him to show his sketches?" Daniel shook his head in wonder.

"She told me it was magic."

Matt was happy for his friend. Charlie was a class act. A good woman was hard to find, as Matt well knew since the fiasco with Noah's mother. After Irene, he wasn't taking any risks. He had a hard enough time keeping Noah's nannies around, let alone a girlfriend.

"Have you seen Will and Harper?" Matt asked as they moved down the impressive line of Sebastian's artwork. Elbowed out of the way by a woman demanding a closer look, he stepped back before she punctured his foot with her stiletto heel.

"I saw Jeremy earlier." Daniel chuckled. "He said they're going to watch from the mezzanine above so they could be close to the real food as soon as it's served."

Matt smiled. Jeremy was great. Sure enough, he noticed three figures on the second level. Jeremy saw him and shook his arm at them so hard Matt feared he might topple into the fountain, but Will's hand was on his shoulder, his other arm around Harper. Will would never let either of them fall.

"What about Susan and Bob?"

"Over...there." Daniel pointed.

Standing by the fountain, Susan waved at them. Bob had his hand at her back and Matt thought his foster father looked a little overwhelmed by the press of people.

"Honey, I'm so glad to see you." Susan threw her arms around Matt in a huge hug. He remembered all the years as a pipsqueak kid when her hug was the only thing that made him feel safe. He would love her forever for that.

They moved in close to hear each other over the voices and laughter. "Sebastian and Charlie will be so happy you made it."

She sparkled with joy. "We wouldn't miss it for the world."

"It's all she's been able to talk about," Bob agreed. "That and wedding plans."

But Matt knew Bob was equally focused on getting everything ready for Harper and Will's wedding. Susan had revealed he was already working on the trellis. It would be a white Christmas wedding in Chicago with a small gathering, the nuptials to take place in Susan and Bob's living room.

"And now we have another wedding to plan." Susan was in her element, her eyes starry with the thought of more grandchildren. She adored Noah and wanted more, more, more.

Susan gave her son a huge hug while Matt clapped Bob on the back in greeting. "This is a real swanky place," Bob said, lifting his gaze to the sky above. "When are you boys moving in?"

The Maverick Group was taking the twenty-ninth floor. "Next week."

"How's Noah? You didn't bring him today?"

Matt spread his arms to encompass the packed lobby. "I didn't want to risk losing him in this crowd. Will let me drop him off for a few hours with Mrs. Taylor." Will's housekeeper was a very sweet lady, and Noah adored her chocolate chip cookies. Come to think of it, they all adored Mrs. Taylor's chocolate chip cookies. "You'll see him at the barbecue tomorrow."

"Mrs. Taylor?" Susan's antennae had popped up. "Oh dear, what happened to your latest nanny?"

Matt felt the darkness rise up in him again, and he clenched his fists to tamp it down. "I caught her yelling at Noah when he knocked over a glass of milk."

Matt wasn't a violent man, but when he'd walked in on the woman's tirade, he'd been closer to losing control than at any time in his life. Even with all of Irene's crap, he'd never felt that kind of rage.

No one abused his kid, not ever.

"I'm glad you fired her ass."

He laughed. Susan always knew how to defuse the tension. "Yeah. I fired her ass. So now I need *another* nanny."

"Oh, sweetie." She gave him a hug for all his woes.

"You must have tapped out all the nanny services in town," Daniel drawled beside him.

It was the unfortunate truth. He didn't know how he'd managed to find every bad caregiver in the area—but he had. He'd have to look farther afield and hope the candidate wanted to move.

Above the din, the tinkle of metal on glass gathered attention. The sun was a foot from the fabulous fountain. Matt glanced at his watch. It was closing in on noon.

Rapping his champagne flute with a spoon, Sebastian stepped onto a small dais erected by the fountain. As the crowd began to quiet, he pulled Charlie up beside him.

"Oh my," Susan said in a breathy voice. "She's absolutely beautiful."

Matt had to agree. Her black dress was short and flirty, her back draped with strands of pearls, her red hair pulled up. Even from here, he recognized adoration brimming in Sebastian's eyes.

"That must be her mother." Bob indicated the elderly woman seated close by in a chair brought especially for her. "Sebastian told us her story, and she's a marvel. Even with her terrible arthritis, she walks a mile every day."

"I can't wait to meet her." Susan said. "I have so much to thank her for. Raising such a marvelous woman who's so perfect for Sebastian."

Sebastian held up his hands, and the last of the noise died down. "Thank you all for coming to celebrate the opening of my new headquarters here in San Francisco. In a few moments, the sun will be at its zenith, and you'll all see why I chose this space. Because it's a special spot, I needed a special sculpture to do it justice." He put his arm around Charlie, kissed her temple. "In the process I found this very special, brilliant woman who has agreed to be my wife."

The crowd erupted with *ooh*s and *aah*s, and Susan wiped her eyes.

It was then that Matt saw Whitney, to Sebastian's right, with Evan slightly behind her. If looks could kill, every last one of them would be dead. Whitney didn't like all the attention going to anyone else. Sometimes Matt wished he could fire her ass too.

But only Evan could do that.

"Step back, folks," Sebastian called out. "The sun's coming."

Those closest to the fountain shuffled back as the sun crept up the first tiles and they burst into glowing rainbows of color.

"I present to you *The Chariot Race* by Charlie Ballard." Sebastian waved his arm, and the silk drape was whisked away, disappearing somewhere above the mezzanine.

A pin dropping in the fountain's waters could have been heard at the other end of the lobby. Four magnificent stallions strained against their harnesses, racing into the sky. The fountain's waters began to churn and hiss, billowing up like the dirt and dust beneath the animals' charge as they dragged the broken chariot behind them. They were triumphant while their driver had been lost in defeat.

As the sun hit the metal, the splendid animals came to life and Matt could almost hear the roar of their hoof beats. With no driver, the reins blew wild in the wind, and their copper tails flew out behind them like flames. Everything was awash in color, even the mosaic gleaming on the platform of the fallen chariot as it was exposed by the oncoming light. The spectators were utterly in thrall of the sculpture's power as the sun moved over it.

He heard whispered words like *genius* and *brilliant*. On the other side of the fountain, Charlie glowed as brightly as the chimera she'd created. Matt was in awe that she could produce such beauty from all its disparate parts—pitchforks and bicycle wheels, tractor seats and pipe fittings. She made sense out of senselessness. And in turn gave power and strength to everyone who gazed at her masterpiece.

The sun revealed new facets like diamonds sparkling in radiant light. His gaze followed its path until he saw a woman beyond the fountain, hidden in the shadows until the sun found her.

Her long blond hair turned a fiery gold as the light hit her, and she was suddenly the only thing Matt could see, young and lithesome, pretty and wholesome, pure and sweet.

It was the girl from the group home, the one who'd played with Noah. Ariana.

Noah had adored her, and she'd been so good with him, endlessly patient, her smile angelic as they played in the dirt. *Would she want to be Noah's nanny?*

Matt usually had older caregivers for Noah. Young women wanted to date, they could be flighty, or they moved on too soon. But he sure hadn't been batting a thousand with anyone he'd hired so far.

Maybe it was wishful thinking. Maybe it was something extraordinary about *this* young lady that set her apart from every other woman who'd walked through his front door. Maybe he'd been alone way too long.

Whatever the reason, when Ariana suddenly turned, her gaze met his like a lightning strike. He had no idea what her story was, or if she'd even consider becoming a nanny, but he put down his drink and headed straight for her. Damn good thing a Maverick always knew how to get what he wanted. Because today, Matt knew exactly what—and who—he wanted.

Ariana.

~ THE END ~

ABOUT THE AUTHORS

Having sold more than 5 million books, *New York Times* and *USA Today* bestselling author Bella Andre's novels have been #1 bestsellers around the world. Known for "sensual, empowered stories enveloped in heady romance" (*Publishers Weekly*), her books have been *Cosmopolitan* magazine "Red Hot Reads" twice and have been translated into ten languages. Winner of the Award of Excellence, *The Washington Post* has called her "One of the top digital writers in America" and she has been featured by *Entertainment Weekly*, NPR, *USA Today*, *Forbes*, *The Wall Street Journal* and, most recently, in *Time* magazine. She has given keynote speeches at publishing conferences from Copenhagen to Berlin to San Francisco, including a standing-room-only keynote at Book Expo America, on her publishing success.

Sign up for Bella's newsletter at:
http://bellaandrefans.com/Newsletter

Visit Bella's website at:
www.BellaAndre.com

Follow Bella on twitter at:
http://www.twitter.com/bellaandre

Join Bella on Facebook at:
http://www.facebook.com/bellaandrefans

New York Times and *USA Today* bestselling author Jennifer Skully is a lover of contemporary romance, bringing you poignant tales peopled with hilarious characters that will make you laugh and make you cry. Writing as Jasmine Haynes, she's authored over 35 classy, sensual romance tales about real issues like growing older, facing divorce, starting over. Her books have passion and heart and humor and happy endings, even if they aren't always traditional. She also writes gritty, paranormal mysteries in the Max Starr series. Having penned stories since the moment she learned to write, she now lives in the Redwoods of Northern California with her husband and their adorable nuisance of a cat who totally runs the household.

Newsletter signup: http://bit.ly/SkullyNews

Jennifer's Website: www.jenniferskully.com

Blog: www.jasminehaynes.blogspot.com

Facebook: facebook.com/jasminehaynesauthor

Twitter: https://twitter.com/jasminehaynes1

Made in the USA
Middletown, DE
22 February 2021